SHROUDEATERS

A Vampire Novel

Maria Arena

'There is no fate that cannot be surmounted by scorn.'

The Myth of Sisyphus
Albert Camus

'There is a limit to our life, but to knowledge there is no
limit. With what is limited to pursue after what is
unlimited is a perilous thing; and when, knowing this,
we still seek the increase of our knowledge,
the peril cannot be averted.'

Zhuang Zhou translated by James Legge (1891)

Prelude to Romance

I whisper: 'Cut yourself. Bleed for me.'
    She answers: 'Tell me you love me.'
    Silence.
    'Tell me.'
    A breath, to infuse sincerity: 'I love you.'
    Oh Hollywood, are you proud of your acolytes?
    Her turn. 'I love you too.'
    And she (*melodramatic pause*) cuts.
    Deep.

Awakening

We're bored, so we fuck.

I watch her eyes; they're focused inward on the lyrics pouring into her ears. Her hips move to a different rhythm to the one I want. I push, make her pay attention. I can't hear her gasp over the music playing in my head, but I see her mouth open, her eyes on my face. She gets what I want; we find the beat, continue. Her world, my world, our bodies melded at the groin but—

It's all so pointless.

Released, I fall over the scars and fresh wounds decorating her breasts. She shoves me off, flicks on *Entertainment Today*, and is lost in another Paris adventure.

Meaningless.

In the afterglow, I search the Net.

'Hey Lucy, have you seen this?'

She flops over on my bed. 'What?' she asks, as I scroll to the top of the webpage on the screen in front of me. 'Oh Christ, I'm so over Facebook. Why can't people just get a life?' She yawns to prove her point before finding an iota of interest. 'Okay, who's bitching about who now?'

I ignore her white noise. 'Check this out.'

She sighs as her feet hit the floor. The scent of her envelops me; her hair tickles my shoulder. 'Is she for real?'

I swivel in the chair, pull her onto my lap, lift her hair as she reads. I bite her neck, softly. 'I hope so.'

Blog One

Hail the Vampire

I am going to kill my parents.

You losers love to hear that, don't you? It rocks your little worlds. Excites you because you think I'm joking. You think this is a *PlayStation* moment you can enter and exit at will; except this is anything but a game, and there's nothing remotely funny about it. I *am* going to kill my parents and every other blood-kin I can find. And I'll tell you why— because they killed me, and everything I held precious in this world.

Oh, you think you can relate, don't you? You with your Internet and smartphones, your designer-torn jeans and Frappuccino tastes; your blood fantasies. You have no idea what this existence is like. How could you; you're mortal.

That's right. I'm a vampire. No, not like Akasha in *Queen of the Damned*; not some literary villain, but the real deal. And no, I'm not six thousand years old; I'm seventy-seven in vampire years. That mightn't sound like a long time but, trust me, every day is a millennium when you're watching all that you love die.

I was twenty-three when I met my parents and I had everything to live for. I was - am - gorgeous: golden hair that hangs to the middle of my back; green eyes flecked with yellow; full lips and an elegant nose; high cheek bones that would make a supermodel envious; slender body that turned many a man's head. And I was intelligent in that cool, rational way of men. *Cogito ergo sum*, Descartes said: *I think, therefore I am*. Though I was young, I understood my mind and knew what I wanted from my life: to learn, to travel, to love.

My ability to rise above the simpering stupidity expected of girls in my era took me to unexpected places and introduced me to men of fine calibre. They were drawn by my youth and beauty, only to be surprised to find a woman with whom they could converse on subjects ranging from commerce to the political nightmare developing across the border in Germany.

One of these men was my fiancé, Didier. He was twenty-five, a law student, and handsome in that smouldering Parisian way. We met at *Café de la Paix*, three days after the strike that closed most of Paris' restaurants, bars and cafés. Didier and his friend, Michel, were engaged in a heated discussion with the café's owner over the rights of the *grévistes* to hold the city and its occupants to ransom for a few extra francs in their weekly wage.

My friend, Isabeau, and I took a seat near the window and watched the men argue as we waited for our coffee to arrive. Didier and the owner of the shop, Monsieur Beauchard, were inches apart and it seemed they would come to blows at any moment. Their fervour was exhilarating and I found myself staring at Didier's mouth, wondering if he would kiss me with the same intensity. The thought surprised me into action.

'Juliana, don't,' Isabeau whispered as I stood to approach the men.

I ignored her. 'What difference is there between the objectives of the *grévistes* and those that grow in the dark heart of Germany?'

A hush filled the shop. 'Return to your coffee, girl, and don't speak of what you cannot comprehend,' Beauchard said, giving Didier one last disgusted look before returning to his bar.

'I know that to give dispensation to the *grévistes* is to suggest a surrender to those who watch for signs of weakness in France,' I said, directing my response to Didier.

His eyes surveyed my body and explored my face with deliberate slowness before he answered. I waited under his inspection, unmoved. 'By supporting the proletariat in their struggle for just reward, we defy the darkness,' he replied, holding out his hand. 'And you are?'

'Juliana Celeste.'

'Didier Villette,' he said, bending to brush his lips across my hand. 'Enchanté.'

Six months later, I agreed to be his wife. Six months after that, my parents killed me.

My parents: Callisto and Constantine.

We met them, Didier and I, in the lengthening shadow of the Eiffel Tower. They sat on a wooden bench seat; he perched on the back while she leaned against his leg and read aloud a passage from *Ulysses*. There was something about them that drew the eye; they were exquisite. Callisto was dark as a gypsy princess, while Constantine observed the world from behind a proud Gaelic face.

As we approached, Callisto looked up and I was caught by the silver glints that flashed across her black eyes. She smiled and beckoned me with a finger. My feet turned of their own accord and, before I understood how I came to be there, I was sitting with them, laughing, as though we were old friends separated by time but not affection. Didier, who stood away as was his custom with new acquaintances, waited patiently as Callisto and Constantine spoke of themselves and inquired after me with tender interest. It was only when Constantine suggested we take refreshments at a bar he knew in Pigalle that Didier stepped in, but by then I was so enthralled that I waved away his concerns and happily linked arms with Callisto as we walked to the closest Metro.

As the entrance in the sidewalk opened before us, Didier took my hand and drew me aside. 'I don't think this is a good idea,' he said.

'Why not?'

'There is something strange here.' He shook his head, 'I don't feel right about this.'

'What is there to worry about, mon cher, we will only have a little drink, yes?' Callisto said, wrapping her arms around his waist. He politely disengaged and moved further away.

I glanced at Didier; while reserved by nature, it was not like him to be obstinate. I searched my own feelings and picked up a tremor of disquiet, but then Callisto caught my eye. A song entered my mind, the melody soft and inviting, although the words were indistinguishable. I listened, letting the sound fill me. 'I think we should go,' I said.

'No,' Didier replied, folding his arms across his chest.

I should have listened to him but, instead, I let Callisto draw me into the underground. It was the last time I saw Didier as a mortal woman.

The bar was vibrating with energy, and at its centre were Callisto and Constantine. They knew everyone. Men fawned at Callisto's side, paying her compliments and offering her all manner of enticements, which she refused with a rush of silvery laughter. Women flocked to Constantine, touching his arm, his hand, running their fingers along the line of his jaw. He indulged them, but his eyes always returned to Callisto— and to me.

A swirl of people surrounded me: women trying to discover my connection to Callisto and the nature of my relationship with Constantine; men trying to discovery if I would go home with them, *despite* my relationship with Constantine. I danced with strangers: they touched me in the smoky darkness, filled my mouth with Seltz, and kissed me, until everything was a blur; and always on the edge of my mind was that elusive melody, reassuring in its presence.

Then we were on the street, moving through the crowd that spilled into the warm night. I was between Callisto and Constantine, my protectors, and it felt as though I was flying, my feet barely touching the ground as we descended into the Metro again.

'Where are we going?' I asked above the rhythmic clatter of the train.

Callisto spoke through unmoving lips: *Home*.

I wanted to reach out and investigate their stillness, but my limbs were heavy and I nuzzled into Constantine's hard shoulder, needing to be in my bed. The train came to a shuddering halt and, as we disembarked, I stumbled. Constantine swept me into his arms, carrying me up the stairs and into a silent pre-dawn, which I glimpsed as sleep overtook me.

Consciousness returned with the pressure of lips against my neck. I was lying between them, on a bed in an unfamiliar room. My heart kicked with panic and I heard a moan beside my ear. I tried to turn, but strong fingers held my head at an angle that exposed my throat. Other hands held my wrist and legs pinned me to the softness of the mattress. The panic grew and I began to struggle.

'Be at peace, child,' Callisto sang in my mind.

Her song was one of love; of desires satisfied, and it filled me with a strange calm that stayed with me even as her fangs slid into my wrist and his pierced my throat.

How to describe the moment of my death? Did it hurt? Was I afraid? What else would you like to know, mortal?

Come back next week and I may tell you.

Curing Mediocrity

It hits me like a comet slamming into the earth. There's a vibration in my feet and hands, racing to the centre of my body, yet pushing against my skin with its cosmic energy until it feels like I'll split from the inside out. My mouth is dry and I feel around for a bottle of water, keeping my eyes squeezed shut because the room is pulsing. The water is good, sliding down my throat, but then I forget it as a new sensation cleaves my skull.

Music.

Death metal screaming.

I start to move to the glorious howling melody, my body thumping to the beat, until my heart's about to burst— like a seedpod.

Awesome.

Moving at the speed of light, I stumble outside, lost in the sound, so free: to touch the sky, kiss the moon, swim in the ocean of my own soul.

The ocean?

Drowning!

I hold my breath until someone punches me in the back. Laughter spills out of my mouth; a frothing, foaming hilarity. The shadows around me inhale, swirl, exhale, and I grin at those gorgeous white-faced freaks, silver flashing in pouting lips and flickering tongues. Their eyes are carnival glass rimmed in black; their limbs long, snapping like flags to the gothic hymns pouring out of the speakers.

I want to touch them, but—

I'm flying, a hundred feet off the ground and the sky never looked so huge; a billion stars are born and die as the heavens turn red and—

I'm falling, fast. I beg for a crash landing, to feel the impact in the cracking of my bones, just so I can experience *something*. I want it. That pain. My heart fills up with my desire and it hurts; a beautiful maudlin agony that deserves to be shared. Where is—

Lucy?

Blog Two

The Virgin Vampire

You are fascinated by death, aren't you? You play with it. Fantasise about it. Make up stories about all the ways you could do it. Dare each other to try it. Use it as a weapon against those who love you— but you don't *really* want it. That eternal ending. What you want, or think you want, is what I have. The gift; the curse. Immortality.

Immortality is the reason so many of you are enamoured with the famous; those fake idols whose lives you make more important than your own. How you allow them to consume the minutes of your day, as though you had that many to spare. You watch them, living their dreams in the pages of your magazines and on the screen. All that drama and sex and money and celluloid beauty. You're already dead without knowing it. And this is the life you want to live forever?

Lucky you.

But have you ever stopped to consider what that means? Living forever? No, don't rush your answer.

Think, if you are capable of independent thought. What would it mean to be truly immortal?

Not sure?

Well then, allow me to enlighten you.

Dying didn't hurt. It was the awakening that killed me.

I felt my life ebbing away as they drew the blood from my body. My heart beat in erratic bursts as the reason for its existence disappeared from my veins. Callisto's voice swirled around my mind, singing. I waited for it to be over and soon it was.

Constantine withdrew first and stood with the sluggishness of someone who had over-indulged. He looked down on me and smiled as he reached out and brushed the hair from my face. 'Welcome, child,' he said, and was gone. I didn't see him again as a fledgling.

I felt Callisto move beside me and I realised that her lovely song was no longer filling my head. I tried to look for her, but I couldn't move. There was no pain, just the knowledge that I was alone in the room; my parents had abandoned me to my fate.

Death seemed like the next logical step, but the moment of release never came. Instead, I waited in a dismal twilight as the sun crawled across the ceiling. I tried to cry, but there were no tears; I tried to call out, but my voice was as weak as my body. Yet, while I lay on the bed, I could feel something growing inside me; a need I couldn't understand.

The feeling grew stronger as night came on, withering in my belly. I was parched; my throat raw as the need grew and grew, becoming more monstrous than the fact of my continuing existence. Fire burned in my limbs and I ached in every joint as though they were seizing up for want of lubrication. Finally, when I thought I could stand it no longer, Callisto appeared above me. In her arms, she carried a child of about six - a warm-blooded little girl, sleeping with her thumb curled into the corner of her mouth. She put the child on the bed beside me.

'A gift,' Callisto murmured. 'To ease the Thirst.' As she spoke, I heard the echo of her song in my head and knew she had placed the child in her thrall.

You may think it evil, but I didn't hesitate. I took the girl and drained every drop of blood from her small body. The child made a small murmur as she passed from this life and, as I felt her go, I wondered why she had died and I had remained. I pushed her body away, feeling my strength return as I sat up beside Callisto. Rage overtook me and I reached out to strike her for making me into this bloodthirsty monster, but she was lightning quick, as only a vampire can be, and I could not get close enough to deliver the blow.

'Stop this foolishness,' she ordered.

And I did stop. Not because she demanded it, but because the surge of strength was waning as the agony of the Thirst returned like an inferno. I curled up, willing myself to die, but death would not come. It had abandoned me. Rather, I heard Callisto inside my head, instructing me in the ways of our kind. Shroudeaters, she called us: the immortals. How I shuddered when she said that, as though we are some higher order of being rather than the monsters we truly are.

Time crawled, each second a torment, and Callisto stayed with me through it all until, mad with the Thirst, I begged her for death.

'This one thing I cannot give you, ma petite amour,' she said, from the doorway to the room, 'but I can ease your pain.' A short while later she returned with another child, this one a boy who looked about ten. She watched me feed with a contented smile.

I learned in the years to come that Callisto's behaviour during those early hours was unusual for our kind. Shroudeaters are, as a rule, solitary creatures who shun others vampires as a matter of self-preservation, even those newly born to our ways. Perhaps this sounds harsh, but it is the capricious nature of humans, with all your childish curiosity and contemptuous fears that moulded our existence. Even our moniker, which your kind bestowed upon us, speaks of your desire for, and your terror of, our ability to tear through the veil of death. No wonder we stay hidden, even from each other.

I didn't know at the time why Callisto chose to nurture me, but she brought me a human every few hours during that interminable twilight. Sometimes she would arrive with a docile adult, but usually it was a child, some neglected innocent, and she would sing them to their deaths while I feasted.

Whatever it was that compelled Callisto to stay was short-lived, and one night I woke to find her gone. I waited for a while to see if she would return. When she didn't, I lay down on the bed, unsure of what to do. My uncertainty didn't last long. The Thirst was raging, and I was forced into the night to hunt.

It was frightening how quickly I adjusted to my new instincts. I trailed humans along the street and watched them from around corners until I found a likely target; an old man who had made his home beneath the Pont Neuf. I followed him into the shadows, my mouth dripping as the smell of warm blood filled my nostrils and the sound of a living heart, so rhythmic, filled my ears.

I silently scuttled up to him, and then rose to my full height as my fangs slid down from my gums. In the instant before I took him, he realised I was there and he turned his watery eyes to me. They brimmed with fear and I hesitated as a small part of my mind - the last vestiges of my human self - screamed out against the travesty I was about to commit, but I couldn't deny the Thirst.

It wasn't a clean kill. There is, however, something in the essence of the vampire that is an excellent teacher and, before long, I was hunting and killing with stealth and precision; most of my victims died in ignorance of their final fate.

In those early weeks, I searched the city for Callisto and Constantine, but could find no evidence of their presence. They had moved abroad or gone to ground, leaving me to figure out this existence on my own. Their abandonment sowed deep seeds of bitterness. I was alone in the teeming city, driven by an impulse I didn't understand, but couldn't deny. My only company were the people I had to kill. I followed Callisto and

Constantine's example and seduced my victims with dinner and drinks, filling their last night with dancing and revelry. Later, I would lure them to my lair beneath the catacombs where I would sing them to death, satisfying the Thirst, but not the hunger in my soul.

It was in my third month as a vampire that I remembered Didier. I was following a young woman along a street, enjoying the quick, sharp click of her heels on the pavement, when I looked across the road and saw *Café de la Paix*. I came to a halt, the sound of the woman's shoes fading as the shadow of my human life touched my vampire's mind.

Didier.

A deep shame filled me as I watched Monsieur Beauchard sweep the pavement outside his shop. How could I have forgotten the man I love? I killed the woman in heels quickly and, as I gulped her sweet blood, I decided to find Didier that very night. It was a decision that sealed Callisto and Constantine's fate.

A Prayer at Dawn

They have a million questions, but I'm too fucked up to answer. I just want quiet; a space to clear my head. All these concerned strangers. Who the hell are they anyway? If they'd shut up, maybe I could think.

Except, I don't want to think; I want to be told a story— her story.

'Do you know what she took? Was it Ice? Crack? E? Was it PCP?'

Yep.

'Damn you kids, when will you learn?'

One of them grabs my arm. 'Hey c'mon, this is important.' He shakes me, like a naughty puppy. 'Look at me. Can you hear me?' I consider smashing him in the face, but who needs the extra chaos. He releases my arm, disgusted. 'Christ, what a waste of space.'

'Forget him, concentrate on the one we can save.'

Yeah, man, forget about me and do your job. Please.

I can't take the whiteness of the walls anymore; they're too stark. It's as though they're oozing snow, which means it should be freezing, but it is a thousand degrees and I'm sweating worse than a gym junkie. The alien green floor shimmers like water trapped under ice.

I cling to the snow-white-wall because I know how fragile ice can be; one misstep and I'm screwed.

Inch by inch, I make my way to the exit, where I look back as the doors slide open. Machines beep in protest while the doctors go insane. One bangs her chest: 'Breathe, girl, damn it!'

I know she'll forgive my absence.

Around the corner and down the street, there's an internet café called *Choice 24*. I saw it as I drove to the hospital, talking to Lucy all the way, trying to keep her alive with the sound of my voice. Ain't the human mind amazing? Here's my girlfriend, puke smeared over her face and clinging to her hair, froth on her lips, zombie eyes freaking me out, and still I notice the cyber café.

Mad, right?

The place is empty except for the guy behind the counter, who looks like a myopic ferret. I hope he thanked his parents for *that* gene combination. I sidle up to the cash register and hand over my last ten bucks; there's a special on between two and five in the morning: the dead hours.

Ferrety rings up the sale as if he's scored big on the Lottery and points to a machine in the corner without looking at me. I ease into the chair, bump the mouse, pass the start-up screen, jump on a browser, wait – *shit connection* – type: www.thegoddessisavampire .com. Jack my phone into my ears. Breaking Benjamin gets deep and meaningful, and I wonder what people would see in my eyes, if they cared to look; would they see my evil mind?

I strangle the idea.

What happened with Lucy has messed with my head and I try not to think about it as the blog loads, but the thoughts keep coming and, with them, a needling of resentment. I warned her about buying shit from Trent. She laughed, as she always does when I try to look out for her, and told me to get a grip. That was Lucy: indie-girl, party-girl, OD girl lying on a bed with a tube stuck down her throat.

Yeah, seriously mad.

I rub my hands through my hair and over my face; I'm so damn tired. Maybe I should go home, catch a few z's before I face Lucy's parents. The Crossings. Now there's a conversation I want to have.

Christian, my boy, you really screwed the pooch this time.

I focus on the blog, connect to the vampire: Juliana Celeste.

Get lost in her story.

It beats reality.

Blog Three

A Vampire's Love

"To love another person is to see the face of God."

Have you heard this line, mortal? It is from one of the most beautiful operas ever written. *Les Misérable*. It is spoken at a moment between life and death, when the ghost of Fantine comes to take Valjean to Glory, when all trespasses are forgiven and the only thing that remains is Love.

Can you understand this? Or have you been tainted beyond redemption by the popular culture version of love, where nothing is unconditional and everything is in service of the self? Do you even know what Love is? Do you understand the concept of self-sacrifice?

Perhaps I am being too hard on you, expecting too much? After all, you are only human, and your role models do leave much to be desired. Okay, I will give you the opportunity to learn the power and strength of true Love.

Heed the lesson.

I thought finding Didier would be easy, but I underestimated his need to leave behind the life he had lived with me. I began my search for him at his home in République, where we had shared many romantic interludes, but it quickly became apparent that he had moved on when a woman and her young child entered the apartment. Bitter disappointment filled me and I considered killing them in the kitchen where my beloved had cooked me dinner; lucky for them, I had already fed.

My next avenue was the university where Didier had been studying. I haunted the grounds for many nights before cornering one of his former lecturers. The good professor required some convincing before he would give up the information I needed - the name of a law firm in the Latin Quarter.

I'm sure the university community mourned the professor's passing in an appropriate manner.

It was late in the evening when Didier stepped into the street and pulled up the collar on his jacket against the chill. My stomach clenched at the sight of his face as he brought a match to the cigarette between his lips. How handsome he was to my vampire eyes. He scanned the road in both directions, searching for a taxi, but the street was empty. A wrinkle of annoyance creased his brow. I drew a breath as a flood of memories came to me, all those small things about him that I loved: the sound of his laughter, the colour of his eyes, the shape of his hands and how they felt holding mine. My heart ached and I wanted to go to him, but I could not because, under the desire to hold him again, was a stronger need and I knew that, to protect him from what I had become, I could only watch from a distance.

He turned down the street, heading for the Metro. I followed. At the entrance, he stopped to look over his shoulder. I melted into the shadows. He searched the sidewalks, his face serious; he had always trusted his instincts. After a few moments, he descended the stairs but I knew from the frown on his face, he wasn't satisfied that he was alone.

To avoid enflaming his suspicion further, I let him go. It was an easy parting; after all, I had an eternity to find him again.

We spent the next two years learning how to exist in this world. Didier worked long hours at the firm and even longer hours in his small apartment in Saint-Germain. He cooked simple food and walked along the Seine. He dated occasionally; the women never lasted more than an encounter with my beloved.

I developed my skills as a vampire and learned what it meant to be a 'creature of the night'— a laughable description. I searched the city for signs of my parents, but Callisto and Constantine had vanished. The only evidence they had been in my life at all was the perpetual Thirst that possessed me. Eventually, I gave up the search and devoted my time to studying the arts, watching the political madness in Germany, and following Didier.

Then war came and Europe was plunged into darkness.

I watched the city of my mortal birth struggle against her oppressor and did as much as I could to assist in defending her freedom; German blood, no matter what the propaganda said, was no different to French blood. Our efforts were futile: the country fell and Didier, though he abhorred violence, joined the Résistance.

Oh, the terror of those nights, watching him participate in clandestine meetings and sabotage, knowing I couldn't interfere despite my vampiric talents. Then came the night he encountered a group of German soldiers, hell bent on savagery.

We were crossing the city, Didier on his way to his apartment and me following across the rooftops. I was alert to them before he was; four men, hiding in the shadows, the sound of their hearts loud. Didier was among them before I could intervene. They surrounded him, jostling and pushing as they demanded his papers. Liquor slurred their voices and twisted their faces into masks of unreasoning hatred. Didier was in serious trouble.

I watched from above, fear sitting in my throat like a stone, as Didier reached into his jacket. He was retrieving his papers, but the soldiers chose to take it as an act of provocation and, in an instant, a gun was pressed to his throat.

Rage, driven by the power of my love, impelled me and I flew down upon them. The one with the gun was dead before the others were aware of my presence. Then, although it hurt my heart to do it, I slammed Didier into the wall, rendering him unconscious. He slid to the ground in a boneless heap. I turned to the remaining soldiers, a smile on my lips, and said, 'Vive la Résistance.'

I carried Didier to his apartment and laid him upon his bed. An ugly purple bruise was rising like a foreign sun on his forehead. My heart swelled and blood-tears trailed over my cheeks as I kissed his closed eyes. I lay beside him, my head on his chest, listening to the slow, steady thud of his heart, grateful for the chance to be with my love one last time.

When the dawn threatened, I rose and kissed him goodbye. His eyes fluttered and he gripped my hand as he lifted his head and tried to focus his gaze upon my face. 'Juliana?' he asked.

I was silent. His fingers lost their strength and he slipped back into unconsciousness. I looked at the sun as it touched the horizon. Thoughts of Callisto and Constantine surfaced and, with them, the beginnings of a plan.

My ideas developed as I observed Didier from afar. All through the war years, never interfering but always close by in case some ill fate should befall him, until one night about six months before the Germans were finally swept from Paris.

It was early in the evening and I was sitting outside a small crowded café on the Rue de Rivioli. Didier was working late at the headquarters of the Résistance and I took the opportunity to hunt. I watched the customers in the reflection of the mirror that lined the back wall of the café. I felt a swelling contempt for the women who fraternised so openly with our enemy and I amused myself by contemplating which one I would kill. I choose a dark haired beauty, who had spent almost an hour sitting in the lap of a German soldier, giggling and drinking while she fended off his roaming hands. I imagined what her blood would taste like and how I would whisper of her betrayal as she died. I stirred the untouched coffee in front of me, the spoon making a soft *clink* with each revolution of the cup as I waited for the couple to leave. I would kill him too; it was my patriotic duty.

The girl stood and waved to her friends, who laughed knowingly. I got to my feet, but as I turned to follow them, a figure in the mirror caught my eye.

Callisto.

I was arrested for a moment, held in breathless wonder at her appearance. For years, I had searched for her and my father without a sign and now here she was, across the road, watching the same young couple as they stumbled down the street. She hadn't changed; if anything, she seemed more beautiful. The sight of her caused an ache somewhere inside and I pushed it away. It wasn't the time to feel anything, but rage.

Callisto strolled across the road and trailed after the soldier and girl. She moved with the grace of a skilled hunter and, despite myself, I admired her. I let her get a little ahead before I followed, allowing some space between us so I could consider my next move. It was strange to feel such uncertainty; I had played out this encounter in my mind a million times. I would overcome her and she would beg for mercy as I chained her to the wall of the dungeon I had prepared, but a different emotion found me: loneliness.

A streak of agony flashed across my body, and I realised I wanted the company of others of my kind, someone who would understand the dilemmas in my soul. I hated Callisto and I wanted to make her suffer, but she was the only 'family' I had.

The couple turned into a narrow side street and Callisto followed, looking over her shoulder. I recognised the gesture; always check to make sure no one is watching. Her eyes widened when she saw me and, without a moment's hesitation, she fled.

I chased her through the city, almost catching her before she streaked away. I knew she was playing with me, but there was something she hadn't counted on; my persistence. Everywhere she ventured, I followed; every tactic she tried, I countered until finally just as the sun tipped the horizon, I captured her.

She laughed. 'Hello daughter,' she said, and raised a hand to my face. 'It has been too long.'

Words crowded my mind. There was so much to say, so much anger, so much hurt, but also the urge to hold her and be grateful to have found another like me. She read all this in my face and her hand slipped into mine as she said, 'Come, let's rest until the night and then we can talk.' I could only nod; my throat was closed. I allowed her to lead me to her hiding place and lay in the cold circle of her embrace, content for the moment.

Callisto was gone before the Thirst called me to awareness. I searched for her, sending out my senses to scan the dark city, but she had disappeared. Fury scorched me; why hadn't I taken her when I had the chance? I cursed the softness of my heart, that mortal weakness.

I snatched my first victim from her life and did not sing her into death, relishing instead her terror and pain. As the blood seeped out of her, my anger eased. I would find Callisto and she wouldn't escape her punishment again. With the burden of the Thirst subdued and my determination fortified, I went in search of Didier. The city felt taut as I crossed through the arrondissements; the streets were mostly empty of mortals, except for those forced into the open by necessity. I sensed that some change had occurred while I was playing cat and mouse with Callisto, and I hurried towards Didier's apartment, a terrible certainty brewing in my stomach.

The front door was open, the imprint of a boot close to the shattered lock. I stepped inside, expecting the worst. I wasn't disappointed. There was evidence of a struggle in the living area: chairs knocked over, the coffee table overturned, a few drops of blood on the papers scattered across the floor. I recognised the work of the SS.

Although I knew it was futile, I searched the bedroom and the bathroom; empty and with no clue as to where he may have been taken. Heartbroken and terrified, I stood on his tiny balcony and scanned the city for the second time, but Didier, like Callisto, was gone.

Family Matters

'You can't fucking make me.'

'Don't speak to your mother that way, Lucy.'

'Why not? She's trying to ruin my life.'

'Actually, you're doing a fine job of that without my help.'

'Fun-*ny*.'

'Your mother didn't put you in hospital, my girl. You managed that by yourself.'

'Just 'cause things got a little out of control doesn't mean I should be sent away.'

'A little out of control? Is that what you call ending up unconscious in the ER? Lucy, you almost died,' Peter Crossing says.

'Yeah, well, I didn't. But I will if you try to send me to live with Aunt Marguerite. In fact, I'll make sure of it,'

'Oh please, it's a little late for the melodramatics, don't you think?'

'Fuck you, Madeline.'

'You little bitch.'

Peter Crossing steps between the women in his life. 'Honey, why don't you wait outside while I talk to her?' Lucy's mother turns on five-inch heels and strides past me, her face stiff with anger. 'Maybe you should wait outside as well, Christian?'

'He stays.' Lucy holds out her hand. I cross the room and lace my fingers through hers.

'This was a close call, princess,' her father says, refusing to be baited, and Lucy sticks out her tongue, gagging. 'You need to take this seriously. We could have lost you.'

Lucy is remorseless. 'Don't go all drama queen on me, Daddy. I'm still breathing.'

A sigh escapes Peter Crossing and he wipes a hand down his cheeks. The rasp of stubble is not a sound I usually associate with Lucy's father; the morning's antics have taken their toll on the CEO of Crossing International. 'This situation has become untenable, sweetheart. These *friends* you're associating with are leading you down some very dark paths, and your mother and I are concerned that if we allow this to continue.' He pauses, looking at the monitors attached to Lucy's body and shakes his head. 'Well, let's just say we think a new environment, with some new people, will do you the world of good.'

'Daddy, I don't care what you and Mother want. I'm not going to Paris or anywhere else.'

Peter Crossing considers his daughter. I can see he's got more to say, but he swallows the words and turns to me. 'You talk to her, Christian. Maybe she'll listen to you.'

I nod. He thinks I'm a saint because I got Lucy to the ER after she collapsed at Trent's party. The guy's got a good heart, but he's as blind as the worm in a bottle of tequila; I'm more fucked up than his precious daughter will ever be.

The door whispers shut behind him and I turn to Lucy. She's sitting up in the bed, a stack of ransacked pillows behind her. A halo of blonde hair flows over the pristine whiteness. There's a quiver at the corner of her pale pink lips, and the grey of her eyes, so much like her mother's, still contain the fog of the OD.

She watches me, waiting to hear what I have to say. 'You really do look like a princess.'

'Screw you,' she says, throwing a pillow at me.

'Anytime,' I reply, although, in my distraction, it sounds as sincere as the promise of a snake-oil salesman. I hand the pillow back and Lucy fluffs it into comfort. 'So how serious do you think they are?' I ask.

'About Paris?' Lucy puffs a breath over her lips and shakes her head. 'Madeline's serious. She's been trying to get rid of me for years, and since she leads Daddy around by his dick.' She shrugs. 'Guess she'll get her way.'

The thought makes my stomach clench. 'So who's this aunt?'

'Don't really know. I've only met her once, when I was seven or something. Did you tell the cops anything about last night?'

I walk over to the window. There's a park across the street. It's a palette of greenery: lime, emerald, olive, jade. Trees stretch their crooked limbs towards the sky. My eyes follow. Up there, invisible against the blank vault of daylight, are billions of stars, clusters of galaxies and other universes; the great mystery. I touch the cold glass and wish for the night. 'Where does your aunt live in Paris?' I ask.

'How the fuck should I know? What about the cops?'

'I haven't talked to them.'

'Well, what're you going to say when you do?'

'What's to say? I was off my face, can't remember a thing. Let's go to Paris.'

'*What?*'

On the street below, tyres screech. 'Forget it,' I say, heading for the door.

'Christian, wait,' Lucy demands. I look at her over my shoulder, hand resting on the handle. She pats the bed. 'Come here.' It's not an invitation.

I let her wait for a few seconds.

When I'm perched beside her, she takes my hand and kisses my fingers, one at a time. My heartbeat quickens as I slip my other hand inside her hospital gown, cupping the swell of her breast. I lean in to kiss her, squeezing her nipple as my mouth touches hers. Lucy gasps. Her hand covers mine, squeezing harder.

The kiss ends and Lucy pulls away, lying back against the pillows. Her cheeks are flushed, but her manner is cool as she glances past me. 'My parentals will be back any second,' she says.

I can barely hear her over the blood surging through my body, and I curse her teasing ways as I fight to re-gain control.

Lucy sees my struggle and touches my face. 'Wait 'til I get out of here,' she promises.

My heartbeat slows. 'Yeah,' I say, and look out the window.

'So, what's the go with Paris?' she asks.

I shrug. 'Could be a good move, don't you think? Getting away from here and all the shit we have to deal with, especially after last night.'

Lucy rolls her eyes. 'Yeah, the trolls will love this. I reckon by the end of today, I'll have screwed everyone at the party, died three times, and be on remand to juvie.' She laughs then grows serious. 'It'd be good to get away for a while I guess. Imagine if we just disappeared; they'd go nuts trying to figure out what happened.'

'And it's not like we've got a lot going on here.'

She raises her eyebrows. 'Uni?'

I lift a shoulder. 'One semester. No biggie.'

Lucy runs her fingers down my arm. 'I don't think Daddy and Madeline had you in mind when they thought up their little plan.'

I get off the bed. 'Probably not, but I'm sure you can convince them to let me go,' I say, kissing the side of her mouth. 'After all, someone has to protect you.'

'My knight in shining armour? As if,' she says, pushing me away. 'Why do you really want to go to Paris?

'Just to be with you,' I reply as the door swings open. Peter and Madeline bustle in; round two. I drift over to the window; look down on the empty park. I haven't lied to Lucy, exactly, but there is another reason to go to Paris: a vampire.

A *real* vampire, whose name has found its way into my soul.

Blog Four

All the Heroes are Dead

You're back again? Well, perhaps that's not surprising, given the smallness of your life and the prosaic nature of your concerns. What a disappointment you must be to your creators, human and divine alike; those who had such high hopes for your future.

Not that their displeasure bothers you. No, not you, the burgeoning I-Generation; corporatised, digitalised, sanitised. You spend your lives in search of the next instant of gratification, experienced in the expectation that it will give meaning to your existence and subdue that restless feeling that gnaws at your stomach like a sharp-toothed rodent.

I know why you return to these pages. I know what you need. I know what is missing from your life.

What you seek is a hero; someone to place on a gilded pedestal and raise to the Heavens. Oh, you can deny it, but you know it is true. You are dying for a hero, someone to take you by the hand and teach you what it means to *live*. Sure, there are those among you whom you lionise - the sports star, the environmental warrior, the humanitarian - but they are all too human and subject to the whim of your own fickleness. Love them today; loathe them tomorrow. Isn't that how you roll?

The problem is, the world you have helped fashion is festooned with the mundane and the average and you are desperate for something that glitters. That is why you make heroes out of us, the Shroudeaters: beautiful, noble, death-defying life-thieves. Yet, we are fool's gold. Do you understand that? Do you care?

I didn't think so.

Fine. Read on, but take note, mortal: stop posting your deluded requests on this page. I am not your heroine, and I cannot save you, even if I thought you were worth the effort.

I have failed as someone's heroine once. I will not do that again.

The fear inspired by the *Schutzstaffel* was well founded. They were ruthless in their suppression of my fellow citizens, brutal in their methods, and merciless in the pursuit of their orders. No one was beyond their reach and nowhere was safe from their gaze. Yet, they possessed an almost vampiric ability to disappear when it suited their purpose; a fact I discovered as I searched Saint-Germain, block-by-block, looking for Didier.

That they could frustrate my vampiric abilities sparked a simmering anger that I held in check as I peered through windows and listened at doors. *What is the point of being a vampire if I can't find Didier?* I thought, scrambling down avenues and boulevards, knowing the question was aimed at the real targets of my ire: Callisto and Constantine. *Is there no benefit to this prison of immortality?* I demanded of them but, of course, my parents remained silent, even though I knew Callisto, at least, was somewhere in the city. Perhaps I would find her again during my search and then there would be a reckoning. In the meantime, heaven help any German soldiers I encountered; SS or not, they would pay the price for the theft of my beloved.

By the time I covered Saint-Germain, daylight was spilling into the sky, turning the horizon into a bruise. Accompanying the sunrise was the heat of the Thirst, rising fast like a thermostat turned to high. Although loathed to quit the search, I had to find a place where I could wait out the daylight hours, and I had to find a human to smother the inhuman flame that scorched my veins.

On the edge of the arrondissement, I turned into a narrow street and spied, about halfway along, the marquee of a movie theatre. The light bulbs that once lined the awning had been shattered long ago as had the glass in the display cases. Most of the posters inside had been torn from the wall, but one remained, faded but intact: a tribute. The title of the film, *The Devil is a Woman*, was emblazoned across the top of the poster. Below the words, Marlene Dietrich regarded me with her beautiful, haughty gaze.

When I was a teenager, Dietrich had been my idol. She was everything I thought a woman should be: intelligent, independent, and utterly desirable. I loved her sensuality, her daring and, to my parent's horror, I spent a summer wearing my father's clothes and puffing cigarettes in imitation of her. Years later, when she refused to join the Nazis, I added audacious and principled to the list of qualities I admired about her.

Before the war made such things impossible, I had gone to see every one of her movies, sitting in the half-dark, mesmerised by her face and words. This particular film, *The Devil is a Woman*, I had seen with Didier not long after we meet. We sat in the centre of the theatre, holding hands as always, yet completely unaware of each other. That was the power of Marlene.

I took the poster as an invitation and went over to the doors to investigate the chain wrapped around the handles; a pointless gesture as the wood and glass panels on either side had been kicked in to give access to the theatre. As I yanked the chain away, a pile of litter in an alcove beside the box office shifted to reveal a human.

'Spare a franc, sister?'

The Thirst shuddered through me as stared at her, taking in her wretched state: thin, filthy, little more than rags to protect her from the cold, teeth rotting in her mouth. She was another miserable bit of flotsam washed up by the war.

'Yes, my dear,' I said, holding the door open for her. 'Step inside and you'll want for nothing ever again.' She came eagerly enough and I began my song as I glanced at Marlene's poster, catching the cold sparkle of approval in her eyes.

At the first inkling of dusk, I left my resting place and resumed the search for Didier. The hours of slumber had done nothing to ease my fury. Nor did my first kill of the night, a young German soldier who stumbled upon me as I hunted through the apartment he had occupied.

'What are you?'

He choked on his words as I turned to face him, letting him see me as I truly am: eyes blazing with blood-lust, fangs extended, fingers hooked into claws, muscles coiled ready to spring; a single-minded predator in human form. I leapt at him, knocking him backwards, and he gave a strangled scream as his ribs snapped under my weight. His breath, tainted with sauerkraut, rushed into my face and I grimaced as I shoved his head aside, tearing tendons and dislocating his jaw. He cried out again, his hands flailing uselessly at my side as his jack-booted feet drummed a death knell against the floor. Unmoved, I went for his throat, for the place where the jugular bulged against his skin, and drove my fangs into him. Hot blood spurted into my mouth and I swallowed greedily, all vestiges of my humanity lost in the warm saltiness that flowed from his body into mine.

When I came back to myself, the soldier was dead. I didn't know when he died or how much he suffered, and I didn't care. His blood had sated the Thirst, but my anger and frustration remained, driven by the knowledge that the longer the SS held Didier prisoner, the lower were his chances of survival. I pushed away from the corpse and crossed the apartment to the kitchenette where I cleaned the blood from my face and hands. A breeze, light as a sigh, slipped through the window and drew my attention outside. The city was still and dark, with only a few pockets of light: guard posts and the occasional entertainment venue, no doubt teeming with German soldiers and collaborators trying to save their own skin. Yet, quiet as the streets appeared, I could hear hearts beating behind barred doors, in secret alcoves, attics and basements, and the sound filled me with despair as the impossibility of finding Didier struck me.

I gripped the edge of the sink. *I cannot lose him. I will not,* I thought, but the simple fact was that I couldn't search the entire city, not when it had taken a whole night to cover a dozen blocks of one arrondissement. *And what if the SS have taken him out of the city, into the countryside, or out of France altogether?* The thought sent a stab of terror through my heart. Fighting panic, I climbed through the window and dropped to the pavement, starting the search again in spite of its futility. I needed to keep moving, for to stop meant surrendering to my fear.

Robbed of certainty, my path grew erratic and I blundered through the streets until I came upon the Théâtre de l'Odéon, which blazed with light. On the steps leading to the main foyer were three German soldiers, bayoneted rifles held at the ready as they watched the road. I skidded to a halt and ducked into the shadows as one of the soldiers turned in my direction. Cursing my impulsiveness, I waited to see if he would come to investigate. He peered into the dark, indecision on his face, before calling to his comrades and pointed to where I was hiding.

'Fools,' I muttered, readying myself to eradicate more sons of the Fatherland, but as they came down the steps, a truck rumbled out of the street opposite and pulled up in front of the theatre. The soldiers hesitated, shot a glance at each other and another towards the place where I hid and, after a brief exchange of words, they turned towards the truck.

The crash of the tailgate jarred the night and mingled with the demands of the soldiers. 'Aussteigen,' they yelled, jabbing their guns at the people who lurched into a haphazard line in front of their tormentors.

They were a disparate bunch: three women and five men, although two of them were hardly more than boys, street urchins arrested, no doubt, for pickpocketing or some other petty theft. Tears streaked their dirty cheeks. My gaze shifted to the two women, one auburn-haired, the other blonde, on the end of the line. They were around my age, gaunt but pretty under the rouge and brilliant red lipstick. A soldier sidled up to the blonde, leering, and shoved his hand inside her dress, pawing at her breast. She didn't flinch, but kept her eyes on the soldiers moving inside the theatre, resigned to what lay in store for her.

The three remaining people, a woman and two men, stood a little apart from the others. They were formally dressed, as though they were attending a matinée performance at the Odéon, and they held themselves erect, chins high in defiance. From their demeanour, I guessed they were business owners or academics. For a moment, I wondered if they were collaborators of the Vichy regime, but I dismissed the notion. Collaborators rarely found themselves outside the Odéon, which had become infamous as a place of execution for members of the Résistance.

I searched the faces of the three, but they were unfamiliar, although that didn't mean they weren't acquainted with Didier. A desire to question them washed over me but, as frustrating as it was to lose a potential source of information, I couldn't act upon it without exposing myself and I had to let the opportunity pass. The last thing I needed was the whole Wehrmacht hunting me across the city while I sought after Didier.

Across the street, a blue-coated milicien officer appeared between the columns of the Odéon; his beret sat at a rakish angle and a cigarette hung from the corner of his mouth. Pinned to his chest were two gleaming medals and around his waist was an empty pistol belt; the gun was in his hand. Hatred blazed in my heart. None were more loathed than the Vichy's militia; puppets of the Germans and traitors to their people, they were as vicious as the SS and twice as dangerous because they could blend in and infiltrate the citizenry at will.

The urge to kill the officer was strong, but as pointless as the desire to speak with the résisters, yet his appearance had the benefit of stirring a new idea. *Perhaps the milice had taken Didier.* The thought gave me hope for, if it was the milice, I knew who could help me in my search.

On the steps of the Odéon, the milicien officer flicked his cigarette away, adjusted his lapels, and strode down the steps towards the people beside the truck. He came to stand in front of the auburn-haired woman and, without a word, he raised his pistol and shot her in the forehead. As she fell, he stepped in front of the blonde and, as the gunshot rang out, I leapt for the rooftop, unwilling to wait for him to reach the boys at the end of the line.

Le Voltaire was alive with the clink of crystal glasses and clatter of fine china plates. Waiters, moving with the precision of surgeons, sliced between the tables, serving *Soupe à l'oignon, Coq au vin* and *Sole á la Meuniere* to customers animated by conversation. Delicate aromas teased the air; champagne corks bounced against the ceiling. Light and music spilled into the night, chasing each other across the street to the edge of the Seine.

Under the table, hidden by a heavy linen cloth, Didier held my hand and gently turned the engagement ring on my finger while his father toasted our future. My own parents sat opposite us. They nodded as Monsieur Villette spoke, and glanced at Didier and me to offer a smile of encouragement. I couldn't recall ever seeing them so happy.

Beside me, my younger sister leaned close and whispered, 'They're just pleased to have you out of the house, you know.' With my free hand, I pinched her leg and she squirmed away with a low giggle, bringing the stern eyes of Madame Villette our way.

Didier's mother was a petite woman with deceptively delicate features, who possessed a fierce creativity that she worn like a crown. She painted in the style of Delacroix, with the same expansive colours and movement, and with the same passion for capturing the dramatic or exotic but, as befitting her stature, she did her work in miniature. At the time of my engagement to her son, she was the darling of the Parisian cultural scene, sort after for exhibitions and public appearances both in Paris and overseas. Yet, for all her success, it was her husband and children that meant the most to her and, as her expression suggested, she would tolerate no disrespect to them.

Chastened, I inclined my head towards her in apology before nodding towards my sister and lifting my shoulders. Madame Villette's expression softened and her gaze shifted to Didier's two siblings, who were home from school for our party, and back to me. She was smiling and my heart swelled with the understanding that I had a friend and ally in my soon-to-be mother-in-law.

Monsieur Villette finished his speech with a flourish. 'To Didier and Juliana. May God grant them a long and fruitful life!' he said, and raised his glass high. Around the table, our friends and family hoisted champagne glasses and, as they shouted our names, the other patrons in the restaurant joined in until it seemed that Didier and I had taken the place of the sun at the centre of the universe.

The memory glowed around me, vivid as a summer's day, until from somewhere across the river, a machine gun chattered and, although I fought to hold onto them, the lights and music in *Le Voltaire* vanished. The restaurant was closed in compliance with the curfew and all I had left, like Marius from *Les Misérable,* were 'phantom faces at the windows and phantom shadows on the floor.' A longing as intense as the Thirst filled my heart. *This* was the life that Callisto and Constantine had drained from me; a glorious human life woven with the threads of love, joy and pleasure, all stolen away.

How I loathed them for their thievery.

How I would make them pay for every lost moment.

But first, Didier.

I crossed the empty road, leaving the Seine to its quiet meandering, and entered a side street that would take me to Rue de Lillie. At the far end of this thoroughfare was the apartment the Villette family used during the spring theatre season and on those occasions when Madame Villette exhibited her work in one of the prestigious galleries on the Champs Élysées. I knew she was having just such an exhibition as I had followed Didier to *La Galerie Elusia* the week before his disappearance. Of course, I could not wander through the exhibition and discuss the work with him; I left that to the sable-haired girl on his arm— whom I killed the next evening, drawing her blood slowly to punish her for her impertinence.

Madame Villette's exhibition was the talk of Paris, although not every conversation was about her artistic talent. Some held her up as the heroine of French culture, who thumbed her nose at the Nazis and refused to be oppressed, while others saw her as a self-interested collaborator. The truth, it seemed to me, was somewhere in between. She had children to feed and protect and so couldn't afford the silence of Guehenno, nor the exile of Breton. Instead, she chose to stay in Paris and, like Picasso, to continue her work with a polite deference to the enemy that never extended to fraternisation.

There was another reason for Madame Villette's compromise: she had family on both sides of the political divide. On the one hand, her husband and Didier actively supported the Résistance. Monsieur Villette worked alongside Albert Camus on the newspaper, *Combat*, gathering intelligence and publishing articles that encouraged the citizenry to oppose the enemy, while Didier went into the field to carry out sabotage and help the persecuted escape France. On the other hand, there was a favourite uncle who held a position high up in the milice and a renegade son, René, who had been involved with the Nazi regime for years.

I knew little about René; his father had banished him well before I meet Didier and the family never spoke of him. There were no photographs or portraits of him at their country estate as there were of the other Villette children. He was a blank space on the wall. The one time I asked Didier about his brother, he had replied, 'Respect my father's wishes,' and, because I loved him, I did. Now, with Didier missing, I wished I had been more insistent. Still, it was not René who bought me to the Villette's apartment — like the rest of the family, I thought of him as a lost cause — but the uncle, Pierre Darnard.

To human eyes, the building across the street appeared empty. Of course, I am not human, so I saw the traces of candlelight that seeped around the blankets covering the windows. They were in residence. A spark of hope ignited in my stomach and I had to fight the urge to rush in on them unannounced. After all, it had been seven years since they'd last seen me and, back then, I was a vivacious human woman, not the monstrous creature of my current existence; I didn't want to scare them to death.

I crossed the street and faded into the dark entrance to the building, puzzling over how I could approach them without inspiring terror. Perhaps a disguise of some kind, or a mask, like the one worn by Marlene Dietrich in *The Devil is a Woman*? No. Procuring such things would mean delaying questioning the Villette's, and that was a delay Didier couldn't afford. Perhaps a note under the door?

As I pondered my options, I caught the sound of movement from above; heavy footsteps, the clink of ice thrown in a glass, and two hearts thudding. The noise drew me from the shadows to look up at the second floor balcony. I thought back to the last time Didier and I had dined with his parents, drawing forth the layout of the apartment. They were in the parlour, which was to the left of the balcony. Then came the sound of their voices and, without another thought, I took a few steps backwards, ran and leapt, catching the railing and landing noiselessly beside the parlour window.

'—Pierre must know.'

'He doesn't.'

'So he says.'

'Why would he lie, Henri?'

'Everyone lies in these dark times.'

'Pierre is family. If he knew anything about Didier, he would tell us. As it is, he has risked much asking questions of his superiors.'

'Maybe he is too concerned with saving his own skin to ask the right questions.'

'If Pierre says the milice don't have Didier, then I believe him. And, what's more, I think we should follow his advice and contact René.'

'No! And you will not mention that name in my presence again.'

'He is our son.'

'He is dead to me.'

'Henri, please. He could help.'

'We don't need his help.'

'Didier does.'

'Enough, Estelle, enough.'

A door slammed inside the apartment and, after a moment, I heard the bitter sobbing of Madame Villette. The nostalgic part of my heart wanted to go to her and offer what comfort I could, to tell her that she was not alone in her search for Didier. The Thirst, awakened by thoughts of being close to a living body, wanted to bleed her dry. Disgusted with myself, I vaulted over the railing and raced away from the apartment, creating safety with distance, as I did with all whom I loved.

I know what you're thinking, mortal. It was heroic of me to spare Madame Villette's life that night, admirable, even. Huh! Tell that to the four strangers I slaughtered before sunrise to ease my blood lust. Or tell it to the Villettes who, with the end of the Occupation in sight, were snatched from their country estate and deported to the horror that was Dachau. Or tell it to Pierre Darnard, whom I terrorised with a prolonged demise to ensure he was as truthful as Madame Villette believed. Or tell it to Didier who, despite all of the deaths I delivered, was still no closer to rescue.

So much for the heroic vampire.

Foolish human; can you hear me over the beating of your quixotic heart?

Midday in Suburbia

Lucy's the consummate politician; given enough time, I'm sure she could convince God that he doesn't exist. I admire her for the skill and usually enjoy the benefits, but I'm not in the mood for her politicking, so I leave her to work on her parents. She glares at me and mouths the word *coward* as the door to her hospital room swings closed.

I don't take the insult to heart, and I don't stay.

My parents live half an hour from the hospital; an easy drive down the highway into suburbia, where ordinariness is the number one criteria in the building code. I pull into the driveway, kill the engine, and climb out into silence. The entire neighbourhood is at work, or school, and the quiet is so complete it's as though I've entered a nuclear testing zone. I glance at the sky, waiting for the superheated shockwave that will annihilate me.

Nothing.

Almost disappointed, I go inside.

In the kitchen, I raid the fridge, scoring left over pizza and a can of Coke. I take them to my room at the back of the house. A weight lifts from my shoulders when I close the door. It's dark, soothing. The strain of the last few hours slips away as I take the familiar path to my computer. I dump the pizza and Coke on the desk and boot up the machine. Seconds later, a selfie of Lucy fills the screen: eyeing the camera, mouth pouting, the swell of her breasts rising from her low-cut top. I consider the icon that sits over her left nipple: a little fox encircling the world, and wonder if the next instalment of the vampire's blog has been uploaded. My hand hovers over the keyboard, but a yawn cracks my jaw and I grab the Coke instead.

Crawling onto my bed, I stretch out and lift my gaze to the ceiling. Photos of galaxies, nebula and star clusters from deep space jostle for my attention; the universe looks down on me. When I turned twelve, my parents brought me a ridiculously expensive telescope, which we took to my Aunt Susan's hobby farm on my birthday weekend. I spent the day bored stupid, but when night fell and my dad set up the telescope in her backyard— Wow, talk about mind-blowing. I looked through the lens of the scope, straight into the heart of the Andromeda galaxy, and everything I thought I understood about my world changed.

I took my eye away from the lens and stared at my dad, who had always been the centre of my world. He ruffled my hair, pleased to have shared some new experience with his neophyte offspring. I let him have his moment, and then dismissed him, returning my attention to the night sky, *knowing* there was something bigger than him; something more powerful, more intelligent, and infinitely more wise. Don't misunderstand me; I love my dad but he's only a man and he doesn't have the answers to the mysteries of this world, or any other.

And I want those answers. I want to know what holds all this - the universe and everything in it - together. The question is, how do I find those answers in one lifetime? The philosophers - Plato, Spinoza, Nietzsche, and their like - couldn't do it. Nor could Copernicus, Einstein, or Newton, and while Hawking and his contemporaries carry on the search, they will solve only a miniscule part of the puzzle before death takes them, leaving the full breadth of the mystery veiled.

Such is the frustration of a single human lifespan.

I open the Coke and settle my obsession with a sugar hit as my thoughts turn to Lucy and the plan I've set in motion. It'll take her a few days to talk her parents into letting me go with her to Paris, but that's okay 'cause I need time to work on my mum and dad.

They'll be reluctant at first, especially since I'll have to hit them up for a loan for the ticket; 'assistant manager' might sound flash, but the pay is shit. I've got enough saved to get to Paris; getting back though is another story. Not that I need a return ticket, since returning isn't part of the plan, but there's no way Mum will agree to me going if I don't have one. Even then, with that hurdle crossed, she'll still have a dozen reasons why I shouldn't go:

It's too far away if something goes wrong.

(How will I mother you if you get sick?)

It'll cost a fortune.

(*How will I keep an eye on your finances?*)

There's no support network.

(*Lucy is wonderful but she's not family*)

You're too young.

(*Don't leave me*)

I sigh. Paris is sounding better by the minute. I haul myself off the bed and flick on the desk light. The glow reaches up the wall and lights the words I've painted onto a black canvas:

'The life of mortals is so mean a thing as to be virtually un-life.'
Empedocles

The quote leapt out at me while I was researching for a paper on causality and freedom for a cosmology class. I wrote it down and transferred it to the canvas a few days later. Something about the words struck me as important. I'd think about them during uni lectures or during slow periods at work, tossing them around in my head, trying to find some consensus with Empedocle's position.

I could see how he might arrive at such a thought. When I watched the drones around me who, like ants, scurried through their lives repeating the same tasks, having the same conversations, fighting the same battles over and over again, his pessimistic view of human life had a sort of eloquent, if depressing, validity, but could I buy into his vision? Did I believe my life was so small that it was meaningless? Did the things I filled my life with give it purpose? Was I just a drone too? I thought hard on these questions, feeling a teetering in my mind; the potential for a collapse of will. Then, out of some distant synaptic corridor, came the voice of Macbeth:

> ...*Out, out brief candle!*
> *Life's but a walking shadow, a poor player,*
> *That struts and frets his hour upon the stage,*
> *And then is heard no more. It is a tale,*
> *Told by an idiot, full of sound and fury,*
> *Satisfying nothing.*

The murderous king and sceptical philosopher were in agreement, it seemed: life was nothing. Part of me reared up in protest, fist clenched in defence of my existence, denying in a raw voice that I had no purpose. *There has to be meaning, otherwise what is the point of going on?* that voice argued.

Macbeth laughed. Empedocles shook his head, and I turned from them in a whirl of confusion.

When I'm troubled, I usually turn to the stars to find solace. Getting lost in the beauty and wonder of the constellations soothes my mind but, that night, the sky was blanketed with cloud from horizon to horizon. So, to escape the mockery of Macbeth and Empedocles, I turned to the internet. Slouching in my chair, I opened my browser, searching for a distraction. Images flashed before my eyes as pages uploaded: music, sex, cars, sport, cats, sex, movies, food, sex, music, but still the question remained:

Is life meaningless?

Then something registered: *The Truth about Vampires.*

Lucy was the one who got me interested in vampires. Before we started dating, I'd watched the odd vampire movie - *Dusk 'til Dawn; 30 Days of Night; Blade* - for the body count, not understanding the deeper motives of the creatures on the screen. It was make-believe, and pretty crap most of the time, but Lucy saw something different. She introduced me to ancient - so she claimed - tomes of vampiric lore, to the myths and legends, all the way back to Lilith, the first wife of Adam, who was cast down for refusing to lie beneath him and became a daemon that sucked the life from small children. When I pointed out that the plight of Lilith was just a story, Lucy replied, 'There's a grain of truth in every story, Christian,' and to prove her point, she lead me to a darker place.

The club was predictably subterranean. We threaded between the press of bodies filling a descending staircase, down into throbbing music, where strobing lights flickered across pale powdered skin and caught on fangs - fake, or filed into reality - and in red, violet, and gold contacts, to a bar where every glass was filled with a deep red liquid.

Wide-eyed, I yelled into Lucy's ear, 'Blood?'

She shook her head and curled her finger. 'C'mon.'

We passed through a beaded entry to another room: smaller, darker, couples talking, kissing, groping, and beyond another doorway with a heavy curtain, where the first thing to hit me was the scent: coppery, familiar. My eyes adjusted to the gloom; more couples, sometimes a threesome: lips locked to flesh, tongues lapping at thin rivulets of blood, glint of a blade, a hiss, a moan, eyes rolling with ecstasy. Lucy's face was flushed and she pressed her fingers to her mouth, and then ran them down her throat to her breast as she gazed at me.

We didn't try it that night, but I woke the next morning with claw marks across my stomach and the impression of Lucy's teeth embedded in my bicep. When I showed her the damage, she laughed, told me to suck it up, and continued to dress. Before she slipped away to join her parents at Mass, she kissed me, bit my lip gently, and promised we'd go 'all the way' next time.

I stayed in bed after she left, dozing and half-dreaming about what it'd be like to taste her blood but, away from the bewitching surrealism of the club and the heat of Lucy's desire, the idea brought a twist of revulsion. Surprised by the feeling, I came fully awake and rolled onto my back, cupping my hands behind my head as I gazed up at the galaxies on my ceiling.

What are you thinking, Christian, I asked myself, *buying into the girl's mad game?*

It was a good question. Fun as Lucy was, and as much as I liked being with her, sometimes there was a darkness in her that rivalled my own. Maybe that was what drew me to her. Yet, did I love her enough—

The rest of the thought vanished and the simple question remained: *Did I love Lucy?*

And a small voice whispered: *Does it matter?*

Maybe.

Maybe not.

We were good together; our parents were happy we were a couple, and our friends were envious of our relationship. We fitted expectations, rebellious piercings and scar tissue aside, and followed social conventions. Did it matter that our relationship was a sugar-coated placebo rather than the real deal - whatever that was? Wasn't it more important that I protected Lucy from the truth? To do otherwise would hurt her and I refused to be responsible for causing her pain. Besides, one of these days, she would come to realise the truth of her own feelings, then she would let me go, pain-free.

Before that revelation came to her, though, I knew she'd want to do the vampire thing. I sighed. *Maybe I'll come to like the taste of blood*, I thought, and shuddered.

Pushing off the doona, I got out of bed and headed to the shower. As the water sluiced away the scent of Lucy's body, I wondered about the obsession felt by the people at the club: was it blood lust, the desire for eternal beauty and youth, the strength to live above human and natural law, the ability to cheat death? All of these? None of them? I was sure of only one thing; to Lucy's friends, vampirism was Religion.

'Delusion and fantasy,' I muttered, so sure of my judgement.

Until: *The Truth about Vampires*.

The article was persuasive. The author wrote about vampiric history, confirming all Lucy had told me, and went into detail about the physical and psychic state of the vampire, explaining their emotional patterns and how they fed on the life energy of their victims:

Ingesting the pranic force of a mortal slows the aging process and extends the life of the vampire far beyond that of the normal human life span.

Now that sounded promising. I sat back in my chair and looked up at Empedocles' statement, and a certainty filled me: he was wrong. Life was not meaningless, but it would take more than one human lifetime to prove it.

My fingers found the keyboard, and Juliana's blog filled the screen.

It's strange the way destiny works, how all the events of our lives flow together. What would Empedocles say if he knew where his outburst of pessimism would lead? Would Shakespeare reconsider Macbeth's cynicism? Would Lucy avoid her flirtation with Ecstasy? Probably not, yet each one has contributed to bringing me to this point; to the place where my destiny is bound to cross with Juliana's, somewhere beneath the City of Love.

Blog Five

Until Death Do Us Part

Why are you so fascinated with my kind? Everywhere I look, there is a new vampire film, or a new vampire book. There are songs, bands, documentaries, mockumentaries, games, websites, and fashion lines, all dedicated to the immortals - as though we are not individuals, but clones made on a production line, solely for your entertainment. What gives you the right to impersonate us? To chisel your teeth to points; to paint your nails black; to sleep in coffins. As though we would be so crass.

Your myths are rabid dogs feeding upon each other until they are more violent, more romantic, and more epic than we could ever be. There is *nothing* impressive about this deathly existence. It is an agony of waiting, of passing endless nights, of inflicting pain and loss upon the innocent. You are blind to these realities, and your ignorance is a bliss that protects your self-absorbed world.

What draws you to the vampire? Is it the idea of eternal youth, beauty, and passion, of stopping the world and halting time? What you forget is the price of such feats of magic. That price is a handful of dust; the remains of your life, which trickles through your fingers, leaving you utterly and terribly alone. But you - deluded mortal that you are - can't see beyond your own selfishness, and you have no concept of sacrifice.

A vampire knows about sacrifice; immortals know all about being alone.

A woman's laugh caught my attention one evening about eighteen months after I lost Didier. I had only recently returned to Paris, having travelled through Germany in search of my beloved and his enigmatic brother. Nowhere did I catch sight of Didier in that blighted country and, although I heard the occasional rumour about René, the brothers appeared to have been swallowed by the black beast of war.

Desolate with failure, I hunted the broad, tree-lined avenue of Jardin des Tuileries, searching among the lovers for a suitable couple to quench the Thirst. The night was crisp, but many people were out strolling, holding hands and smiling, their eyes lit with romance. They made me sick.

The woman's laughter was whimsical. The sound floated between the trees, accompanied by calliope music from a brightly lit carousel. I hated the owner of that laugh without laying eyes on her, and I knew she would be the one to satisfy my hunger that night; her and her lover.

I edged closer to the carousel, but stayed hidden amongst the shadows, waiting for her to appear. White horses meandered up and down their poles, while a pair of elephants stood stoically side by side, their wide backs offering a steady seat to the less adventurous. The carousel turned, coming almost full circle, revealing a white swan with arched wings spread behind its graceful neck. From within this protective alcove came her laughter, this time blended with the unmistakable baritone of a male companion.

The carousel slowed, the music winding down, and I saw a hand grasp the edge of the swan's wing; there was a plain gold band on the ring finger. Then the woman appeared. Dark hair fell around her shoulders, framing a small face with delicate features and eyes of deep green. She was perfect; just to my taste.

Her laughter rang out again as she held out her hand to the man who remained in the swan. He, it seemed, was being obstinate, for she stomped her foot and demanded he leave the carousel, *at once*! I waited to see my second victim. He stood, making the swan sway, and leapt down in front of the woman, his face lit with a smile.

A smile I recognised.

There are moments when the world stops turning, when sensation ceases, and the mind becomes a white void. These moments are so significant that they break you apart and show you the truth of who you are. I am a vampire. A killer: deathless, soulless, but, in the silence of that moment, in the light of that smile, I knew I was also still capable of joy.

Didier was alive, and I drank in his presence like the blood of my first victim. From the shadows, I marvelled at his face, at the line of his jaw, at the pulse in his throat that beat strong and steady with life. There were new lines around his mouth and eyes that spoke of some distressing experience, but he was as handsome and vibrant as the day I met him, and he was *here* right before me. My heart soared. Then he caught the woman in his arms and kissed her, the wedding ring on his finger catching the light from the carousel.

There are other moments when the world spins with sickening speed, when every sensation is a gaping wound, and the mind collapses into darkness. As I watched Didier with his bride, I died for the second time.

They strolled away from the carousel, arms entwined, and passed close to where I was standing. I could not move, even though, if he had glanced up, Didier would have seen me, but the woman absorbed his attention and I was merely a shadow among the shadows. They continued along the avenue towards the Musée du Louvre and, as though pulled by an invisible cord, I followed, weaving between the trees, keeping them in sight.

I was a riot of emotion. One minute I hated them and wanted to end their lives and their love. The next, I was reminding myself that Didier was alive, and that it was a blessing he had found love again. Then, he would touch the woman's face with a tenderness I remembered so well and I would want to destroy her. I was insane with contradiction; it tormented me as I trailed them onto Quai des Tuileries and across the Seine at Pont Royal. I knew I had to leave them, or they would pay the price for my pain, but before I could, I needed to know where to find them again.

They lead me to an apartment building on Rue des Saints Peres, not far from Le Tabou, a club Didier and I had frequented when I was mortal. I felt the clench of jealousy around my heart again as I pictured Didier and his wife dancing through the night, lost in the rhythm of the jazz and each other. Bitterness rose in my throat and I dug my nails into my palms, fighting the urge to annihilate.

Didier and his bride disappeared inside the building and I waited until I saw a light come on in an apartment on the third floor. A silhouette appeared at the window. Delicate; fragile: the woman. She was joined by Didier, who took her into his arms. I turned away, unable to watch, and went in hunt of a couple who would satisfy my hunger and the rage that turned my heart to ashes.

He saw me coming; a beautiful creature with eyes full of glittering hatred and a smile that revealed the sharp canine teeth sliding over my bottom lip. He paled and his mouth opened to let out a cry, but I didn't give him the chance. I grabbed him by the shoulders and used the hardness of my body to propel him to the ground, wrenching his head back to expose the muscular neck. He gave a thin shriek and bucked beneath me. He was strong, but I was stronger and more agile. I brought my mouth to his throat and bit deeply, feeling the gush of blood against my face. He screamed, and I pushed my fist into his mouth, shattering teeth as I gorged.

A movement pulled my attention away from him, and I glared at the woman who was making a pitiful bid for freedom. 'Don't bother,' I said, and saw her eyes widen as she took in the blood smeared across my mouth and her dying lover in my arms. 'You're deep beneath the catacombs, and even if you could escape me, you will never find your way to the surface.' She slumped against the wall, and I returned to the man, finishing him off with a snap of his neck.

I turned to the girl, eyes narrowed, spiteful. She stared at me, resignation evident in the slump of her body. *Where's the fun in that?* I thought, wiping my mouth with the back of my hand. I dropped the man and strode across the room, dragging the woman to her feet.

'Do you want your freedom?'

She whimpered and I almost dispatched her on the spot out of disgust, but I controlled the urge and sent her reeling into the hallway instead. 'I'll give you a ten minute head start.' The girl chewed her bottom lip, glanced into the darkness and looked at me, uncertain. 'The passage leading out of the catacombs is that way,' I said, pointing left, 'you have nine and a half minutes.'

The woman ran in the direction I'd indicated. It seemed she was not as cowardly as I had presumed. I stepped back into the room and took care of her paramour's body as I counted down the minutes in my head and kept track of her frantic flight through the passageways that made up my lair. I realised this was an unfair advantage but, the fact was, I'd already hunted her once and, while I like a challenge, I wasn't prepared to search too hard for her when her real purpose was to alleviate my anguish.

My mind turned to Didier and his wife as I dragged the body of the man to its final resting place; a pit in the bowels of my lair where the rats and roaches delighted in my deeds. *What am I to do about this woman who has invaded Didier's life?* I wondered. Could I get rid of her when it was so evident they were in love? Shouldn't I be happy that Didier had found joy?

'No,' I raged, pounding my fist on the crumbling mortar. 'He's mine.'

Maybe once, when you were a mortal woman of warm flesh, my mind whispered, *but now you are a creature of blood and death, thanks to Callisto and Constantine.*

Oh, how I hated those names. I tried to focus, gathering my fury to send my senses in search of my makers in the city above, but the voice would not be silenced. *You have two choices: leave Paris forever or continue to watch over Didier, and his wife. Protect them, and perhaps you can redeem your soul, in time.*

Anguish whipped through me. This was to be my lot? Well then, so be it, but I would not suffer alone. I closed my eyes and listened. The woman had unwittingly circled back to the room from whence I had sent her in search of freedom. She was pressed against a wall, panic-stricken and without hope.

Excellent, I thought, moving through the dark. The Thirst was gnawing at me again, and I welcomed it with a lover's delight.

The Princess and the Liar

Parties are not my thing, but Lucy insists we go to every lame celebration of our impending departure for Paris, even those organised by the wannabe's at the far edge of her social network. After two week of beach barbeques, dinner parties, and late-night drinking fests in seedy bars, I'm pretty much over it, and she knows it.

'Hey,' she says, dropping down beside me on the chaise lounge. Her silk dress rustles against the leather as the material rides up her thighs. She lifts her hips and smooths the skirt with a wriggle until it sit demurely above her knees. Below the hem of her dress, her bare legs hold onto summer, although I suspect it may be a bottled version of the season. A pink cardigan covers her arms and shoulders, protecting against the chill June wind. Her hair is pinned at the back of her head, half up half down, framing her neck while hiding the small nicks in the skin below her collarbone. She's a vision and, although I'm annoyed about having to be at this contemptibly ritzy dinner, I'm also sort of proud to have her by my side, especially when I see the way other guys look at her and then at me.

'Are you coming back in? Daddy's making his speech soon,' she says, straightening the tie I pulled loose so I could breathe.

Before I can answer, a girl calls to Lucy from the doorway to the banquet hall. She hurries across the reception area towards us, short skirt snapping, fingers pressed over her lips, eyes wide, as though she might explode at any second. When she reaches Lucy, she grabs her hand and drags her to her feet as she exclaims, 'O.M.G, Lucy, you'll never guess who just turned up.'

Lucy laughs and allows herself to be drawn away by one arm as she holds the other out to me. I make a show of standing, then sit again as the girls disappear into the throng of guests who've come to wish us *Bon Voyage*. I'm not ready to hear another 'When I was in Paris' story, or to see another insinuating wink when someone mentions that Paris is the city of love.

I yank the tie askew again and undo the top buttons of my shirt as I try to place the girl who'd stolen Lucy away. I'm pretty sure her name is Milynda, but I remember her as a pale-faced Goth who hovered around Lucy like a dark fog all through junior high before she was transferred to some private school down South. Somehow, between then and now, she'd morphed from mumbling shadow girl to giggling glam goddess.

Girls; who could work them out?

Maybe the change shouldn't surprise me since Lucy has also undergone a transformation since her junior high days. When I first meet her, she was a bitch-princess: fifteen going on twenty-five (or so she thought), with long ebony hair, dressed in black, wearing five inch platform boots, silver buckles, pins and spikes. She was nasty to her clique (who adored her anyway), rude to her parents (who loved her anyway), sarcastic with anyone who tried to reach her (who were tolerant because they thought they could change her) and, in my eyes, totally intriguing. Not because of the attitude - we all had that - but because I could see it was an act and, as always, I wanted to solve the mystery of who she really was behind that vicious veneer.

It took a while to break into her inner circle and longer to make her curious about me but, once she decided I was worth her attention, we were soon hanging out most afternoons and all weekend. What I discovered about her in that first year was that she wasn't putting on an act - she really was a bitch, but only because she refused to accept the insipid crap most people wanted to feed her. Lucy was honest, but people couldn't handle her honesty, so they labelled her - anti-social, delinquent, outsider - and, in response, Lucy amped up the attitude and meet their expectations, tenfold.

What those people missed was the girl behind the attitude, but I saw her: astute, funny, curious, and loyal almost to a fault. This was the girl I came to know and care about on those wet weekends when we played *COD* or *Halo*, battling it out until our fingers ached and our stomach hurt from laughing; the girl who volunteered at the animal shelter and cried every time a dog or cat was taken through 'the door'; the girl people didn't see, the one Lucy kept hidden from everyone, except me.

Although I knew her parents credited me with the change, it was Lucy who decided to let the dark princess die a natural death. We didn't talk about it, or acknowledge it in anyway, she just did it; a slow shedding of the outer layers of her persona that took almost a year and concluded one summer's night, at her parent's beach house, with our first real kiss.

In those moments when our mouths were pressed together, I celebrated her and everything she meant to me. But, when the kiss broke and she looked into my eyes, I wondered how I could ever fulfil all of the expectations I saw in her smoky gaze. She smiled as I brushed hair from her cheek and turned her so that her back was against me. I tilted her chin towards the sky and whispered, 'I will never forget the stars tonight.'

Becoming lovers was the obvious next step, and one I was more than willing to take, but it still came as a surprise when her father introduce me to a business associate of his as 'Lucy's boyfriend'. Somehow, I figured what was between Lucy and I went no further than us. I was wrong. Soon, I came to realise that Lucy thought this way about us too, which seemed to make her happy, and I couldn't bear to hurt her by asking for more time to find out if I could be all that she wanted. Now, a year later, I'm pretty sure I can't be.

Lucy's back at the banquet hall door, hand on hip this time. I give her a wave and stand, buttoning buttons and straightening my tie as I walk towards her. Beyond her, the guests have taken their seats and the

MC is at the microphone. He's making a joke about a man who proposes to the wrong woman after climbing the Eiffel Tower.

'What're you doing?' she says.

I slip my arm around her waist. 'Thinking about you,' I reply, as the MC reaches the punch line and laughter breaks around us. We weave through the tables to the front of the room and sit as Peter Crossing is invited to the stage. My mother looks over at me. She's wearing her: *Where have you been?* expression.

Man, anyone would think I'd ditched the bride at my wedding.

I'm saved from giving some kind of response by the whine of feedback. There's a collective groan from the guests and Lucy's father taps the microphone. 'Sorry about that, folks,' he says, and someone heckles him from the back of the room. There's a smattering of laughter and I control the urge to roll my eyes at the predictability of these people.

'Thanks for the input, Jon,' Peter Crossing says, unfolding a square of paper.

I lean close to Lucy and murmur against her ear, 'He's written a speech? He does know we're only going for six months, right?' She reaches behind her and gives my knee a warning squeeze. 'A little higher, babe,' I whisper again, and she digs in her nails.

Peter Crossing looks at Lucy, and I sit back. 'There comes a moment in every father's life when he has to face the fact that his child is no longer a child, but a fully-fledged adult—'

My phone vibrates against my leg; a notification. The vampire has posted a new blog. Lucy glances over her shoulder, her eyes daring me to check the feed. I lift my hands away from my phone and she returns her attention to her father. She's been weird about the whole Juliana thing for the last couple of weeks, sort of sceptical and jealous at the same time, especially after she put two and two together: the blogs and my desire to go to Paris.

We were vegging out at my place the first time she decided to voice her disapproval and, as always with Lucy, she didn't bother to sugar-coat her feelings. 'That skank is taking up all of your time,' she announced.

Stretched out on the lounge, laptop resting against my legs, I was reading about Didier's disappearance and flicking between websites on wartime Paris, like a detective searching for clues to a long-unsolved mystery. On the TV, Sherlock Holmes was interrogating the soon-to-be executed Lord Blackwood. As they bantered, I imagined meeting Juliana in some dark mossy cell where I would reveal the whereabouts of her lost lover and, to show her gratitude, she would take me in her arms and—

A cushion smacked me in the head. 'What the hell, Lucy?' I said, flinging the cushion back at her.

'Jerk-off, you're ignoring me.'

She was huddled in a beanbag with a copy of *Let The Right One In* resting on her knees and a scowl on her face. Careful not to sigh, I put my laptop aside and went over to lie beside her. The bag lifted as the beans shifted to accommodate my body. On the TV, Watson was bemoaning Holmes' lack of manners.

'Where are you up to?' I asked, taking the novel and opening it to the bookmarked page: Eli had just crossed, uninvited, over the threshold into Oskar's apartment. I knew the scene and loved the description of the dainty pearls of blood that rose on Eli's forehead, which - to Oskar horror - burst and poured in rivulets down the vampire's pale skin.

Lucy pulled the book from my hand and dropped it on the floor. 'Still ignoring me,' she said, and shook her head. 'What's with you today?'

'Sorry, but it's a cool story, hey?' I replied, ignoring the real intention of her question.

Lucy sighed. 'Yeah, it's cool. All that blood; totally gruesome. It'd suck being a kid forever, though. Poor Eli, always relying on someone else to survive.'

'Maybe it wouldn't be that bad.'

'But forever? That's a long time.'

Juliana's words appeared in my head: *Have you ever stopped to consider what that means? Living forever?* 'I don't know. Look how quickly time goes when we're together,' I said, and nuzzled her neck.

Lucy gave a short laugh and pushed my head away so she could look into my face. 'Seriously, Christian, you realise it's bullshit, right? The blogs and all that.'

'Yeah, of course.' The lie sounded convincing to me but Lucy tilted her head and gave me her sceptical look. 'Okay, wait here,' I said, crawling out of the beanbag.

In my room, I hunted through the junk on my desk, looking for last month's *New Scientist*, which I spied underneath a draft physics assignment that was a week overdue. Quashing a twinge of guilt, I shoved the paper deeper into the pile, and headed back out to Lucy.

'Whatcha got there?' she asked, over the sound of an explosion.

I glanced at the TV. A fury of splintering wood and flames engulfed Watson and Holmes as a wharf exploded. Another close call for the intrepid duo, I knew, since I'd seen the movie half a dozen times. I held up the magazine, hoping I'd be as successful at diverting Lucy's attention as Holmes was at avoiding death. On the front cover was a picture of two foetuses, foreheads touching, floating in an amniotic sac. The caption beside the photo read: *Cloning Consciousness, Defeating Death*.

Lucy took the magazine and looked over the cover. 'Yeah, so?' she said.

'So— it's not the vampire stuff that interests me.' I tapped the image on the cover. 'It's our desire for immortality. We don't want to die; we never have. Death is not a gift to us. Think of the immortals we've created during our existence; gods for every circumstance, enduring when we can't. And, of course, the vampire is the perfect vessel for this desire because they occupy the same plane of existence that we do, and not some celestial space beyond our reach and understanding.'

Lucy raised her eyebrows.

I shrugged. 'It could make for an interesting paper next year.'

'You're an astrophysics major.'

'You don't think there's a connection between our search of the heavens and the desire for immortality?'

'I think you're a dreamer who needs to face reality. Vampires are fun, as we know, but hardly the answer to some great cosmic mystery.' She flipped the magazine onto the coffee table and fixed her eyes on me, her expression serious. 'What's the go with this Juliana Celeste woman? You seem a bit obsessed.'

I pushed the magazine aside and sat on the table in front of her. 'Babe, the only person I'm obsessed with is you.'

'Aw, you're so sweet,' she said, as her hand shot forward and pinched the flesh above my hip.

I twisted out of her grip. 'Shit, Lucy, that fucking hurt,' I said, lifting my shirt; my skin was bright red, warm and pulsing. 'That's not cool.'

Lucy raised an unsympathetic shoulder. 'Stop avoiding my question. What's the deal with Juliana? You're going to try and meet her in Paris, aren't you?'

I fought the urge to sulk and went on the defensive instead. 'Yeah. So? What of it?'

'What of it? Ah, what if she's a psycho?' She picked up the novel from beside the beanbag and waved it at me. 'What if she really believes she's a vampire and tries to rip out your throat?'

'Don't be stupid.'

'Me? Stupid?' Lucy jabbed a finger in my direction. 'You want to meet a woman who claims she's a vampire, in a *blog* of all things, and I'm the stupid one?' She folded her arms and glared at me.

I glared back, even though I didn't want to fight with her. Aside from being pointless, since nothing she said would change my mind about finding Juliana, I couldn't afford to piss her off too much in case she decided to ditch the whole idea of going to Paris. I let my features soften and reached out to touch her knee.

'Babe?' She moved away. 'C'mon, we don't have to do this.' Her face remained stiff. I hung my head, thinking of what to say, then sighed and looked at her again. 'Okay, if this is really bumming you out,' I shook my head, 'I won't try to meet her. It's no big deal. She was interesting to me 'cause of the whole immortality thing and, you know, aside from everything else, at least she was articulate about it.' I laughed a little, 'Unlike some of your vampire friends at the club.'

Lucy leaned forward, relaxing now she had the upper hand. 'Christian, I'm not saying you can't meet her. It's your life, you do what you want. I just want you to be straight with me about it, and I want you to be careful too.' She reached into the front pocket of her jeans and pulled out a necklace, at the end of which was a crucifix. 'This was my grandmother's. She gave it to me before she died. She said it always protected her from the bad things in the world. I want you to have it.'

'I thought you didn't believe Juliana's a vampire?'

'I don't, but she seems to, so you need some protection,' Lucy said, fastening the chain around my neck. She adjusted the crucifix, centring it against my chest. It was plain, silver and glinted in the light.

'You don't really think this will work, do you?' I said.

'No, but that freaky vampire woman might.' She smiled. 'And when she goes to suck your blood, it'll give you the chance to escape.'

I lifted the crucifix, testing its weight and thought, *What if I don't want to escape?*

Satisfied, Lucy pushed out of the beanbag, scooping up the remote control as she got to her feet, and snuffed out Lord Blackwood in the middle of his 'I will rule the world' speech. 'C'mon,' she said, taking my hand, 'let's get outta here. I want gelato.'

Peter Crossing isn't a megalomaniac like Lord Blackwood, but he still enjoys the sound of his own voice and, as he drones on about how proud he is of his little girl, I wish I had a remote control, with a large, all-purpose fast forward button. My mind is about to drift into more memories of Lucy and our spats over Juliana - she might've conceded to me meeting the vampire but that doesn't mean she likes another woman taking up my time - but I hear my name.

'— puts my heart at ease,' Peter Crossing is saying, his eyes on me. I feel the weight of that look: the plea, the expectation, and I shift in my chair as the rest of the guests turn their gazes to me. 'You will look after her, won't you, Christian, and bring her home safe?'

Strangely, despite all that I'm planning, I feel no hesitation when I stand and place my hand on Lucy's shoulder and say, 'You have my word, Mr Crossing.'

The room erupts into applause as Lucy stands and hugs me, and only I hear her say, 'And who will bring you home safe, Christian?'

Blog Six

Peripheries of Existence

There is a myth about a king called Sisyphus, a man notorious for his deceit and greed, and his readiness to murder to satisfy his vices. Weary of his mischief, Zeus ordered Sisyphus chained in the Underworld, but the crafty king tricked Thanatos, the Spirit of Death, into wrapping himself in chains, thereby preventing mortality for Sisyphus and all humanity.

And what did the living think of this audacious act? They *complained* to the Gods:

'Our enemies do not die on the battlefield.'

'Look at my diseased body, how am I to continue in such a state?'

'When will the burden of this life end?'

To quieten the whining of their mortal charges, the Gods - in their wisdom - liberated Thanatos, restoring the only thing of which humankind can be assured; Death, the gift of release.

Sisyphus, of course, was the first to receive this gift, but the cunning life-monger ordered his wife not to perform the traditional burial ceremonies when he died. And so, upon reaching the underworld, Sisyphus protested to Hades that his wife had failed in her duty and he sought permission to chastise her in the mortal realm.

Once restored to life, Sisyphus refused to return to the Underworld and spent his days revelling in the joys of living. Finally, the Gods grew weary of his impertinence and forcibly returned him to Hades where, for his defiance, Sisyphus was allotted the task of pushing a boulder to the top of a mountain, only to have it roll down again when he reached the summit, for all of eternity.

Now, what can you glean from Sisyphus's torment, human? What does his tale tell you about the Shroudeaters? Come on, I am trying to help you - although the Gods only know why - what is the connection?

Must I spell it out for you?

Sigh

It seems I must.

Imagine, if you can, Sisyphus struggling with his burden and you might understand the anguish of the next fifty-eight years of my existence. I followed Didier and his wife - Geneviève - as they moved through post-war Paris: taking jobs, buying their first house, entertaining their splendid friends, and all the time, I raged.

It should have been me at his side.

How many times, in those first years, did I think about killing Geneviève as I watched her live *my* life:

cooking his meals, washing his clothes, spending an hour choosing a dress and doing her make-up before he came home from work, kissing him hello and later, in the subdued light of their bedroom, loving him with all of her body, enjoying my ecstasy, my joy, my happiness.

The torment of those moments was more than I could endure and I banished myself from them, leaving my voyeurism to hunt and feed, and destroy without mercy. Yet the blood and my victim's agony didn't quench the fire of my jealousy, and I returned to my vigil unsated.

How many nights did I haunt their house in the hushed hours after midnight and before the dawn, wandering through each room, a wraith made silent with fury, touching the everyday things that made up their life together. A cup left on the sink, a shawl draped over the arm of a chair, a book-marked novel - *L'Invitée* by Simone de Beauvoir, which I stole - lavender soap in a dainty dish, an umbrella by the front door, a hat, a jacket, gloves, infused with Didier's scent.

Inevitably, on those long nights of prowling, I would find myself drawn into the parlour, to the mantle above the fireplace. On one end was a bible inscribed inside with Geneviève's name, a date and the words, 'Live in the Love of the Lord', which I assumed she'd received at her First Communion. On the other end was a pair of porcelain turtledoves, the male with his tail raised and splayed, while the female peered dotingly at his puffed chest - a thing that could only be a gift from a well-meaning, yet clueless relative - but neither of these things interested me. Rather, it was the photograph in the centre of the shelf that drew me night after night.

The wedding portrait was displayed in a simple wooden frame. Geneviève wore a modest white dress, cinched at the waist with a sash. Her hair was pinned away from her face, which was turned to Didier. Cradled in her arms was a bouquet of Calla lilies. Didier was dressed in a white shirt, dark trousers and suspenders. His head was bare, although in his time with me, he had favoured a hat, and his face was clean-shaven. He had a protective arm around Geneviève and eyes that saw only her.

Although I had studied the photograph a hundred times, I would lean closer, looking for a detail I might have missed, a nuance I hadn't considered, a crack in their blissful veneer. They were standing in front of a hedge, running wild with the joy of summer and a lack of trimming. Around their feet was a tangle of grass. Over the top of the hedge was the fire-blackened steeple of the church where, I assumed, they had married. I wondered, bitterly, if the priest had tolled the bell in their honour.

With nothing new to see, I would concentrate my attention on Didier, trying to feel myself in Geneviève's place. I would imagine the warmth of the sun, the chirping of crickets hidden in the grass, the whisper of wind through the hedge, the lingering tang of burnt wood and spent artillery shells on the air. I imagined until I felt the pinch of the new shoes on my feet and the weight of the lilies in my arms, their delicate scent rising to envelop us. I imagined until I felt Didier pressed against me, solid, real, the promise of his love in every breath. I imagined until a sound came from their bedroom - the creak of springs as they turned in their sleep - and my imaginings were shattered.

How many times did I leave that photograph to stand beside their bed, fangs bared, the Thirst rampant, wanting to kill them both, to end my torment? How many times did I look upon Didier's contented face as he held Geneviève in his arms, and turn away to hunt among the human detritus?

How many times?

So many, I lost count.

Perhaps you think my reticence was foolish and contrary to my vampire nature? Perhaps you are thinking: *Just kill them already and be done with it!* Yes, you'd like that, wouldn't you, human? A little more innocent blood spilled. Yet, the simple fact is, to kill Didier would have been pointless because his death would not have released me from my suffering; his life would have ended, but my love for him would not.

It was for this reason that I refrained and, instead, watched as he bought her flowers and red wine on his way home; or took her driving in his new car; or slow danced with her on the bank of the Seine to music only they could hear; or held her as she cried at the end of *La Belle et la Bête*. All of the things he would have - should have - done with me.

Nor could I kill Geneviève. Although I would have very much liked to follow Françoise's example in *L'Invitée* by removing my rival, Geneviève was not

Xaviere; she lived not for herself, but for Didier and, though I was loathed to admit it, he lived for her. They were not separate entities, but one noble soul; to annihilate her was to destroy the man we both loved.

So you see, my love for Didier was my Sisyphean dilemma: frustrating, futile, yet inescapable. Loving him was the boulder I pushed before me up the mountain of my immortality, never to reach the pinnacle - the heaven he shared with Geneviève - and I was condemned to carry that burden for all eternity.

Then came the twins: Zoé and Éloy, but I cannot write of them now. I have dwelt too long in the ghostly house of my beloved, and still the tale is not told.

Be gone, mortal, goddamn you. Leave me to my torment.

In the Realm of the Gods

Lucy wants to join the Mile High club.

I glance up from my laptop and look at her blankly in the dim cabin light.

'You know,' she whispers, smiling as she nods towards the aft toilet.

I weigh the benefits, and decide they're not worth the hassle. 'Later,' I say, stowing the laptop and pulling the thin blanket over my shoulder. Undeterred, I feel her hand at the button on my jeans. A moment later, her head disappears beneath the blanket.

Her mouth is warm.

I close my eyes and try not to breathe too rapidly. Paris fills my mind; Juliana murmurs in my ear, her voice echoing across a vast distance. Lucy re-emerges, disappointed. She gives me a sullen look and turns towards the window.

Damn.

I button up, and then touch her shoulder. 'Hey,' I say, coaxing her around to look at me. 'We'll have plenty of time for that when we get to Paris. After all, it's the city of love.' She doesn't budge from her sulk and I stifle the urge to roll my eyes. 'And we're *only* sixteen hours and forty-two minutes away,' I add, with a laugh that's half euphoria and half exasperation.

Lucy groans, but it's fake; the excitement has caught her too, and she smiles. 'You're right. Sorry. Just feels like we've been locked up in this plane forever.'

'I know, babe. Maybe try to get some sleep? It'll make the time go faster.'

'Hmm guess so,' she replies, pulling her bag up from the floor. She rummages inside and brings out a small box.

'Birth control?' I ask, frowning.

She smirks. 'Not quite. A parting gift from Trent.'

'You're kidding me?'

'Relax,' Lucy says, popping two pills from their protective plastic cells. 'They're just moggies. You want?'

'Nah.'

She shrugs, swallows both pills with water, and makes herself comfortable against my arm. I watch the movie playing on the screen in front of me until I hear her breathing, deep and easy, then I close my eyes. Sleep comes swiftly and I dream of a French vampire, standing on the summit of a mountain, searching the sky, looking for me.

Blog Seven

The Balm of Innocence

Old-fashion decorum would suggest I owe you an apology, human, for the abruptness of my departure from the last entry in this blog. It was, one might say, analogous to breaking off in the middle of a funeral speech, or turning up the houselights halfway through a movie. Unforgivable, really. Fortunately, we exist in a world where such courtesies are discretionary, at best.

Not that you even considered the need for an apology, so busy are you laying bare your own tortured soul, as though we share some sort of *connection*. Then there are those of you who presume to offer me advice, as though you could possibly understand my experiences. Yet, the sycophants and agony aunts among you continue to fill the comments section of *my* blog with your endless, mindless, drivel.

What do you want from me?

Sympathy?

Gratitude?

Whatever it is, I cannot help you, and I don't need you to help me. You may be lost but I know my purpose - to eradicate the Shroudeaters; my kith and kin.

It is not my purpose to write for you. Nor should you think I am providing a forum for you to express your discontent and perceived allegiances. Understand - you mean nothing to me beyond the blood that flows through your veins. And whatever you do, don't let my compassion for those I loved fool you. In one beat of your heart, I would send you to join them in the Underworld.

Still feel like you know me?

Still want to be my 'friend'?

Still want to hear my story?

No?

Yeah, right.

I missed the announcement of Geneviève's pregnancy, which was a small blessing I owe to the prostitute whose cry for help I answered in an apartment on the outskirts of the city. My habit in those days was to leave my day shelter and hunt in a quadrant of the city I hadn't visited in at least three months; a practice suggested by Callisto in the first days after my vampiric birth. *The wise vampire's life is a travelling feast,* she had murmured, watching me draw the lifeblood from the elderly man she had gifted to me. It was advice I took to heart.

On this evening, I was in the sixteenth arrondisse-ment. The area had survived the Occupation unscathed, although it was somewhat de-populated since many of the wealthy residents had decided to wait out the war in friendlier climes. I spied a couple staggering along the street, obviously the worse for an afternoon of imbuing their favourite tonic, which, from their scent, was a robust vin de Bourgogne. As I tracked them through the streets, waiting for the best opportunity to strike, I thought of where I would dispose of the bodies. Bois de Boulogne was not too far away and, as the park had once been the sanctuary of thieves and murderers, it seemed an appropriate choice.

Ahead of me, the couple stopped on a corner to embrace and share a passionate kiss, and as always, my stomach clenched at the display of intimacy. The Thirst rose and a quiver ran through my body with its intensity, but I cautioned myself to wait as the man took a set of keys from his pocket. Arm in arm, the couple stepped off the curb, then halted as a muffled scream breached the night. The man and woman sent a fearful glance in the direction of the shriek and, without a word, they dashed across the road and hurried into the darkness.

The Thirst urged me after them but I hesitated as another cry, softer and wracked with pain, reached me. I glanced after the couple, feeling a moment of regret, and turned into the street. On the side of the first building was a sign: *Rue le Sueur* and I felt a jolt of recognition. Four years earlier, the street had been the talk of a horrified Paris, when it was discovered that one of their own had been murdering their fellow citizens and destroying the evidence of his crimes in what the newspapers called 'a charnel house'. No wonder the couple had fled; so close to the home of a monster.

Human monsters, of course, were of no concern to me, especially one who had meet his own demise on the guillotine but, as I passed the house, my senses tingled at the scent of carnage - blood, cinders and lime - that lingered around the building. Yet, I knew this was not where the cries had emanated from and, as if in confirmation, I caught the sound of a strangled sob accompanied by a distinct grunt that lead me across the street and three houses down. A dim light burned behind a curtained window on the first floor. I smell blood and sweat, and the aroma that only the monstrous can detect, fear.

'Please, no more.'

The words fell like autumn leaves, hope sapped from them. Something tugged inside me, something more than the Thirst. I forced the door in the façade open and crossed the courtyard to the stairs. Darkness filled every corner; the other apartments were empty. Tainted light seeped beneath the door I wanted; the handle moved easily when I gripped it and pushed.

I knew in an instant that the woman was almost dead. She was lying on the faded carpet in a pool of her own blood. Scattered around her were an array of tools that had been used in her torture. Her face was swollen and bruised; her naked body was contorted with pain. I listened for her heart and caught its slow, erratic beat.

Leaning over her, humming, was a dark-haired man, who was just as naked and gore-splashed. He looked at me and straightened, a smile blooming on his handsome, boyish face, but I saw the calculating flick of his eyes as he assessed the change in his situation. He held up a blood-smeared hand and his mouth opened, words ready to pour forth to buy him an advantage.

I was on him before he uttered the first syllable. Surprise flashed across his face as I grabbed his hand, snapping the fingers as I drove him into the wall, taking pleasure in the crack of bones and his shrieks of agony. His eyes fluttered and I slapped him, shattering his jaw. His eyes rolled back in his head and unconsciousness took him.

The Thirst demanded that I drain him, but I dropped him on the floor and turned to the woman. She was too broken to try to escape; still tears leaked from her eyes as I approached, and the fear rose from her like a mist. I sat near her, close enough for her to see me, but not close enough to touch her. Searching for her mind, I found it racing, the thoughts careening from the horror of the last hours to her childhood and through her short life. I settled and watched what she had to show me.

Her name was Annika. She had four older sisters. Her parents had loved her. A radio broadcast: 'Poland invaded'. A train rattling to Paris. Her favourite aunt in death's repose. Annika on the streets, running from German soldiers, fighting to survive. A friend, finally, Hanna. Sharing stolen bread. Sick with fear: *Where, oh where is Hanna?* Kissing a Résistance fighter, Gaël; exchanging hand-made rings. Screaming beside his body. A procession of men in Bois de Boulogne until—

Her thoughts broke away, returned to her childhood. I disengaged from her mind, my heart heavy with her suffering. 'Annika.' Her eyes focused on me. 'I'm going to kill him,' I said, pointing to the slumped figure on the floor. 'Do you understand?' A few moments past, and then she nodded, although I could see it caused her pain to do so. I lowered my hand onto hers. Her fingers twitch. 'Before I do, I can release you from this life, if you wish.' The nod came quicker and was accompanied by fresh tears. Her lips moved and I lifted my hand to cover her mouth and nose. 'The time for words is done,' I said, shifting closer to her until we were lying side by side.

When she was gone, I let the Thirst fill me and, like a predator released from a cage, it leapt forward, sharpening my senses. Instantly, the rapid heartbeat of Annika's attacker boomed through the room and I narrowed my eyes. He was conscious and waiting for an opportunity. *You little snake,* I thought, smiling as I stood and walked over to him.

The moment he sensed me above him, he struck, rolling onto his back and stabbing a long, thin blade into the air where I had been standing. 'You'll need to be faster than that, sweetheart,' I said, breaking his wrist as I disarmed him. I drove the blade through his stomach, pinning him to the floor. He howled.

The sound and the heavy scent of thick, warm blood pushed me over the edge. I dropped to the floor beside him and twisted his head towards me. 'This is for Annika,' I said, as my fangs slid forward.

Fear filled his eyes and, through blood-lined lips, he said, 'Monster.'

'You should talk,' I replied, biting deep into the sweet place beneath his jaw.

It wasn't until I was carrying Annika's body through the trees of Bois de Boulogne that I thought about what I had done. The realisation was so profound that I staggered to a stop. For years, I had killed humans to satisfy the Thirst or dull my rage. Why hadn't I just killed and drained Annika? Why had I cared about her suffering? Why did I want to ease her pain? Was this some kind of new weakness?

I shook my head, trying to clear the questions, and hefted the body, wrapping the sheet tighter as I headed towards the clearing where the prostitutes gathered. It was late and many of the women were engaged in their particular business, so I placed Annika's body on a well-worn path close to one of the 'privacy rooms' that the women constructed out of branches and other litter. As I straightened, I was struck again by the question of what I was doing. Why should I care if the body was found? What difference did it make to me for Annika to find a final resting place among the only family she had at the end of her life? What the hell was wrong with me?

I fled the forest and made my way across the city, killing two vagrants and the teenager who was terrorising them on the way, to satisfy the Thirst and reassure myself that nothing had changed. By the time I took up my vigil in Didier's home, I was almost convinced that my behaviour with Annika had been an aberration until a small voice whispered: *Prove it. Kill her, and him.*

Once again, I found myself standing over Didier and Geneviève as they slept, the Thirst burning. They were facing one another, hands clasp between them, legs entwined under the sheet. Their foreheads were tipped towards each other, as though they were sharing their dreams, and there was a glow about them that made me think they were made of light rather than flesh and blood.

Do it, the voice demanded and my fangs slid forward. I leaned over Geneviève, ready to snatch her out of Didier's grasp, and that's when I heard it. Heartbeats: two strong and steady belonging to Didier and his wife, and two others, quick as rabbits, coming from inside Geneviève.

I recoiled, backing away from the bed as though it contain a pestilence. A single thought pounded through my head: *She's pregnant, pregnant, pregnant.* The horror of it; the unfairness, the hopelessness, overwhelmed me and I ran from the room, crashing through the house, not caring about the noise I made, wanting the world to know that I existed. As I dashed out of the front door and into the shadows across the street, I heard Didier racing after me.

'Stop, thief!'

Hearing his accusation brought me to a halt. Me? A thief? *Me?* No, I was the one who had been robbed. I was the one who had been wronged. I was the one who had been discarded. I was the one living in the shadows of the life I was meant to live: he was *my* love; they were *my* babies; that was *my* house. The Thirst blazed inside me and I took half a dozen steps, gaining speed, ready to slam him to the ground and draw every last drop of blood from his cheating body. Then Geneviève was at the door, wrapping her arms around him and I pulled up as those rapid heartbeats, safe in her living womb, drummed across the night.

How could I kill them now?

For the second time that night, I fled, seeking the darkness of my lair, where I wandered the corridors and roamed the caverns with only the roaches and rodents for company. The Thirst blasted through me with the heat of a forge, but I was determined to ignore it; let it reduce me to a cinder, if that was possible. Better to be incinerated than to face a world where Didier was playing happy families.

Nights passed. The darkness deepened and I found myself on my hands and knees, dragging through the muck and filth, the Thirst intolerable. I felt my inside drying while the skin on my body flaked and shed like tiny fish scales. My mouth tasted of ashes and my hair became as brittle as straw, and still the Thirst savaged me, insistent and demanding as a newborn baby. And, as my physical suffering intensified, so did the clarity of my mind until I was aware of every vein on the verge of collapse, and of each cell ready to crumple upon itself.

My existence became unbearable but I was so weak that I could no longer stand, nor even crawl to save myself. At the same time, it was obvious that the deterioration in my body was slowing, not stopping but dragging out as the Thirst fought to keep my form together in case a blood source should come along.

What terrible demise have I brought upon myself? I thought, mournfully.

In answer, Annika came to me.

It is the long death of the Shroudeater, she murmured, her form gathering from the dust of my body.

Annika? What are you doing here? I set you free.

You came when I needed you. Now you need me.

Are you here to set me free?

A laugh flittered through the darkness. *Blood will set you free. Or time.*

Then I choose time, I muttered.

Why? Because of the babies?

I nodded.

Foolish. Anger flashed through me, but I could find no voice for it. *Why did you intervene that night?* she asked.

I thought back, remembering Annika's plea. *You asked for your pain to end. It seemed— right.*

You wanted to protect me from further harm.

I guess.

Why have you watched over Didier all these years?

I gave a weak, dismissive wave. *Okay, I see where you're going with this and I don't want to hear it.*

They will need you, she replied, her form breaking apart.

I don't care. I won't watch the life that should be mine any longer.

When Annika spoke again, her voice seemed to come from everywhere. *There is a vagrant asleep two caverns over. Take the blood slowly.*

I don't care.

Silence for a few seconds and then: *If you perish, who will make Callisto and Constantine pay for the life they stole?*

Good question.

I visited Didier and Geneviève less during the months of her pregnancy, but every few weeks I would return to their bedside and gazed - sometimes in amazement, sometimes in dismay - at the ever-increasing roundness of Geneviève's abdomen. Faced with the blatant evidence of her biological purpose, my hands would press against my own firm, flat belly, sheltering a womb of dust, and I would lament my lack of fecundity.

Of course, the futility of this grieving was not lost on me. Vampires are takers of life, of hope. We steal the future. It is as simple as that; even birthing a Shroudeater is a theft, as I well knew thanks to Callisto and Constantine. Yet, despite my rationalising, as Geneviève grew more voluptuous with life, my sense of inadequacy deepened.

Unnerved by the feeling, I made the choice to stay away from the house for a month, giving myself a reprieve from the yearning I felt whenever I was near Geneviève. The night I returned, I found Didier sitting on the front stoop, smoking a cigarette as he stared moodily into the street. At his feet were half a dozen black-tipped butts. I faded into the shadows and, although it was not my habit to pry with Didier, I sought his mind.

His thoughts were scattered, flitting from what he must do to protect Geneviève in her delicate state, to how he would care for their child when it came, to whether he was even ready to be a father. He swept a hand through his hair, took a long drag on the cigarette and flicked the butt away as a new idea occurred to him: would Geneviève love the baby more than she loved him?

A wave of despair lapped at his mind as he considered what this would mean for his marriage, and I was surprised by the undercurrent of fear swirling beneath the thought. I had never imagined Didier afraid, not even during the war years. My heart ached for him as he stood and turned for the door, and I had to resist the urge to go to him with the reassurance that loving him wasn't something so easily put aside.

I pulled out of his mind and tracked his movement through the house until he entered the bedroom. As selfish as it may sound, I was glad for Didier insecurities. They made me feel better about my own sense of inadequacy, and connected me to him in a way I hadn't experienced since Geneviève came into his life.

Satisfied with seeing him, I wandered down the street, contemplating where I would hunt, but I got no further than the corner when a commotion broke out behind me. I didn't need to turn to know what it was about; I could smell the scent of blood and amniotic fluids on the air.

The twins were on their way.

Hospitals are no place for a vampire: too many lights, too many people, especially ones with a keen eye for sickness, but I followed them there anyway. I waited in the garden, pacing back and forth, one minute imagining I was beside Didier as he paced the corridor inside; the next, imagining I was with Geneviève, urging her to bring his children safely into the world.

With dawn nearing, I broke my vigil and, despite the risk of exposure, I went into the hospital to hunt. It didn't take long to find my victim; a quick check of the registry lead me to the coma ward. The choice was straightforward; only two beds were occupied. In one was a woman, her head wrapped in fresh bandages. Tubes snaked out of her body and attached themselves to the machines around her.

In the other bed was a young man, not yet thirty according to his medical chart. Straps held his thin body in place but, otherwise, he seemed to be sleeping. On a shelf above his head was a photograph of him in uniform. I stroked his cheek; the skin was soft and warm. He didn't respond to my touch. I lowered my hand to his chin and turned his head toward the window, exposing his throat. He made a low sound and I hesitated, watching him, but there was nothing more. I took his hand in mine, feeling the blood flow just below the surface of the skin, and lowered my mouth to his neck. His heartbeat fluttered as I slid my fangs into him, singing my thanks, and with the rush of his blood, I thought of Geneviève, somewhere below, labouring to bring life into the world.

With the Thirst satisfied and the sun clawing at the horizon, I hurried out of the soldier's room. I needed to get back to my lair and wait out the daylight. By the evening, I figured, the twins would be born and I could return to the hospital to see them. Excitement settled over me as I raced the sun; it would be a long day, but I would endure it, as I endured everything else in my existence.

I left my lair in the mid-hours of evening, early enough to not be suspicious, but late enough to miss the majority of human traffic at the hospital. The maternity ward, as I had hoped, was dimly lit and quiet with only a few last minute visitors and shell-shocked fathers lurking in the corridors and rooms. Didier, I knew, had returned home and was sleeping.

The ward where the newborns slumbered contained twenty small cribs. About half were full. In one of the cribs was a pink wrapped bundle and beside it, in a crib drawn closer than the others, was a bundle swathed in blue. I placed my hand against the glass, feeling a sob inside my chest.

You should have—

'Bonsoir madam, may I help you?' The nurse looked at me with a mix of curiosity and expectation. 'Visiting hours are almost over,' she said.

For a moment I could only look at her; it had been an age since I had spoken with a human about anything but death. I took a breath and calmed myself. 'Forgive me. I have travelled far to see my new niece and nephew.'

'Oh. The twins?' the nurse said, excitement shining in her eyes. 'It's been so long since we had twins on the ward. They are little celebrities.' She laughed with delight.

I joined her, although my laughter sounded peculiar to my ear. 'Would it be possible to hold them?' I asked.

An uncertain expression crossed the nurse's face. 'Well, the mother is asleep and we've just settled the babies.'

'Geneviève is asleep?' I let consternation fill my voice. 'How unfortunate for me. Alas, such is the price we pay for helping others. Never mind, I will try again in a few days. Thank you anyway.'

The nurse ran her gaze over my face. 'You help others?'

'Yes, returned soldiers mostly,' I shook my head sadly, 'how they suffer so from the effects of the war.'

Uncertainty rose around her and I pushed into her mind, just a little, to help her make the decision. She looked into the nursery and then back to me. 'I can't wake them,' she said, smiling, 'but I could bring them closer to the window, if you would like?'

'I would be grateful,' I said, and meant it.

She left me by the window and shortly after appeared on the other side of the glass, moving with exaggerated care so as not to wake her charges. Soon she had the two cribs beside the window and, using the same care, she eased the blankets away from their small faces.

I thought I knew what love and hate were but, whatever I had experienced to that moment, was a mere shadow of the fierce emotions that cleaved me in two as I looked down on the twins. Love for them billowed inside me like a ship's sails, only to be flattened by the black hatred that I harboured for my own unnatural parents.

The nurse rearranged the blankets around the sleeping babies and glanced up at me, the smile on her lips vanishing as she caught the hellfire in my eyes. Instinctively she moved in front of the cribs, putting herself between the twins and the monster she saw staring at them.

'Brave girl,' I mouthed, and left her to her night-mares.

The twins came home and I returned to my nightly visitations, although with more caution as the babies were ridiculously unpredictable, responding to the whims of their needs at all hours of the night, drawing their tired parents from their beds, yawning. It was a trait I admired for I was also a creature of needs that *had* to be satisfied. The similarity bound me to the twins and very soon, I began to think of them as my children and I fussed over them in the night. I watched their narrow chests rise and fall, marvelling at their small fingers and tiny toes when they kicked off their coverings. I soothed their murmurings when dreams plagued their tiny souls and patted them back to sleep.

Sometimes they were awake when I crept into their room and they would watch me approach through the muslin covering their cot, wide-eyed but unafraid. I would sing to them on those nights, snippets of old songs from my youth, and, for once, remembering the time when I was still full of life didn't make me sad. When they were old enough, smiles greeted my arrival as they raised their arms to be held. It was only months later that I realised the danger to which such familiarity had exposed them.

What a shock it was to see her luminous face pressed to their window. She was dark-haired and elfin, with green eyes that blazed with the Thirst. The window scaped faintly as she lifted the frame, inch by inch with all the patience of our kind. I was in a darkened corner of the room and she was unaware of my presence; a sure sign that she was newborn. My parents, it seemed, had been up to their mischief again.

She climbed over the sill, silent as moonlight, and approached the bed, reaching for Éloy with urgent fingers. He looked up at her, smiling, and raised his pudgy hand. I moved out of the shadows. Her eyes widened and then narrowed as she turned for the window. I grabbed for her, but she was gone, leaving me with a handful of air. Éloy babbled softly as though asking the fledgling to come back. I pressed my fingers to his lips and place a kiss on his smooth forehead, urging him to sleep. When he was breathing deep and steady, I turned for the window and leapt after the intruder.

My head swirled with emotion as I sent my senses across the city: anger and fear warred with surprise and curiosity. I wanted to destroy the vampire for daring to harm the child and yet, she was the first of my kindred that I'd seen since Callisto and Constantine had birthed me. *How many more of us are there,* I wondered, picking up her scent.

I followed her through the night, keeping pace but not overtaking her. I needed to think about what I wanted to do with my blood sister before I confronted her. She twisted and turned through the city, trying to shake me as the need to appease the Thirst grew. Her flight became more erratic: she stopped in a schoolyard, sniffing after a band of gypsies; next was a homeless man on the docks beneath Notre Dame; then a student at the back of Shakespeare's bookshop but, in each instance, I came upon her too soon and she fled before she could taste their blood. How frustrated she grew until finally, as dawn flushed pink on the horizon, she entered the Cimetiére du Pére Lachaise and stumbled to a weatherworn sepulchre. Her glance at sky as she closed the door told me where her fears lay; she would battle the Thirst through the day, but not risk the madness that came with exposure to sunlight.

Interesting; perhaps she had some character after all.

Whether it was this, or that the twins had softened my heart a little, I took pity on the fledgling and backtracked to Rue Spinoza, where I had spied a vagrant asleep in one of the doorways. By the time I returned to her day shelter, gift in hand, I had decided what I would do with my blood-sister, but before I put my plans into action, I needed to ask her a question about our parents.

She fought me at first, until the lust for blood overwhelmed any sense of loyalty she felt towards Callisto and Constantine. Then she came mewling, reaching past my leg to snatch at the unconscious vagrant that I held just beyond her grasp. 'Answer my question, le petit mon ami,' I said.

She hissed at me and gave her answer, which stayed with me through the long day. By the time I returned to Didier and the twins late in the evening, I knew that, to protect those I loved, I would have to leave them in the care of Geneviève, if only for a short while.

Paris Interludes

Lucy's aunt is my first impression of Paris.

Marguerite is an elegant, slender woman of undefinable age, with black hair and the same sultry grey eyes as Lucy. She's standing in the middle of the concourse at the arrival gates, wearing a long red jacket that makes stark the pale lustre of her skin. There's an unlit cigarette between her lips. Tourists flow around her, throwing curious glances at her face, wondering if she's famous. She ignores them, as though she is.

When Marguerite sees us, her haughty manner vanishes. 'Bonjour, bonjour,' she calls, pulling the cigarette from her mouth and waving it above her head like some 1930s starlet. She drags Lucy into an embrace, kissing her cheeks. 'Bienvenue à Paris. Ça va Lucy?'

Her niece rolls her eyes. 'Yeah, good thanks.'

'Français ne parlant pas aujourd'hui, ma chère?' Marguerite asks, drawing on her cigarette.

'Umm, you know that cigarette's not lit, right?' Lucy says, stepping around her aunt. 'So, where's the baggage carousel?'

'Politciens fichus.' Marguerite glances at me as she snaps the cigarette in two and throws the pieces into a pot plant. I like her already. 'You must be Christian?' she says, switching to English.

'Oui. Il est agréable de vous rencontrer,' I reply.

Marguerite smiles. 'French is a beautiful language, oui?' she says, looping her arm through mine as we follow Lucy.

'Oui.'

'Lucky we speak English then,' she says, and pats my hand.

By the time we collect our bags and find our way onto the Metro, Lucy has come around. She chats to her aunt, the language flowing off her tongue as though she's lived in Paris all her life. I listen, not understanding a word, but loving the sound of their conversation. Soon though, my attention is drawn outside the train.

Parisian suburbs flash past: concrete, steel, glass. Bland apartment blocks, squat commercial buildings, pre-fabricated walls coloured with graffiti. Black ribbons of road; piles of rubbish blown against a leaning wire fence.

It's like home: disappointing.

Marguerite touches my hand. 'Beauty is rarely found at the extremities, rather at the heart. Wait, Paris will delight you.'

She's right; as we come out of the Metro at Marais, the city enfolds me, and for the next three days, I almost forget my purpose for being here.

I'm not into the tourist thing: unthinking sheep, preyed upon by tour guide wolves. Marguerite's no wolf, though; Marguerite's seriously cool. She takes us to the majors: the Eiffel Tower, the Louvre, the Champs-Élysées, and Notre Dame, but we don't stay long in these tourist swamps.

Instead, we visit unassuming, awe-inspiring art galleries hidden behind easy-to-miss wooden doorways, and quirky shops selling everything from the latest techno must-haves to aphrodisiacs. She takes us to moody cafes where we meet her equally moody friends, and to decrepit theatres presenting obscure plays that, Marguerite assures us, will take Paris by storm.

Lucy and I are enchanted.

By the fourth day, Marguerite's over it. 'I must work,' she announces over a cup of steaming black coffee as we sit in her favourite breakfast café (she has two or three haunts for every meal). 'So today you are on your own.'

Sweet. I know where I want to start: the Catacombs; Juliana's lair.

Between bites of a warm, buttery croissant, I ask Marguerite about the catacombs. She raises her eyebrows. 'That depends on what you want to experience. Like everything in Paris, there is what the tourists see, and there is what the Parisians know.'

After our days of exploring the city with Marguerite, this doesn't surprise me. 'I'll take the local knowledge.'

She nods and leans forward as though she's about to impart a state secret. 'Most people know the catacombs as a few narrow tunnels lined with bones. What they don't know about is the kilometres of tunnels and chambers that lie under the entire city. Nor do they know of the secret entrances to these places.'

Excitement stirs in my stomach: Secret places? Vampire places?

'Boring.'

I glance at Lucy, but she keeps her eyes on the magazine she's not reading. The pages flick, distracting, annoying. I'd grab her wrist to make her to stop but her aunt is watching. 'Do you know a way in?'

'No, but there is someone I know who could take you down and show you around, if you like?'

'Sounds good,' I say.

'Sounds like shit,' Lucy says.

Her aunt and I ignore her. 'What's down there?' I ask, wondering if she's heard any stories that hint of Juliana.

'A whole other world,' Marguerite replies.

Blog Eight

An Aside

I've been a little harsh with you in these blogs, haven't I? I should apologise; tolerating fools is not something I do easily, and it grows more difficult the longer I endure this existence. You wouldn't understand this, of course, because, for you, time is one of the attractions of my kind. Infinite time. All the time in the world. An eternity. Forever. And you don't see what there is to endure.

Perhaps you're right. What am I complaining about? After all, an abundance of time gives me more opportunity for contemplating things— like revenge. Sounds good huh?

Yes, and it would be if time actually existed.

Are you frowning? Shaking your head? Wondering what I mean? Maybe I should hold onto that apology for a while longer?

Okay, listen, it's simple if you think about it. Everything humans do is controlled by an invisible mechanism that ticks down the microseconds of their lives. This construct is called time and it organises everything that occurs: sleeping, eating, working, playing, according to the hour, the minute, the second. Even birth and death are fitted into these neat little compartments, as though humans have some influence over when these things will occur. Time is humanity's greatest vanity and its strongest prison. Why? Because time is an illusion created by you, to control you.

Don't believe me? Okay. Did you know, human, that the second and the minute didn't exist until the middle of the sixteenth century? It took the discovery of the pendulum for these useful little concepts to come into being, and what a yoke they have proven for your kind. Thank you, Master Huygens. So, if the second and the minute are an invention, how can anything about time be true?

But! But! But! I hear you say, the sun rises and sets, and the seasons change. What is that if not time, passing?

How clever you think you are. Except you are confusing the Earth's natural cycles with humanity's chronic need to control those cycles. The sun sets and rises according to a rhythm. Humans overlay those natural rhythms with the artifice of time. Tick tock tick tock. It's a lie.

Before you get too outraged, relax. I'm not criticising you *per se*. In fact, illusory as time is, it is still a gift for you mortals, one that we Shroudeaters would gladly kill you for, if only we could steal it away. This is because there is no rhythm to a vampire's existence; it is a flat-line for all of eternity. Yes, the sun comes up and sets, the seasons change, things are born, grow, mature and die, but a vampire exists in a perpetual now with nothing to indicate the passage of time: days and nights blur; months and years slip by with nothing to mark them as significant; and there is no end in sight, just more of the same. It is a torture.

I understand it is hard for you to think of our everlasting existence in these terms, but that is because you have death to look forward too - although you won't understand this either. Perhaps all I can do is show you and hope you'll see the light. You shouldn't, however, take this as a sign that I've come to like you.

I don't.

Excerpt Travel Diary: 10th April 1949.

... Foreign as the feeling is to me, I can barely contain my excitement at leaving Paris. It has been years since I ventured beyond her borders and, back then, I travelled rough, concerned only with finding Didier. Tonight, I travel by train and sit in the lap of luxury, surrounded by gleaming mahogany, red velvet and gold fittings, like a Russian princess.

Delightful.

The train is headed to Brussels, the birthplace of Patria, my little Belgian blood-sister. It is a shame, some may say, that she will never lay eyes on that old city again, but such is the consequence of hunting my family. I only hope I may swiftly find Callisto and Constantine and bring them to the same fate.

But enough longing for the future. I must enjoy this experience for what it is, which is not difficult for I am enamoured with train travel and have been since my mortal days with Didier: the rhythmic sway of the carriages, the rush of air beyond the window, the vivid sparks that flare and die on the tracks in the darkness. Yet, how much more special it is with my vampire senses.

I catch every nuance as we fly across the ever-changing landscape: the trees that rear away from the juggernaut in their midst; the battered crops, bowing their heads; a lake excited into ripples; the impassive mountains, unconcerned with the fleeting, or the man-made. There is blood being spilled out there too; hunters at work, pouncing on their prey, and it pleases me to know I'm not the only killer abroad tonight.

Not that my fellow travellers - if they knew of my presence - need be concerned; I satiated the Thirst before boarding the train in Paris and, although stirred by my exhilaration, I should not need to feed again before I alight in—

The conductor has just left my cabin; the poor man. He came to check my ticket and, instead, he encountered, well, me. And what an effect I had on him! The moment he saw my face, he lowered his head, but not before I caught the widening of his eyes and the sudden tension in his body. I smiled to myself; mortal men are so predictable.

Now, I know it is unsporting to toy with humans, given the weakness of their minds, but sometimes it is irresistible, so I made him wait while I took a slow tour of his person. What a fine specimen he was with his dusky skin and beautiful almond-shaped eyes. I drew a breath; hints of baharat and harissa drifted from him.

Delicious.

His head came up, like a deer sensing danger, as I informed him that I didn't need a ticket. He stood, unmoving, a battle between his will and my vampiric suggestion waging inside him. I could have pushed harder - and would have to avoid killing him; a missing conductor would only disrupt my journey - but I enjoyed watching him fight for his autonomy, even if the struggle was only fleeting. After a few moments, he inclined his head again and wished me bonne nuit as he stepped backwards and closed the compartment door.

I can hear him as he moves from cabin to cabin; the warm, welcoming cadence of his voice and the sharp click of his ticket punch …

Extract Travel Diary: 26th August 1949.

… My parents are not in the city, nor is there any sign that they have been here, at least not recently. I curse myself as a fool. What was I thinking, choosing to leave Didier and the twins because of the ranting of a starving fledgling? Or perhaps Patria was more cunning and loyal than I anticipated? There is a lesson to learn from this; trust no one, especially not my blood-kin.

Not all is lost, however, for I have felt the presence of another Shroudeater. So, while it pains me to be away from my loved ones, I have decided to stay on in

Brussels a while longer, to see what I can discover about my Dutch kin …

Extract Travel Diary: 3rd October 1950.

… What an adventure tonight has been. A culmination! A triumph! Oh, to be so full of this satisfaction every night; I feel as though I have gorged on blood. Yet, I haven't touched a drop, as the Thirst keeps reminding me. *Soon*, my unquenchable mistress. There must be a balance to this account if I am to do better next time. For, although I have succeeded, in truth, the task I set myself has taken far too long.

Yet, could such a delay be avoided? After all, the difficulties I encountered have their roots in the very nature of the Shroudeater, and my vampire cousin was typical of our kind: aloof, cautious, solitary. Luckily, he also shared our egotism, which made him careless with his leavings. Perhaps this is an age thing? As best as I can tell, he's been roaming the streets of Brussels since before Napoleon's defeat at Waterloo in the early 1800s. Perhaps the longer a vampire exists, the more reckless and contemptuous they become? It wouldn't surprise me.

For all the months I've spent tormenting him - interrupting his hunting and feasting, for which he vehemently cursed me - and following him across the city, I was nearly caught unaware when he leapt at me tonight. Agility kept me out of his filthy clutches and, once the chase was on, I dashed along the route that I'd laid out weeks before. Still, there were a few close calls; he was quick and his knowledge of the city gave him the advantage, and once or twice, I found myself almost cornered. Ah, the thrill of it!

Although I lead him a winding chase through the city, I had a destination in mind and, as midnight slipped past, I drew him up Treurenberg Hill to the Church of St Michael and St Gudula. What a discovery the church had been: gothic and beautiful, with its high ceiling and arched enclaves, its alabaster columns and dark choir. How I love the statues of the saints and the apostles - did I imagine the frown on St John's brow when I stood beneath him? - and the baroque pulpit with its terrifying depiction of Adam and Eve being chased from Paradise by a skeletal figure. Yet, it was what lay beneath the church that was of most interest to me.

The old vampire didn't hesitate to follow me onto consecrated ground; in fact, his thoughts - garbled though they were - had a distinctly gleeful tone to them. He thought he had me trapped and I was happy to let him think so as I lured him down into the burial chambers, then lower still into the crypts of the original church ...

Extract Travel Diary: 27th October 1950.

... I am done with my blood cousin. Roeland is as stubborn as he is uncouth. If he knows anything of Callisto and Constantine, he refuses to divulge it, and even the enticement of blood brings forth nothing from him but pointless threats and vitriol. The barbarian; let him rot to dust!

Extract Travel Diary: 5th November 1950.

… the blind gypsy was in the Grand-Place again this evening, in her usual spot to the right of the entry to the Town Hall. She was swathed in layers of ragged, mismatched clothing with a tattered blanket thrown over her shoulders. Beside her, a small fire burned in a brazier to ward of the freezing night. As is her habit, she called to the few unfortunates trudging home through the gloom, asking for food or a spare franc. Mostly they ignored her, although some felt offended enough by her presence to spit in her direction and fork the evil eye.

Humans are so strange.

My previous observations of the gypsy have been from afar, but tonight I felt impelled to speak with her. I crossed the square, fast and silent as always, yet she turned her withered face toward me as I approached, her milky eyes tracking back and forth as she sniffed the air. A hand darted out from under her garments and dragged the fire closer. I expected her to mutter something superstitious, an ancient invocation against the forces of darkness, or some such nonsense. Instead, she demanded I stay back and accused me of having 'their' stench upon me.

What was I to make of this?

Although her own odour left much to be desired - a combination of grime, pungent tobacco and rot - I knelt before her and asked what she meant. In response, she pressed her lips together and raised a hand, palm open. A surge of distain rushed through me; the opportunism of mortals is astounding. Resisting the urge to slap her, I drew several francs from my pocket and dropped them into her hand with a comment about deals with the Devil. She gave an ugly cackle and made the coins vanish with the skill of Robert-Houdin.

Without further ado, she launched into a tale of encountering a 'repellent fellow who carried about him the stench of death, much like you' in the Parc du Cinquantenaire late one evening. The gypsy shivered and pulled the blanket tighter around her shoulders as she explained how he had toyed with her, whisper of her impending doom while he poked and prodded her from different directions until she was in a whirl of confusion. She fell silent, swept up in the horror of the memory, until I pointed out the obvious; that he hadn't killed her.

A look of annoyance flicked across her face and she started to turn away, muttering about the rudeness and ingratitude of some 'creatures'. I almost laughed at the audacity of her, but knew it would be imprudent if I wanted the rest of her story. To entice her to continue, I took a few more francs from my pocket and jingled them together, which had the desired effect. Apparently forgetting whatever transgression I'd made, she raised her hand, but rather than crossing her palm with the coins, I asked her why the stranger - I didn't use the word vampire as it seemed clear that, while she knew we were different, perhaps even evil, she hadn't guessed our true nature - hadn't gone ahead with his threats. Her answer gave me pause; it seems another male 'reeking of the pit' had interrupted her tormentor.

I felt a flush of hope. Was this Constantine?

Dropping the francs into her hand, I asked her to go on. She did her vanishing trick with the coins again and grinned at me, revealing a row of black stubs. In the firelight, her eyes had a watery yellow gleam and it struck me that she was dying. The gypsy nodded, as though she'd read my mind, and then launched into an account of how she had listened as the two 'men' fought at a blurring speed until one had the other pinned against a tree.

I interrupted her at this point to enquire if there had been a woman involved in the fracas. For, if one of the vampires had been Constantine, then surely Callisto would've been nearby.

The woman shook her head. She hadn't heard any but the two males, which - she spat on the ground at my feet - was enough wickedness for one lifetime. I took her meaning and drew a final two francs from inside my coat. Her blind eyes locked on the sound of them in my hand and when I asked if she could tell me anything further, she was quiet for a moment as though held mesmerised by their glitter. I didn't press her as I knew she was re-visiting that night, searching for the detail I needed, and I felt strangely grateful to her. Finally she shook herself, took the money, and offered what she remembered: the name of another city.

I left her alive, or as alive as the disease consuming her allowed, and returned to this room for a last day of rest. Tomorrow night I leave Brussels and journey to Prague …

Extract Travel Diary: 21st March 1951.

… Prague is a dead loss and I want nothing more than to return to Paris. Oh, how my heart yearns for the vibrant mecca of my birth, for the gorgeous symphony of my native tongue, and for Didier; the only light in this dull existence.

I can take no more. Home it must be …

Extract Travel Diary: 14th July, 1951.

… Curse my stubborn nature. One hint of my parents, one faint echo of their existence, and I find myself further from Didier than ever. Istanbul, oh Istanbul, how beautiful this most ancient of ancient cities. I am constantly lost down its winding boulevards and narrow cobble-stoned streets, and within its aromatic bazaars, pulsing with life and crushing humanity.

Here and there, I find evidence of Shroudeaters as they go about thinning the human herd, but never do I catch a full sighting. Tantalising. Frustrating. Is it Callisto sipping from the wellspring of this glorious city? Is it Constantine? Yes, I believe they've been here. I feel the memory of their presence imprinted on the walls of the Sultan Ahmet Camii and hovering at the Basilica Cistern, but there is also another; the *Other*, the one the blind gypsy encountered.

I admit to a growing obsession with this vampire, one which he feeds. It is as though he's playing with me, daring me to follow where he goes; it is a challenge I find difficult to resist. Nights pass as I search for him, uncovering one resting place after another but, always, he has moved on. Who is he? Why does he taunt me? Is he a stooge for my wicked parents? If so, he will perish alongside them.

Perhaps tonight I will find him and end the mystery ...

Extract Travel Diary: April, 1953.

... The jolting of the carriage is abominable. The road - if the tortuous strip of dirt below the wheels can be called such a thing - is pocked with holes that jar the spine each time the driver finds one. Indeed, I'm sure the fiend is aiming for them, but I had no other choice except to hire him if I wanted to continue my hunt.

Yet, as we slip further behind the Iron Curtain, I have to admit that I question my reasons for this mad crusade. What happened to the rational woman of my mortal years? Dead. Gone. Displaced by a creature obsessed beyond rationality; a depressing thought made bleaker by the sombre landscape beyond the window. Did no inch of Mother Russia escape the ravages of war? Blasted and ruined, she seems. Shattered woods, gouged farmlands, decimated towns, and the people: impoverished, starving, each one haunted by a dream turned nightmarish. Nowhere amid the wretchedness do I hear a lament for Papa Stalin.

By comparison, my misery is an embarrassment. Worse, it is a misery of my choosing. At any strike of the clock, I could abandon the hunt for Callisto and Constantine and return to Paris and my beloved family. I am tempted too, except I sense that Moscow is the place where my nights of searching will come to fruition. And I know that Didier would want me to continue, to finish what I started - what *they* started - so I can return to him and the twins with the dust of the Shroudeaters on my hands and peace in my heart ...

Extract Travel Diary: September, 1953.

... The air was heavy with expectation as I strolled around Patriarshiye Prudy this evening. I don't know what caused the feeling; it was as though the trees, the water, the very buildings were waiting for something to burst forth, like the finale of magic trick. So distracting was this feeling of pending greatness that I almost missed the vampire scaling the apartment block on Bolshoi Patriarshy Pereulok.

She was quick and confident, and didn't hesitate for a moment as she worked the latch on the window to the apartment she had chosen. I jumped the fence surrounding the pond and hid in the shadow of the trees, watching for her through the leaves. It wasn't long before she re-emerged, a sated smile on her lips and a flush in her cheeks. She scuttled down the building's façade, landing on the pavement with a cat-like spring, took a quick scan of the street in both directions and stopped, her eyes on the place where I stood.

A sharp thrill of excitement twisted through me and I prepared to give chase when she raced for cover but, instead of running, she strolled towards me. My excitement dissolved into uncertainty as I tried to decide whether to flee myself, or wait to see what she wanted. It was only when she was a few feet from me that I realised the decision was no longer mine to make.

I sensed another presence behind me and turned. He was taller than me but thin, with deep-set green eyes that gave me an appraising look as his voice invaded my mind: *Comment t'appelles?*

I stepped back to keep both vampires in my line of vision and opened my senses, searching for their intent, but I felt no threat coming from them. Rather, they were curious and somewhat amused. I responded to his request with my name and he replied with his own, Ilya, before introducing his companion, Yelena...

Extract Travel Diary: December, 1953.

... Tonight I hunted with the clan. How surreal and strangely exhilarating it was to be part of a pack when I have been on my own for so long. Yet, I am also sickened by the experience for it has revealed the full depth of my vampiric depravity. Still, there is no point in losing myself in self-flagellation, nor can I allow myself to be caught by romantic ideas of belonging. Instead, I must keep my purpose for being in Moscow at the forefront of my intentions. Still, what an evening...

Mayakovskaya Metro was the meeting point for the night's adventure. Ilya and Yelena arrived together, as always, slipping like shadows down the icy length of Tverskaya Ulitsa. They were brother and sister in their mortal lives and were birthed on the same night by Grigori and Lizaveta, who dropped from the snow-dusted rooftop of the building opposite the metro's entrance.

From what I have gleaned, Yelena and her brother are only slightly older than me in vampire years, and they are Lizaveta and Grigori's first born. The bond between the four appears strong for, whenever I hint at my resentment for Callisto and Constantine, the children look at me without understanding. This lack of comprehension, I've come to realise, stems not only from the bond they share with their parents, but also from a *liking* of my own.

This was made evident to me one night as we prowled Red Square. Lizeveta had overheard me trying to explain my feelings for my parents to Ilya and Yelena and a frown creased her lovely pale brow. Then she surprised me by claiming to know of Callisto and Constantine. Stunned into silence, I trailed after Lizeveta as she spoke in a friendly tone of the 'capricious French vampires' who came to her city on occasion and treated it as though they owned it. She laughed deep in her throat, amused by the absurdity of the idea. When I asked her if the vampires were in the city at present, she spread her hands before her, shrugged, and strolled after Grigori.

I left them that night before the hunt and returned to my day shelter in the Novodevichy cemetery, where I sent my sense out across the city, seeking the slightest hint of Callisto and Constantine. I found nothing but I wasn't disheartened. The city was vast and my parents could be hiding anywhere, or they may have moved on. Either way, I was sure my Muscovite cousins would have some useful information about them and, maybe, they might even know something of the other vampire who continued to elude me.

Tonight's hunt was to provide me with the opportunity to question them further.

The youngest of the clan is Anya, who is only a few months into her eternity as a vampire. She is still depressingly human, but sweet and she laughed as her family crowded around us. There was an electric excitement crackling around them that was infectious. I felt the Thirst flare within me and - to my chagrin - I didn't try to subdue it.

The metro had been closed for half an hour and all was quiet on the street. Not that it mattered; our quarry was below ground. Grigori lead us to the maintenance entrance and we descended to the platform. The vampires moved fast, heading for the tunnel at the far end of the station. I tried to keep up, but the beauty of the hall slowed my feet; we could have been running through a palace. Grey, white, and pink marble gleamed on the walls, ceiling and floor. Colonnades shone with embossed steel and polished stones. On the vaulted roof, niches filled with colourful mosaics pulled at my attention. I've always admired the Paris metro for the uniqueness of the stations, but this— this was a work of art.

'Торопитесь!' Grigori called, as he leapt onto the tracks and was swallowed by the blackness of the tunnel. Anya captured my hand and urged me forward. I nodded and together, we jumped after him.

Although it pains me to admit, something happened to me in that crushing darkness. Some restraint I had unconsciously maintained, even during my most savage days, collapsed and I became one with the pack. My mind and will retreated and the Thirst rushed to fill the void. I was aware only of the other vampires; their heat as the Thirst raged in them; of the ground beneath my feet; the air flowing over my face, carrying the scent of metal, earth and blood - Yes! Blood. My fangs slid down and I felt their wonderful sharpness with my tongue.

We raced down the tunnel, taking a left branch and following its gentle curve until we reached a junction. Without slowing, Grigori lead us to the right, along a tunnel lined with thick black cables that snaked out of holes in the ceiling like tentacles. We moved downward, deeper into the earth, flying past long forgotten doorways and metal-lined passageways with dirt floors.

Some part of me noted them and filed the information for later consideration.

Then came a sound.

Heartbeats.

The Thirst pressed against my skin; a living thing wanting to escape its cage.

'Migrants,' Yelena murmured beside me, as though I might need some justification.

I didn't.

Ahead was a door outlined by a weak yellow light; it didn't slow us in the least. The clang of metal against stone stunned the humans inside the bunker and, for one long moment, they could only stare at us, confounded by the horror that had found them. The same could not be said of us.

There were twenty of them in the room, which reeked of their humanness; a heady wine that blotted out everything except the need to feast. Grigori snatched a woman from a rough blanket on the floor and drove his fangs into her neck. Blood sprayed around them and she let out a gurgling scream. He drew a great draft from her, gulping her hot peppery blood, and then pushed her away, mortally wounded, and went after a teenage boy, who was rooted to the spot beside an ember-filled brazier, until the vampire touched him. Then he sprang away like a young antelope, straight into Anya's waiting arms. She laughed, childlike, as she wrench his head to the side and bit into his smooth, pulsing throat.

Panic descended on the humans. They rushed for the door only to swerve when they saw Ilya blocking the way. He snagged the shirt of a man and pulled him into a deadly embrace. The man was large and possessed with a will to live but, against the Thirst, he might as well have been a lamb. Ilya's bite drove him to his knees. The man's eyes were wide with pain and disbelief. As his life drained away, he raised a hand towards a woman and small girl, who were caught between Lizeveta and Yelena. The child's life was drained in an instant and the woman died with tears for her husband and daughter sitting bright as diamonds in her eyes. Ilya finished off the man, shoved his corpse into the tunnel behind him and reached for the next fear-crazed human who passed within his grasp.

The slaughter continued and I, too, feasted: a girl; a grandmother; a wiry youth who, bless his valiant heart, tried to fight me; a man who cowered under a corpse, pretending to be dead - as though I couldn't hear his hammering heart. Their blood filled me, flowing to my extremities, cooling the Thirst.

Too soon - and yet, not soon enough - the massacre was over and we fell amid the dead, sated. My Russian cousins murmured to each other in satisfied exhilaration, and I would be a liar if I didn't admit to sharing their feelings, at least in the initial minutes, but as the echo of our victim's screams drifted away, my disgust rushed back to me. The taste of blood soured in my mouth and I felt bloated with wickedness. I stood, gazing at butchery we had wrought, struggling with my shame and loathing for the monster that I am.

Unable to bear the accusing eyes of the dead, I stumbled towards the door, drawing questioning looks from Grigori and Lizaveta. Waving away their concern, I made a feeble excuse about over-indulgence, to which they smiled knowingly, and passed into the passageway. Ilya came out behind me and, in his impeccable French, asked if I was all right.

Not wanting to address his question directly, I inquired as to where he had learned my mother language. By this time, I had walked far enough away so that the bunker was out of sight and I felt slightly better. I stripped off my blood-soaked jacket, dumped it on the floor, and leant against the wall. Ilya leant beside me and talked of his travels to France before the war, when he had still been human. Then he chuckled and I glanced at him as he revealed that it was Callisto who had 'truly clipped his barbarous tongue.'

His fondness for my vampire mother was evident in his tone and I cautioned myself to curb the hatred I felt at hearing her name. Instead, I spoke of my desire to see my parents again and how I had scoured the city with my senses, searching for a trace of them, but found nothing. Ilya shook his head and gave my forearm a gentle squeeze as he informed me that Callisto and Constantine had left Moscow a few years before.

Speaking with a nonchalance I didn't feel, I asked if he knew where they had gone. He looked away from me and I thought for a moment that he wasn't going to answer, but then I heard, as only we can, the subtle sounds of his clan moving along the passageway in our direction. As Yelena came around the bend and Ilya went to embrace her, he whispered in my mind: *North, to Finland.*

I can't say this news brought me any joy for, although I hadn't been able to sense my parents in the city, I had harboured a secret hope that they were still in Moscow. Now what stretched before me was more travel, more searching, more days turned to dust when all I really wanted was to return to Paris and Didier.

Lizeveta saw the gloom on my face as she and Grigori strolled by and inquired after the cause of my distress. I lied and said I was concerned about the corpses we'd left behind in the bunker. A glance passed between Ilya and his mother, who smiled warmly at me as Ilya explained that if the bodies were found, which was unlikely as the rail system was vast and had many secrets, blame would most certainly be direct towards the Party.

'There are many rooms filled with horrors down here, and most of them are not of our doing,' Ilya said. His mother patted my arm and bid me not to concern myself with such matters.

We ambled on, moving steadily upwards towards Mayakovskaya station. The vampires were right; the system was a vast array of tunnels and passageways, but I hadn't realised we were below the main branches until I heard a train rumble over our heads. I looked up in surprise; had I been that caught up in the hunt that I had missed our descent?

Turning to ask Ilya about our whereabouts, I found Yelena smiling at me with a knowing wistfulness. Drawn by the mystery of her expression, I moved closer to ask the meaning of her smile. She twitched her slender shoulders and dropped her gaze, suddenly shy, and stunned me by saying that I wasn't the only vampire who'd gotten lost in the labyrinth of the metro. At first, I thought she was referring to herself, but as she continued, I understood that she was referring to another vampire who was not of the clan.

It could only be Constantine, or the Other.

I pressed her with questions, sensing that - *finally* - a revelation was at hand, but before Yelena could speak further, Grigori was standing between us. He loomed over Yelena and she cringed away as he ordered her to speak no more of such things. His voice was low, dangerous, and he shot me a look of warning before pushing Yelena ahead of him down the tunnel.

Ilya appeared at my side. 'Some ideas transcend the boundary between the mortal and immortal, no?' he said, apparently unmoved by Grigori's temper. He indicated that we should follow the others and I fell into step beside him, but my mind was already on the surface, searching for any small vibration that would lead me to the Other…

Extract Travel Diary: February, 1954.

… The clan are hiding the truth from me. They know who the elusive one is, but whenever I broach the subject, they refuse to provide the information I need and their reticence only convinces me that I *must* know his identity. My frustration is at a peak; I want to leave

Moscow and continue my search for Callisto and Constantine, but I cannot until they give up the information I want.

Strangely, it pains me to do what has become necessary, for I had considered sparing them the fate of Roeland and the others, but they have forced my hand.

I know their weakness: poor little Anya.

I know the deep secrets of the city: what wonders human paranoia creates.

I know they'll come for her and when they do, I will be waiting.

Extract Travel Diary: November, 1955.

… It is time to admit what I knew six months ago. Finland is another dead end. I've travelled its width and breadth, but there is no sign that Callisto or Constantine were ever in the country. If fact, I can find no trace of any vampire, not even here in Helsinki. This leads me to wonder why Ilya sent me on such a meaningless search; was he protecting my parents? Did he sense my ill intent? Was he playing a game?

Perhaps one day I will return to Moscow and ask him before he perishes.

In some ways, I am glad not to have discovered more of my kin in my travels around Finland. After those last months with the clan, I don't think I could face another incensed, pleading, or ravaged Shroudeater. Of course, I can rationalise that time as a necessity; to find Callisto and Constantine I must know where to look but, as I've discovered during my lonely trek through the villages, towns, and cities, there is a price to be paid for necessity.

Below me, the streets of Helsinki are empty; the human populace is tucked away from the cold and biting wind. Even the homeless have found shelter for the night. Over us, I sense a full moon, although I cannot see it for the cloud blanketing the sky.

I wonder what the weather is like in Paris tonight?

Such ponderings, I know, are pointless. I may be closer to my home city than I have been in a long time, but I am no closer to returning. Instead, I will leave this glorious cathedral, which has sheltered me during these last weeks, and resume my hunt for my parents in Scotland.

Ah, Edinburgh.

Why hadn't I thought to start my search there? It was not like Callisto and Constantine had kept their association with the 'Empress of the North', as Sir Walter Scott called the city, a secret. I can only say in my defence that Patria - clever little fledgling that she was - managed to convince me of the truth of her assertion that our parents had gone to Brussels.

Tricky vampire. Much like Ilya.

What is this strange loyalty that drives these vampires? What do they stand to gain by protecting Callisto and Constantine, and the Elusive One, who mocks me with his evasiveness? No matter what I threatened, no matter what enticement I offered, none of the clan would give even a hint of his path. Why? What is so special about him to them?

Such vexing questions.

The cathedral clock has struck eleven and the time has come for me to depart, once again. I expect this journey will end in Edinburgh, for me and for my parents, and although the mystery of the Other one may not be solved, I believe I can exist with that …

Extract Travel Diary: January 1956.

… Side-tracked again. Apparently, it is not in my nature to allow a mystery to remain unsolved. Damn my stubbornness. I picked up the trail of the Other in Stockholm and followed it across Sweden into Norway. Along the way, he left bodies behind him like Hansel dropping breadcrumbs, and I have no doubt he wanted me to follow his trail. Of course, he could also be just a careless, arrogant idiot, in which case I should abandon him to his fate, but my instincts tell me there is more to him. They also tell me he is playing with me, but why? If he wants my attention, wouldn't it be more useful to make himself known to me? At least then, I would know his purpose and could respond appropriately. On the other hand, perhaps he has encountered *my* handiwork and is unwilling to expose himself to the same fate as our kin. All of which is no more than frustrating conjecture. Bah!

The trail ran cold in Bergen. I scoured the city and searched the mountain villages, but I could find no more bodies, no further clues. So it seems, no matter my tenacity, the mystery remains beyond my reach.

With no other recourse, I've taken passage on the TS *Leda*, which will sail me to Newcastle on Tyne where I can resume the pursuit of Callisto and Constantine. It is my second time on a ship - the first being between Helsinki and Stockholm - and I am quite taken with sea travel: the rhythmic swell of the white-capped waves, the quiet power of the turbine engine drawing us ever on to our destination, the sharp, salted air, even the humans are attractive with the blush of cold in their cheeks. I have not taken from the herd on board the ship, of course, for, as with train travel, it would not do to have a passenger disappear when they are listed on the manifesto...

Extract Travel Diary: February, 1959.

... I feel somewhat agitated this evening, a state of being that could easily be blame upon the atrocious weather beyond the window. How malicious the Cailleach Bheur must be, to create such a brew of snow and rain, and winds strong enough to flay the flesh. What love does the old hag have for her people? None, I would say! Indeed, I have often wondered during my time in Scotland, why any human - or vampire, for that matter - would want to live here. Agreed, the summer can be lovely, but it is over before the sighs of relief at its arrival have left the air, and it does not compensate for the long hours of dreariness that fill the rest of the year.

Of course, the weather is not really the cause of my consternation. After all, what does a vampire care for the cold and dark? They are our allies, cloaking our movements and confining the human flock to their homes, where they are easy pickings. No, the reason for this disquiet is that finally, after all the years of searching, I am but one night from confronting Callisto and Constantine. Yes, finally, I know where they are; I've seen them.

My parents have taken up residence in Blackness Castle on the banks of the River Forth.

It was a fluke, really, that alerted me to their whereabouts. After months and months of fruitless searching across the country, I had returned to Edinburgh, despondent and ready to revisit my old methods of finding information about my parents. I knew of at least one vampire in the city who was likely to know something of Callisto and Constantine. I named her Esmeralda, as her beauty and seductive way of enticing her victims reminded me of Hugo's doomed heroine.

Heading out of Waverley Station, already planning how to trap Esmeralda, I noticed a discarded newspaper lying on a bench. The sensationalist headline - *Deaths Darken Blackness* - did its job and caught my attention. I picked up the paper. Below the by-line were two paragraphs about a village called Blackness that had been struck by a strange malady, which had carried off ten of the residents in the last few weeks. Rumours about Blackness Castle were circulating through the town as old superstitions took hold. A resident, Hamish

Muir, had told the reporter, "Some folk think an evil force has moved into the castle. Some say it's the Devil himself." I finished the article, knowing Hamish was right on one count at least.

I took the first taxi I could find to Blackness.

The village seemed almost an afterthought, with a few dozen houses, a church and an inn, where I took a room. Further along the shoreline, the castle dominated in that dramatic way Callisto loves and I wasn't surprised to find her here. The next few nights were spent watching their comings and goings while I carefully masked my own presence. Although I had no idea what had drawn my parents to this particular isolated part of Scotland, I was certainly pleased with their choice of location.

Now, the nights of watching are done and tomorrow night I will bring this episode to an end. Yet, here I am, struck by this odd reticence. What is its cause, I wonder? Could it be that I have come to love the chase more than the capture? Or do I fear what I will feel in the presence of my makers? Am I afraid they will dazzle me and soften my resolve?

Or it is knowing that soon I will be able to return to Paris, to Didier and the twins, and that I fear what has changed in their lives during my absence, and all that has remained unchanged in my own …

Extract Travel Diary: February, 1959.

... They are gone.

Did I sense this last evening? Was this the reason for my mood? Did I allow them to slip away in the wild of the night? Did they get wind of me even though I've been so careful to mask my presence the whole time I've been in this wretched country? Was it, perhaps, the Other who warned them? No, I don't think so. I've sensed no other Shroudeater close by, only Callisto and Constantine. Yet, there is doubt they have moved on.

The castle is empty; its stone corridors and rooms are deserted once more and there is no evidence that vampires have been in residence there. No blood, no bodies, no bones. And no clues as to where they have gone.

What am I to do now?

My heart says return to Paris, demands it even, yet I can't give up when I am so close. To do so would make a mockery of these past ten years ...

Extract Travel Diary: January, 1960.

... When I was mortal, Didier and I spoke of taking a trip to London on the Night Ferry. The conversation would come up as we waited at Gare du Nord for the train that would take us to his parent's estate for, inevitably, the Night Ferry would be disgorging its passenger onto the platform across from us. How happy they seemed as they retrieved their luggage from the harried porters, and we would lose ourselves in dreams of romantic dinners and private cabins.

How far removed I am from those splendid imaginings. Instead of making love with the man who filled my heart with joy, I am alone and tormented by the pain of failure and an unbearable yearning for home. How I long to see Paris and my beloved, yet how my stomach churns with the knowledge that Callisto and Constantine remain free. Not even the gentle sway of the carriage can soothe my emotions. All I have to sustain me is the knowledge that I will soon be close to Didier again ...

So there you have it, mortal. Cut and pasted for your reading pleasure: eleven years of my existence, over in a half an hour, or maybe an hour, if you took your time. This is what it is like for a vampire, all the years spinning by, spinning out, but never ceasing, while around us all the things we love move closer to becoming dust, memory, nothing.

Contemplate this, my misguided devotees, and then tell me you still want this existence.

Memories from the Underground

When Lucy first lays eyes on Marguerite's friend leaning against the railing around the Colonne de Juillet, she refuses to go anywhere near him. She is already pissed at me for getting her out of bed at four in the morning and the sight of Remi adds insult to her injury.

'You're kidding me?' She pulls on my hand as I start to cross the ring road. 'He looks like a fucking murderer,' she says, with that particular distain she reserves for those she perceives as beneath her.

I have to admit, Remi is quite a sight. From under a black cap, a mass of twisted greying hair hangs to his shoulders; an equally matted beard covers his face, which is creased with deep lines. He's wearing an army jacket that has seen better days, over a jumper stained with I don't want to know what. Around his neck is a faded scarf; on his feet are mismatched runners, grey with grime. As I appraise him, he regards me in equal measure and I see in the candour of his gaze a fierce intelligence and the suggestion of some lofty position attained before fate dealt him a sucker's hand.

'You don't have to come, Lucy,' I say.

'Right, like I'm going to stay here by myself.' She glances over her shoulder and shudders as though someone's stalking her. 'Seriously, Christian, what are we doing out here?'

Can I tell her the truth? *Well, babe, we're hunting a vampire, and since vampires are nocturnal, we need to sneak up on her while she's sleeping through the daylight hours. Don't you watch the movies?* Yeah, that'll work.

'This was the only time he had free.'

'What the hell? Does he have a day job at Estée Lauder or something?'

I laugh and hug her. 'Listen to you, funny even before sunrise.'

She smiles a little and slips her arms around my waist. 'Why do we have to go down there with him?'

I follow her gaze across the road. Remi is scraping something from under his fingernails with a small pocketknife, which he wipes on the sleeve of his jacket while he considers at us. 'Think of it as an adventure,' I say. She gives me an uncertain look and I squeeze her again. 'Don't worry, I'll protect you.'

Lucy moves out of my embrace and steps onto the road. 'Famous last words,' she replies.

As I suspected, she's wrong about Remi. He leads us through the tunnels and chambers, staying close - too close in Lucy's opinion - and provides a running commentary on life in the true Parisian underground. His knowledge is vast like some of the caverns we move through and his sense of humour is as black as the darkness that pushes against our torchlight. As he talks, I listen for clues to Juliana's whereabouts, but if

Remi knows of her, he gives nothing away, not even when I hint at her presence.

But I know she's here; I can smell her.

The air carries a hint of decay, of rotting things left in the dark. There are dead things down here. Not the ancient dead, dry and crumbling, but the newly dead. Something is in residence besides the rodents and cockroaches, and fist-sized spiders whose webs glitter in the beam of our torches.

'Jesus,' Lucy yelps, grabbing my shirt. 'What the fuck was that?'

'Mademoiselle? Are you okay?'

Remi shines his torch at her chest and I see the white of his teeth in the reflected light. He doesn't seem to mind the graveyard smell.

'I'm fine,' Lucy says, pushing the torch away, and I catch the smirk on his face as he turns down the passageway. She looks at me, her mouth pressed into an unforgiving line. 'Remind me again why we're down in this disgusting place.'

I take her hand and start after Remi. 'History, babe.'

'Great,' Lucy says, her voice echoing off the walls. 'Couldn't we just go back to the Louvre?'

Not for vampire history, I think, trying not to let her distract me. My skin is tingling; a warning? I scan the dark.

Nothing.

'The Louvre?' Remi says, his voice laden with scorn. 'Dead things from a dead past. Down here is living history. Down here there is a battle to survive and live free.' As he speaks, we enter a cavernous room. There are rows of crates, split into two sections, facing a smooth, high wall. Between the sections is a rope of thick electrical cables, which snakes along the floor, ending at a metal box.

'Is that a projector?' Lucy asks. She shines her torch at the roof. 'Are we in a movie theatre?'

Remi scowls and spits against the wall. 'The police shut us down, as though we don't deserve a little entertainment.' He scratches his unwashed cheek and I wonder how Marguerite came to have him as a friend. They seem worlds apart. Then I remember something my father told me, back in the day.

We were finishing up at a soup kitchen in the city - his attempt to instil gratitude and humility in me - when I'd asked how the people let themselves get into such a situation. He'd placed a hand on my shoulder and said, 'We're all just two disasters away from destitution, Christian'

'Why two?' I'd asked.

His gaze rested on the people gathered around the tea and coffee van. 'Most of us can deal with one disaster: the loss of a marriage, the loss of a job, the loss of a child, perhaps even a psychological problem. But when such things combine, they can easily switch us from this side of the table,' he pointed to where we were standing, 'to that.' He nodded to a homeless man carrying a cup of tea in one hand and all his worldly possessions in the other.

With my father's voice fading, I consider Remi as he prattles on about life in the 'bowels of Paris' and I ponder what two disasters brought him so low? The question has just finished forming in my mind when Remi's torchlight pins me to the spot. I squint in the sudden brightness.

'You're a curious one, aren't you?' he says. At first, I'm not sure what he means; am I nosy, or am I strange? Maybe he means both, which is closer to the truth. Then he clarifies, 'You want to know my story? How I ended up down here?'

'Do you mind?' I ask, indicating the torch. Remi lifts a shoulder, grunts in that peculiarly French way, and points the torch at a spot somewhere between us, illuminating both our faces. Lucy clings to my side. 'I don't need to hear your story. That's not why I'm here.'

A sly smile creeps across Remi's face. 'Oh, I know why you're down here. You're here for her.' My faces flushes and he stabs a finger at me through the torchlight, the smile becoming a laugh, rich and sardonic. 'I knew it.'

'Who's "her?"' Lucy asks.

I shoot a warning look at Remi and say, soothingly, 'You, babe. He's talking about me trying to impress you by coming down here.'

Remi makes a derisive sound in his throat. 'Trying to impress a woman always leads to a man's downfall. Just ask Adam.' He raises the torch to the roof of the cavern, as though his history is written on the stones up there. 'My life was perfect. I was a Professor of Philosophy, heading a successful department. I had a beautiful, intelligent wife, who loved me. There were houses, cars, and dinner parties, conferences all over the world. Then, one day, at a conference in Amsterdam, that woman turned up, that she-devil, and I lost it all.'

She-devil? My skin flushes hot and then cold as my heart beat accelerates. *He does know Juliana,* I think, and a urgent need to press him for more information grips me but, in the next instant, I want him to shut up so he doesn't tell Lucy something I'm not ready for her to know. Torn, I wrack my brain for a way to discover what I want without giving away what I need until Lucy - typically - makes the effort unnecessary.

'Just ask Adam? What a crock,' she says, loosening her hold on my arm. 'You men always blame women for your inability to keep your dick in your pants. It's pathetic.'

Remi swings his torch down to her face and she responds by shining her light in his eyes. They squint at each other. 'Is that so?'

'Yeah, it is.'

'Lucy,' I say, pushing her torch towards the floor. 'That's not polite, babe.'

Or smart, I think but don't add. Lucy's candour is a quality I appreciate in her; she's a no bullshit kind of girl. Sometimes, though, she opens her mouth without considering the consequences, and it seems to me she's forgotten just where we are and why we need the man she's busy insulting.

As though setting out to prove my point, Remi clicks off his torch and does a neat trick of vanishing into thin air.

'Nice one, Lucy,' I say, as the beams of our torches cross and re-cross the carven in search of our guide, but we're alone.

'Aw, relax. He's in the next room,' she replies, and stomps across the theatre to a rough-cut archway. The blackness barely retreats before her torch. In fact, it seems to leach the brightness from the beam as she swings it back and forth.

'So?' I ask. The question comes out sharper than I intend because I have this uncanny feeling that the dark behind me is gathering, like a rogue wave, and that soon I'll be crushed beneath its immensity.

'He's not in there,' Lucy says, scurrying back to me, the darkness getting to her too. 'Who just takes off like that? The jerk.'

'Maybe if you hadn't insulted him.'

'It wasn't an insult; it was the truth.

'The truth according to Lucy, huh?'

'Don't start, okay. Let's just get outta here.'

I regard her in the reflected beam of my torch. She's biting her lip, peering into the consuming blackness, looking for a danger she can't name. 'Sure. Do you know the way?'

Lucy looks me straight in the face. 'The way what?'

'Out,' I say.

'That's not funny, Christian. Weren't you paying attention?'

'I didn't need to pay attention. That's why I brought a guide.'

Panic crosses her face as my words sink in, but it only last a few moments. Lucy's never been one to be cowered by a situation; she's too wilful for that. She gives a quick shrug, dismissing the complication, and shines her torch across the theatre chamber to the door she thinks we came through. 'Fine, we'll backtrack until we find the entrance.'

Her optimism is sweet and I don't really want to shatter her confidence, but— I raise my torch and point it towards another entry to the cavern. 'I don't think that's a good idea.'

'Shit.'

'We could be wandering around down here for hours, trying to find our way out.'

Lucy shakes her head. 'Well, that's just great, Christian,' she says, dropping onto the nearest crate. 'What do you suggest we do?'

'Wait.'

'That's the best plan you've got?'

I pull a crate over and sit in front of her. 'Remi'll come back. He's your aunt's friend, so he can't go back without us. Marguerite would have his balls, for sure.' I take her hands and rub my thumbs across her knuckles. 'We just have to wait 'til he feels like he's taught you a lesson.'

'A lesson in what? Lying to yourself?' Lucy replies, raising her voice so that it bounces through the chamber and into the passageways beyond. I sigh and let go of her hands. 'What?' Lucy asks, leaning towards me. Her fingers find the rip in my jeans and slip inside.

I press my hand over hers. 'Your mother's right about you,' I say. She digs her fingers deeper as she raises her chin and tilts her head questioningly. 'You're a wicked girl.'

'That's why you love me, right?' she says, and kisses me.

Her mouth is warm, and a tantalising contrast to the coolness of the carven. I draw the kiss out, brushing my lips over hers and playing with her tongue, partly to enjoy the feel of her, but mostly, so I don't have to answer her question because the truth is, right at this moment, I don't love her much at all.

In fact, I'm kind of pissed at her for the way she treated Remi. What could I learn from him about Juliana? And how much time is being wasted while he sulks? What if I've miss my opportunity to find the vampire while she sleeps, all because Lucy had to get on her soapbox? Annoyance surges through me and I bite her lip.

Lucy pulls away with a hiss of pain, but before she can complain, Remi's voice fills the theatre, accompanied by the reverberations of his clapping. 'All right! I love a bit of porn.' Lucy and I stand together, searching for our guide. He clicks on his torch and we find him sitting on a crate against the wall, near one of the entrances to the chamber. 'Please, don't let me stop the show,' he says, with a laugh.

'Jesus, where the hell did you go?' I ask.

Remi gets to his feet. 'Up,' he says, looking passed me to Lucy. 'Needed some fresh air. Ready to on?'

'No,' Lucy says.

'Yes,' I reply.

'Christian?'

I turn on her. 'Listen, I want the rest of the tour. If you don't want to come, stay here and we'll come back for you.'

'Non,' Remi says, pulling at his ear. 'We won't be coming back this way. I'm meeting a friend at an exit on the other side of the city.'

'That settles it,' I say, and Lucy glares at me with enough venom in her eyes to stop a heart.

We leave the theatre and travel down a narrow, sloping passageway. Despite her anger, Lucy stays close, although she doesn't touch me; a sure sign that I'll have a fight on my hands later. The air grows colder as we descend and Remy continues with his commentary as though he hadn't left us alone in the dark. I listen carefully, trying to find a gap where I can turn the conversation to the woman who brought him undone, but he prattles on almost without drawing a breath until we reach a small chamber.

The graveyard smell is stronger and the hairs on my neck stir as I sense— something.

'Do you feel that?' I ask.

'What, Monsieur?'

'Yep, I feel it. Tired. Cold. Grossed out. In need of caffeine. Can we fucking go now?'

'Lucy, shut up.'

'I couldn't agree more,' a voice whispers, and Lucy is flung against the wall. She falls in a heap as I hear a scream, but I don't know if it's Remi or me. The vampire swoops, her fingers pierce my shoulder as she twists my head. She breathes against my neck, ice cold, and I only have time for one word.

'Juliana.'

Blog Nine

What Becomes
of the Broken Hearted?

Have you heard the expression 'babes in the wood,' human?

Do you know where it comes from?

A story, yes? A tragic tale of innocent children betrayed by greedy, callous adults. Sound familiar?

I heard this story from my mother. No, not Callisto, but my mortal mother. When I was a child, she would come into my room in the evening and lay beside me in the semi-dark. She would ask about my day and tell me some funny episode from hers, which would lead her into a tale…

'… the woman looked so wretched that I hesitated to take the baguettes from her hand, and I wondered if she was a cousin to the husband and wife who died, a long, long time ago, of a terrible wasting disease, leaving behind their two small children; a bright-eyed little girl with blonde curls and her twin brother, a scallywag who chased frogs and caught crickets to put in his sister's hair.'

'How mean,' I cried, affronted.

'Indeed,' my mother agreed.

'What happened to them?'

'They died.'

I gasped. 'Because the boy was mean?'

'Because they weren't smart enough to survive.'

My mortal mother was no maternal sentimentalist, but she did love me, and she taught me resilience, a trait that has served me well during this abysmal existence. She was, I think, a good parent to my sister and me and, perhaps if I had survived my encounter with Callisto and Constantine, she would have guided me towards become a loving parent myself. But this was not to be the fate of either of us; for she was killed in the London Blitz, and we all know what happened to me. Rather, it was from Didier and his wife that I learnt - if only as a consequence of my haunting them - what it means to be a parent: the joy, the sacrifice, the suffering.

So much suffering.

Do you understand what I'm talking about, human? Have you an appreciation for the suffering of your own parents? Have you thanked them for bringing you into the world? Oh, I know they are not perfect - no human is - but they gave you *life!* Surely, that is worth your gratitude?

You don't think so, do you?

Of course not, as the pitiful comments against your makers that you leave for me to read make abundantly clear; as though the wrongs they have done you could possibly compare to the injustices perpetrated by the thieves who stole my life. What difference, I ask you, is there between those rapacious vampires and the insidious humans who condemned the 'babes in the wood' to starvation?

How poetic it will be to bring them to the same end.

But we are talking about you and your parents aren't we, my faithful, warm-blooded sycophants. Perhaps it time you telephoned them, or hugged them if they are nearby? What will it hurt you?

Do it now, before it is too late.

Go on... I'll wait.

Didier's children had grown into fine strong mortals while I had been traversing the continents, looking for my parents. They were a pleasing blend of their father and mother: Zoé delicate and dark, with a determined brow even when she slept, and Éloy, as dark as his sister was, but with a carefree abandon in his outflung limbs. I hovered around their beds during those first few weeks after my return, afraid to miss a single night for fear they would grow to adulthood before I had the chance to revel in them as children. Already, I had missed so much.

Around their rooms was the evidence of their busy lives: crowded bookshelves, rows of records, posters of pop stars - over Zoé's bed was a picture of someone called Johnny Hallyday, who I thought I might pay a visit to one night - musical instruments in the corner (a guitar for Zoé, alive with her fingerprints, and a violin for Éloy, shining with neglect), sports trophies and pendants on the wall, and photographs of friends. In Éloy's room was a separate shelf for his miniature models of iconic bridges. I recognised the Tower Bridge, Brooklyn Bridge and Golden Gate, and a half-finished Rialto Bridge. On the end of the shelf was an unopened box with a picture of the Sydney Harbour Bridge on the lid. In this way, I came to know his vision for his future.

The children grew fast, as human children do, broadening their experiences, testing their boundaries, succeeding and, sometimes, failing, discovering love and losing it, as they worked out who they were going to be in the world. Through it all, Didier and their mother were there to guide them as good parents should. Still, I knew their children better, for I was witness to the secret conversations; the ones that happened when Éloy and Zoé were alone and angry, or lonely, or giddy with ardour. I was there in the night to listen to the murmur of their dreams and soothe them as they slept.

And for four years, my heart was content. Then came the night after their graduation.

Didier and Geneviève hugged Éloy and Zoé, fussing as they cautioned the twins to keep watch over each other and to return home by their midnight curfew. I waved goodbye from the shadows on the roof, having decided to stay behind instead of trailing after the children on their night of revelry; like all astute parents, I knew the time had come to loosen the reins. Their musical laughter drifted from the car as they turned out of our street and headed into Paris.

It was a long time before we heard laughter again.

Midnight had been and gone when I made my way back to Didier's house after quenching the Thirst with the help of a gentleman who thought I would be an easy mark for his violent intentions. I'd taught him, before he died, that the night belonged to me. Returning through the back garden, I expected to find Didier's house dark and silent, with the twins snuggled in their beds, exhausted from a night of fun. Instead, every light was on and a pitiful wailing filled the street. Curious, but not yet alarmed, I concealed myself in the shadows near the kitchen. Even then, as I saw Geneviève flailing at Didier, sobbing and howling in her hysteria, I thought I was witnessing what I'd long hoped for - the argument that ends all arguments between a husband and wife.

It is strange how the prism of our own yearning can distort our interpretation of what we see, but I did not - could not - remain blind for long. *How can the children sleep through such a racket?* I wondered, slipping around the corner of the house towards their rooms, '*and with every light ablaze?* Part of me clucked, like a maiden aunt, at the thoughtlessness of their parents.

Having spent many a-night watching over them, I knew the twins slept deeply, but even the neighbours were stirring: lights coming on, faces appearing at windows. *Why aren't the twins awake?* I crept along, staying close to the wall, until I reached Éloy's window. The room was empty. The bed was neat, the top sheet turned down, waiting.

For a moment, the emptiness held me transfixed. What did it mean? The twins were good teenagers: hardworking students, fun loving with their friends, and always respectful of their parents. Why would they break curfew? Surely, they would know the worry this would cause us? I sighed. *They are growing up so quickly, but still they are babes at heart.*

Zoé's bedroom was on the other side of the house, and I needed to check it before heading into the city to track down our wayward children. The street was filling with neighbours wrapped in nightgowns, hair mussed from their pillows. To avoid them, I scaled the drainpipe and scurried across the roof, stopping beside the dormer when I saw a police car parked outside the gate. I paused in the darkness. *A police car?* Inside the house, the wailing had stopped but I could still hear Geneviève's distraught sobbing.

A denial-filled voice whispered in my mind. *A police car? For breaking curfew?*

Dropping to the lawn, I circled around the house, back to the kitchen. Geneviève was sitting at the table, her head lowered onto her folded arms, black hair spilling around her like ink. Tremors shook her body. Didier stood beside the refrigerator, one white-knuckled hand clasping the handle. His face was still and had a ghastly grey sheen, like the smooth surface of a lake. A police officer was talking to him and taking notes in a small book. Didier nodded or shook his head as required, but when the officer gestured to the door, he refused to move.

'Pardon, Mr Villette, I am sorry to insist, but you must come to identify the bodies.'

Bodies? I pressed against the side of the house. What was this madman talking about? An urge to dash inside and rip out the officer's throat swept over me. *The Liar!* I would teach him to play such a cruel joke, but Didier's broken voice held me in check.

'I can't,' he said.

The officer reached out and gripped Didier's shoulder in sympathy as Geneviève's chair scrapped across the floor. She stood, pushing her hair away from her face, which was blotched with grief but, at the same time, dignified and filled with tenderness as she spoke to Didier. 'We will go together,' she said.

I waited only long enough to hear which hospital the twins had been taken to before racing ahead of their parents. Crossing the town, I headed for the train station, where I secured the services of the sole taxi and offered the driver triple his fare if he could get me to Paris within fifteen minutes. The man nodded and hooked his thumb towards the backseat, gunning the engine and pulling away from the curb before I had the door closed. The streets were empty and, as the taxi sped into the city, I prayed that the nightmare was untrue. Needless to say, God wasn't listening.

The young nurse who escorted me to the viewing room was sombre in her duty and utterly susceptible to my suggestion that I was family. Her shoes made a faint squeak against the polished floor as she walked and her uniform whispered against her stockinged legs. The watch she wore pinned to her pinafore ticked softly and accompanied the healthy beat of her heart. How I detested her for being alive. I felt the Thirst stir, turning lazily like a well-fed cat, but ignored it. I didn't want to harm the girl, not really; it wasn't her fault that she was alive while the twins were dead.

We moved deeper into the hospital, walking down corridors and passed wards. The nurse maintained a respectful silence, for which I was grateful, and guided me with a series of hand gestures. As we came to a set of double swinging doors, she opened one side for me, but I stopped short of passing through as I felt the presence of a Shroudeater nearby.

It had been months since I'd last sensed one of my brethren and years since I'd had any direct contact with them. Not because they weren't in Paris and getting up to their usual mischief, but because I had made a deliberate practice of masking my presence and avoiding hunting grounds frequented by other vampires. Call it pessimistic but, after failing to capture Callisto and Constantine, I didn't have the will to continue with the task I'd set myself all those years ago when I'd travelled to Brussels.

The nurse was looking at me, her eyes full of compassion. 'Mademoiselle?' she said, and I realised she thought I was reluctant to continue to the viewing room. I waved her onwards and the Shroudeater's presence lessened as the door closed behind us, although my skin still tingled with their energy.

Ahead of the nurse was a steel door with a sign that read: *No Unauthorised Admittance*. She didn't hesitate and I followed her into a small area with two doors, one either side of the room. Beside each door was a simple, sturdy-looking chair. We stepped through the door on the left and I was confronted with the bodies of the twins, lying side by side on separate trolleys, with white sheets draped over them and pulled up to their chins. The nurse stood at my elbow, alert for my reaction, ready to assist if emotion should overwhelm me.

'May I have a few minutes?' I asked.

She dipped her head in agreement. 'I'll be right outside.'

Death is no stranger to me: I have experienced it, witnessed it, and dispense it, and this bothers me not one iota but, standing between Éloy and Zoé's remains, I discovered an understanding of death that had eluded me. Death, in the young at least, is not about the loss of life - which is par for the course of human existence - it is about the loss of potential. When I touched Zoé's waxy cheek and brushed a hand over Éloy cold forehead, I mourned not for their life, but for all of the things that *could have been* if they had lived.

How alike we were, the twins and I; a drunk driver had stolen away their potential to be musicians, architects, friends, lovers, fathers, mothers, grandparents, and geriatrics; to be whimsical and hateful, to be fervent and melancholic; to experience all the spice of living. Callisto and Constantine had stolen the same from me. They had killed me young and birthed me into the bland existence of a vampire, where all I would taste for eternity was the bitterness of blood and loneliness. At least, Éloy and Zoé had been spared that.

Aware of the danger of encountering Didier and Geneviève the longer I stayed, I kissed the brow of each twin and murmured, 'You were the children I was robbed of, but I have loved you as my own. You will live forever, if only in my memory.'

The nurse stood as I came through the door, her expression a mix of concern and detachment. I whispered into her mind, easing the concern and encouraging her dispassion, which would help her forget that I existed.

'I can make my way out,' I said.

She squared her shoulder. 'Fine,' she replied, turning abruptly and pushing through the steel doors. Once again, I followed her, but this time, her stride was brisk and in a half a dozen steps, she had left me behind.

I saw her again at the nurse's station, listening to Didier and Geneviève as they spoke in low, distraught voices. The police officer from the house hovered behind them. He glanced at me as I approached, but I wasn't worried about him; like the nurse, it was easy enough to turn his mind elsewhere. It was Didier who made me anxious. Pulling up the collar on my jacket, I hurried past the group and made it to the exit without drawing their attention. Relief swept over me but, like Lot's wife, I couldn't resist taking a peek over my shoulder.

Didier was looking straight at me, a frown on his weary face. As our eyes met, I caught a flash of recognition, which was immediately replaced by disbelief. *No, not now! Not like this!* I thought, bringing a hand to my face. *Don't see me,* I begged, whispering into his mind. Didier rubbed a hand across his eyes, giving me the opportunity to flee before he could question my existence any further.

If Didier remembered seeing me at the hospital, the memory was soon lost in the darkness that accompanied the days following the twin's death. Each night for weeks, I sat above their window and listened to the grief that threatened to consume them; and I pondered the hole left in my heart and wondered how I would fill it? I could see this wound in Geneviève and, perhaps for the first time, I felt empathy and a lessening of my desire to kill her, but it was for Didier that my heart ached.

He became a shadow, creeping around the too-silent house. He refused to talk and he avoided his wife as though she was responsible for bringing the torment of loss into his life. Geneviève begged him to work through his grief with her, but he was in a place where he could not hear her pleas and eventually, unable to stand the accusation in his eyes, she left.

A savage joy swept through me. Didier was, once again, mine.

It was a short-lived feeling for I soon realised that, while Geneviève was out of the way, Didier was lost in his memories. When I returned from hunting in the late evening, I would find him in Éloy's room, studying the model bridges. He would stand in front of the shelf and peer at each miniature, looking - it seemed to me - for his son's fingerprints. Sometimes he would carefully lift one and raise it to his nose, drawing a breath as though searching for Éloy's scent and, finding nothing, tears would roll down his cheeks. When he had cried himself out, he wandered to Zoé's room where he would take up her guitar and strum the strings, but the sound only brought more tears. Sobbing, he'd put the instrument aside and lay on his daughter's bed, pulling the blankets over his head, like a child afraid of monsters, and fall into an exhausted sleep.

For weeks, Didier lived this half-life of sorrow and I yearned to ease his anguish. It drove me like a compulsion and brought me to a point where I wanted to reveal myself to him, openly, once and for all. I imagined the ways I could do this without terrifying or, worse, repulsing him but, when the moment came, I found myself unprepared.

I had gone to hunt along the Seine in the early evening, choosing my victims from amongst the homeless who pitched their government-supplied tents on the banks of the river. It was a quick, careless feast, my mind more occupied with Didier than with my victims.

With the Thirst satisfied, I returned to the house expecting to see Didier involved in his nightly mourning, but he was not in Éloy's room. Perplexed, I checked Zoé's bedroom. It was empty, as was the rest of the house. Panic twisted my stomach and I turned my senses outward in search of him. I didn't need to search far.

At the bottom of the garden was a wooden shed sitting beneath the spreading arms of an oak tree. Didier had built it when the twins were small; it was his place of retreat from the world of women and children. As Éloy had grown, it became a centre of male creativity; the place where Didier took his son to teach him the lessons of manhood. They had built go-karts and volcanoes in the shed; practiced karate and talked about the responsibilities of men. When Éloy was fourteen, his father bought a vintage Renault and the shed became a weekend workshop, dedicated to restoration.

I ran through the house to the back door and stood on the stoop. Light spilled across the lawn from the shed's partly open door and I felt a rush of relief. If Didier was tinkering with the car again, surely that was a sign he was beginning to heal. I stepped onto the path to the shed, intending to peek through the side window; to take one last look at my darling before leaving him for the night. Then, on a breath of wind, came a familiar scent.

Crossing the yard in seconds, I reached for the door, but hesitated before touching the handle as the voice of reason spoke in my mind. *What if it's not Didier's blood? What if he really is tinkering with the car? What will happen if you expose yourself this way?* That voice was right, but I didn't care; the time had come and I couldn't deny it any longer. I dragged the door open.

Didier was crumpled beside the wrecked car in a spray of shattered glass. I hurried to his side, kicking away a hammer that lay inches from his hand. There was so much blood and I shivered with an unspeakable desire before pushing the Thirst down: *It is Didier, you fiend!* Kneeling beside him, what had occurred was immediately obvious; deep gashes opened the skin from his wrist to elbow and the blood flowed rich as red velvet.

'Oh, my beloved,' I said, and gather him to my body.

His eyelids fluttered and I remembered the long-ago night when I had saved him from the German soldiers; it was the last time I had been this close to him. I touched his pale face, my fingers tracing the contours of his jaw and finding the pulse in his neck. It was fast and seemed to be keeping time with his breathing. *Not good, sweetheart,* I thought, reaching for a rag on the workbench behind me. I tore strips from the cloth and cinched them around his arm, staunching the flow of blood.

Didier moaned. 'Geneviève?'

Her name on his lips was a dagger through my heart, but I put the pain aside and whispered, 'Don't give up, my love. I will bring her to you.'

'Who—' he asked, slipping away before he could finish the question.

Geneviève wanted to know who I was, too. 'An old friend, come to pay my respects,' I replied and returned the telephone to its cradle for the second time. She wouldn't be long in arriving; the loss of her children ensured that.

Through the back door, I could see Didier lying on the floor of his shed. I desperately wanted to go to him and steal a few more precious minutes together before his wife arrived. Instead, I left the kitchen and climbed onto the roof, nestling in beside the dormer like a shy gargoyle, to wait for the rest of the night's drama to unfold.

In the distance, a siren wailed while, from the opposite end of the street, came a splash of headlights, moving fast. The mortals were converging, coming to rescue Didier and, as always, I would fade into the background of his life, his invisible guardian; a dark angel eternally condemned.

The Truth of a Dream

Her voice comes out of the dark. 'How do you know my name?'

I can't opened my eyes; I'm afraid of what I might see, even though I'm the one who's come looking for her. One thought spins through my head: *She's real. She's real. She's real,* but it doesn't comfort me. Instead, I'm terrified; this must be what Moses felt like when God spoke to him from the burning bush. The myth is reality, but this one has the potential to kill me. I know I'm being a coward - *Where's Lucy?* - but I keep my eyes shut, hoping to fool her. It doesn't work. Maybe it's my breathing that gives me away.

Cold fingers brush my neck. 'Not your breathing; your blood.'

Eyes wide open, I'm blinded by the light of a discarded torch, but I scramble away from her anyway, press against the wall. I glance left and right - *Where the fuck is Lucy?* - searching for the way out. The door Remi lead us through is gone, or if it's there, she's concealing it somehow. Dammit, what the hell was I thinking, coming here?

The vampire watches me with beautiful, inhumane eyes of gold-flecked green. I slide to the floor, curl up; try to be small, inconsequential, not worth killing. 'Why do you cower? You would be dead already if I meant to harm you.' Juliana drifts to the other side of the room and leans against the wall. Beside her is the door. I know she's deliberately pointing it out to me, proving I'm not a prisoner, that there's nothing to fear.

Not true, not true, my mind whimpers. *You're trapped in a room with a real vampire who's blocking your only escape route. That's the definition of fear, my friend.*

Maybe, but the vampire hasn't moved. She seems relaxed and, if anything, amused rather than threatening. Keeping an eye on her, I find a shred of courage and get up off the floor, reminding myself that she's the reason I came to Paris. Still, I keep the distance between us as I look around for Lucy. She's not in the room.

'Where's my girlfriend?' I ask.

'Safe, for now,' Juliana replies moving towards a dark bundle against the far wall. The vampire looks at me, a gleam of malice in her eyes. She kicks the bundle. Something snaps and there's a groan.

I shudder. *Lucy?*

Juliana licks her full crimson lips. 'Not Lucy, more's the pity, but you did interrupt me.'

The hairs along my arms and neck stir. 'Sorry,' I stammer, 'I didn't know you were— busy.' It sounds pathetic and I look at the ground.

'That's okay,' Juliana replies, and my head jerks up.

She's standing in front of me, though I didn't hear her move. My spine aches with tension; I want to bolt, but my feet are planted. The vampire smiles and I catch a glimpse of her wickedly sharp canine teeth.

'Are you going to explain how you know my name? And what you're doing here? Or do I have to *draw* it out of you?'

Sweat trickles over my ribs, even though it's cool in the room. 'Don't you know why I'm here?' I ask, buying time. Now that I've found the vampire, the thought of those fangs sliding into my neck freaks me out.

A slithering sound distracts me. Across the room, the bundle is moving. A grimy hand creeps across the floor, searching. I barely see Juliana move. She kicks the hand; vicious, bone breaking. There is a grunt of pain and a drained, white face lifts in the gloom. My breath catches in my throat. It's Remi. I step towards him and the vampire turns her gaze on me. The golden flecks in her eyes flare red as rubies as she rolls Remi onto his back and places her booted foot over his throat.

With the fierceness of a lion, Remi fights her, clawing at her leg with his good hand as she increases the pressure. His feet flail, making his body buck, but the vampire doesn't move an inch. The sound of his choking is nightmarish, worse than any horror film I've ever watched.

'Please, stop,' I whisper. Juliana shrugs and shifts her weight, applying a quick downward pressure. Silence fills the room.

My hands are freezing, but my body is furnace hot. *Holy fuck, she killed him. She killed him!* Bile rises from my stomach and I clench my jaw, struggling against the urge to puke. *She killed Remi. Oh my God, Remi!* I feel jittery inside, as though I'm gonna shake apart. I don't know what to do; I've never seen a real person killed before. *Shouldn't someone stop this?* I look at the door, wanting the good guys to burst into the room, but no one comes to save the day.

Leaving the body, the vampire wanders over to me, pausing inches away. 'You haven't answered my questions,' she says, continuing our conversation as though nothing's happened.

Her words are like a dousing of cold water. Calmness returns to my mind and body as I realise she's not going to kill me; not yet anyway. I don't know what's keeping her in check, curiosity maybe, or perhaps she's got another agenda, but it doesn't matter. What she's giving me is time and I run with it.

'You didn't answer my question,' I say.

Her eyebrows arch again, and I find it hard to breathe. She is exquisite and dreadful all at once. Eyes like jewels. Hair of pale gold spilling down beside her face and across her shoulders. No scar or blemish marring her skin. Her body, narrow and almost boyish except for the swell of her breasts. Heaven help me; she is a dream and a nightmare.

'Do I know why you're here?' the vampire says, touching my chest. I shudder, graze my shoulders on the rough wall to escape her touch. She snickers and glides to the centre of the room. 'Not everything is clear to me, but I know you've come from a distant place - I can smell it on you - and I can guess at your purpose. Mortals only ever seek out my kind for two reasons: to bring death, or find death. Which is it for you?'

I glance at Remi's body. 'I didn't come for that.'

'You came to bring death to me then? Well, I should at least know the name of my killer?'

'Christian Carfax.'

'Oh, perfect,' Juliana laughs, soft and dangerous. 'What are you? An avenging angel? A warrior for God come to dispatch the unholy vampire?' The tension grows in her body as she prepares to spring at me. 'I hope you're ready to meet your maker, *Christian*, because better men than you have tried and failed to rid the world of me.'

'Wait, Juliana,' I shout, holding my hands out, though it's a useless gesture. The seconds tick by as I wait for her to attack, but instead she takes my hands in her own and examines the scars etched into my forearms.

'Interesting,' she says searching my face. 'What's that about? Some type of ritual, or were you involved in a battle of some kind?'

'They're for Lucy.'

'Your girlfriend?'

'The love of my life,' I reply a little too quickly.

She releases my hands. 'Love?' she says, a sceptical lilt in her voice. 'What do you know of love?'

'I know your story.'

She touches her mouth; runs her thumb over her bottom lip thoughtfully. There is blood around the cuticle. 'My blog?'

I nod.

Juliana turns away, wanders to the other side of the room, unhurried, comes back to stand in front of me. 'You think you know my story, but you don't know all of it, and you haven't understood what I've told you so far, otherwise you wouldn't be here.' She shakes her head; there's disappointment in the movement. 'What do you want?'

I can't speak. Here's the moment I've planned for, dreamt about, and it feels so important that it blocks my throat, locking my voice inside. I swallow. 'I'm not here to kill you,' I say, forcing the words out, 'and I don't want you to kill me.' The possibility of my death makes me feel giddy, like I'm standing on the edge of a dark bottomless crevice. Weird, I realise, but death's never been part of my plan. 'I want what you have,' I say, keeping my eyes fixed on the vampire. 'I want immortality.'

I'm ready for any reaction: arrogance, derision, laughter, even anger, but not this; a word, simple and definitive.

'No.'

Blog Ten

A Gift for the Enemy

So, human, are you still convinced that immortality is for you? Is it still something you crave? If I were standing behind you right now, would you arch your neck for me? Would you allow another of my kind between your legs? Hmm, that's the way, open up. It won't hurt all that much; the initial stab of pain as we pierce your flesh, followed soon after by a strange collapsing feeling as your body empties and an erratic clenching in your chest as your heart tries heroically to pump your dwindling supply of blood. This is when you'll panic. Yes, you will. Everyone panics. It is a biological compulsion; you may think you want immortality, but your body knows better.

I would listen to your body, if I were you - but I'm not, and you won't, so why am I bothering? After all, it's not like we are friends or anything, although I suspect you could use a real friend or two instead of the flatterers you surround yourself with like mirrors in a fun house. Those pretenders who reflect back to you only what you want to see and never the truth of who you really are. Perhaps if you had true friend, you wouldn't be sitting there, fantasising about an encounter with me, a death-dealing monster. Perhaps you would be *living* every moment you have left.

But what do I care about what you do? I am not your friend. Vampires don't have friends. We have prey and memories of friendship, neither of which fill the void at the centre of our existence.

Is that what you want?

Another sacrifice to immortality?

Would this make you happy?

Let's see if that's true.

The question philosophers ask of Sisyphus is: *Can such a man be happy?* If I were to use Didier as the exemplar, I would have to agree with Camus and say yes. The death of his children was the boulder Didier was condemned to push to the top of the mountain; an incredible burden that almost overwhelmed him time and again in the years to come. Yet, when he reached the pinnacle of his suffering, before his grief rolled to the bottom of the mountain and he turned to retrieve it, I could see his acceptance of his struggle, and in that acceptance - when he embraced the pain and loss - he found a sort of happiness.

Perhaps, unlike Sisyphus, the burden for Didier was eased by the presence of Geneviève. I watched this woman, my greatest rival, as she dealt with the loss of her children, admiring her strength in the significant moments - birthdays, Christmas, anniversaries of that terrible night - when she soothed those around her, and felt for her in the private moments, when she would crack apart like an eggshell.

Didier never saw this woman, screaming her anguish to the heavens. To him, she was a comfort: listening when he raged against God; holding him as he poured out his tears; waiting in silence as he made his way back down the mountain. For this, I gave her my grudging respect.

I say grudging because women have never been my favourite creatures. Even from a young age, when I watched my mother and her sisters as they embroidered around our kitchen table and gossiped about various women from the neighbourhood, I felt dubious about them. Why did they take such joy in deriding other women? And how could they, upon seeing those same women in the marketplace, behave as though they were the best of friends? The hypocrisy of women confused and frightened me; did they talk and laugh about me when I left the room? Surely my mother wouldn't? Yet, I'd overheard her speak poorly of her sisters when they displeased her. Such observations taught me to step carefully around women and to be cautious of whom I allowed close to me.

This changed went Isabeau entered my life.

I meet her on the first day of high school. Like me, she was standing on the outer rim of the students, watching the popular girls sitting in the centre giggling and whisper behind their hands. Our gaze meet across their heads and, to my surprise, she twisted her face into a grotesque mask, crossing her eyes and poking out her tongue. I supressed a laugh, not wanting to draw attention to myself, and she nodded towards the Elm tree at the bottom of the school grounds. Choosing to follow her that day took a leap of faith, but it was a choice I never regretted.

Isabeau was the opposite of any girl I'd ever meet; she was quiet and considerate, only speaking when she had something she thought worth saying. To Isabeau, words were like gems, each one precious and given with intention. By comparisons, I was wanton with my words, making up for all of the conversations I'd held inside over the years of my childhood. Isabeau never rebuked me for my chattiness but, as we moved through high school, she encouraged me to talk less and think more so that, by the time we graduated and prepared to enter university, our discussions had matured along with our friendship.

Not that this seriousness meant we didn't have fun. Isabeau shared my love of Dietrich and my interest in Surrealism - for a short while, she was madly in love with Max Ernst - and we visited exhibitions and films whenever we could afford to go. In winter, we skated at the Rond Point des Champs Elysees because Isabeau loved the feeling of gliding across the ice, while during the long summer days we relaxed at the Piscine Deligny and read passages from our favourite novels to each other between bouts of sunbaking and swimming.

Although we took different paths during our university years - teaching for Isabeau and nursing for me - we studied together and went on double dates on the weekends, or to family picnics where our aunts always tried to match us up with whichever bachelor-cousin was their favourite that week, despite our eye rolling and protests. They were good times, made better because we were more than best friends; we were sisters.

Didier's arrival in my life created a seismic shift that rippled across my friendship with Isabeau. In those early weeks, I would have given away everything that I'd worked for just to be in his arms. Of course, Isabeau, sensible as always, cautioned me not to lose myself and I tried to listen to her, but the lure of my lover was too powerful and I was soon skipping arrangements that I'd made with her to be with Didier.

Yet, true friend that she was, Isabeau was patient and when I did make time for her, she never criticised but listened as I prattled on breathlessly about the wonders of my relationship with Didier and how amazing our life together was going to be once we were married. In the pauses between my commentary, she managed to slip in some details about her own life; her new job at an exclusive girl's college and her own romance with a young doctor she'd meet at a café on one of the occasions that I'd left her waiting. His name was Simon Cohen.

I knew the name. He was a smooth-talking Austrian, who was the subject of gossip among the nurses at the hospital where I was working and, from what I remembered, none of it had been complimentary. I reached across the table and rested my hand over Isabeau's as I told her what I had heard.

Her face was still when I finished and I saw the shimmer of tears in her eyes. 'I'm sorry to be the bearer of bad news,' I said, my heart aching for her.

She withdrew her hand abruptly and grabbed her purse, shoving it into her lap as she glared at me. 'You're not the only one who deserves to be loved, you know.' I gaped at her as she stood and, by the time I had found something to say, she was through the door and crossing the street. They were the last words to pass between us; a week later, I encountered my vampire parents and lost everything that made me human.

Despite our falling out, Isabeau didn't forget me. She kept a photograph of us, taken at the Piscine Deligny during our seventeenth summer, on her mantle beside her wedding photographs - how radiant she looked standing beside Simon - and a year after my humanity was stolen, she named her daughter after me.

I watched over Isabeau and her family as often as I could in my early years as a vampire, sometimes spending the evenings when Didier worked late sitting on the balcony above their apartment, listening to their life unfold. They were a close and joyful family but, as the possibility of war loomed and anti-Semitism increased across Paris, fear crept into their lives and I worried for them.

With the fall of Paris, I was busy keeping track of Didier but, whenever I felt he was safe - the grand illusion - I checked on Isabeau and her family. It was not hard to find them as Simon had been fired from his job and they were essentially confined to their house.

Terror had taken the place of joy in their lives and was eating away at them; Isabeau was thin with worry and her hands shook whenever she reached for her little girl. Simon paced the room or, when his wife and child slept and the house was dark, he peered from behind the curtains, watching the street.

His surveillance was justified when the first of the round-ups took place. When I caught word of it, I raced across the city to Isabeau's apartment, dreading finding the rooms empty, but the family was there, huddled together, sharing a prayer before eating. Once the meal was over and their daughter was tucked into bed, Isabeau and Simon stood together at the window.

'Do you think they'll come for us?' Tension stretched Isabeau's voice.

'Not tonight, and not ever for you, my love,' Simon replied, slipping an arm around Isabeau's waist. She laid her head against his shoulder, neither of them voicing the concern inherent in Simon's comment.

What could I do? My best friend's family was in peril, but I couldn't just re-appear in her life as though the last three year didn't exist, not as I was now; an unnatural creature, feasting on the living. No, I couldn't destroy her memory of me; it was all I had left. Once again, I cursed Callisto and Constantine for their selfish indulgences.

Then came the night when I had to act.

I'd been trailing Didier through the back streets as he made his way towards his apartment when he was interceded by a contact from the Résistance with information about a major milice operation to round up

Jews from across Paris and confine them to the Vélodrome d'Hiver to await deportation.

'How many this time?'

'Twenty-two thousand.'

A look of incredulity filled Didier's face. 'Not just the men then?'

'No, women and children too,' the contact replied, and my heart filled with fear.

Didier closed his eyes and I knew he was thinking of the Jewish people whom he'd counted as friends over the years. He spoke as he opened his eyes, which were bright with anger. 'We've got to warn as many as we can—'

I leapt away before he finished. Isabeau and her family had to be warned of the impeding danger and I could get to them faster than any member of the Résistance. Doubt plagued me as I took to the catacombs and the secret thoroughfares beneath the city. *You're a vampire,* it said, *all you will do is scare her to death. Let the past lie. Let the future take care of itself. You can achieve nothing by exposing yourself!* On and on the thoughts went, but I didn't stop until I reached Isabeau's front door.

Pressing my ear to the wood, I listened to the voices within; so familiar, so frail, so dead if I didn't do something. I knocked and stepped back into the shadows beside the stairwell. Footsteps vibrated the board beneath my feet, a bolt withdrew, the knob turned and a crack opened between the wall and the door. Simon's face appeared in the gap, his eyes narrowing as he searched the dimness.

Send out Isabeau.

I projected the thought with enough power to make him act without questioning, yet I noticed a slight hesitation before he turned and felt a flicker of hope. He was strong-minded, like Isabeau, which was just what his family would need to survive this night and all the long nights to come.

The door opened wider and Isabeau stood in the opening; back straight, chin up, eyes lustrous with defiance. 'Who's there?'

I spoke from the darkness. 'It's Juliana.'

A hand fluttered to Isabeau's mouth and she stepped into the hallway. 'Juliana?'

'Please don't come any closer. I'm only here to warn you. They're coming for you and your family. Not just Simon, but all of you. Do you understand? You must leave Paris tonight.'

Isabeau stepped closer, a hand reaching for me. 'It's been three years, where have you been?'

'Stop,' I ordered, and she did, her face awash with confusion and longing. 'I know it's a shock for me to be here. I know you have many questions, and I wish I could answer them, but there is no time. Isabeau, you must take your family and flee. On our friendship, which I know you still hold dear, promise me you won't delay. Promise me you will leave within the hour.'

The urgency in my voice broke through her surprise. She glanced past me, down the stairwell, and drew her shawl tighter around her shoulders as she moved back towards the apartment. 'Yes, of course. But, are you sure? We've heard no rumour—'

'Have I ever lied to you, Isabeau?'

Tears filled her eyes. 'Where have you been?' she whispered.

It tore at me to see her pain, but I couldn't encourage the sentimentality. 'Take as much food as you can carry and jackets; you'll need to sleep rough. Head north, travel at night. Good luck.' I turned to leave.

'Thank you, Juliana.'

Hesitating on the top step, I fought the urge to hug her to me, for to do so would reveal the strangeness of my being, and the last thing she needed was to know that there were other monsters in this world. The *Schutzstaffel* and milice were terror enough for any mortal.

'Be safe,' I replied, and bounded down the stairs before my love for her betrayed us both.

I crossed the narrow street and swung up onto a first floor balcony of an empty apartment, which gave me a view into Isabeau and Simon's home. True to her word, Isabeau hurried from room to room, gathering what she thought they would need for their journey. As she packed, she spoke to her daughter of the adventure they were about to embark upon and the little girl, with all the seriousness of her mother, offered assorted items that she thought they could use on the trip - two pencil, a tattered doll, a piece of ribbon. Isabeau took each one and slipped them into the pockets of her jacket, kissing the child's head after each addition.

Simon was in the kitchen, filling a small suitcase with food. When Isabeau came into the room, he stopped her and whispered fiercely, 'Are you sure we can trust this friend of yours?'

'With my life,' Isabeau replied, with her usual economy, and a spasm of loneliness twisted my heart. She was the only person who had truly understood me and now we were separated for all eternity.

I hung my head as sadness overwhelmed me, but my grief was interrupted by a sudden, shattering burst of machine-gun fire and I was instantly on my feet. Didier was out there, somewhere in the city, unprotected. Isabeau and Simon heard the shots too and it gave them a new urgency, but I couldn't stay to see them on their way. Didier was my first priority.

As I climbed onto the railing surrounding the balcony, I saw Isabeau take my photograph from her mantel. She wiped the glass, a nostalgic smile on her face, before placing the frame into her bag. It was a sweet gesture, and I sent her my love as I dropped to the street and went in search of Didier, knowing she would understand my choice.

The round up tore thousands of Jews from their homes and set them adrift on a sea of uncertainty that, for all but a few, washed up on the horror-filled shores of Auschwitz. I'd like to think Isabeau and her family escaped the fate that was forced on so many that night, but I don't know for certain. The following evening, I returned to their apartment, which was empty except for two of the bags that Isabeau had packed, including the one containing my photograph. The sight of that bag sent a chill down my spine.

Were they taken to the Vélodrome d'Hiver? Maybe. I wasn't able to get close enough to the building, which was guarded by armed police officers day and night, to find out. I hope not, for the sounds of torment coming from inside that place were soul-destroying, even for one like me.

Not knowing the truth of something can be a blessing. I have tried, in the long years since those terrible nights, to hold onto my memory of Isabeau as I last saw her; a tender lioness doing what needed to be done to protect her family. It is the only way I can honour her and the friendship we shared.

Years later, watching Geneviève nurture Didier through the loss of the twins, I was reminded of Isabeau, of her unwavering patience and understated resilience, and I thought that, if the flow of events had been different, perhaps the three of us could have been friends. Fate, however, is a fickle thing with a twisted sense of humour and, instead of enjoying the company of gracious, strong women, each of us was struck by tragedy.

It hardly seemed fair.

If there was any good to come from losing the twins, it was the shift in my attitude towards Geneviève. No longer did I feel the need to eliminate her from Didier's life. Indeed, I came to see that she was his reason for living and so I looked out for her. Not that this meant I wasn't still jealous. Rather I was like a best friend who coverts her best friend's husband; I protected her because it bought me more time with the man I loved.

Without the twins to brighten and complicate their lives, Didier and Geneviève slipped into quietude. He took a job with a small law firm in Sévres, which paid the bills but didn't tear away chunks of his life. Geneviève filled her days helping out at her local church. Some evenings I would follow her back from her visits to the poor, where she would cook them a decent meal, or just sit and listen to their sorrows. The woman was a saint, really.

In this way, the years drifted by and their pain faded into shadows beneath their eyes and lines around their mouths. They stayed close to each other, bonded by love, but also by the lurking presence of Death. Not that their unity prevented Him from arriving at their door again. This time he came, clothed in disease, for Geneviève.

I arrived at Didier's house in the early hours of morning, having spent the evening chasing a vampire who had recently arrived in Paris. He was from Algeria, young and strong, difficult to catch, but I had the advantage; the city belonged to me. To my surprise, the kitchen light was on and Didier and Geneviève were drinking red wine as they sat at the table, holding hands. A pang of jealousy shot through me as it always did whenever I caught them in a tender moment and I turned to leave, not wanting the exhilaration of the night to be tarnished, when Geneviève spoke.

'We've survived worse than this. Have faith. We'll beat it.'

Didier reached for his wine glass and I saw that his hand was shaking. He sipped, swallowed, and cleared his throat. 'You're right. Lots of people survive. That's what Doctor Pascal said, right? And you're strong. We'll get through this.' He took another swallow of wine. 'Yes, we will.'

Geneviève offered him a gentle smile. 'We will, sweetheart. I promise.' This was not the last time I heard Geneviève lie to Didier to help fortify him during the dreadful months when Death toyed with her.

Often I would find them in the kitchen or sitting on the back step in the hours after midnight, when sleep was impossible for Geneviève. They would talk of the past, or of the following day's treatment - but never of the future - and Geneviève would keep their conversation light, laughing frequently, and leading Didier back to her whenever he began to slip into sadness. When a silence grew between them, he would ask if she was comfortable and she would pat his arm, or snuggle closer to him and murmur, 'I'm fine,' although it didn't take a vampire's eyes to see that the opposite was true.

Her strength, which I thought I had seen the limit of with the twins, was admirable. Never did I hear her lament her situation, not even when she was alone, nor ask for sympathy from any of the people who came to visit with her. Eventually, however, when her body was ravaged and she could stand her suffering no longer, she waived; and who could blame her.

I hunted nearby that night, sensing that Death was closing in on Geneviève. When the thirst was sated, I made my way to the house and took up my usual perch in the shadows over the main bedroom, arriving just in time to hear Geneviève beg Didier to bring her life to an end.

Horror strained Didier's voice as he replied, 'Don't ask that of me, Evie. Please. I can't. There's still time and things that can be done.'

Tears sat in Geneviève eyes, but she lifted her hand and inched it over Didier's hand. 'Yes. Okay. You're right. We'll keep trying.' She drew a slow breath. 'Would you bring me some coffee, dear?'

Relief filled Didier's face; coffee was something he could do. When he was gone, Geneviève turned her head on the pillow and sobbed softly. My heart ached for her; perhaps Didier couldn't fulfil her last wish, but I could.

Geneviève wasn't aware of my presence until I took her in my arms. She was almost weightless and her skin was paper-thin. I could smell the disease eating her. It had made her blood rancid. Thankfully, there are many ways to end a life.

'Are you an angel?' she asked.

'I am whatever you wish me to be,' I told her, and began to sing as I pressed her to my chest. She didn't have the strength to struggle and I held her long after her last breath, and then laid her upon the pillow, arranging her hair and hands into peaceful repose.

Moments after I closed the window and resumed my position on the roof, I heard the crash of the coffee pot and the shattering of Geneviève's favourite cup. I waited for the howl of grief from Didier but none came. When I decided to risk a look into the room, I saw him sitting beside his wife, holding her hand, his head bowed. He stayed that way for the longest time.

It was a different grief that took Didier. There was no rage, no fist waving, or cursing of God. There was a profound sorrow and loneliness but, as he conversed with his remaining friends, I realised there was also tranquillity. He faced his burden because he knew Geneviève was no longer in pain and that they would soon be reunited.

So, even in death, he loved her more than me.

Was there no escape from *my* burden? Was it to be my eternal punishment to love this man? A man who had lived, loved, and suffered before my eyes, while I just existed? This was the true travesty of Callisto and Constantine's indulgence all those nights ago. Didier would die and his yoke would be broken, but there was no release from this mortal world for me.

Like Sisyphus, my suffering was to be everlasting but, unlike Sisyphus and Didier, it was a suffering that I couldn't find happiness in, and one that I was unwilling to bear alone. No, there was going to be a reckoning for the burden that I was forced to endure.

Exposés in the Dark

'I cannot.'

'Why the hell not?' I don't mean for the question to come out like a petulant demand, but I'm crushed, and I can see from the coldness in Juliana's expression that she's immovable on the subject.

Her mouth curves at the corners. 'You're angry?' she says, as though it's a new experience. She turns her back on me, letting me know what my anger means to her, and crosses to the door. Air rushes into the room as Juliana steps into the corridor. 'Walk with me, Christian.'

I hesitate. It's dark out there. My hand creeps to the crucifix beneath my shirt: Lucy's idea.

Juliana glances over her shoulder. 'Are you coming?'

'Yeah, sorry,' I say, dropping my hand away from the crucifix.

The vampire tilts her head to the side. 'What's beneath your shirt, Christian?' she asks gliding back in to the room.

'Nothing.'

Juliana stops a metre from me. 'Really?' she says, raising her eyebrows. 'Let's see about that.' She makes a show concentrating. 'Are you hiding a foolish trinket on your person, Christian? Hmm yes. Pure silver? Expensive. Very nice. Any other trinkets or potions? No garlic, Holy Water, wooden stakes?' She laughs and my skin crawls at the coldness of the sound. 'Honestly, Christian, do you think these things will protect you from me?'

I swallow; violence radiates from her.

'Let me tell you a little secret about my kind, Christian. Garlic, Holy Water, and crosses will not keep us at bay. I could baste you in garlic and still drain you dry, no problem. As for your precious silver cross. It would serve you better if you hawked it at the nearest pawn shop.'

Despite what Juliana says, I reach for the crucifix, needing something to ward off the chill of danger that's skittering up my spine. Juliana sniggers, closing the distance between us until she's centimetres from my face.

'Shall we clear up a few other things while we're here?' She thrusts her chest forward. 'Feel my skin,' she demands.

I don't want to touch her, but my hand rises by itself. My fingers brush over the swell of her breasts, which should be soft and warm. Instead, I find the hardness of cold, smooth marble.

'Don't you see Christian? You cannot harm me,' Juliana says, pushing my hand away. 'If you were to try to drive stake through my heart, it would only ruin my shirt and infuriate me.' She digs a fingernail into my chest, right over my heart, her eyes sparkling with spite as I wince. 'I cannot be burnt or frozen, stabbed, decapitated, or shot, not even with silver bullets.' She titters at her joke. 'I am impervious to poison and electricity. And I cannot be drowned. In short, Christian, my kind cannot be killed by the likes of you, while your kind - so frail, so pathetic - has no protection from the likes of me.' She steps away as she speaks, returning to the door.

I don't know what to say. I thought I knew everything there was to know about her kind. I've studied vampire lore, watched every vampire movie ever made and read every story written about them. I know her vulnerabilities. Is it all a lie?

Yes, she answers inside my mind.

I touch the centre of my forehead, rub the spot where her voice seems to come from; I don't like her being in there. The room tightens around me. What else am I wrong about?

Everything; a whisper.

Get out of my head; a plea, not a demand.

Of course.

I can't be wrong about everything; Juliana's existence is proof of that.

The vampire leans against the doorframe. 'I *am* real, Christian, but the rest of what you think you know is a lie. Humans invented 'Vampire Lore' to help them cope with our presence among them. Such stories allow them to feel less vulnerable, especially when they include a 'weapon' for our destruction. But that's all they are, Christian; stories told by frightened children.'

I think over what she has told me, wondering how it affects my plan and decide that it doesn't; I'd never wanted to kill the vampire anyway.

If Juliana hears the thought, she lets it go. 'Why don't we forget all this nonsense and take a walk.' She turns into the passageway and her voice drifts out of the darkness like curling smoke. 'Or don't you want to be immortal?'

She's changed her mind. The thought rushes through me and I almost leap after her. And stop. The passageway is not the one Remi brought us down. I'm in a different section of the catacombs and whatever notion I had of getting out of here is totally blown.

Juliana calls to me, 'Come Christian,' and I follow her voice as though it's a beacon.

The ground sucks at my shoes and the smell of dirt is strong. I'm not sure if we are moving upwards or downwards. I can only just make out Juliana in the gloom. She's an apparition, floating. Sometimes she's close, whispering in my ear. At other times, it's as though she's talking to me from around a corner. I want to stop, get my bearings, but I can't; what if I lose her down here, in the dark?

Shoving the fear down, I keep after Juliana. Still, I need to know I'm not alone, so I ask, 'If all the lore is an invention, what is the truth about vampires?'

Juliana is suddenly beside me. I draw a breath, relieved to have her close by; the darkness is cloying and my sense of direction's shot. Disoriented, I almost grip her arm as we walk along the passageway.

'What is truth, Christian, but a matter of perception? Is it not so that what is true for you may not be true for me?'

I know the philosophical game she's playing, but I don't want to join in. 'What's the truth about vampires,' I persist.

'How about I tell you what isn't true?' She doesn't wait for me to agree. 'Fallacy number one; we can't see ourselves in mirrors. Who invented that one do you think? Bram Stoker perhaps? What a lot he has to answer for.' Her voice is coming from somewhere above me, and I wonder if she's levitating. When she speaks again, she's behind me. So quick.

'No, not Stoker. A priest? They like to keep the faithful in a state of constant fear. And they're very concerned about souls, which apparently we don't have. Although how anyone actually knows that particular 'fact' is a mystery to me. How, indeed, do they even know that humans have souls?'

The vampire becomes downright chatty, but I don't mind; the sound pushes back the grinding darkness. She's ahead of me again and I stumble on, following her voice. 'Fallacy number two; that we drink the blood of lesser creatures.' She makes a disgusted sound. 'How could anyone drink the blood of a rodent?'

'I would, if it saved a life,' I say.

Juliana stops and I crash into her; it's like hitting a granite wall. I bounce off and land on my arse in the dirt. *Damn.* She pulls me to my feet and I smell her scent - coppery - as her fingers grip my arm.

'Vampires drink human blood, and only human blood. If you were to become one of us, you would kill humans, at least one every day for all of eternity. You cannot fast - the Thirst won't allow it - and you cannot quench your need with other fluids. Just as a human must breathe, we must feed, and feed, and feed.' She releases me, but doesn't move on.

'I'll only kill the evil-doer,' I say, full of bravado.

Juliana laughs. 'How noble of you, Christian,' she says, walking on. From over her shoulder she says, 'Except, won't *you* be the evildoer?'

There are a dozen things I want to say in response to her mockery, but I say nothing because I realise I can see the walls, the ground, the vampire. Further down the passageway are two rows of lanterns, glowing yellow. I've never been so grateful for light in all my life.

Suddenly, Juliana is standing beside me. Her ivory skin glows and I'm tempted to touch her. I don't. Instead, I gazed at the lights again.

'Humans love the light, don't they, Christian? They think it makes them safe, but death comes in the light as often as it comes in the dark.' She starts down the hallway, not waiting for my answer, and adds cryptically as she reaches the first lantern, 'And not just to humans.'

I stop walking as an idea hits me. 'Sunlight,' I say. The word comes out like a sigh of relief. 'You can't go into the sunlight because it will burn you to ashes.' As I say it, a benign look fills Juliana's face; a teacher obliging a slow student.

'Did you *really* read my blogs, Christian?'

'Yes.'

'Then you should know vampires can travel by day or by night. We elect not to go into the sunlight because the Thirst becomes intolerable and we're forced to hunt and feed more often, but sunlight will no more kill me than it will you. In fact, with all your frailties, you are far more vulnerable to the sun than I will ever be.'

Juliana must see the dismay on my face because she shakes her head as we continue walking and turn into a shorter passageway with maybe a dozen rooms on each side. At the far end, I see a large metal door barred by two heavy metal poles. On both sides of this door is a pile of bones stacked neatly in rows reaching to the roof.

A long, low howl erupts from the end of the hallway. My skin shrinks against my bones. 'What the hell is that?'

'Your destiny,' Juliana replies.

Blog Eleven

The Withering

Oh, how amusing some of you are! What acid tongues you possess. Leaving your trite comments, or lengthy diatribes, as though this blog is in any way about you. As though you - a mortal! - have the wisdom to lecture me.

The arrogance.

What do I care if you think I am narcissistic? Or petty? Or evil? How do your inane compliments - "the Goddess, Juliana" indeed - alter my existence? Empty platitudes; empty slurs. And please, as if I need worry about your small plans for extermination. In the name of God, no less. Your capacity for delusion is exceptional, and that's about the only thing you've got going for you.

So tell me, human - I know you won't be able to resist - what is it you think you can change with your words? What power do you think you possess, exactly, sitting there before that screen, in your underwear? Really? Well, let me set you straight: you might be a hero in WoW, or a warrior in COD, or a cyber-God in *The Sims*, but in the real world, you are powerless to affect change. Why? Because you cannot stop the march of death. It's coming and there are no '1ups' available to you.

No, don't point to me. We've already discussed this; I do not live. I exist, and there is a big difference between the two. But we do have something in common; I cannot affect change either and maybe that makes me as pathetic as you—

No, it doesn't.

Now, go troll somewhere else before I decide to demonstrate the fragility of your existence.

Frustration.

This is the core aspect of a Shroudeater's existence. The world moves, but the vampire stands still. Life is created, ripens, expires, but a vampire remains unchanged: forever youthful, forever strong, forever beautiful. The perpetuity should be wonderful; it is not.

Throughout human history, we have been called 'unnatural' for defying death, drinking blood, and killing humans. Yet, this is not what makes us unnatural. Indeed, other creatures share these qualities. Consider the butterfly, which dies to one form and is re-born in another, more exquisite, form; or the *desmondontinae*, which draw blood from their prey to survive. And, of course, even a cursory glance at history reveals the human penchant for killing each other, and every other species on the planet. No, these characteristics are not what make us unnatural; it is our inability to change that sets us apart from the natural world.

This is what truly kept me from Didier; a fact that was never more profoundly evident to me than in the years after Geneviève's death.

I can't say why I hadn't noticed the changes in Didier earlier; perhaps it was Geneviève who kept him youthful. Or perhaps it was my jealousy that clouded my vision; I coveted Didier as long as he belonged to Geneviève. When he was free, I suddenly saw him as he was; an old man puttering through the remainder of his life. This did not diminish my love for him, for he was as handsome as ever with his wrinkled skin and greying hair, which was a testament to the life he had lived.

When I looked at my own face, or ran my hands over the smoothness of my skin, which had not changed since the night of my immortal birth, I felt myself to be a meaningless void. Oh, I had moved over the surface of the world: I had taken life in countries across Europe; I had raced through the snow, hunted in the rain, dance in the moonlight, and greeted the dawn with blood-smeared lips; I had mesmerised and seduced, terrified and released, but none of it had made a mark on me. I was a blank. Nothing.

Some nights, when I was feeling more generous with myself, I tried to reason that the changes my existence had wrought were written inside me, that they were invisible to all but me, but the fancy always collapsed with my first kill of the evening. Who was I kidding? Shroudeaters don't change: we exist, we hunt, we kill, we envy. There is no more.

With this in mind, how could I go to Didier and re-claim my rightful place at his side when I was caught in this fixed state, this endless moment? Of course, there was always the option of bringing Didier over to the ways of the Shroudeater, which would halt the changes happening to him, changes that would eventually steal him away from me and deliver him into a different sort of forever, but I would not do it. I would not succumb to the selfishness of my vampiric parents, even if I could find another vampire to participate in the birthing.

So what was I to do? Finally, Didier was free to be mine; finally, I could go to him. Yet it was impossible, for one look at my beautiful face, unchanged despite the passing of five decades, would reveal to him that I was a monster.

Such was my frustration, which ate at me and made me careless.

Geneviève had been interred beside her children at the Cemetiére d'Auteuli. Once a week, Didier made the trip across the Seine and into Boulogne-Billancourt to visit the graves of his family. I always knew when he was going because a vase of roses would appear on the kitchen table the night before: red for Geneviève, white for Éloy and yellow for Zoé.

A strange combination of emotions took hold of Didier on those nights. Where he usually ate his evening meal in the lounge room in front of the television, he would place his plate on the table and sit before the flowers. Melancholy radiated from him and he often spoke to the roses as though they were his family sitting with him, sharing a meal and a glass of wine. When the meal was done, he would wash the dishes and tidy the kitchen, leaving it exactly as it had been on the night Geneviève died. Then, although it was early, he would retire, thinking perhaps to get a good night's rest before the visit. It never happened. Hours after getting into bed, he would still be awake, staring through the window while his hand rested on the pillow where Geneviève had drawn her last breath. As dawn broke, he would rise, wash and dress in his finest suit before going down to the kitchen to make coffee and toast, which he never ate.

Nerves, I guessed, taking my leave of him as the night receded.

I never knew how his visit to their tomb went but when I saw him in the evening, he appeared relaxed and somehow content, as though he had purged himself. Sleep found him easily on those nights and took him deep into its embrace. When he was snoring gently, I took the opportunity to slip away to the cemetery for my own visit with the dead.

This was not a new practice. I'd been visiting the twins since the night after they were buried. Like any parent, it made me feel closer to them. This became a little strange after their mother was buried with them and, at first, I was resentful of her intrusion, but I soon got use to the idea of Geneviève's presence and even found a few words to share with her on some of my visits.

On one particular night, I was sitting beside a grave adorned with the life-size statue of a cloaked woman leaning over the prostrate form of her love. She was kissing his hand and, although there was an endearing tenderness about the figures, I was annoyed. Didier had been to visit the twins and Geneviève that day and returned in his usual peaceful state. Later, as I entered the darkened cemetery and made my way down the gravel path towards their tomb, it occurred to me that this was another thing of which I had been robbed - where was my grave? Where was the commemorative to my short human existence? Where was my statue of lovers torn from each other by death? Where could Didier go to mourn for me, his first love? Nowhere is where. Only the dead were acknowledged for their existence. I had disappeared into the crack between life and death. I was gone, but not dead; how could anyone mourn for me? How would anyone remember me?

The unfairness brought my rage to the surface. In every way, I had been removed from Didier's life and, although I loved the twins and had accepted Geneviève, I felt a burning resentment towards them for having everything that should have been mine: Didier's love, his grief and, in the end, his memories.

Balling my hand into a fist, I prepared to demolish the figure of the prone man when a voice spoke from behind me.

'That one's my favourite.'

I turned. A teenage girl in a long dirty jacket was leaning against the side of a small sepulchre. Above her head was a cherub tinged with patina. 'I think she really loved him,' she continued, scratching a match on the wall and lighting a hand-rolled cigarette. She drew deeply and let the pungent smoke leak from between her lips. It swirled around her, distorting her features. 'You understand how that is, don't you?'

'What do you mean?' I replied, scouring the cemetery for other humans. Her sudden appearance was perturbing; the living didn't usually sneak up on me.

She puffed on the cigarette and took her time answering. 'The old man.'

I narrowed my eyes. 'What old man?'

'The one who comes to their graves,' she said, and pointed to the twin's tomb. She finished the cigarette and dropped the butt, grinding it under the heel of a scuffed boot. 'Comes every week, all sad and lonely looking, talks to them for about an hour, then goes away with a smile on his face. You know him.' It wasn't a question. She pushed away from the sepulchre and came closer.

'And how do you know that? Are you a spy?' I asked.

The idea seemed to please her. She pulled up the collar of her jacket so that it covered the lower half of her face and darted her eyes around the cemetery. Then she shrugged the jacket back into place and laughed. 'No, not a spy. I live up there.' She pointed to the roof of the apartment block across the street.

'Which apartment?' I asked, thinking I might need to pay her family a visit if they were as nosy as the girl.

'Not in the apartments. On the roof. There's an old pigeon coup up there.' She didn't elaborate further.

'So you've been watching— the old man?'

'Sure. I watch everyone who comes to the cemetery,' she said, and looked at me, 'but you're the only one who comes in the night, after the gates are locked.' She waved a hand at the high stone fence around the perimeter as she dug into her pocket and pulled out another cigarette.

'I worked days,' I said.

She blew out smoke. 'Right, and Sundays too.'

I laughed quietly and the tip of her cigarette twitched. 'Observant, aren't you?'

'Gotta be,' she said, her tone implying more than she was willing to share. She stood and wandered around the grave, coming closer again. 'So, what are you? A ghost?'

Her directness surprised me. 'Why would you ask such a thing?' She shrugged as though it was obvious and watched my face for a reaction. I kept a smile to myself, liking her boldness, which was so different from the usual human reaction to me. 'You're not afraid?'

'Of a spirit?' she said, dragging on the cigarette.

'What if I'm not a spirit?'

She blew the smoke out in a rush and looked me up and down. 'You do look more solid than I expected,' she said, and I caught the note of uncertainty in her voice. She took a quick step backwards, some of her bravado slipping away.

I remained where I was, not wanting to frighten her. 'That's because I'm not a ghost.'

She took another step and glanced left, then right, judging the best avenue of escape. 'What are you then, 'cause you sure as hell aren't human?'

'Is that so?' I replied, turning from her. I wandered over to Éloy and Zoé's tomb and made a show of picking up the vase of roses beside the door, looking to put her at ease so that she would stay and talk with me. It had been a long while since I had carried on a conversation with anyone. 'Well, I guess I am a spectre of sorts,' I said.

'What does that mean?' the girl asked, her voice coming from behind me again.

I smiled - curiosity gets humans every time - and turned, changing the course of our discussion as I faced her. 'Aren't males funny creatures? See how the old man, as you called him, arranged these flowers? Each colour in its own block, as though they are contrary to one another rather than merely different colours.' As I spoke, I rested the vase on top of a headstone and lifted out the bunch of yellow roses.

The girl watched me mingle the flowers and chewed her bottom lip. It was clear there was an argument going on in her head; stay or flee? When her hand dipped into her pocket again, I knew which voice had won. She put the cigarette between her lips and hoisted herself up onto the stone fence surrounding a pair of matching graves. When she was comfortable, she took the matches from her pocket and the cigarette from her mouth and held both in her hand.

'My father was strange like that too, but with his shirts.'

'Was?'

'Yeah, he left.'

'And your mother?' I asked, expecting the woman to be dead.

'She went to find my father.'

I paused in my arranging of the bouquet. 'Without you?'

A hard look came into the girl's eyes. 'She didn't have the money for us both to go,' she said, defensively.

'So she left you on you behind?'

'Of course not, she's my *mother*. She wouldn't just abandon me.'

I slid a yellow rose between two red ones. 'No?'

'No. She asked my aunt and uncle to take me in.'

I ran my gaze over her tattered clothes and allowed my eyes to linger on her face, which was coated in a layer of grime. 'Let me guess, that didn't work out for you?'

She shrugged one shoulder. 'They were mean to me, so I left.'

I nodded, as though I cared. 'And now?'

'I'm going to find my parents.'

'Ah,' I said, starting on the white roses, 'then you and I have something in common. I am also looking for my parents.'

A sceptical expression flashed across the girl's face. 'They left you?'

'Indeed.'

'Do you know where they are?'

'They travel.'

'How long have you been looking?'

'Much longer than you, little spy,' I said, finishing with the flowers. I held them out to the girl for her inspection. She gave a faint nod before lifting the cigarette to her mouth and lighting it. As she inhaled, I asked, 'What does the old man do when he comes here?'

She puffed the cigarette and thought for a second. 'He usually clears the leaves away from around the tomb first and sweeps the gravel from the step. Then he empties the vase of the old flowers and puts in a new bunch.' The girl paused, puffed again, and continued, 'And he polishes the cross on the door. Then he prays for a while. I don't usually watch that bit. It feels, you know, like intruding on something private.'

'That's considerate of you,' I said, picturing Didier on his knees, with his head bowed. Somehow, after all of the loss he had suffered during his life, I was surprised to know he still prayed; certainly, it wasn't a practice he performed at home. Perhaps he wasn't praying to God. Perhaps he was praying to the twins and Geneviève, but how would I know? It wasn't as if I could ask him.

The dry hand of frustration stroked my anger again and I struggled to keep my voice even as I said, 'What does he do after praying?'

The girl flicked her butt away. 'He eats, and talks to them,' she pointed to the twin's tomb, 'which is sort of crazy. He gets odd looks from people sometimes but he doesn't seem to notice, just babbles on until he's run out of things to say. Then he packs up his stuff, kisses the cross, and shuffles off.'

Visions of Didier's visit played across my mind and I tried to savour the second-hand account of his life, but the unfairness of the existence forced upon us deflated my pleasure. The truth was, while I carried on a half-existence, Didier's life was slipping away from him, and me. How long would it be before I was arranging flowers outside his tomb? One year? Five? Next week? And then what?

An eternity without him?

Intolerable.

It occurred to me then, that maybe I was wrong; maybe I should bring Didier over to the way of the Shroudeater? It would mean a temporary change to my plans, but it could be done, and we would be together, forever. The idea was so tempting and I may have implemented it that very night, except— I knew Didier. He would not thank me and the thought of him hating me for all of eternity was worse than the thought of losing him forever. Once again, the actions of Callisto and Constantine had stymied me.

I turned towards the twin's tomb, returning the flowers to their spot beside the door, keeping my face hidden from the girl. If she saw the fury in my eyes, she would run and I wasn't ready for that. 'And what of me? How did you connect me to the old man?' I asked.

The sound of her shoes landing on the gravel, loud in the tranquillity of the cemetery, preceded her answer. 'Well, it wasn't hard. You visit the same graves.'

'True,' I conceded, wandering down the row.

The girl kept pace in her row. 'Course, at first, I didn't get why you visited the same graves 'cause there's two kids and a woman buried in there and I figured she was his wife and they were his children, but who were you?' She stepped up onto the edge of a grave, balanced to the end and jumped down again. 'And why did you only come at night? That made me curious. So I waited for the old man to visit and I came down to the cemetery and pretended to be visiting a grave close to his family, and I listened.'

A pang of jealousy pierced me as I thought of the girl being close to my love. 'And what did you hear?'

'The usual stuff. What he'd been doing, how much he missed them, then he said a prayer and asked God to watch over them.' She paused and stopped walking, looking over at me from between two vaults, 'And someone called Juliana.'

I could only stare at her.

'That's you, right?'

He prays for me?

Of all the things I had experienced in the years since Callisto and Constantine had cursed me with this existence, never had I felt as shattered as I did in that moment. Didier hadn't forgotten me. My legs buckled and I gripped the corner of a marble pedestal to keep from collapsing.

'It *is* you,' the girl said, and clapped her hands. 'I knew it. So, were you his secret lover? Or his first wife?' Her eyes gleamed with excitement. 'Did he kill you? Is that why you haunt the tomb of his family?'

I gathered myself and straightened. 'You know nothing.' My tone was hard, abrupt, although I hadn't meant it to be; it was my habit with humans who thought they knew me.

Stillness came over the girl. 'I know you're not human,' she said, bringing us back to where we had started.

'That's true,' I admitted, and for the first time, I caught the scent of real fear on her. I spoke softly, trying to put her at ease again. 'Do you have any more to tell me about the old man?'

She shook her head.

'Alright,' I said, holding her gaze with mine, wanting her to see my gratitude. 'You've given me a great gift. Thank you.'

She took a step backwards. 'I'm going to go now,' she said, and glanced over her shoulder to the apartment building behind her.

'Yes, you should go. A cemetery at this time of night is no place for a young girl. Before you do, though, do you want to know what I am?'

'No,' she whispered, but I showed her anyway.

Oh, seriously!?

What did you expect, mortal? Of course, I killed her. I'm a vampire. If you don't like it, stop reading. You *can* make that choice, you know.

Cells and Souls

Seconds pass. We stand in the passageway amid muffled growls and shrieks. My skin is prickling with goose flesh, but Juliana is silent, unmoved. Horrifying as the noise from beyond the barrier is, I can't stop my gaze from finding her. I remember her first blog: *I am gorgeous.* I'd taken the comment as an egotistic boast - everyone online says they're beautiful even if they look like shit - but she hadn't lied. I watch her face, her mouth, her eyes; fall in love. Just a little bit.

She turns her head and catches me with her dazzling smile. My heart skips, and I almost smile in return, but then I notice the smugness in her eyes and realise she's been snooping on my thoughts again.

My jaw tenses. 'I told you to stay out of my head,' I say, feeling like a teenager whose secret crush has been revealed. 'It's rude.'

I don't see Juliana move. One moment she's on the other side of the passage, the next she's in my face, pressing me up against the wall, fingers clamped around my throat. 'Do you want to die?' she asks, and I discover an interesting thing about myself; I'm not ready to die, not in the forever sense anyway.

'Sorry,' I mumble.

A howl rips apart my apology.

Instinct grips me and I struggle against Juliana, wanting to bolt. She holds me firm as the howl becomes a shriek, spiralling toward some inhuman octave before cutting out, abrupt as a blackout. Juliana releases me and I skitter away, putting distance between the door and me. 'What was that?'

Her gaze is cool. 'That, dear Christian, is the sound of a vampire's suffering.'

My body shakes. 'What?'

'You're asking the wrong question. It is not what, but who?'

I force my head to clear, think for a few moments. 'It's her, isn't it? Callisto? You've got her locked up down here?'

'She's not the only one.'

'Constantine?'

Juliana smirks. 'Yes, he's here too. And most of the others. Those I could find. Only one or two elude me, and soon I will have them too.'

'Your revenge?'

She shrugs and starts down the passageway again, towards the door. I follow her, even though it's the last thing I want to do, but it's like I'm in my own horror film; I know I should run in the opposite direction, but I can't help myself. A lantern burns above the lintel, creating a pool of murky yellow light. There is an inhuman chorus coming from behind the door. The hairs along my arms and at the back of my neck rise and fall, responding to the fear surging through my body. I can't make out individual voices, which are muffled by the door, but inside my head, I feel their need and hear their intentions. Simple, clear, unremitting; they want blood.

My blood.

A metre from the door, I come to a standstill. I can't make myself take another step. Every nerve is a siren screaming a warning. The demands of the imprisoned vampires leaks from under the door, rising like the hunched shadow of Max Schreck.

'*Cést vin que?a ma?och.*'

Silence descends like a benediction.

'Jesus,' I say, rubbing a hand over my face.

'You may need something a little more tangible to put your faith in, Christian,' Juliana says, easing down onto the floor. She sits back against the passage wall, unmindful of the dirt.

I don't want to talk theology with her; it's an argument I know I'll lose. 'Why do you make them suffer like this?' I ask.

Juliana sighs and draws her legs towards her chest, dangling her wrists over her knees. Her hands are pretty; not the hands of a killer. She lifts them, rubs at the blood caught around the cuticles. 'You're right, Christian,' she says, 'I'm a slave, not a killer.'

I frown, annoyed that she's dipped into my thoughts again, but I'm too curious not to encourage her line of thought. 'How are you a slave?'

The sigh comes again. 'What does Sisyphus push up his mountain?'

Her change of tack throws me for a second, and I rush my answer. 'A rock.'

'Don't be plebeian, Christian. Think deeper.'

The rebuke stings a little, and I move away from her, towards the door, but change direction when I hear something inside the chamber stir. *Focus*, I tell myself, staring at the stones in the wall. If Sisyphus is a vampire cursed with immortality, as Juliana insists, then the rock is a metaphor. I come back and sit in front of Juliana. 'His suffering and he's a slave to it because he can't escape.'

'Good, you're beginning to use your mind,' Juliana says, and I feel a touch of pleasure at her praise until I realise she isn't complimenting my astute thinking. 'Should I fill in the blanks?' she asks, dropping the pretence. 'It may save time.'

'Time doesn't exist,' I say.

Her pretty fingers are against my jugular. 'It does for you, human,' she murmurs. My heart jumps. The vampire licks her lips and settles back against the wall. I breathe again.

'It's simple, really. What Sisyphus pushes ahead of him is the Thirst; the burden of every vampire. You asked me why I make them suffer. I don't. It is the Thirst that makes them suffer. They are slaves to it and it's killing them.'

'You said nothing could kill a vampire.'

'You haven't been listening,' Juliana says, her tone patient. 'What I said was the myths you've been fed about killing us are untrue. I didn't say we were immortal; that's your assumption.'

'Vampires aren't immortal?' The idea blows my mind.

Juliana stands. 'We're close to immortal, but everything dies. Eventually. Under the right conditions.'

'The right conditions?'

She nods towards the barred door. 'The Thirst is what drives a vampire; the slave master we can't ignore. Imagine a desert seared by a thousand suns and it still doesn't come close to the inferno of the Thirst, burning through a vampire's body. Human blood subdues the ferocity, but it's never gone, no matter how much blood we take, and if we don't take blood, or can't, eventually the Thirst consumes us.'

Images from a dozen movies fill my mind. 'You mean like in holy flames?'

A flash of annoyance crosses Juliana's face. 'This is reality, Christian, not Hollywood. What happens to a human body without nourishment?'

'Starvation?'

'Yes, indeed, starvation.' Her tone is matter-of-fact. 'Only much worse.'

'How could it be worse?'

'Do you know anything about the process of starvation in humans?'

'A little.' Juliana raised her eyebrows, waiting. I search my memory; regurgitate what I remember. 'In the first stage, the body breaks down carbohydrates and turns them into glucose. In the second stage, it breaks down fats. Then, if things get really bad, it breaks down proteins, the muscles. At that stage, there's pretty much no going back without medical help since the body's too weak to metabolise food anyway.'

'Very good,' Juliana says.

'Yeah, God bless the Internet.' I don't mean to sound sarcastic; it just comes out that way.

Juliana lets my comment slide. 'What about the psychological symptoms?'

'Umm fatigue, weakness and confusion first, then irritability in the early stages. In the later stages, delirium, hallucinations and convulsions. From what I've read, it's pretty unpleasant.'

'Yes,' Juliana says, looking at the barred door.

I wait for her to say more. The vampire remains silent, her attention shifting beyond the door. Instinct takes over and I slip passed her before I think of where the hell I can go.

Juliana's hand wraps around my wrist. 'That's not the way out for you, Christian.'

I don't try to resist; what would be the point? 'So how is starvation worse for a vampire?' I ask.

'There are all of the physical processes, the body turning on itself for survival, but none of the psychological symptoms. A vampire is aware of every change, right up to the moment their bodies can no longer sustain form and turns to dust. They beg for madness, but all they get is more clarity as the Thirst consumes them. It's a purification,' she says, pushing me towards the door.

'Wait.' My voice bounces off the walls. Behind the door, the chorus suddenly cranks up and I scramble away, putting Juliana between them and me.

She laughs. 'Brave little Christian.'

The voices inside are hysterical. They screech through my brain and fear sinks into my stomach. *What if they smell my blood?*

I don't hear Juliana speak, but the quiet tells me she's silenced them again. 'So, now you understand what you've asked for, Christian,' she says, brushing her fingers across my forehead. The tenderness in her touch surprises me. 'Do you still want to be one of us?'

The vampire's question hangs between us. She watches me with the patient eyes of a predator; her body relaxed and tense at the same time as though she's gathering her energy, making ready to spring the moment I give her the opportunity. The intensity of her gaze sends pinpricks of warning skittering across my skin and locks my mouth shut, but she's not the only reason for my silence. The vampires inside the chamber are listening for my answer - even in my human state, I can feel their longing - and there's something else too.

Singing.

I'm pretty sure I know whose voice it is that I hear: Callisto, and although I can't understand the words, the melody is soothing, like the warm caress of a mother's hand against my face. A feeling of ease settles over me, diluting the sense of imminent peril, calming my mind and filling me with the idea that all will be well.

Juliana edges closer, snapping my attention back to her, and the singing stops, leaving me alone with the vampire. 'Time to deliver you into the hands of Fate,' she says.

'Not yet,' I reply, holding up my hand, as though it could stop her.

A mock expression of consideration flashes across the vampire's face and is gone. She grabs my arm at the bicep, her grip like a manacle. 'Yes, now,' she says.

'What have you done with Lucy?' I blurt out, panic twisting my voice so that I barely recognise it.

This time the considering look on Juliana's face is genuine. 'Why do you care?' she asks.

I sense the chance of a reprieve as she releases me but, strangely, the question throws me a little and I have to think about how to respond. *Why do I care?* I go with the easy answer. 'She's my girlfriend.'

'What does that have to do with anything?' Again, I feel confused by the question and Juliana sees it. 'Come on, Christian, it's not like you love her.'

My reply comes in a rush. 'I do love Lucy,' but even as the word fall out of me, I feel the need to qualify them. 'In my own way.'

Juliana gazes at me. 'In your own way? How romantic.' Her voice is deadpan.

Her attitude arcs me up. 'What do you know about it? Not everyone has a grand romance like you and Didier, you know,' I say, unable to contain the sneer that colours my tone. 'Lucy and me, we help each other through the crap that life throws at us and that's more important than some flimsy, bullshit notion of love.'

Flickers of red flare in Juliana's eyes as she says, 'Wrong answer, human.' In an instant, she has me shoved up against the door, pressing me into the metal until it feels like my shoulder will pop.

'You're hurting me,' I gasp.

'Better you than Lucy,' the vampire says acidly. She reaches into the pocket of her jacket and produces an old-fashioned wrought iron key. The metal scrapes as she pushes the key into the lock. The sound is faint but it's enough to stir the vampires inside the room. They howl and gibber like inmates in an asylum.

I can't stop a shiver of horror.

Juliana bangs her fist against the door, right in front of my face, and I feel the vibrations race through my bones as my head rings. Her brethren quieten. 'You sought me out so I would make you a vampire, but no vampire alone can do that. In this room, there are two who could do what you wish. They're mad with the Thirst, and I'm certain you won't survive the experience, but if it is still what you want, then go to them.'

Her hand disappears inside her jacket again and she brings out a silver key. 'But if you decide you want to retain your humanity, you should stay in the centre of the room, well clear of the walls. At the far end, you will find another door for which this key was made. On the other side of that door is the human world.' The vampire releases her hold on me. 'The choice is yours,' she adds.

'That's it? You're not going to kill me?'

'Not today.'

'And Lucy.'

Juliana's smile is cold. 'No longer your concern.'

I'm about to protest when she turns the key and pulls on the bars, sliding them into a recess in the wall.

The door opens. Inside is darkness. All thoughts of Lucy vanish.

'I can't go in there,' I say, turning, ready to plead, but the passageway is empty. Juliana is gone. There's just me, the bones of the dead, and the vampires waiting for me beyond the door.

Blog Twelve

The Vampire's Curse

I have no lesson for you today; just a warning.

It ends with me.

Didier died on a winter's night. He was ninety-six; a shrivelled old man, bent across the back, his face a map of his life, lined and roughened, although his eyes were lively, right until his final breath.

I stirred before dusk, knowing our time had come to an end. I dressed in an outfit similar to the one I was wearing the night we met Callisto and Constantine and twisted my hair into a French knot, just as it had been the last time Didier saw me alive. He was sleeping when I entered his room, a childlike figure with the blankets pulled up to his chin. A fire was burning below the mantle, its light touching the strands of his silver hair. I had dispatched his nurse, and the Thirst was a distant murmur like the ocean heard through a conch shell. We were alone but, as always, I waited in the shadows.

It was a strange feeling, watching the man I loved on the cusp of death. Memories of the time we had spent together as mortals came to me. I could hear the rich, warm laughter of his youth and see, in visions that played out across my mind, those traits - his wry smile, the way his eyes widen in surprise at some unknown fact, the lift of his brow in consternation - that had endeared him to me all those years ago. I remembered the touch of his hand, the smell of his skin, and the way he looked *into* me, as though he were searching for my soul.

Those were the happiest days of my life and they had been stolen away. Callisto and Constantine had condemned me to the periphery of the life I should have lived and the loss was as bitter as the wind shrieking outside the window.

I left my shadowed alcove to stoke the fire. Sparks burst around the iron poker. In their red embers, I saw the reflection of my rage. I pushed it aside as I sat at the foot of the bed and stared into the flames, thinking on the years spent watching Didier, re-visiting his life with Geneviève.

My resentment towards her had mellowed since her death and I was almost grateful they had found each other. The last ten years of Didier's life had been full and interesting as he kept himself occupied with his friends and garden, but I often sensed his loneliness and longing for Geneviève. His yearning saddened me, but how would his life have been without her? A solitary man, pining for a lost lover? It didn't bear thinking about. Instead, he had experienced joy and loss, burden and reprieve. With Geneviève, he had lived a human life; it was all that could be expected.

The sharp crack of a log on the fire brought me to my feet. I looked around at Didier and felt my insides constrict as I realised he was staring at me. For a long moment, neither of us moved. Time ceased; death was in abeyance. Then he drew a breath that rattled through his lungs and he pushed himself up on the pillows. His eyes were bright with recognition as they shone out of his weary face.

'Hello beautiful,' he whispered, and my heart crumbled.

Shaking, I walked to the side of his bed and knelt on the floor beside him, taking his fragile hand in mine. The faint beat of his pulse echoed through his veins and I knew we didn't have long.

'Are you real?' he asked.

'Yes,' I responded, and brought his hand to my lips. A lifetime of longing filled me and I kissed each knuckle softly and brushed them against my cheek.

'Where have you been?'

I heard the strain in his voice as he struggled to speak. 'I have always been with you,' I replied, placing his hand beneath the covers. 'Now hush, we are together at last. Be at peace.'

There was a pause. I listened for his heart and heard a faint beat. He drew a breath and looked at me. 'I've always loved you.'

'And I you,' I murmured, as his eyes slipped closed.

It was not until death took Didier that I realised how I had measured the passing of each night by the beating of his heart; how I had listened for it and been comforted by its steady rhythm. In the silence that followed his passing, I felt lost in nothingness. What was to be my purpose now, for all of eternity?

I lay on the bed beside him, feeling the warmth ebb from his body as the night moved towards dawn. I stayed with him through the day and into the night, waiting for some sense of what came next. And as I lay there, my anger grew. Was there really any question of what I had to do?

No.

Now that Didier was gone, there was nothing to restrain me, nothing to draw me away from the hunt. Callisto and Constantine were my quarry; I would not rest until I found them, and made them pay for the lives they had ruined.

The Gauntlet

The silence that descends is creepy.

The passageway behind me fades into darkness. Nothing moves in the pool of light outside the door. Across the threshold, the vampires are waiting, pent-up like a held breath. I look at the key in my hand; a choice Juliana said.

Some goddamn choice.

Taking stock, I consider: I could take my chances in the corridors and tunnels of Juliana's lair, and the catacombs above but, without the vampire to guide me, I know I'll be lost in no time. Or I could stay where I am and wait for Juliana to return, but then what? I thought of Remi; death, that's what. And not the vampire's death I'd come looking for, but the all-to-human, light's-out-forever death.

The door then.

I put my hand on the handle, which is cool against my palm. A low growl, like a rusted turbine, rumbles out of the room. The sound is dry, grating, unlubricated. My heart hammers; there's no way I'm going in there. I look down the passageway; the darkness is slick as oil. I'll get lost, and Juliana's down that way too, but anything's better than facing whatever made that noise. Choice made, I turn, take a step, and that's when I hear the singing again.

Callisto, in my head: *That way is death.*

I stop, uncertain.

She will kill you, Christian. You know too much.

Her voice is reassuring, but I take another step towards the darkness anyway. At least with Juliana, I know what I'll face. Behind the door is a horror best left unknown.

This way is escape, Christian. Don't be afraid. I will protect you.

I glance at the door.

Juliana didn't lie; you do have a choice. Death or freedom. The singing is hard to resist. The melody wraps around me. Warm drowsiness fills my bones and I want the comfort promised by that voice. *Come, child. There is peace to be found through the door. Peace and love*, she sings. *And Lucy.*

Lucy? What did Juliana say? *She's safe— for now.*

I move back towards the door, rest my hand flat against the metal. I'm not one for all that macho rescue-the-damsel-in-distress bullshit; I'm no Vin Diesel, but Lucy is in danger because of me and the responsibility for her plight drags on my conscience. Time to man up; I clench the key in my fist, push the door open, and step into the room.

The smell smashes into my face. Dust dry decay; flesh shrinking, crumbling bones, dried blood, livers, kidneys, lungs, desiccating. The air is hot, acrid, scorching my throat as I breathe. Spontaneous combustion seems a distinct possibility. The chamber is an incinerator filled with waste and ruin. I cover my mouth and nose, but then the sound comes - a freight train loaded with agony - and I have to cover my ears, or lose my mind. They shriek out of the darkness: howls of hunger-driven rage and madness. Chains clink, rattle, grind and, through the protection of my hands, I hear the gurgle of strangulation. I don't want to see them, but light follows me across the threshold and the horror of Juliana's revenge is made plain.

They're in various stages of decomposition. Some are little more than animated skeletons; sightless, hairless, bones clicking, fangs gnashing grooves into jaws. Others are worse. Their eyes are shrivelling balls in the cavern of their sockets; they reach for me with arms draped in strips of skin, hands tipped with curling nails as they try to form words with tongues turned to leather.

I shake my head; it's too much. How could Juliana inflict this on her kin? I want out of here. There must be another way. I can't go through this room.

You must. The chamber falls silent again and the shambling, reaching monstrosities retreat into the darkness as Callisto speaks. *This will be Lucy's fate too, Christian.*

'No.'

Yes. I know Juliana's mind. She will drain Lucy and coerce a kindred to finish the birth. She will allow her to roam free until the Thirst has her deep in its grasp, then she will bring her to this prison, chain her to the wall and let her suffer the slow death of starvation.

'No.'

If you would save her, you must come through. She sings again, softly, sweetly. *Look ahead, Christian.*

I think of Lucy amongst those horrors - the idea is appalling - and do as Callisto asks. At the end of the chamber, maybe four metres away, there is the second door. The dim light is drawn to its metal surface; the keyhole is a promise. In my hand, the key is warm.

Four metres.

Think of Lucy, Callisto sings.

I lock my eyes on the door, develop tunnel vision, and steer a course down the centre of the chamber. Shapes stir on either side of me. The urge to run - to fucking sprint - to the door is powerful but I restrain myself. To stumble is to die. *Focus on the door,* I think, *you're almost out. Focus on the door.* The words become a mantra, blocking out the terror.

The door grows larger the closer I get, like a promise about to be fulfilled, and I notice there is a shelf beside it, recessed into the stone. In the centre of the shelf is a glass jar, half filled with something. I squint through the gloom, trying to make out the shapes inside. There is a jangle of chains and a solid *thunk* behind me, and the shapes suddenly make sense; keys. A jar half-filled with keys; no prize for guessing what they fit.

A bony hand swipes out of the gloom, trying to hook my leg. I jump away, almost fall. Hungry panting fills my head. My heart slams against my ribs as a gaunt face looms out of the shadows, its eyes large and round like a starved child.

'Come here, mortal,' it hisses, dagger-sharp teeth bared. I skitter backwards towards the darkness on the opposite side of the chamber.

'Hush, Constantine,' Callisto murmurs, right beside me. 'Hello, Christian,' she says. Her eyes roam over my body, but she doesn't close the distance between us. 'I've been listening to your conversation with Juliana.' Her daughter's name is greeted with hisses and curses. Callisto waits until quiet returns, watching me with an indulgent smile. 'Have you made your decision? Will you accept the gift from us, or will you flee into the mortal world?'

'This is not what I wanted,' I say, moving around her towards the door.

She makes no attempt to stop me but, as I slip the key into the lock, she says, 'What is there in the mortal world for you, Christian, now that you know the truth about us?'

My fingers grip the key. I imagine I feel a subtle vibration coming through the metal; the rumble of traffic. Paris is alive, humming with potential. I think again of all I want to do with my life, of the endless possibilities that are not possible within a finite existence. I think of the questions that plague me; of the mysteries I want to solve:

What is the universe?
Who or what is God?
Where did we begin?
How will we end?
What is the point?

Seeking out Juliana was supposed to buy me time to discover all I want to know, to experience all there is to experience, to give meaning to Empedocles' life so mean. I hadn't considered that she'd have her own agenda, although she'd stated the fact bluntly on her blog: *I'm going to kill my parents.* Why couldn't she be the uncomplicated Hollywood version of the vampire, driven by bloodlust, recklessly colonising humanity, struggling for power with other unnatural forces? Instead, she has to be all too human; seeking revenge and destroying my dreams in the process.

'Look, I'm sorry Juliana has done this to you,' I say, without turning. I'm afraid I'll lose my nerve if I face them. 'But if I trusted you enough to turn me, she would only track me down and I would end my days in this tomb too.'

'Not necessarily,' Constantine says. The chains binding him rattle and, despite myself, I glance over my shoulder. 'We could protect you, help you feed, develop your strength.'

'It is the only way to save Lucy,' Callisto says, coming out of the shadows. 'Even now Juliana has your love in hand.'

'Juliana has Lucy? Is she alive?'

'Yes.'

'You came for immortality, Christian. We can give you that,' Constantine says. His tone reminds me of Peter Crossing when he's talking up some business deal. 'I know you are afraid, but there is a larger picture to consider. We don't want to perish down here, wasting away until we are dust.' Callisto shudders and I imagine she's thinking of all the years that stretch before her. 'You can end our agony, protect Lucy, and be granted immortality, if you're brave enough.' The last part of his 'deal' is a challenge.

Like that'll work.

'What we want often manifests in unexpected ways, Christian,' Callisto adds. 'The secret is to recognise the opportunity when it is presented, no?'

She has a point.

I look around the chamber: dark, reeking with decay, the air heavy with the vampire's Thirst. This is not the place I imagined for my turning. I had pictured a tiny grotto, smoky with shadows, the lights of Paris spilling through a window, Edith Pilaf crooning softly. Lucy calls me a 'romantic idealist'; perhaps she's right.

'Will you trust us, Christian?'

Choices; endless choices.

'Will it hurt?' I ask, although I know the answer from reading Juliana's blog. Funny what we fear.

'No more than you want it too,' Callisto says, gently, and I hear her singing inside my head as I step into her embrace. Her voice fills me as her fangs sink into my neck, drowning out the snarls of the other Shroudeaters. There is pain, but it recedes quickly. Numbness creeps into my body, starting at my fingers and toes. Callisto's song is the sweetest sound I've ever heard; a lullaby drawing me away until I feel my arm rise, exposing my wrist to a second set of fangs.

I pray they will be the last.

Blog Thirteen

Reunion

Well, how nice to see you back here, mortal.

Don't worry; I'm not softening towards you. I just thought that perhaps you had embraced the latest undead craze, although why anyone with even a spark of intelligence would choose a shambling, oozing, walking carcass over the sophistication of a Shroudeater is beyond me. Still, I suppose zombies have a certain charm. They're not bias, for one thing; everyone is equal to a hungry zombie, and they never fight amongst themselves. In fact, they are like *The Three Musketeers* - 'all for one and one for all' - don't you think? Hmm, perhaps you humans could learn something from your gruesome fictitious creations.

Now, don't look so disappointed. I know you think a zombie apocalypse would be awesome - ah for the chance to chainsaw, batter, and behead while saving the pretty girl (or boy; take your pick) - but the truth is the realm of the undead is the sole province of

Shroudeaters, or what's left of them, and you're not welcome here.

Oh, stop pouting; it's unbecoming.

It is interesting to me, however, watching you mortals lose your minds over zombies. Why can't you be satisfied with life? Are you so afraid of death that you would rather exist as a foul, decaying caricature of the living? When will you see that the life you possess is the greatest, indeed the *only*, asset you have?

Let's re-visit with Sisyphus for a moment.

In case you haven't worked it out yet, Sisyphus *is* a vampire. He is undead. This is his *punishment* for trying to cheat the Gods, to gain a longer existence than was deemed appropriate. Do you see? Eternity, immortality; these are not gifts. Sisyphus can never escape his punishment. He can never die. He will push that rock up the mountain *forever*.

You mortals, on the other hand, have the gift of the finite; an endowment wasted on you because you cannot appreciate anything of prodigious value, but perhaps I can help you understand. Okay, here goes:

The human lifespan has two significant moments: birth and death. Agreed? One gives life and the other gives *meaning* to life. When you know your time is finite, you love, learn, adventure. In between those joyous moments, you suffer: pain, grief, heartache, loneliness. These are the sacred increments of your life, and when you have loved enough and suffered enough to absorb what you need to know about yourself, there is death: blessed release.

For Sisyphus, for the vampire, even for your unfortunate zombie, there is no end to suffering; there is no transcendence. We are condemned to push our burden before us for all of eternity.

Unless, of course, something intercedes.

Existing was harder without Didier.

In the nights following his death, I found myself caught in tempests of habit and history, which forced me to seek shelter in the places where he had spent his life. I haunted his house, the park where he played chess, his favourite cinema, all in the grief-stricken hope that they would hold an echo of his presence, which I could cling to so my own existence was bearable. It was a hope in vain.

On the evening after his burial, I returned the Cemetiére d'Auteuli and broke into his tomb. He had been laid to rest between the twins and Geneviève. Their sarcophagi were dust-covered - old tragedies - while his stood in stark contrast, clean as my pain. I sank down on the cool stones and rested my head against the lid, as close to my beloved as I would ever be, now that he had gone where I could never follow.

A great weariness weighed on me; all the years that stretched ahead without hope of release from their burden. How could I face them without Didier? It seemed impossible and I forced my mind from them, lest I go mad with their desolation, and thought instead of my parents and the revenge I had planned for them.

Straightening, I turned towards the door, my lassitude lifting as I considered my options. It was obvious that chasing Callisto and Constantine across the globe would not accomplish my goal; I'd tried that and only succeeded in losing precious years with Didier and the twins. No, this time I had to bring them to me, and as far as I could see, there was only one way to do that.

Exposure.

If I had learned anything from my kindred as I tracked Callisto and Constantine, it was that Shroudeaters fear that humans will stumble upon confirmation of our existence. We must remain a fiction, wrapped in the myth, half-truths, and outright lies, with which the humans frighten themselves. Exposure would be inconvenient and, well, messy.

History provided numerous examples of how humans responded to apex predators, either of their own species or another. They exterminated them or made them into Gods and, while divinity had a certain appeal, there always came a time when humans decided to throw down their Gods. Knowing this, the unspoken 'law' of the Shroudeaters was discretion: take of the human herd, but leave no trace of the feast; move through the human world, but remain invisible. The only time a human should know of us was when they were in our arms as we sang them into death, or so Callisto said one night before she left me to fend for myself.

The thought of exposing the Shroudeaters - and by extension, myself - brought me no pleasure. I did not want the scrutiny of the human world; their misguided attention was already too extreme, but if it was what I had to do to bring my parent's within striking distance, then so be it.

Satisfied with my decision, I left Didier's tomb and jumped up onto the cemetery wall, crouching in the shadows below an overhanging tree. The Thirst was rising; it infused my senses, heightening every aspect of my surroundings: the glittering city stretching into the distance, pulsing with life, awash in the tantalising musk of the teeming masses. Closer; around the corner and approaching unhurriedly, footsteps. A youth from the strong beat of his - yes, his - heart, enveloped in cheap cologne and cigarette smoke. Faint music reached me, low thumping bass, and the quick tap of his finger against glass; texting. I smiled. Like most of his generation, he was oblivious to the world around him, which made him easy prey for the likes of me.

I dropped off the wall and leaned against the stonework, still in the shadow of the tree, and watched as he strolled into the street. Slender, blonde-haired, fresh-faced and, best of all, distracted by his technology. When he drew near enough, I stepped into his path. He looked up, not particularly concerned until he saw what was standing in front of him. Then the panic came, but it was too late to save him. I wrapped my arms around him and leapt, taking him to the top of the wall and over in one smooth movement. He cried out as we landed, the sound bouncing between the gravestones. I forced a hand over his mouth and pushed his head backwards, silencing him and exposing his throat at the same time. His pulse pounded against his skin and I nuzzled the spot, tenderly.

I slipped inside his mind: *Please don't, please don't, don't, don't, don't.*

I replied: *I have to, lovely*, and began my song.

The Thirst was strong, flaming through me, as I sank my fangs into him and drew his blood from him in greedy draughts, gulping at the warm, sweet-saltiness. He struggled at first, fighting for his life, and I changed the melody of my song, urging him towards peace and acceptance. Slowly, he calmed and as he relaxed, I held him tighter, pouring my song into him even as I drained him into death. The moment of his release sent a shudder through us both: him as a last spasm of life; me as a grief for that which I would never know.

When I was done, I let him fall away and sat back against the cold marble of the closest grave, lightheaded with the flow of his blood through my body. There was an ecstasy in the feeling; a re-capturing of what had been stolen from me by Callisto and Constantine - the semblance of being alive. For some time, I lost myself in the sensation and imagined myself mortal; warm, supple, and capable of death. Yet, too soon, the feeling faded and my cold vampiric reality returned.

Sighing, I knelt beside the boy and gathered him into my arms again, his limp body less resistant but, strangely, more awkward to manage without the spark of life. I carried him through the cemetery to the opposite wall and jumped to the top, surveying the surrounding streets before dropping down and loping away. It was risky, moving a body through the open, but I wanted to preserve the sanctity of Didier's resting place to ensure I could return to his tomb as I pleased.

Bois de Boulogne was only a few kilometres away and I reached the outskirts without incident. At three in the morning, the park was quiet and I turned into Avenue de Saint-Cloud and carried the boy down the road until I saw a parallel path between the trees. Here I laid his body, knowing an early morning fitness fanatic would discover it in a few hours. I gazed at his face before leaving him, memorising his features. There was a part of me that wished to know his name, but that would come soon enough once the media got hold of his story.

As I continued along Avenue de Saint-Cloud towards Avenue de l'Hippodrome, my thoughts circled the idea of a second victim. The boy's death might warrant an article in *Le Monde* or perhaps *Le Parisien*, especially when details of his bloodless state were revealed, but to reach Callisto and Constantine, the story would need to go national and be picked up by the international media too. Two victims, killed in the same manner and found in the same park on the same night, would stir some interest. After all, journalists - and their readers - loved nothing more than a lurid vampire-killing spree, even when the killers turned out to be psychotic fakes and not true vampires at all.

Unlike me.

My second feast of the night had just arrived for work at Lagardére when I happened upon him. He was crossing the car park, carrying a sports bag in one hand and a laptop in the other. A silver whistle hung around his neck and bounced as he hurried towards the complex. The faint odour of chlorine lifted from his skin. I slipped ahead of him and stepped around a tree as he approached the main gate, smiling softly.

He hesitated and the usual play of expressions flittered across his face: mild lust, confusion, and a touch of annoyance. 'Can I help you?'

'Yes,' I replied, and took him.

'I got your message, daughter.'

Although I had baited the trap, the sound of Callisto's voice immobilised me. I forgot to sing, and the woman beneath me gave a sudden cry and wrenched her neck away from my mouth. She gasped, soft cries of terror coming from her as she scrambled backwards, pushing with her feet. The cries grew louder and more hysterical when she saw my face leering over her, fangs exposed, dripping with her blood. She clamped a hand over the wounds I had made and drew a sharp breath, readying for a scream.

Callisto slipped passed me and gripped the woman by the head. She twisted her hands; a quick, merciless action that snapped the woman's neck before her scream could be realised. 'Perhaps we could dispose of this one properly?' she said, letting the body drop.

I stood and wiped my mouth, eyeing her. She was as striking as the day she had stolen my humanity and looked relaxed in jeans and a dark red pullover, but I could see the tension in her limbs. 'Are you angry with me, *mother*?' I asked.

'You've been careless,' Callisto said, her eyes flaring with silver filaments.

'Not at all,' I replied, thinking of the news headlines splashed across the evening edition of *Le Figaro*: SIXTH VAMPIRE KILLER VICTIM FOUND. 'I've been strategic.'

'Is that so?' Callisto said, and toed the body between us with the tip of her shoe. 'There are easier ways to get our attention.'

'I've tried to find you,'

'We know.'

'You do? How?'

'We have our ways.'

'And, you decided to ignore me anyway?'

'You were okay on your own.' She smiled with all the warmth I remembered. 'How is Didier anyway?'

A cold wind blew through my heart. 'He died,' I said, and leaned over to lift the dead woman into my arms, hiding my pain from the monster who had brought it upon me.

Callisto made a low clucking sound with her tongue. 'Such is the mortal journey,' she said, although I heard no sympathy in her voice. 'Leave that here.'

Surprised, I glance at her. 'Why would I do that?'

'Because we have to diffuse the interest in our kind that you've stirred up over the last few weeks.'

'And how will you do that?'

'Same as always. A human pasty,' she said, and laughed when I frowned. 'Oh, come on, you didn't think this was an original plan, did you?' She pointed to the ground, encouraging me to release the body. 'You children, so impetuous.'

I lay the women back on the grass, close to a hedge where she would not be easily seen and murmured a few words of apology for the way her life had ended; it had not been my intention for her to pass so violently. When I stood, Callisto was already walking out of the park where I had lured the woman. I dashed after her and caught up as she started down the street. 'What about the body?' I asked.

'Constantine will take care of it.'

'How?' I asked, feeling strangely childish, as though we were truly mother and daughter.

'Read tomorrow's newspapers,' Callisto replied, haughtily.

I pressed my lips together. If only the stories humans told were true; I would stake her on the spot. Instead, I swallowed my irritation and asked, 'Where are we going?'

Callisto stopped and looked at me, her expression just short of unfriendly. 'I'm going to hunt and then to check on someone I haven't seen in a while. I don't know where you're going.'

Panic rushed through me. After all this time and all the effort I had put in, I couldn't let Callisto slip away again. 'Who are you going to check on?' I asked, and sent my mind towards hers, probing for an answer that would give me the upper hand.

The superior smile that I loathed surfaced on Callisto's face. 'No one you know.'

But she was wrong. I did know.

For all Callisto's vampire prowess, she had a weakness, a gap in the fortress of her mind, opened by her attachment to her children, and in that gap was Patria. I thought fast. 'You'll never find her.'

Callisto's smile disappeared as she measured me with her gaze. Although I couldn't feel her, so subtle were her skills, I knew she was trying to pry into my thoughts, looking for what I knew about her youngest daughter. I increased the noise that protected my mind and Callisto immediately dropped her gaze and drew away.

'You know Patria?'

'Intimately,' I replied, and started walking in the opposite direction to which Callisto had been going, towards the nearest entrance to the catacombs. As I expected, she followed and I felt a flare of anticipation as the opportunity for revenge finally presented itself. 'I can take you to her, if you like.'

Callisto appeared in front of me. She was quick; I had to give her that. 'Where is she?'

'In the catacombs,' I replied, sidestepping her and continuing down the avenue.

'The catacombs? What is she doing down there?' Callisto asked, matching my stride.

'Waiting.'

'Waiting? For what?'

'Why you, of course,' I said, as we arrived at a narrow door between a church and a bakery. I knelt down and reached behind a drainpipe that clung to the wall, producing a key with a flourish.

Callisto was unamused. 'What are you up to? she asked.

I thought over her question as I slipped the key into the lock and opened the door. Darkness retreat as the streetlight invaded its territory, but not very far. 'What am I up too?' I mused, mirroring Callisto's question. I didn't see an advantage in lying to her, so I decided to play it straight. 'I want an exchange,' I said, stepping through the door and moving aside, inviting Callisto inside.

She remained on the threshold. 'Me for her?'

I smiled. 'Now you're catching on.' The silver filaments appeared in Callisto's eyes again and she trembled ever so slightly. 'Shall we?' I asked.

Callisto glanced left then right, surveying the street, perhaps looking for Constantine, but nothing moved; no humans, no vampires. With a shake of her head, Callisto moved passed me and walked to the top of the stairs, where she waited while I locked the door. I showed her the key before placing it in the space between two brick. 'In case you ever come back this way,' I said, taking the lead.

The darkness around us was complete but offered no challenge to my vampire's eyes. I set a quick pace, eager to get Callisto to the chamber, while preventing too many of those questions that plagued her. She stayed on my heel, following me down the stairs into the first level of the catacombs, where the corridors opened out a little, allowing her to come along side me.

'How long has she been down here?' Callisto asked, with a note of accusation.

'What is time to a vampire?' I replied.

'In this place, time would mean something to any creature,' Callisto said.

We reached the intersection that would take us into the lower sections of the tunnels, towards my lair and the chamber beyond. Callisto didn't seem to be paying much attention to where we were going, and I realised she was searching the tunnels and listening for signs of her daughter. Of course, she would find no such sign, at least, not from Patria.

I kept moving, drawing her closer to the chamber, but Callisto's pace slowed. 'Are there others down here?' she asked, her forehead creased with concentration.

Again, I saw no value in lying. 'There are,' I said, listening to the clamour of voices that muttered inside my mind. Some of them were aware of Callisto's presence and were working themselves into quite a frenzy. 'Shall we continue?' I asked.

Without a word, she came on, but I could feel her distress, like a heavy hand on the back of my neck, and I was almost relieved when we turned the last corner and the chamber came into view. An expectant silence filled the passageway as we drew closer to the door, and I imagined the vampires inside straining against their chains, desperate with the thought that Callisto had come to free them; a thought Callisto apparently shared with them.

'You must release them at once, Juliana,' she said.

I considered her demand for half a second. 'No, but I will free Patria if you take her place,' I said, unlocking the door. Instantly, we were engulfed by wails and howls as the vampires pleaded for their freedom. Callisto seemed stunned by the onslaught and she reached for the wall to steady herself. 'Don't worry, you'll get use to their racket.'

Callisto stared at me, her face filled with anguish. 'How can you be this heartless?'

'You should know, you made me,' I replied, my voice flat.

The tone of my response surprised me. I had imagined my confrontation with Callisto a million times since the beginning of my vampiric existence. Always the clash was ablaze with emotion, an epic struggle to right the wrong that had been done to me. Never in those imaginings had I thought that, when the moment came, it would feel so— prosaic. The realisation disgusted me; even this, the revenge I had planned for so long, had become, in the face of eternity, a non-event that, more than anything, I just wanted to be over.

I stepped inside the chamber. 'So, Patria?'

'But the others?' Callisto said, looking through the doorway. The vampires called to her and she moaned. 'My children.'

'Better to save one than none.'

Callisto swayed, hesitating. 'I don't sense Patria,' she said.

I almost rolled my eyes. 'She's been here the longest. Her mind is protected in a way the others are not. They still hope to see the night sky and taste the warm blood of the herd,' I said, taking a few steps deeper into the chamber and drawing Callisto forward.

Around us, the vampires listened with the intensity of the obsessed; my description of their desires was not a lie. 'Patria is different. She is not yet completely lost but, almost.' I smiled. 'It has been intriguing to watch.'

'You are a monster,' Callisto said, rushing me.

I was ready for her. At my feet was a length of chain attached to the wall at one end and fitted with manacles at the other. I swept these into my hand as Callisto barged into me. Twisting, I looped the chain around her waist and pulled as I drove her backwards into the wall. She was strong, but her surprise gave me the upper hand. Holding her with my shoulder, I gripped her arm and snapped the manacle over her wrist, clicking it shut as she howled her rage. Her children joined her, their voices creating a nightmare din. I ignored them and yanked on the chain, tightening it as I capture her other arm and slammed on the manacle. She kicked and bucked, smashing her body against mine, but to no effect; I was as hard as she was, and far more determined.

When it was done, I step away to gather the shackles for her feet. The vampires, as they usually did when their hopes were dashed, had fallen silent and there was only the sound of Callisto testing the chains. She hissed at me and spat, her eye gleaming with the silver light of her fury as I looped the second chain around her waist and fastened the shackles around her ankles.

'You won't get away with this,' she said.

'You don't think so?' I asked, when she was firmly secured. To emphasis my point, I ran my gaze over the other vampires I had captured. Taking their cue from

Callisto, they snarled at me. 'I think the odds might be in my favour.'

Callisto pressed against her fetters. 'Constantine will come for me, and you'd better be far from here when he does.'

'Of course he's coming for you.' I touched her shoulder, 'I'm counting on it.'

She glared at me until I removed my hand. 'He won't be so easily captured.'

'Maybe. And that's why I've prepared something special for him.'

'What do you mean?' Callisto asked, her eyes narrowing to slits.

I wagged my finger at her. 'Uh-uh, don't want to spoil the surprise.'

Disgust filled Callisto's face. 'You're evil.'

My humour dropped away. 'Really? Who started this?'

'Isn't it about time you got over that? Callisto demanded.

'Well I would, except for a small thing called *eternity*,' I replied, my voice rising.

I didn't mean to yell, but her line of argument struck me as unfair. Who was she to judge when all I was trying to do was clean up the mess that she and Constantine had made. I strode to the far end of the chamber and stood with my head hanging until I felt some of my rage recede. When control returned, I walked back to her and said, 'Anything else you would like to discuss?'

'Where's my daughter?'

I tilted my head as though I needed to think about it. 'By now? Dust in the bottom of some long forgotten tomb.'

Callisto shook her head and the chains rattled pleasantly. 'She was your kin, Juliana. How could you do that to her?'

'It was a just punishment. She went after Didier's twins.'

'Those babies were human; they were born to perish. Not like Shroudeaters. We are immortal.'

'Nothing is immortal, Callisto, as you will discover, one day.'

I took my leave of her then so I could prepare to meet Constantine. She didn't beg, or protest, or demand to be freed as the others had, but she watched me; the silver in her eyes the last thing I saw as I closed the door.

Born Again Christian

Those lying fucks.

Why didn't they kill me?

Send me to the other side.

Heaven.

Hell.

I don't care.

Anything would be better than the inferno raging through my collapsed veins. I'm driven from the ground where Callisto and Constantine birthed me. The earth tilts beneath my feet as though trying to rid itself of my infected touch. I reach for something solid to bind me to the world, and touch hard flesh; the hand of my mother.

My mother?

The hand I hold draws me closer. Callisto. I can smell my blood on her breath; the aroma is maddening. 'Hush, my son,' she murmurs.

'He needs to feed,' Constantine says.

'Will it be you or me, my love?'

'You are his mother.'

Callisto sighs, and the air is suddenly drenched in the coppery scent of blood. A riot erupts as the starving vampires snarl and strain to get at her. Constantine hisses a warning and they fall back, withdrawing into the dark.

'Thank you, darling,' Callisto murmurs, brushing a finger down my cheek. My head turns. I feel my gums split apart, fangs sliding out as I latch onto the wound above her breast. It's so Hollywood B grade, I should laugh, except something else is in control now. I clamp my mouth to the hard flesh. Tepid liquid rushes down my throat.

The Thirst retreats. Sweet relief.

I hunch over Callisto, pulling the blood - *my* blood - from her body until she begins to struggle. 'Enough,' she says, her fingers coming between my mouth and her chest. 'Enough!' There is command in her voice and I lift my eyes to her face. Constantine grasps my arms, pulls me away as the wound over Callisto's breast closes, becomes a scar; a memory.

She staggers against her chains. 'Now we must both feed. Christian. Free us from our bindings so we may hunt together.'

'Yes, free us—' Mutters of agreement from the dark.

My mind is clearer with the blood, although I'm still weak. My limbs feel paper light; all substance gone. How much blood does the human body hold anyway? I look at the ground.

Bad move.

Head swirling, I notice they didn't spill a drop.

Somehow, this repulses me more than anything else: the stench, the decay, the darkness, the loathsome cries. I *can't* be one of these creatures. Greedy, deathless *things*. What was I thinking? I have to get out, have to find Lucy, have to go home to Mum and Dad, and my room, the Net, my friends. I have choices to make, a *life* to live. Pain jolts through me, napalming my thoughts. At the same time, every cell in my body contracts.

'You don't have that choice any longer, fledgling. You are what you are, accept it.'

'He's right, my child. I know you are hurting, but there are ways to manage that and, if you free us, your father and I will guide you.'

'Fuck you. You're not my parents,' I say, bending over my knees.

Callisto rests a gentle hand on my head. 'It takes time to stop thinking like a human, Christian, but you'll get there. Believe me.'

Thinking like a human? Good suggestion. I fight off the next wave of fire and stand straight. *Defiant*, I think. I look at the door and the key waiting in the lock. What are humans best at?

Survival. Like cockroaches.

I take a few steps.

'You're not human anymore, Christian.' A spasm twists through my body, leaving me on my hands and knees, panting. When it eases, I sit against the door.

'The Thirst grows stronger. Soon it will have you crawling in circles like a rabid dog,' Constantine says. There's no sympathy in his voice.

'You will not survive the day without our help. Already Juliana suspects your decision; she will be waiting for you to emerge.' Callisto walks towards me, coming as far as her chains will allow. 'Abandon us and die. Or give me the freedom you promised and survive. These are the only choices left to you.'

She's right. Stringing two thoughts together is almost impossible, and my body is so light, I'm worried it will disintegrate with the first breath of wind. Then there's the Thirst, which is growing at an abominable rate. I look at the smooth skin above Callisto's breast and accept that I'm screwed without them.

'All right, but just you and Constantine,' I say, reaching for the jar of keys on the shelf beside the door.

There's a chorus of protest. Callisto glances over her shoulder and they quieten, though I can feel the desperation flowing from them.

'As you wish,' she says.

'No, Callisto, you cannot…'

'Mother, free us too…'

'I must feed…'

'Be at peace, my kin,' Callisto says, as I work through the keys, looking for the one that unlocks her manacles. 'I will feed and nurture the fledgling, then return for you.' She looks into my eyes as the chains fall away.

I think she's lying.

'Callisto?' Constantine's voice is dignified. The vampire raises her hand for the jar of keys. She smiles and I shiver with the Thirst. 'Callisto.' More insistent.

'Coming, my love.'

As she removes his bindings, I unlock the door and step into the passageway beyond, but I can't go any further. My knees unhinge and I slide toward the floor. I wish for death, but I fall into a baked red desert, where undead things shamble and scream.

The First Sacrament

Spiced plums. Desert sand. A hint of mint. And blood: warm, pulsing, calling. The girl presses into the far corner of the room, watching me with dark, almond shaped eyes. Her head is covered by her khimar; delicate hands, white against the cobalt material, hold the headscarf to her body.

She is wrapped; a gift.

I shift in my corner, the one opposite her, and battle the Thirst.

To take my mind from the inevitable, I piece together the journey to this room. I remember being lifted from the floor, the beseeching howls muffled as a door closed. I remember dripping passageways and a spiral staircase. I remember Callisto and Constantine supporting me, arms around my waist, hustling me forward with unnatural speed. They were silent, but I caught snatches of conversation passing between them when the pain receded and allowed my mind to clear.

…wait here until the day is ended?

Yes…

…to rue du Cardinal Lemoine?

…she could be nearby.

I don't feel her...

...she's masking her presence.

...must hunt.

A door opened, and a new world of pain crashed over me. The city was a living thing: roaring traffic, crushing humanity, lights of every hue, each one bright as a sun. The air rank: sweat, shit, piss, blood, coffee, red wine, and everywhere, perfume. Paris flattened me; pushed me up against a wall like a thug.

Callisto took my head between her hands. 'Christian?'

'I can't—' I wanted to say something, but I couldn't think passed the city. I wanted the silence of the catacombs, the slow drip of water, and the stagnant air. I tried to turn towards the door.

'It will ease, Christian,' Callisto said, holding me. She began to sing, the words filtering into my mind and dulling my senses as she lead me through the streets. Their conversation continued.

We must hunt soon.

I know. Not much further. Across the river. Notre Dame. The gypsies. You remember?

Constantine laughed. *How could I forget? What of the fledgling?*

The room at L'Hôtel.

She knows it?

No. They exchanged a glance. *A mother has her secrets.*

Their voices faded as we crossed the Seine. The smell of the water was brutal: fish, oil, diesel, garbage, and the tang of silt covering the bottom of the ancient channel. I gagged and clamped a hand over my mouth as Callisto hurried me to the other side.

'Poor Christian,' she murmured. 'Never again will water be a cleansing tonic.'

I felt like crying. It wasn't supposed to be like this. Being born again as a vampire was about invincibility and power, not this torture of the senses, this agony of craving, this goddamned vulnerability and weakness.

'It will pass, my child, once you have fed,' Callisto said, urging me forward.

I shook my head and the world spun until it was a blur.

System overload.

When I came to, I was lying on a bed looking into the face of my first victim.

The girl.

A gift from Callisto and Constantine.

I hear her move; she's crawling for the door. My body tenses. I imagine this is what a leopard feels moments before it springs, every muscle bunched and throbbing with energy. The girl freezes, halfway to reaching for the doorknob. The hesitation should be her downfall, except I still can't give in to the Thirst. Not when she's looking at me with those beautiful dark eyes, full of fear, and something else.

That 'something else' reminds me of another woman; a beggar. I think of that woman to protect the one in the room with me.

She, the beggar woman, was in the Metro as Lucy and I came into Paris with Marguerite, standing at a junction of tunnels, her back to the white tiles, eyes lowered. I slowed as we approached. Lucy and Marguerite strolled ahead, oblivious to the woman. She wasn't the first beggar I'd seen; there were dozens on the route from Charles de Gaulle, each peddling something: trinkets, talismans, talents; cheap and nasty for sure, but something to exchange for a coin. This woman offered nothing. She kept her head down as I stopped in front of her. The cup of her hands was empty.

Emotions swirled through me: anger, pity, indignation, contempt. Why was she just standing there? Why didn't she *do* something if she wanted help? Why didn't she do *something* to change her life?

As these thoughts shot through my mind, she raised her head. Her face was a study of dignity. She knew her plight, she understood the choice she'd made, and she accepted both with a gentle serenity. I saw this in her eyes and something more; she knew *my* thoughts, had read them on my face.

I felt a new emotion; guilt.

She read this too.

Fumbling in my jacket pockets, I searched for a few euros. She waited, patient as a flower for the rain, but when I held out the five-euro note, she folded her hands into her chest and lowered her eyes. Rejection: her graceful answer to my anger, and my guilt.

These are the qualities I sense in the girl crouching on the floor before me: dignity, serenity, and grace; her gentle humanity. They are not enough to save her. I rise up in my corner, legs shaking, lips pulled back, teeth pushing through my gums. There is no finesse in my movements. I want her. In my eagerness, my foot catches the bed sheets and I sprawl across the floor.

Rising up again, I'm looking into her face.

There are tears in her eyes.

She holds her hands out to me.

Not begging; accepting.

Like Sisyphus.

I turn away from her, using the last ounce of *my* humanity. 'Get out,' I rasp.

She doesn't wait to be told twice. The door crashes into the wall and I hear her footsteps racing down the hallway. I have no strength to close the door behind her. The Thirst is my world now. Thought is gone; compassion is gone; the last vestige of my humanity is gone. The only thing left is a blood-starved vampire.

God help the next person who enters the room.

He is not human.

He is a beating heart. A pulsing jugular. A solution to the Thirst.

I take him before Callisto crosses into the room, ripping him from her arms. She pushes us backwards and I stagger, dragging him to the floor. Bones snap under my weight and he moans, feeling the destruction through the anaesthetic of Callisto's song. I can't stop; his pain is nothing compared to mine.

My mouth.

His throat.

My fangs.

His skin.

Tearing.

Blood.

He's dead before I finish. His heart gives a final thud and stops. The flow of his blood eases to a trickle, and then gives out altogether. Wrenching my mouth free, I push the body away, feeling a wave of revulsion at its husked appearance. I cough up a gout of blood, start to crawl away, look at the bright splash, turn back; God-curse-me.

Far from easing the Thirst, the blood has enflamed it, like petrol on fire. I twist towards Callisto. Her eyes are soft with concern. 'Come, Christian, this time you hunt,' she says.

'I'm not ready.'

Callisto looks at the boy's corpse, the blood on the floor, and me. 'The Thirst says otherwise.'

Antecedents

Paris is unnatural in the slow hours before dawn.

The city is almost silent: its horde of tourists consigned to their matchbox rooms; the thundering traffic immobilised by the lateness of the hour; the citizenry locked in sleep, and only the most debauched of creatures scurry through the dimness. The city is an undead thing, waiting for resurrection.

No wonder I feel at home.

My senses are snapping as Callisto guides me down narrow cobblestoned streets. I can smell the people behind the walls in the apartment buildings around us. I can hear their measured heartbeats. I can taste the saltiness of their sleep-sweat like a mist on the air. I want to visit them, but Callisto refuses to stop.

We knife through the city, heading northeast. Callisto glances at me, and I know she catches the longing in my face. 'I remember this city in its infancy,' she says.

'How long has it been for you?' I ask, accepting the diversion.

There is laughter in her eyes when she answers. 'Ah poor Christian, it will be some time before those human limitations fall away.' She touches my hand in sympathy. I'm tempted to pull away, but I don't. I need her, and not only because I need (*want, want, want*) to feed.

Soon my child, Callisto whispers in my head. Aloud, she says, 'We don't count the minutes, or the hours, or the years. What would be the point in the face of eternity?'

'That was Juliana's argument too,' I say, sniffing the air: the tang of gunpowder and blood wafts around me. A murder in the night. I feel appalled by the violence, but I also ache to taste the blood. 'But she was lying. She counts the years, every last minute of them.'

Callisto nods, a crease appearing between her eyes. 'She was always different, that one. In hindsight, perhaps we should not have birthed her, but it was the passion of the Thirst, and that can never be denied.'

I shake my head.

'What is it?'

'Who—' I pause, the question awkward on my lips. 'Who *birthed* you and Constantine?'

We take a sharp turn and race along a dimly lit alleyway. We're moving so fast I'm sure I'll start defying gravity at any second, but Callisto's voice is even, as though we're strolling through the metropolis.

'The Ancients,' she says, leaping up to a balcony and jumping down again; a gymnast landing a perfect ten.

Callisto laughs and, as I wonder at her behaviour, an odd shimmer happens inside my mind, like a curtain fluttering in a faint breeze. A space appears between my thoughts and I'm drawn through the gap. Beyond, I catch a glimpse of Callisto's mind.

There are two versions of her, sitting in a forest of tall, red-leafed trees. One is the shackled nightmare from Juliana's dungeon: hunched, parched, skin cracked, eyes sunken, hair brittle as kindling. The other is a pale-skinned, clear-eyed beauty, who leans over her monstrous self and rubs a salve of blood into the wounded skin. I push forward a little and they look at me, surprise in their eyes.

Suddenly my head is filled with the tortured voice of a soprano and I'm slammed out of her mind. I stagger and Callisto catches my arm. 'What the hell,' I say, as she steadies me.

'No uninvited exploring, fledgling,' she says, her voice mild.

'I didn't mean to,' I reply, rubbing at my temple. 'What was that song?'

'*Un bel di vedremo*. Do you know it?'

'I do now,' I reply, wondering if I'll ever get the soprano's voice out of my head.

'I'm sorry, Christian. It's a defence to protect my mind from others of our kind, who as we know, don't always have my best interest in their heart.' She pulls on my arm and we continue through the streets, vampire quick. 'It's a technique you'd be wise to learn.'

I think of Juliana and her probing of my human mind. 'Alright,' I say, as the Thirst rushes forward, gnawing at my body. I need a distraction. 'So, how about that history lesson?'

Callisto nods and slows to a walk. I'd be happier running, but I keep pace with her, letting her voice take me away. 'Constantine and I were born to our vampire lives on the same night, in a forest that grew beside the Aveyron River,' Callisto says, a wistful smile touching her lips. 'We'd known each other since childhood, when his family arrived in my village after fleeing the clan wars in Scotland. I liked him immediately, especially his funny way of speaking, and I took it upon myself to teach him French. In return, he taught me to hunt and to play, for I was a serious child, given to more refined pursuits. My favourite game, which he taught to my friends as well, was Barla-Bracks about the Stacks.'

'What's that?'

'A game of chase played in pairs, where we had to hold hands and, sometimes, there was kissing.' She covers her mouth as though she's said something risqué, then laughs. 'He taught me a poem about it. Do you want to hear it?'

'Sure,' I say, happy for any diversion that keeps the Thirst at bay.

'Okay.

> *We two are last in hell, what may we fear;*
> *To be tormented, or kept pris'ners here?*
> *Alas! if kissing be of plagues the worst,*
> *We'll wish in hell we had been last and first.*

I smile, surprised by the perfect Scottish lilt in her recital. 'Wow, you sound just like Constantine except, not so blokey.'

Callisto shrugged a shoulder. 'It was the first thing I learnt in English. I guess the inflection has stayed with me.'

'Makes sense,' I say, thinking about the poem, which struck me as oddly appropriate to my makers. 'So, you and Constantine were childhood sweethearts?'

'Yes. Sometime during our teenage years, we fell in love and were betroth. But we didn't marry immediately, as was the custom in our day, for the Queen of Scotland, Margaret, the Maid of Norway they called her, died just days after I accepted Constantine's proposal, drawing his father and him back across the sea. What dark years they were, waiting, never knowing if the boy I loved would return. Then, three full moons after my twentieth year, he stood before me again. He was no longer a boy, but a man, scarred and hardened, but I could still see his love for me in his eyes. A month later, we married in a lavish ceremony at Sainte-Foy Abbey.

'The celebrations went late into the night and, by the second hour after midnight, Constantine and I could no longer wait to be together. We slipped away and wandered into the forest, laughing and touching each other, making our union real. As we moved deeper, I became aware of a golden light filtering through the trees; it was coming from a fire burning in a clearing. Constantine took my hand and we crept closer.

'Around the fire stood a dozen figures, six males and six females, paired off and facing each other. Each one was exquisite, breath taking, and I was mesmerised the moment I laid eyes on them. Between each couple, lying at their feet, was a naked human, curled like a sleeping infant. As we watched, the hand of one reached for the foot of a dark-haired woman with topaz-coloured eyes. She kicked it away and I gasped at the sudden violence.

'They turned in our direction. "Run," Constantine murmured, but it was too late. We were caught in strong arms and carried to the woman. "Welcome, my children," she said, and I fainted as her fangs slid forward.'

Callisto's face is serene as the memory takes her back to the moment and I realise she has no malice towards her makers. For her, becoming a vampire *was* a gift. I think about Juliana and the hatred that stained her voice when she spoke of her birth and her parents. Will I hate Callisto and Constantine with the same intensity? Will I love them when ten human lifetimes have passed and I am still here? Will I feel as murderous as Juliana when all I love has passed and I am still here?

Something with talons clutches my gut. I stumble.

Callisto catches me. 'It is best not to dwell on such things, my child,' she says, as we dart cross Rue de La Fayette and take a twisting route of back streets until we come out onto Rue des Martyrs, where we hurry past brightly lit shop fronts offering all manner of human delights. I stop outside *Heaven* and consider the art nouveau lamps displayed in the window, their pretty chains and baubles gleaming. They are just the sort of trinkets Lucy loves.

Lucy.

The talons flex again, biting deep. Wincing, I push her out of my mind as I turn from the store window; she's beyond my reach for now. I follow Callisto, listening to her story and the call of the Thirst as it races through my veins.

'My mother's name was Lilith. She was of the first inner circle. My father was her latest mate, Asher. He was of the outer circles.

'What does that mean? Inner circle? Outer circle?'

'It is complicated,' Callisto says, pausing for a few seconds. From her expression, I can see she's looking for the best way to explain. She comes to a decision and continues, 'There are two lines of vampire lineage. The first makes up the inner circles, of which there are three. These circles are closest to the Font - the source of our kind, or so legend say. The second line makes up the outer three circles, which are an evolutionary divergence from the Font.'

'Evolutionary?' I say and laugh, thinking she's joking.

Callisto glances at me as we cross a street and slip into another. 'Yes,' she says, her tone clipped.

'Sorry, it's just a strange word to associate with vampires.'

'Everything evolves, Christian, or it perishes.'

In my mind, I hear Juliana's voice: *Everything dies*, and I'm struck by the gulf between the two vampire's approach to their existence, and I wonder which side of their divide I'll find myself on in the future. 'So, the night you and Constantine found the vampires in the forest,' I say, forcing my mind to move on, 'the two lines of lineage had come together for a council of some sort?' I say, thinking of the countless vampire movies I've seen.

'Not a 'council', a birthing circle.'

'A what?' I ask, as a wave of furnace-hot heat undulates through my body, leaving me parched inside.

Callisto touches my arm, drawing my attention outward. 'Try to concentrate on me. It'll make the next quarter hour easier.' I give her a questioning look. 'ETA to our destination,' she says, picking up her pace.

'Right,' I reply, though fifteen minutes sounds like forever to me.

'Okay, so you already know it takes two vampires to birth one of our kind, but not just any two vampires can accomplish this feat. They must be of different bloodlines; one from the inner circles, one from the outer.

'In my parent's time, this practice was ritualised in a gathering, where specially chosen humans were exchanged and birthed according to the ancient customs. It was a celebration, a blood feast.'

'A gathering? Aren't vampires solitary by nature?'

'For the most part and, considering the current human obsession with our kind, we must remain so now more than ever. But, at the time of my birth, vampires moved and gathered more freely, since the humans were distracted by their own scheming and betrayals. And, of course, we were discreet with our taking from the herd, and our gatherings were scattered and usually sheltered from the eyes of humans.'

'But you found them.'

Callisto nods as her fingers brush the length of her throat. 'A convergence of events that conspired to bring us to that clearing.' She lifts her shoulders and lets them fall. 'It's irrelevant. My last human memory was of being wrapped in their song as they bled me into the death-sleep. When I woke, they brought my first feast and I knew I was where I belonged. The transition was harder for Constantine; he fought the Thirst and refused to feed, but I coaxed him until he submitted. He has been voracious in his appetites ever since. It was his bloodlust that lead to the birth of Juliana; a mistake for which we have all suffered.'

There's sadness in her voice, and she's quiet as we pass along Place des Abbesses. I wait for her to continue. When she remains silent, I offer her a prompt. 'What happened to your parents?'

Callisto waves the question aside. 'Another story, for another time,' she says, pointing to the left fork in the divided road. She dashes ahead, and I pick up my pace to keep even with her. Ahead are the gates of Cimetière de Montmartre. 'For now, we must find Constantine.'

The Gift of Dying

Romani dance in the city of the dead. Their camp is boisterous with music; fire bathes their skin in warm hues. I lick my lips; tongue the sharp points of my teeth. I breathe their scent; a tantalising mix of blood, smoke, wine. Their taste fills me and I inch forward.

Callisto places a hand flat against my chest. 'Wait,' she commands.

Men gather in small groups, talking as they watch the women dancing together, skirts flaring like plumage. A teenage boy breaks from one group, the men slapping his back as he leaves them. He looks over his shoulder, half-cocky, half-uncertain, and they urge him on with whistles and knowing laughter.

The girl he approaches wears a yellow dress, the bodice tight around her breasts; a red bandana covers her dark hair. Her eyes are brown and filled with firelight. She turns those eyes on the boy and he falters, courage gone. The men hoot encouragement from their side of the camp, and I see his shoulders square as he reaches out to touch her hand.

Smiling, the girl tips her head towards the other women, who have stopped dancing to watch. They nod their approval and the boy turns away, walking into the darkness between the gravestones a few metres from where Callisto and I wait.

'He's the one,' she says.

'Won't they know?' I ask, not really caring; the scent of the boy's blood fills my head.

'She'll dance a while longer before their rendez-vous.'

We hunt the boy, moving silently between the tombs, until he stops in the dark beneath a bridge. A moment later, a match flares and the red tip of a cigarette bursts into life.

'Keep quiet and be cautious. Sometime they're stronger than you expect, even with the song,' Callisto says, pushing me towards the bridge.

Fear grips me. 'But what am I supposed to do? Is there some special method?'

'Learn,' she says, and I catch the whisper of her singing.

I hesitate, but not for long; the Thirst is a powerful motivator. I dart across the cemetery, moving low, fast, and quiet, as though I'd been hunting humans my whole life. The boy is at the centre of my attention.

His scent is powerful: copper and salt. His sound is irresistible: the pulse of his heart; the bellow of his breathing; the cascade of saliva as he swallows. He is humming Callisto's song. I ache with need, but as I reach for him, he leaps away like a deer realising danger is near. He runs, and I give chase. It's an uneven race; vampirism has its benefits. I bring him down in a few steps and, although he fights like a young lion as

Callisto warned, I turn his head with a sharp flick, snapping his neck.

His throat is exposed. I sink my teeth deep into the flesh and draw the blood from his body. It's warm and thick but, somehow, wrong. When I'm done, I stand and face Callisto. The Thirst has retreated, but I don't feel satisfied.

'Feeding isn't just about the Thirst, Christian. There is a finesse to it; an art.'

'An art to killing and drinking the blood of our victims?' I say, unable to hide my disgust.

Callisto tilts her chin and her eyes narrow. 'There is a beauty in the death we bring. You are yet to understand this.' She nods to the boy at my feet and points to a nearby grave. 'Hide the body,' she says, turning away.

I bend down beside the boy and study his face. The cheeks are hollow, the lips stretched into a grimace. There is no peace in his face, and I ache with the weight of my responsibility. How could there be beauty in this act? How could there be peace, either for him or for me?

Stop Christian, it is done. Callisto's voice coils through my mind. *You cannot escape destiny and neither can those you will encounter. Accept what you are and learn to love yourself; it is how you will serve them best.*

I lift the boy. *Love what I am?* His body is a dried leaf and I carry him with care, fearing he'll crumble against my chest. *Love what I am?* The idea seems impossible. I push aside the top stone of the tomb with my foot. It slides easily. *Accept what I am?* The idea was foreign to me when I was human; how will it help me now?

Unexpectedly, I hear Juliana in my head: *Ours is a Sisyphean existence.*

I lay the boy inside the grave, amid the ruins of an old casket, and drag the stone into place. As Juliana explains it, vampires are slaves to the Thirst, burdened forever with their need for blood. I turn from the grave and return to the place where the boy waited for his love. The dim red glow of his cigarette twinkles and I press my shoe to the spark, crushing out its light. Callisto seemed to suggest another way to look at our existence, following Camus in his line of thought: Acceptance of what can't be changed.

Maybe Callisto is right. Maybe Camus is right. All I have to do is accept that I'm a bloodthirsty killer, and all will be right in the world.

Yep. Easy.

'Christian,' Callisto murmurs from the corner where she waits, 'we must go.'

I nod, and accept – at least – that there is no turning back.

How Sisyphean of you, Juliana whispers, and I peer into the darkness of the cemetery, unsure if the voice is a memory, or if Juliana is nearby.

'Christian.' Callisto's voice is louder. She gives no indication that she hears anything unusual in the night.

'Okay,' I say and, although I'm not sure it'll work, I fill my head with music – Limp Bizkit hammering through *Break Stuff* – as Callisto suggested.

Just in case.

We hurry down tree-lined boulevards, avoiding the Romani, moving between ornate miniature cathedrals and great crypts of marble and stone with stained glass doors and flowers on the stoop. Angels and cherubs watch from the peaked roofs of sepulchres as we pass, and everywhere is the sign of the cross.

So much for consecrated ground, I think.

We enter a section of the cemetery where the graves are packed together, every inch of the ground occupied except for the narrow pathways that the dead are forced to concede to the living. The quiet is deeper here, and Callisto slows as we approach a fenced grave topped with a plain slab of stone. At the head of the tomb is a dark shape that I presume is the headstone until it moves.

'Shit,' I say, as Constantine leaps over the fence and lands beside us.

'Nice to see you too, fledgling.'

He looks different: his features are flushed, handsome, his manner relaxed. I envy his satisfaction. I've fed twice tonight and the Thirst still tears at me like a wild cat. Callisto takes his hand and brushes it against her cheek, while he tucks a loose strand of hair behind her ear. They move closer and I wander away; voyeurism has never been my thing.

Except maybe when comes to Lucy.

I did like to watch her. That sounds creepy, but it's not really like that. Sure, I like to watch the way she moves her body, especially when she dances, all those lovely curves and hollows. Mostly, though, it's what goes on in her head that gets me. She does shit that I'll never understand, even if I had the genius of Einstein. I guess that's what attracts me to her; the mystery of her nature. Not her as a female - though God knows, that's hard enough to resist - but the person *inside*. I want to solve the enigma of her, just as I want to solve the enigma of the universe; the why and the how.

An intersection lies across my path; a choice of direction that absorbs me for a moment. I can see, with hindsight, that I fucked up with Lucy; coming with her to Paris, taking her with me to find Juliana, putting her in danger. I try to imagine where she is, what Juliana is doing to her, and my heart clenches with guilt. I wander on, choosing neither the left or right path, and console myself with the knowledge that Lucy is alive, and still human. I don't know how I know this, but it's true. I wonder if she'll be happy to see me, as I am, now.

The avenues through the cemetery widen. Tall, leafy trees form an archway, blocking out the night sky. Eyes watch from between the graves as I pass; amber and green, slit with mistrust. An angry hiss warns me away from a cracked stone slab. The cats haunting Cimetière de Montmartre know what I am, and hate me.

Will Lucy hate me? For what I did? For what I am now? For destroying the future she had planned for us?

I turn into another street, moving fast, trying to outpace my thoughts, when I hear weeping. My senses sharpen, locking onto the sound. The Thirst flares. I move between the graves until I see her. The bandana tells me who she is: the Romani girl. She's come looking for her lover and, from her low, heartbroken sobbing, I know she thinks he's abandoned her. Guilt washes through me; I'm responsible for her pain. I want to comfort her, to take her in my arms and make amends. I glide closer, not wanting to frighten her, but she detects my presence anyway. She lifts her head, her cheeks wet with tears, her eyes searching the darkness, shining with hope; looking for him— finding me. We stare at each other for a long moment before she takes a deliberate step backwards like a child retreating from a snake.

'Wait,' I say and she stops, even though I can see by the set of her face that it's not what she wants.

So many things battle inside me as I look at her. I want to caress her face. I want to tell her not to be heartbroken; that her lover didn't discard her. I want to tell her I'm sorry for finding her; for needing her blood.

Wavering between remorse, compassion, and compulsion, I cross the distance between us, and as I do, something new rises in my mind: a song. The words are foreign, but it doesn't matter. Instinctively, I know they are for her, and as I take her in my arms, I sing them into her mind.

The difference between the girl's death and her lover's is immediate and intense. Her blood is sweet, satisfying, and I sense no fear in her, not even when she takes her last breath.

I release her, and tears fill my eyes as I gaze at her, understanding what Callisto told me. This is the beauty in the death we deliver. I fold her arms over her chest and tuck her hair into the bandana; her face is peaceful.

She weighs almost nothing when I lift her and carry her to the grave where I placed the boy.

'Thank you,' I whisper, as I slip her inside and cover the grave.

Stepping away, I marvel at the feel of my body. For the first time since becoming a vampire, I feel no pain, no need; the Thirst has receded to an awareness on the edge of my perception. I know it will be back, but for now, I am content, sated as Constantine.

'Do you see how it can be now?' Callisto asks from behind me.

'Yes,' I say, unsurprised by their arrival. Some part of me sensed their approach as I finished with the girl. 'It doesn't make it right, though.'

'No, but it is bearable, yes?'

'Maybe. Time will tell.'

'Well, you've got plenty of that, fledgling,' Constantine laughs and claps me on the back as I close the grave.

The girl's blood has left me feeling agreeable, so I don't shrug him off. 'What's next?'

Callisto looks at the sky, which is beginning to lighten on the horizon. 'We need to get you into some shelter before the sun comes up.'

'Why? Afraid I'll burn to cinders?' I laugh, dashing away, coming back, circling behind them, bursting with energy. 'Juliana told me vampires are impervious to the sun. Did she lie?'

'Mon dieu, he is like a puppy,' Constantine says.

Callisto is indulgent. 'No, Christian, she didn't lie. But you're newborn, and the Thirst will be intolerable to you in the daylight.' She takes my arm and guides me towards the gate.

'Where do you suggest we go?' Constantine asks.

'Basilique du Sacré Coeur. We can hide below the crypt, in the caverns.'

'What caverns? There aren't any caverns beneath Sacré Coeur,' I say.

'Not everything is in the travel brochure, Christian,' Callisto says, as Constantine breaks into a run. She tugs on my hand and we leap after him: her lover; my father.

House of God

My human parents spent the first thirteen years of my life trying to convince me that God resided in our local church. I was sceptical; Sunday after Sunday, I searched St Luke's for God but, it seemed to me, the building had about as much spirit as a bottle of flat lemonade. Then, a week after Easter, my best mate, James, was hit by a car. While he fought for life at the hospital, I went to St Luke's. I got down on my knees right in front of the crucifix and I prayed to God to save him.

James died.

St Luke's was just a building: I never went there, or into another church, again.

Now, on the steps of Sacré Coeur, I feel God's presence and I tremble with fear. *Can I cross over the threshold?*

Callisto passes beneath the portico, but Constantine leaps onto the ledge above the three archways and scrambles up a column until he reaches the statue of Christ. He grins down at me as he gives the statue an irreverent high-five before swinging across to the roof. His agility is impressive, and I only realise my apprehension when he reaches the first dome and pushes open a section of window.

'Christian,' Callisto calls.

I wait to see if Constantine will re-emerge before I go to her, but he's disappeared. 'What's he doing?' I ask Callisto. In answer, I hear the locks click behind a door in a deep recess and Constantine's pale face appears.

'Entrée vous, madam,' he says, making a grand sweeping gesture as Callisto passes into the church. He looks at me, 'Monsieur?'

I take a step towards the entry and stop.

The power of the basilique rises around me. The voices of martyrs cry out at my presence. A compelling male voice leads the condemnation; Saint Denis, the Christian beheaded on the butte of Montmartre for returning souls to God. *Pas entrer dans l'esprit impur*, his spectral voice commands.

Constantine grabs the front of my shirt and pulls me into the church. 'Ignore the dead, Christian,' he says, with a laugh, 'They're dead.'

I stumble after him, waiting for some cataclysm to occur, but it doesn't come.

'God plays no favourites, Christian. We are all his creatures,' Callisto assures me.

'How can that be?' I say, staring at the mosaic in the apse, high above the central alter. Jesus, dressed in flowing white robes, his arms spread in benevolence, gazes down on us. 'We steal life. We defy the natural order. Doesn't that make us evil?'

'Why are we evil, Christian? Because we take human life to survive? Humans kill *all* living things, without regard or compassion if it suits their purpose. Yet God forgives them. Shroudeaters take only what we need and do so with love and gratitude for the sacrifice.' She lifts her gaze to the ceiling. 'So why wouldn't God forgive us?'

Constantine moves out of the shadows. 'What does it matter? We are what we are, fledgling. Such ponderings do not change your reality.' He turns to Callisto, 'Come my sweet, the crypt is open.'

Callisto takes his hand and they glide between the pews. I follow them, feeling the eyes of Christ on my back. I want to believe that gaze is forgiving, but I'm not convinced. We descend into the crypt, moving swiftly until we come to a statue of a martyr. Constantine jumps over the kneeling figure, onto the mantel and slips behind the monument. Callisto follows. I wait a second, listening for the sounds of human activity from the church.

'Christian.' Callisto's voice is tinged with motherly impatience.

'Yeah, okay,' I say, clambering over the martyr and onto the shrine. I feel an absurd need to apologise as I grab the woman's cold stone thigh, but the urge passes as I see Constantine standing in the entrance to the crypts.

'Who would have guessed,' I say, as he steps aside to let me pass.

'Paris holds many secrets,' Constantine replies, pressing his hand against one of the stones. A door slides across the opening and I'm swallowed by darkness. Below, a light flickers; Callisto is at the bottom of a narrow set of stairs, waiting in an archway. Constantine prods my shoulder. 'Let's go, fledgling.'

I take the stairs two at a time and follow Callisto into a low-roofed antechamber. Against one wall is a chair and a wooden table, on which sits an old wick lamp, covered in dust. As I pass, I wonder who would sit at such a table, in such a place.

A guardian, Callisto explains inside my head.

For whom? I send back, feeling foolish. I've been a vampire for less than twenty-four hours and suddenly I'm telepathic— Mad.

Callisto doesn't answer, but leads the way through a second arch at the other end of the room. The chamber beyond is much larger. The light of Callisto's torch doesn't reach the ceiling, but I can make out enough to see the rectangular vaults dug into the walls.

For the dead, Callisto murmurs as Constantine leans into one of the recesses and sweeps out the crumbling remains of a body onto the floor.

'There you go, fledgling, nice and comfy,' he says.

I shiver, hating the idea of sliding into the narrow space, but a sapping weariness is washing through me and I know I have no choice.

Callisto shakes her head and places a restraining hand on my arm. 'That's not necessary, Christian. You can sleep on the floor,' she says, sending a withering look to Constantine.

He snorts laugher and drops to the floor, pushing his back against the rough stone wall. Callisto follows his example and I sit next to her, thankful to be at rest.

I'm aware of the sun on the horizon and my eyes flutter open in the dark. The Thirst prowls through me like a beast, ready to hunt. I lick my lips, my senses already searching the church above for signs of life as I climb to my feet. There is a priest in a vestibule somewhere, a withered man with the heartbeat of a mouse. I turn my senses away; the thought of killing him is too much of an offence to consider. I search further and feel the presence of people on the steps of the basilique, moving away.

The Thirst growls: *Hurry, hurry.*

Constantine is gone and I can sense Callisto waiting by the stairs. I feel her need - the Thirst is pressing her too - but she says nothing as I join her and we climb into the church. The smell of humans is everywhere, and I can almost see the shimmer of their heat, like a ghostly residue. The Thirst leaps inside me and I stumble under its demand.

Callisto glances at me. 'Control it, Christian. It's a *part* of you, not all of you.'

'It's hard,' I say, as we come out from under the portico.

'It will become easier.'

'That's what I'm afraid of,' I reply. We cross the lawns beside the basilique and my anxiety vanishes as my senses amp up. Someone is sitting on a bench seat, in the shadows beneath a tree. I breathe, tasting the air.

It's a woman; on her own. I hear her heart: relaxed, rhythmic, hypnotic. Callisto gives my hand a quick jerk, pulling me back, and nods towards the figure. 'Feed, and we'll meet later at L'Hôtel. Do you remember the way?'

'Yes,' I say, but she's already gone.

Moving closer, I consider the woman, trying to decide on the best way to take her. I don't want a repeat of my first two kills, but to give her a death like the Romani girl in Cimetière de Montmartre. Approaching her directly is out; I don't know what my face looks like after my transformation, but my hands have a kind of translucence that makes them almost glow in the deepening dusk. Then there are my clothes, which are filthy with blood and dust. One look at me and she'd run, and the moment she did, I would lose control of the Thirst and any chance of giving her a gentle death.

I sidle up behind her. She doesn't move, not even when I wrap my hands around her throat. Too late, I hear the singing.

Juliana.

'Hello again, Christian.'

The woman between us whimpers. I let go of her and she lies down on the bench, tucking her legs up and wrapping her arms around her body like a frightened child. Juliana considers her without expression, and then she looks at me.

Beautiful.

'Thank you,' Juliana says, pushing the woman's hair over her shoulder, exposing her throat. 'Are you pleased with my offering, Christian? I knew you'd be in need when you woke.' She tilts her head to the side, flirty and challenging at the same time. 'Would you like to—?'

The need for the woman's blood engulfs me; I'm drowning in it, but I'll be damned if I'm going to let Juliana play with me. I step away from the seat, fighting the Thirst for every inch.

Juliana watches me, her expression turning contemplative. 'You're stronger than I expected,' she says, coming around the seat. 'But then, look at your parentage.'

I'm about a metre from her and the woman; I can't go a step further. 'What do you want, Juliana?' I ask. The words are husky.

'Poor Christian. It is such a battle to control the Thirst in the beginning.' As she speaks, Juliana jabs her fingernail into the woman's forearm.

The warm copper smell of blood fills my world. 'Fuck you,' I mutter.

Juliana laughs and licks her nail. 'I see you're in no mood to talk right now, so I'll leave you to take care of your *needs*,' she says, and I feel a surge of anger at her mockery. 'When you're done, find me at *Shakespeare's* bookshop. Do you know it?'

My anger has made the Thirst stronger and I can only nod because I'm not sure what will come out if I open my mouth.

'Good. I'll be there until about midnight, and then I leave Paris, so don't get too caught up in your pleasures.' Juliana smiles, her beauty dazzling, but I can also see the bitterness in her eyes. She steps away from the seat and melts into the shadows. I sense her watching, but I don't care; the Thirst is all that matters now.

The moment Juliana breaks her hold, the woman bolts, but she doesn't make it out from under the tree. I'm on her in three strides. She fights, heaving and twisting beneath me. I pin her against the grass, and she yelps as something pops in her shoulder. Her blood is surging, so close, just beneath the surface of her skin. I want it more than I've wanted anything in my life, but I discover something with her cry of pain.

Control.

The woman under me looks up, tears in her eyes. I smooth her hair away from her face. In the human world, she would be considered ugly. Everything about her is rattish: from her mousy hair, brown eyes, sharp nose, and weak chin, to the soft plumpness of her body, but to my vampire eyes, she is beautiful. Her blood is clean, sweet smelling, rich. I tell her she is exquisite through my song and she stops crying.

Singing, I hold her hand as I lower my mouth to the soft place on her throat. I catch the scent of lavender rising from her skin. Her pulse flutters against my lips, tantalising. I want her blood so much, but I'm gentle, careful not to rush. She makes a small protesting sound as I draw the blood from her. I pull her closer, singing my gratitude and she quietens. Her blood flows into my extremities. My skin tingles with warmth; my muscles fill with energy. I feel alive.

I sing and sing until her heart stops, then I draw away to gaze at the woman; her face is serene. After a moment, I pick up her body and carry it down to the vaults under the basilique, where I know God will watch over her for all eternity.

Leaving Sacré Coeur, I head for the Barbès-Rochechouart metro, eager to get to Juliana. I need to know what she's done with Lucy and what she wants with me. I stick to the shadows and avoid people, though the Thirst is already building and I know I'll have to hunt again before I get to *Shakespeare's*. I'm deep into imagining my encounter with Juliana when I stumble into the lovers making out in an alleyway.

'Fuck, man,' the male says.

'Sorry,' I mutter, and keep going.

He's young, built, and not prepared to let me off with an apology. He grabs my arm and swings me around to face him. 'What's your problem,' he demands, shooting a glance at the girl. 'You fucking blind?'

The Thirst sneaks forward. I sigh. 'Listen Romeo, I don't want to get in a pissing match with you. I said sorry. Let's leave it at that, hey?'

He looks me up and down, taking in the dirt and blood on my clothes. 'Looks like someone messed you up already.' He flicks another glance at the girl. 'And now you wanna go a few rounds with me, huh?'

I try one more time. 'This is not how you want your night to end, my friend.'

He glances at the girl. Her mouth twitches and she gives him a subtle nod.

My fist drops him like a lead club, and the girl barely registers the attack before she's in my grip. Taking them is not as slow and loving as the woman at Sacré Coeur, but I still sing them down, although they don't deserve such easy deaths. I drag the blood from them, feeling it strengthen my body and drive back the Thirst.

When it's over, I look at my clothes. Romeo had a point; I can't ride the Paris metro dressed like this. The man at my feet is wearing a jacket. I take it before tossing the bodies into a dumpster behind Carrefour Market and heading onto Rue de Sofia. The shops are closed and I cruise the street, looking for something I'd like to wear. As I look in the window of a trendy boutique with headless mannequins wearing jeans, t-shirts and obscene price tags, I consider the idea of the slippery slope.

Forget it, Christian, I think as I make for the back entrance to the shop. *You're already at the bottom.*

Blog Fourteen

In Admiration of a Girl

Okay, that's it.

I have tried to steer you away from your ridiculous, romantic notions about vampires, but do you listen? No. Instead, like wilful children, you meddle in things that are none of your business, all because it's what you *want*. Pah! And don't give me that 'the sins of one do not define the character of the many' rubbish. All of you who visit these pages and slavishly read these words would interfere in my world, if you had the chance, despite everything I have shared with you. Don't deny it, I know you would because one of you already has and now, here I am, right back where I started.

Why didn't I kill him when I had the opportunity?

I know part of it was that I wanted to torment Callisto and Constantine, to deepen their suffering by giving them a morsel of hope, a taste of blood to fire the Thirst into a savage, unquenchable inferno. Yet, if this were all I wanted, I would not have given the human the key to the exit, and the chance at salvation.

Was it ego then? He'd read these pages; did I believe he had *listened* to me? Did I think I had finally met someone with enough intelligence to understand the reality of this existence and *turn away*? If so, I overestimated him Or, perhaps it was not the fledgling, but Callisto and Constantine and their determination to survive that I misjudged? Not that it matters; either way, they are free and another Shroudeater - Christian (I know!) - wanders the earth.

You, no doubt, are happy to hear of my error of judgement, aren't you, mortal? I know from your comments that you think imprisoning my parents was wrong. How soft you are! Does their escape please you? Does it give you hope that you, like the fledgling, may encounter ones willing to bring you into the fold? Are you glad that they have won and I have lost?

Well, consider this: were my actions only about punishing Callisto and Constantine? Was it only for the sake of revenge that I chained them to those walls? Or is there more to me? Were my motive's - unlike yours - more profound than satisfying my own desires? I understand this is a difficult concept for you to grasp; after all, your culture teaches you that everything is about *you*, but think, if I erase my parents from existence, whom do I save?

Myself?

Think again.

Who is the real beneficiary of my actions?

That's right, mortal.

You.

Consider how many lives I will have saved over the years to come. Think of how many people I will have kept from the misery of this existence. My actions were not for me; they were for you! For your children, and all the generations to come after them. But, typically, one of you couldn't resist temptation and so, the Shroudeaters continue. Yet, I have not given up the quest to eradicate them - sorry to disappoint you - and the reason for this lies, surprisingly, with one of you. Her name is Lucy, and she is the fledgling's love, or so she believes.

For a mortal, Lucy is remarkably like a Shroudeater. Calculating, ruthless, relentless; she has been trying to manipulate me into setting her free since she regain consciousness in the catacombs. Likewise, far from being afraid, the girl is a born survivor, ever alert for a chance to save her own skin and, although I should have dispatched her immediately, I am somewhat pleased that I haven't had cause to kill her, yet.

It's not just that the girl provides me with leverage for controlling the fledgling but, in some strange way, she reminds me of Didier as they share the same fierce loyalty and assuredness. Like Didier, Lucy believes she is following the correct path, and she is dogged in her insistence that her love for the fledgling is real (she becomes quite sulky when I argue otherwise). Accompanying this insistence is an absolute belief - established once I'd convinced her that he hadn't fallen victim to my rapacious appetites - that the fledgling is coming to rescue her from my evil clutches (her terms, not mine). I have not yet decided whether to tell her that her sweetheart has abandoned her for an existence that she cannot share, although I am sorely tempted whenever she prattles on about marrying Christian, and their future children, and her dream house in some place called Ascot. Blah, blah, blah.

Such vapid aspirations are common to you mortals; it's the 'happily-ever-after' fantasy sold by Hollywood and fifteen dollar romance novels: a bed mate, some offspring, and a cave to dwell in; how far you have advanced. In one such as Lucy, this limited vision would be a travesty - a tiny stage for a tiny life - but she does aspire to greater things and to make, as the cliché goes, a difference, and it is for this that I have come to, shall we say, appreciate her.

Of course, she is young and, therefore, brimming with self-importance and a grandiose idea of just how much she can achieve in her lifetime, but I can't hold that against her; who wasn't exuberant in their youth? And, with enough time and experience, who knows, her enthusiasm could well develop into a mature force for action that may see her bring at least some of her aspiration to fruition.

The problem with this scenario, however, is the fledgling.

I don't presume to know Christian - and I freely admit that his decision to be birthed surprised me - but I do know what it looks like when a man is in love with a woman. Didier was in love with me and, although it still stings to admit, he was also in love with Geneviève. I'm not sure what Christian feels for Lucy, but I wouldn't call it love, which is the only thing that might protect Lucy when the fledgling comes for her. And he will come, out of loneliness, or nostalgia, or to alleviate the horror of the abyss of millennia lying before him, and what then for Lucy? Of course, he will have to convince our parents to bring her into the kinship of the Shroudeaters, but when have Callisto and Constantine ever considered any creature other than themselves?

No, I will not allow them to turn Lucy into an abomination. I would rather kill her myself. But she need not die, as long as I can remove the threat posed by the fledgling and our parents. Indeed, no human - not even you, my fan girls 'n' boys - need ever again fall victim to, or follow in the footsteps of, the Shroudeaters.

This pestilence will end with me.

Lessons from the Last Desert

I learn some things about being a vampire in the human world on the short walk from Rue de Sofia to the metro station. People stop in the street as I approach them, staring at me with wide eyes that follow as I pass. Sometimes they sigh, or make some soft-spoken comment, full of admiration or longing: their loneliness on display. I imagine this is what movie stars experience when they're out in public.

What they don't experience are the more sensitive humans who turn away when they see me; like the mother who hides the face of her young daughter in her skirt and closes her eyes until I turn onto Boulevard de la Chapelle.

What do you see? I wonder, descending into the metro: An angel? A devil? Maybe it's the dirt on my face and the new clothes that confuses them. *I can fix that*, I think, pushing open the door to the nearest men's room. In the mirror, I see— me, but not me.

All the vampire stories I've read or watched screwed up on the reflection thing, just as Juliana said. I see myself: matted blonde hair; smears of dirt on my cheek; stubble on my chin; straight nose like my father's, and my eyes, looking back at me, still brown, but with flecks of gold. I see my mouth: full lips, dark as raspberries; crusted blood in the corner. Inside: canines, longer, the colour of ivory.

I strip off to the waist, turn on the tap, cup my hands under the water, deluge my head and face with water, scrubbing away the filth. When the water runs clean in the sink, I use Romeo's jacket as a towel. With the dirt gone, I see the other changes. My skin is a pearl: milky, smooth, unblemished. No more scars from cutting; no heart for Lucy carved into my chest; no tattoo wrapped around my bicep.

I shiver and grab my shirt, pulling it over my head as the door opens.

A businessman strides in, eyes sweeping the room; they touch me, move on. I keep my head down, focusing on washing the blood from under my nails. His piss hits the urinal and I gag at the stink. I look at him in the mirror, and that's when he *sees* me.

He stares at me for a dozen seconds. That mightn't seem like a long time but it's an eternity when you can read the thoughts behind someone's eyes. I grab my stuff, and turn for the door.

'Wait.'

Fuck, I don't need this.

'Are you—?'

Is he really going to ask the question? And what do I say if he does? *Yeah, man, I'm a vampire. What of it?*

'—looking for a good time?'

For a second, I don't know whether to laugh or snarl at him. In the end, I see him for what he is -

miserably human. 'Jesus, mate, get a fucking life,' I tell him and walk out the door.

I can't stand the way the humans stare at me: Adulation. Accusation. Why can't they be as blind to me as they are to themselves?

At the junction of three metro passageways, a vendor of useless plastic crap is packing up his shop. Tinny carnival music, more depressing than cheerful, jangles out of cheap speakers. The man has some Zhu Zhu pets playing in a pen, having the time of their robotic lives. The Parisian commuters ignore the vendor and his wares; only the tourists stop to marvel.

Idiots.

On one of his stands is a range of 'I ♥ Paris' caps. I grab one as I pass, pull it over my head, and keep moving, hoping he's too involved with the tourists to notice, but the guy's a professional hawker and his eyes are everywhere.

'Hey you!'

Choice: Bail and hope he doesn't give chase, or confront him and hope he backs off.

I turn.

The tourists are staring and the commuters flick nervous glances our way as they hurry on; they've got trains to catch and don't have time for trouble. I get up in his face, quick, before he can say anything more and I focus on one thought.

'Sorry monsieur,' he says, his eyes locked to mine. 'Take it, take it. A gift. A gift for you.'

'Merci beaucoup, monsieur,' I reply, cutting off his babble.

I stroll away, natural as hell. Behind me, the vendor is spruiking his goods again and the tourists are laughing at his antics, but it sounds a little forced. I pick up the pace, wanting to put a train and half a dozen stations between them and me. Moving with the flow of humans, cap pulled low, jacket collar up, I find some anonymity in the crowd until I come to the next obstacle.

Turnstiles.

Great.

Such a simple, every day, thing and all I can do is stand and look at the gateway stupidly. There was money in my old clothes, which are now hidden in a dark corner of the crawlspace above the boutique on Rue de Sofia. I tug on the corner of Romeo's jacket.

This is ridiculous, I'm a vampire, for Christ sake, I think, watching the human tide flow: ticket in; green light; ticket out. Unfortunately, I don't think my newfound powers of persuasion will work on the ticketing machine.

I become aware of the feeling of being watched. Above the turnstile is a camera. A scene from a hundred movies flashes into my mind: a red light blinks, the camera lens opens, zooms in on my face; in a cement room somewhere, a thug gives the order to take me out.

Movies: the opiate of the masses.

I make a show of searching through the jacket. The two outside pockets are empty, but the inside pocket contains a condom - *guess Romeo wasn't a complete idiot* - a packet of gum, and a twenty euro note.

Romeo fucking rocks.

The ticket machine eats the money and spits out my change. The camera follows me as I pass through the turnstile. I'm tempted to shoot them the finger, but why bother. They're just humans and I've got more pressing business.

The train ride is torture.

Humans press against me, their bodies warm, fragrant, pulsing. The Thirst is inside me again, not beyond my control, but building like a firestorm. We're standing shoulder to shoulder; the Friday night revellers and me. Party girls dressed in low-cut, short sparkly dresses, smiling and flirty; slick boys in their t-shirts and tight jeans, pretending nonchalance; whispering lovers bathed in the scent of recent sex. Their mouths contort; their breath comes in puffs of sweetness; sweat seeps from their skin masked by expensive perfumes.

They're psychedelic. Vivid. Delicious. Addictive.

A woman, dark hair swept up to show off her long, graceful neck, smiles at me. I smile in return and wonder how her blood would taste. The Thirst savages me as the train pulls into the station. I have to get out.

The instant the doors open, I jump from the carriage. Keep moving, running up the stairs, out of the metro, into the night where there are fewer humans. Plunging down narrow streets, I wonder how I'm going to stop myself becoming monstrous in a world saturated with humans. I run faster, trying to leave behind the questions, but they keep coming, each one more damning than the last:

How do I stop people from losing *their* humanity and becoming nothing more than a food source? How can I face an eternity with all those deaths lined up ahead of me? I'm already plagued by guilt over the lives I've taken; how will I be in fifty years, or a hundred, or a thousand? The Thirst can't be denied; Juliana and my makers said so, but there must be a way to lessen the burden. I think of Sisyphus. Can I find peace with what I am and the lives I must take?

I race through the park at République, cross the road beside the monument, and come to a stop outside the circle of light thrown by a carousel. The ride is filled with lovers of all ages; awkward teenagers in love for the first time, elderly couples, holding hands and smiling at each other. How can I kill these people? I back away from the carousel and turn towards the monument in the centre of the intersection, ready to start running from the inevitable.

An old man is sitting on the monument steps, watching the traffic. In his hand is a document that he occasionally turns into the street lamps, reading a few lines, before turning his attention back to the cars. I watch him from the tree line, noting the slump of his shoulders and the sad tilt of his head. Curious, I cross the street. He looks up as I approach, a nod his response to my raised hand.

'Mind if I sit?' I ask.

'It's a free country.'

'The traffic gets crazier every day,' I say.

'Oui, but it is interesting to watch.'

As he speaks, a Peugeot darts across the traffic, drawing a chorus of horns and abuse as it disappears down a side street. I look down at his hand and see the document he's holding is a letter. He sees what I'm looking at and waves the letter in front of him.

'From my sister, in Prague.'

'I'm sorry, monsieur, I didn't mean to stare. It's just strange to see a real letter, you know, when we have email and stuff.'

'Technology isn't everything,' he says, settling more comfortably on the stone step. He shuffles the pages of the letter back to the beginning and points to the date: 21st August 1943. 'My sister has been dead for ten years. She sent me this letter during the war and I received it just today.'

'Amazing.'

He shrugs his narrow shoulders. 'Perhaps for some. For me, it's a reminder of how alone I am in this world. She was my last relative and since she passed, I have been waiting for God to call me home, but it seems he is not ready for the likes of Jacques Gravois.'

I study him and it occurs to me that a solution to my earlier questions has arrived in the form of this old man. Leaning close, I say, 'It doesn't have to be this way, Jacques. I could help you, if you want.'

He pulls away and gives me an assessing look, tilting his head to look under the brim of my cap. What he sees doesn't please him. He stands, his face wary as he folds the letter, tucking it away in his breast pocket. 'No monsieur, whatever you're offering, I'm not buying. The days may be long and the nights interminable, but the Lord will take me in his own time.'

I nod. 'If that's your choice, Jacques.'

'It is,' he says, stepping off the monument. 'Adieu, and good luck to you.' He shuffles away as quickly as he can. I feel his apprehension and expect him to check over his shoulder, but he keeps moving, braving the traffic rather than waiting for the red light, to be away from me.

Standing, I walk around the monument; a commemoration of France's third republic and its ideals: *Liberty, Equality, Fraternity.* Above the monument is a statue of a woman. In one hand, she holds a tablet inscribed with words, in the other, an olive branch. Over her shoulder rests a sword. I look into her face and wonder if her sculptors, or the citizens of the Republic, considered the irony of these three symbols: Freedom and peace, preserved by violence.

Oh yeah. There's a worthy credo by which to live, and die.

My cynicism amuses me as I look across the Place de République, searching for Jacques, but he's gone safely into the night. Leaving the monument, I cross the road into Rue du Temple, moving fast, aware of the press of time; Juliana won't be at *Shakespeare's* for much longer. The Thirst is building too, and I know I'll have to detour to hunt.

I turn into the park on Rue Perrée, wondering if the Republic's credo can serve me. I have to kill, but maybe I can do so by bringing peace and freedom to those who want it. *Maybe,* I think, as I slip between the trees, looking for a victim, this one yielding.

Witches Brew

Shakespeare's is closed.

I can see that as I move out of the shadow of Notre Dame and cross the river. The shop is lit up inside, soft yellow light spilling over the abundance of books. So many words; too many to read in a human lifetime.

Lucky me, to be a vampire.

No one moves downstairs, and the windows on the upper floors are dark, shuttered. If there are writers-in-residence shacking up at the bookshop, they're not burning the midnight oil. What would Hemingway and Joyce say about their obvious lack of commitment to their art? Nothing, probably.

Juliana is nowhere to be seen, and I spit out a curse, wondering how the hell I'll find Lucy now.

I hurry over the cobblestones, past the Wallace drinking fountain, where a memory thumps me in the stomach: Lucy and her aunt Marguerite standing beside the green fountain, arms linked, heads tilted, smiling; a photo op. How gorgeous Lucy was that day. How royally I've fucked up, again, hunting instead of coming straight here to meet Juliana.

Walking over to the front door, hoping Juliana has left some clue of where to find her, I cup my hands to the window. Books overflow from the shelves, taking up space on chairs, blocking the steps, poking out from under tables and bench seats. Here and there, sketches and paintings cover the spaces where the books have yet to invade. At the second entrance to the shop, the story is the same - no sign of Juliana.

I slump down on the bench under the window, wondering what to do. It's close to midnight and there are plenty of humans on the streets, but I don't need them; the Thirst is sated by the blood of my last two victims, each who'd answered 'yes' when I posed my question. What I do need is to find Lucy and, with Juliana gone, there's only one option I can think of, although I didn't want to involve them.

Callisto said to meet at L'Hôtel, which is only a few blocks away. I don't know what time they'll be there; hopefully before the dawn and with enough hours for them to get some sense of where their daughter has gone. I sigh, knowing I'll have to persuade them to help me, especially Constantine, but they're my only chance of finding Lucy.

The bells of Notre Dame toll the hour and I look up— into the eyes of Juliana.

She's perched on the wooden seat that rings the tree across from me. Her back is against the trunk, elbows resting on her knees, hands dangling between her calves. Her hair is in a ponytail, hanging over her shoulder. She seems relaxed, and there's a playful expression on her face.

'Did you think I'd go without saying goodbye, Christian?'

I'm not in the mood to play. 'Where's Lucy?'

Juliana rocks forward, her booted feet touching the ground without a sound as she strolls over to me. The way she moves is like the wind: she's gentle on the world but she penetrates everywhere; there's no resisting her. She leans over me, fills up my vision, and I sense her violent potential; at any moment, she could become a hurricane, sweeping me up, tearing me apart, scattering me across the cobblestones, into the night.

Except, I'm stronger now than when I was born; stronger than when I took her gift at Sacré Coeur. Not as strong as her, true, but strong enough to resist, to defend, and growing stronger.

Juliana steps away, but not before I catch the streaks of ruby that flash across her eyes. She knows my strength, I realise, and it pisses her off. 'We should have a conversation,' she says, looking along the street. I take the opportunity to stand. We're centimetres apart. I can smell the blood on her, faint like a whiff of the sea; salty, tasty, tempting. Juliana turns her eyes to mine, licks her pink lips. 'Coffee?'

'What?'

She slips her arm through mine and walks, dragging me along whether I want to go with her or not. 'You know, café au lait, or are you an espresso kind of guy?'

Beside the bookshop is a restaurant, *Le Petit Châtelet*. A few late night couples occupy the tables outside, finishing bottles of wine or drinking digestifs. They touch hands across red-checked tablecloths and gaze into knowing eyes, whispering and laughing in half tones as though they're already naked.

The mood changes as Juliana and I stride between the tables; they stare at us, forgetting each other. Their conversations begin again as we enter the restaurant, but hesitantly. The romance is broken.

A waiter glides out of the dimness, his annoyance evident in the way he grips the menu. He follows us to a table with a window that opens onto the street, which Juliana chooses without consulting him. The waiter says nothing, but I sense his displeasure deepening. He shoves the menu at Juliana, who turns her eyes on him. For a moment, he's still; caught in the hunter's snare and knowing it. Juliana smiles, flashing her teeth. His bottom lip trembles as she takes the menu from him. 'What would you like, Christian?' she asks, flipping through the pages.

'What?'

I've devolved to the level of moronic repetition, but I can't help it; the situation is too damn weird. I can't get my head around being in a restaurant, ordering coffee, as though we're regular humans out for the night, instead of vampires who've both killed and drunk the blood of our victims in some dark back street.

Juliana winks at the waiter. 'Don't mind my friend. He's had a challenging night.' She glances over the list of drinks on the menu and clicks her tongue. 'Yes, I think we'll have two Witches, merci beaucoup, monsieur.'

The waiter's shoulders stoop with relief as she dismisses him with our order. I watch him scurry over to the bar and wonder if he'll be the one to bring the drinks to our table.

'Now isn't this civilised,' Juliana says. She holds up a finger as I open my mouth to respond, 'Don't say "what" again,' she warns with a laugh. At the bar, the waiter flinches as though something hideous has brushed past his ear and dashes into the kitchen.

'Philippe,' the barman calls after him, followed by a stream of abuse.

'Sensitive soul, that one,' Juliana says, smoothing her hair and looking out the window as the barman delivers the drinks to our table.

'Pardon Phillippe, madam and monsieur, he's has had a long shift.'

Juliana's attention remains fixed outside, leaving me to respond to the barman. I send him away with an assurance and five Euros for his trouble, and then I turn to Juliana. 'What is this?'

'Witch's coffee,' she says, picking up the spoon from the saucer and laying it aside. 'Have you tried it before? It's made with Strega. Delicious. It was what we drank when I was human. But don't use the spoon, only a barbarian would mix the coffee and cream.' She lifts the glass to her mouth and draws a breath.

'Are you going to drink that?' I ask; the possibility stuns me.

She lowers the glass, places it on the saucer, takes the spoon, drops it into the coffee, and slowly stirs, turning the elegant, layered liquid into a murky unappealing brown. Pushing the coffee aside, she fixes her gaze on me. 'I miss the little civilities, like smoking a cigarette, or taking high tea, or shopping for shoes, or visiting a library in the middle of the day. I miss the everyday, the ordinary, all the things *they* take for granted.' She turns her head toward the window again. 'Most of all, I miss being anonymous.' Her hand creeps across the table and touches the cuff of my stolen shirt as she looks at me. 'You understand that already, don't you, Christian?'

I think about crossing the city tonight, about the humans I encountered and the way they looked at me. How will I feel after seventy years of their inspection, rejection, desire? How will I feel after an eternity? Will I be as bitter as Juliana?

I look at her beautiful face and catch a glimpse of more than bitterness; sadness lurks beneath the surface too. Is this what really drives her? Will it drive me to reject myself the way Juliana rejects everything vampiric, including herself? I think about Callisto and Constantine, their complete immersion in their vampire-selves. Will I be like them?

'You're too much of an idealist to be like our parents, Christian,' Juliana says, withdrawing her hand, 'and you're not ruthless enough to be like me.'

'That's not polite,' I say, starting up a song to close my mind to her.

Juliana shakes her head. 'You're like an unsecured network, Christian, beaming all those thoughts into the stratosphere. You need to secure that shit, as they say in the movies.' She listens for a second and raises an eyebrow. 'Slipknot? Not my choice, but better than nothing.'

'I'm not an idealist.'

'You're right,' Juliana says, picking up the spoon beside my glass. 'You're worse than an idealist. You're a romantic.' The spoon drops into my coffee, the clang of metal against glass is like an atomic bomb in the quiet restaurant. The barman looks up and I hold his gaze until he looks away.

'We're s'posed to be talking about Lucy,' I say, pushing the glass aside.

Juliana leans back in her chair, her eyes glitter with smugness. 'Hmmm lovely Lucy. A real vixen, that one. What a mouthful she would be.'

My hands clench. 'If you hurt her—'

She raises her eyebrows. 'What, Christian? What would you do?'

I force myself to relax. Now isn't the time to antagonise her. 'Just tell me where Lucy is, that's all I want. I need to get her back to her parents.'

'Really? You don't want to bring her over to the "dark side" so you can spend all of eternity together?'

'No.'

'Don't want to be another Callisto and Constantine?'

'No. I want to take her home.'

She studies me for a few moments, eyes narrowed, assessing. 'How noble of you, Christian.'

I refuse to bite. 'So?'

'You can't have her.'

'Damn it, Juliana,' I say, reaching across the table, but she's quick; the curtain doesn't even move as she leaps through the window. I see her waiting on the street, leaning against a tree, that annoying smirk back on her face. The barman's eyes follow me as I cross the restaurant and open the door; he doesn't look for Juliana.

'Shall we take the evening air,' she says, and strides away before I have the chance to answer. I go after her, keeping pace. We cross the Seine, pass Notre Dame, and head down to Rue de Renard. There is the odd tourist on the street and I feel a twinge of the Thirst at the scent of their blood. Juliana gives me a knowing look, which I ignore.

Ahead is the Centre Pompidou with its inside out architecture glowing against the night. Juliana leaps, effortlessly, onto the ducts that traverse the building. Moving with the nimbleness of a cat, she scales the tubing, heading for the roof. I follow close behind, my feet landing on the roof a second after hers.

We sit above the eastern façade, looking over Paris, and I'm struck silent by the beauty of the city. The Eiffel Tower is a glittering pin, piercing the velvet sky; the Arc de Triomphe, unshakeable, on stone legs; Sacré Coure sitting on its hilltop like a glowing jewel. And all around these iconic monuments, the streets stretch their silver tendrils to the horizon.

When Juliana speaks, her voice is like marble. 'You ruined everything.' I drag my gaze away from the lights to look at her. 'And now, you have to make amends,' she says.

A part of me knows that, vampire or not, I'm in danger; that Juliana is hanging onto her restraint by a handful of cobwebs. But, there's another part me that doesn't give a fuck. I shrug my shoulders. 'You sent me in there.'

Juliana's hands clench into fists. 'Six months without blood. They should have torn you apart.'

'Should've, could've, but they didn't. You underestimated them. Deal with it.'

She glares at me, those streaks of red flaring across her irises. 'I should have broken your neck.'

'Again, you didn't, and here we are.'

Her eyes narrow to ruby-coloured slits as she fights for control; it's obvious she wants to take me out in the worst way, but - lucky for me - there's something she wants even more.

'You want your girlfriend,' she says, standing. I follow her up, knowing she's about to strike a deal. 'I want our parents. You bring them to me; I'll give Lucy to you.'

I stare at her; she looks back, impassive, the anger clearing from her eyes. I shake my head. 'How am I s'posed to do that?'

Juliana touches my arm, soft, mocking. 'You're a resourceful fellow, Christian. You'll think of something.'

I shake my head again. 'They'll never go for it.'

'Then I'll kill Lucy.'

She's standing on the edge of the roof, Paris spread out behind her. A strong breeze, or a well-placed hand, would topple her over the edge. My palms tingle, itching for action.

Step away.

I'm not sure if it's her voice in my head, or my own, but it's good advice and I follow it. Turning away, I walk to the centre of the roof, stop at an air duct, put my forehead against the cold metal, and try to think. Getting Callisto and Constantine to return to the catacombs is about as possible as raising the Titanic, but I'll have to convince them somehow.

'Forget the catacombs.' Juliana's voice drifts down from above me and I realise I've left my mind open to her. I start blocking as I look up. She's sitting on the air duct, feet dangling just above my head. I didn't hear her move. The tingling starts up in my hands again and I shove them in my pockets. 'I'll never return there,' she says.

'Where then?'

'Edinburgh.'

'In Scotland? You're kidding, right?'

'It's where Lucy will be,' she glances at the sky, 'in five hours.'

'Getting Callisto and Constantine to the catacombs would've been hard enough, now you want me to get them to Edinburgh?'

'Compensation is never easy, Christian.'

'But Edinburgh? Come on, give me a break.'

Juliana slides off the air duct and stands close to me. 'Dear, sweet Christian,' she says, her marble fingers brushing against my cheek, 'I have given you a break, in more ways than you realise.'

'Is that so?' I say, standing my ground.

She turns and says over her shoulder, 'Well, you're not chained up in the catacombs, are you?' At the edge of the rooftop, she stops and faces me. 'You have two nights. After that, I will drain Lucy dry.' The wind races up the side of the Pompidou, ruffling her shirt. She spreads her arms and falls backwards, smiling as she disappears into the dark.

To Love is all too Human

I see her from the street, at the window, behind a flutter of curtain. A Shakespearean ghoul; pale, floating, deadly. She doesn't acknowledge me when I raise my hand, although her eyes are on me as I cross the road. When I reach the room, softly knock, enter without being asked, she's still at the window, looking at the night sky.

Dawn is three hours away.

Two assailants do battle over my body: fatigue and the Thirst, which was temporarily appeased by the homeless man I drained on my way to the hotel. I'll have to hunt again before I can rest, but first: Callisto.

The memory of my first victim catches me as I sit down on the edge of the bed. His body is gone, and there is no evidence of the violence I committed to spoil the rich gold and royal blue décor of the room, but I remember the taste of his blood. The Thirst uncoils; I'll have to bring Callisto and Constantine around quickly.

In the living room, a flat-screen TV is tuned to some music video show. The sound is muted. I watch the near naked girl on the screen gyrate against a Ferrari for a few seconds, then reach for the remote control and turn her off. It's not the bare flesh that gets to me; it's the flushed pinkness of her skin, and those red, red lips.

'Tasty,' Callisto says.

'Sure, if you like junk food,' I reply. The joke sounds flat, even to me.

Callisto gives me an appraising look, softened by the concern in her eyes. 'You need to hunt, fledgling,' she says, with a light caress of my cheek.

'Soon. First, we have to talk. Where's Constantine?'

She sighs and crawls onto the bed, making a nest out of the pillows before leaning against the bed head. 'He's gone.'

I shake my head, not because I didn't hear her, but because I don't want it to be true. 'Gone? Where?' I sink my fingers into the eiderdown and clench the material inside my fist.

Callisto raises a pale, smooth shoulder in a half shrug. 'Constantine comes and goes as he pleases. It is our way.'

'So you don't know where he is then?' A hopeless rage fills my bones; I want to smash the room apart. The Thirst burns brighter and there's a taste of ashes in my mouth. I think of Lucy— dead.

'He's in Edinburgh,' Callisto says, flicking on the TV again. A large black man is singing into a 1950s microphone; a diamond chip sparkles every time he open his mouth. Callisto licks her lips. 'I like junk food,' she says, and winks at me.

I'm too stunned to reply for a moment, then the question rushes out. 'How do you know that?'

'Because I was there when the email came.'

'Email? You get email?'

Callisto laughs. 'It is the twenty-first century, fledgling.'

'Yes, I know, but— who'd email you?'

She fakes being offended, and then says, 'Not me, sweetheart.'

I catch up. 'Who the hell would email Constantine?'

Callisto lies down on her stomach, facing the TV, her knees bent, feet swaying as though she can hear the music even though the mute is still on. 'I'm not at liberty to say.'

'Fuck that,' I say before I can stop the words.

She looks at me, eyebrows raised. 'Where have all the gentlemen gone?'

'I'm sorry. I didn't— I just— Look, you've got to tell me who's emailing Constantine and why he's in Edinburgh?'

'Perhaps you should tell me why you need to know so badly?'

'Because Juliana's on her way to Edinburgh.'

She's on her feet and leaning over me, fingers digging into my shoulders before I take my next breath. I feel her trying to get inside my head, but I'm ready for her:

I sing my words
I'm fucked at dealing
with your life's dead bodies everywhere.
You!
Really want me to be a good son, why?
You make me feel like no one.

Callisto narrows her eyes as she tries to hear past Jonathon Davies' growling angst; no chance. She pulls away and looks down at me. 'What do you know, Christian?' she asks.

I could be a smartarse but - despite what Juliana says - time is of the essence. The re-cap I give her is brief and I finish with my own question, 'Why is Constantine in Edinburgh?'

There is an antique chair beside the window: narrow legs, low back, cushioned seat. Callisto swings the chair around and straddles it, her arms resting across the top. 'He's there for a woman.'

'He's cheating on you?'

Exasperation clouds Callisto's face. 'Stop thinking like a human.'

The rebuke stings, but she's right; the old rules and definitions don't apply anymore. 'Okay. Who is she?'

'Her name is Moira. She's the carrier of his human bloodline.'

'Human?'

'Don't look so surprised.'

'But you said you were childhood sweethearts and you married young?'

Callisto takes a moment to think. 'Do you know the work of Màrquez?'

I shake my head and glance through the curtain to the night sky. I feel the pressure of time running out. The Thirst is deepening its grip on me too. 'We have to talk about Edinburgh.'

'*Love in the Time of Cholera*,' Callisto says, touching my knee. I hear the whisper of her song and the Thirst recedes a little. 'And I am speaking of Edinburgh,' she says, standing. She goes to the window to check the sky for herself, and leans against the doorframe. 'Florentino Ariza has a philosophy. He says: "The world is divided into those who screw and those who do not," and he trusts only those who share their love with discreet abandon. Of course, Florentino is a unique man, swimming against the ideological tide that depicts love as black and white: sacred within the bounds of sanctified marriage with anything outside marriage being sinful, taboo. It wasn't so in my human time. Constantine and I, and many of the betrothed we knew, loved each other deeply, and we knew we would spend our lives together, but that didn't mean we stopped loving others.'

'You screwed around?'

'Eloquent as always, fledgling. And yes, we had our lovers. Constantine's was Rachel, a clan woman who, if his path had been different, he may have wed.'

'You weren't jealous that he was with another woman?' I ask.

Callisto laughs. '"One can be in love with several people at the same time, feel the same sorrow with each, and not betray any of them."'

'Màrquez?'

'Ariza.'

'So Constantine got Rachel pregnant?'

Callisto plays with the sheer white curtain, running it between her fingers. 'Yes. And he has watched over the bloodline, generation after generation, ever since.'

'I don't understand. Why would he do that?'

'Won't you watch over your family, Christian?'

The question pulls me up short. I haven't thought about my human parents in any more than abstract ways since Callisto and Constantine birthed me. I'm aware that I love them, but they seem irrelevant to my new existence.

I don't look at Callisto when I respond, 'Of course, but once they're gone—' I leave the rest unsaid.

Callisto returns to the bed and sits, facing me. 'It has always been easier for the child to forget the parent than it is for the parent to forget the child,' she says with no hint of reproach. Still, I feel an edge of impatience - a combination of the Thirst and the will to action - but I force it down.

'There is something you need to understand about being a vampire,' Callisto says. She seems relaxed, but I note the tension around her eyes. 'Every vampire needs their obsession. It's what keeps us grounded when eternity stretches before us.

'Think of it, Christian: year after year, month after month, week after week, day after day; all of those moments winding out into the black abyss of the future. As humans, there is a set timeframe, birth to death. For vampires death is a concept, if that, but we still need a sense of purpose, otherwise we atrophy into stillness. I've seen it happen to the ones who birthed Constantine and me.'

Her eyes grow distant and I feel her pressing at my mind, politely, as though she's knocking on a stranger's door. Then I realise she's opened herself to me so I can see what's in her mind:

Jungle; thick with foliage. Wet, humid, dark.

A hand - hers - pulling away vines.

A face; male, marble white, stained with moss.

Bowls; one flecked with dried blood, one filled with fresh blood.

A second face; female, green lips smeared red.

'After centuries, they went into the deep forest of our land and became effigies, covered in greenery, trapped in a living death.' A sigh brings her back and I'm locked out of her mind again.

'Have they chosen starvation?' I ask.

'No, more like isolation. Although if it wasn't for a few superstitious locals and a daughter who refuses to let them go, perhaps that would be their destiny.' Callisto gazes through the curtains for a moment, and then shakes her head. 'Anyway, we need a purpose. For Constantine, it's maintaining his human line. He watches the carriers of his lineage, protects them from danger, and manipulates their lives so that his seed is carried into the next generation. It's a game, but one he takes seriously.'

'And they know who he is?'

She gives a quick laugh. 'He appears throughout their history, always with a different name and a different role, an eccentric uncle, or a trusted advisor, and always on the periphery of their lives, with them never knowing his true nature.'

'And what about you? What's your purpose?'

'Why, my children, of course.'

'Juliana said we're supposed to be solitary creature, to prevent our existence becoming known to the living?'

'That's true, but we all need some mothering now and then.'

'What about Juliana? What's her obsession?'

Callisto brushes the hair from her face as she weighs up what to tell me. I don't tell her that I already know; that it was obvious from Juliana's blogs. Instead, I wait to see how much I can trust my vampire mother.

'It was Didier, and that's why she's lost her mind,' she says leaving the window. Her footsteps are soundless as she pads through the apartment to the bathroom. The door closes behind her and I hear water splashing in the sink. When she comes out again, her face is moist, but composed.

She doesn't return to the bedroom. There's a lounge opposite the TV, pushed into the corner. Callisto sits, looking at me. 'We tried to warn her not to anchor herself with a human, but she is wilful and wouldn't listen. This is something you must heed, Christian, because I know there is a girl that you care for,' she pauses.

'Lucy.'

'Yes, she's the one. You must let her go, or face Juliana's fate.'

'Which is?'

'Heartbreak, madness, hatred, despair. All these things Juliana has suffered - and inflicted upon her blood kin - because she would not let go of Didier, even when he had found happiness in another.'

'She loved him.'

Callisto gives a soft snort of contempt and says, 'Certainly, but humans die. And to fix your future to something that will pass is foolishness.' Her tone is surprising; it's the closest she's come to expressing anger with Juliana since we escaped her lair beneath the catacombs.

The emotion doesn't last long and her voice is amicable when she continues. 'Juliana was my favourite. Beautiful, feisty, intelligent, passionate. I caught sight of her one evening, as she strolled with Didier along the Rue du Rivioli. Her poise, the haughty angle of her chin, the determination in her stride, these things set her apart from the average Parisian woman of her time - timid little mice that they were back then.

'When I pointed her out to Constantine, he saw these qualities and decided we should bring her into our kinship, but as always, it was I who watched over her in those first hours, helping her through the transition. In the days and weeks that followed, I tried to counsel her in our ways, but she was adamant that she belonged with Didier. Nothing could sway her conviction, not even the war.

'But, like all parents, I knew better. I'd lived longer, had seen more and I understood our world in a way she could not. So, like a good parent, I intervened on her behalf.'

There's an interesting word: *Intervened.* I remember Juliana's first blog: *I am going to kill my parents.* 'Children don't like intervention,' I say, trying to ignore the sudden affinity I feel for Juliana. She has Lucy; that makes her the enemy, and I don't want to empathise with her until I have Lucy back and safe.

'Even if it's warranted?'

My truthful response would be: *Let us make our mistakes and live own our lives,* but I'm curious, so I say, 'Depends. How did you intervene?'

'I tried to get rid of Didier.'

'Pull out the rotten tooth, huh?'

She nods. 'I thought the war would do the job - those SS bastards were ruthless - but he survived. When he turned up after the war, I thought love had succeeded where hatred and violence failed, but Juliana was tenacious in her refusal to give him up. After a few years, I tried a different tactic.'

Callisto falls silent. I wait, seeing that she's struggling with something.

I take a look at the sky and sense sunrise, not too far away. The window of opportunity is slipping shut; in less than an hour, I will have to hunt and sleep. I rub a hand over my face; thinking past the Thirst is getting harder. I need to hurry Callisto along.

As I walk over to the lounge, it occurs to me that the task I need to achieve has been partly accomplished without any effort from me: Constantine is in Edinburgh. I remember Juliana's last words to me on the roof of the Pompidou, and finally understand.

She knew he was there.

Callisto looks at me as I sit on the lounge; her expression is as open as I've seen it so far. 'I love all of my children,' she says quietly. 'They are my anchor against eternity, and I have never wished or wanted ill for any of them. But Juliana crossed the line when she killed Patria. I lost two daughters that night.'

'Patria?'

She nods. 'I nurtured her through the transition, and then took her to Didier's house for her first hunt. She was supposed to kill them all, but Juliana found her.'

'And executed her.'

Callisto hangs her head, letting her hair veil her face. 'I wanted to protect Juliana from the inevitable despair of loving a human.'

Her words ring in my head: I love a human— in my own way.

Callisto reaches for me, her hard fingers crushing my wrist, though - I note with some surprise - with little pain. 'What will keep you grounded, my child? It cannot be Lucy.'

I ease out of her grasp. 'Don't worry. I intend to get Lucy away from Juliana and take her home to her family. That's all.'

'Do I have your word?'

'For what it's worth, sure. You have my word.'

'And to anchor yourself?'

I turn towards the TV. A music clip set in a war zone flashes images of death and destruction across the screen, and I say impulsively, 'I was considering world domination.'

Callisto laughs, and I feel the tension break. 'You may need something a little more concrete to anchor you, fledgling. Perhaps, after you've hunted, you'll feel a little less grandiose.' She stands, stretches, looks at me. 'Shall we?'

I sit still on the edge of the lounge, letting the violent images wash across my vision. I'm a little surprised by the idea of world domination, but I don't think it's grandiose. Maybe I've watched to many vampire movies - which always end badly for the bloodsuckers - but now that I am one, and I know the truths and fallacies (or at least, I'm learning them), why wouldn't we run the show?

I shove the thought out of my head. *Focus on the problem at hand*, I remind myself. 'Juliana is after Constantine,' I say, standing beside Callisto.

To her credit, she barely flinches. 'How do you know?'

'She told me as much, but I didn't realise at the time. It makes sense now.'

'You can't be sure,' Callisto says.

'She knows about Constantine's lineage, doesn't she?'

'Yes.'

'The email from Moira was from Juliana. It's a trap, don't you see?'

'No, he wouldn't fall—'

'He would if she threatened his bloodline.'

Callisto shakes her head, her eyes filled with anger, fear and, finally, acceptance. 'Dawn is three quarters of an hour away,' she says, picking up the house phone.

'Hunt, and return as quickly as you can. We will rest here for the day and be in Edinburgh by mid-evening.'

I take the quickest route to the road: through the window and down the façade of the building as the Thirst fills my body with its fire. I find three victims close by, huddled inside their government-issued tent. They die, unwillingly, with my fangs in their throat and my song rushing through their heads.

It's the best death I can give them, under the circumstances.

Blog Fifteen

Farwell to the Vampire City

'In my humble opinion, humans should never allow themselves to be caught by sentimental reminiscence - your life is too short to waste dwelling in the past.' This was what I said to Lucy this evening when she started her usual pleading to be reunited with the fledgling.

'In my humble opinion, you should see a fucking therapist about your stupid vampire bullshit,' was Lucy's petulant response.

If it had been any other mortal - one of you, for instance, my faithful blog-junkies - who had uttered these words, I would have torn their tongue from their mouth and left them bleeding, but Lucy was having a tough night. She was still groggy from the cocktail of barbiturates I fed her before bringing her to this hotel and frustrated by her fourth night of captivity. Poor petal, she is typical of your kind: never satisfied with what you have; always yearning for what is out of reach.

I guess delivering the news of Christian's conversion didn't help her mood any either, but what else could I do? She had to know, and I did try to be sensitive. Still, it can't be easy to learn that your boyfriend has abandoned you to become one of the undead.

Of course, she didn't believe me, but that doesn't change the facts and she *needs* to face reality, or risk losing her sanity when she sees Christian again, which is the other reason for Lucy's sullenness; we are leaving Paris in a few hours. The tantrum she threw when I told her was spectacular and brought a visit from the hotel manager. At his knock on the door, Lucy drew a breath to scream and, for the first time since I'd woken her in the catacombs, I gripped her by the throat, fangs bared, and whispered a warning. She promptly fainted, which solved one problem, and I was able to sweet talk the manager; crisis averted.

Tell me, mortal, why must your kind be *so* melodramatic?

It seems Lucy really believed I was faking my vampirism because when she came around, she refused to look at me, or speak. I didn't take offense as I understood where she was at; I could see the thoughts on her face as she stared at the wall: *If she's a real vampire, what does that make Christian?* Eventually, she returned her gaze to me and I saw that some of her natural cunning and boldness had returned, which was pleasing to see and validated my decision to protect her from my kin.

'Are you going to kill me?' she asked. As tiresome as this question is to me, I knew she would asked it - funny how when faced with the potential of *actual* death, you humans always choose life. I assured her that I needed her alive and she thought some more. 'Is Christian really like you?' I nodded. She stared at the floor for a while. 'I want to see my Aunt Marguerite,' she said, raising her eyes to challenge me.

Such audacity!

Of course, I refused and, undaunted, she immediately employed all of her charm to try to get me to do what she wanted. Like she had a chance. Yet, the strange thing was, with each argument she presented, I *did* feel myself leaning more towards agreeing with her and, again, I was reminded of Didier.

'Have you thought about a career in law?' I asked when I'd heard enough. A calculating look crossed Lucy's face as she assessed my comment then she took a breath and prepared to launch another argument, apparently thinking I wasn't quite there yet. I held up my hand. 'I won't let you see your aunt, but I will take a message to her.'

Now, don't get all choked up, mortal. You know I'm not that soft, or that generous. I only agreed because I needed to sate the Thirst, and because I wanted to visit with Didier before we left Paris.

Disappointment clouded Lucy's eyes and I realised she had harboured some fanciful notion of escape. I made sure to destroy that hope by placing a bottle of pills on the table next to a pad of hotel stationary.

Lucy's expression turned scornful as she looked at the paper. 'What exactly am I supposed to do with that?' she asked. In reply, I took a pen from the bedside table and held it out to her. She raised her eyebrows.

'This isn't the dark ages, you know. Where's my phone?'

'In my pocket,' I replied, tapping the stationary.

She ignored the gesture and held out her hand. 'Can I have it?'

How wonderfully insolent she is! I thought, letting the urge to slap her hand away pass; she was too feisty to cripple in that way. 'No phone,' I said, lifting the pill bottle and popping the lid, 'but you can have two of these and ten minutes to write 'til your heart's content. How does that sound?'

Lucy scowled at the purple tablets. 'You suck.'

'You better believe it.' I took a bottle of water from the bar fridge, placed it beside the pills, and gave her a nod. 'We don't have all night.' Lucy reached for the pen and I placed a finger against her wrist. 'Pills first.'

She glared at me. 'Whatever.'

I wish you could have seen her right then, mortal, bristling with defiance as she swiped up the tablets and shoved them in her mouth. How she made me want to laugh, for she epitomised the very essence of what it means to be human: that haughty pretence of confidence you all wear, which barely conceals the truth of your vulnerability. *I am not afraid*, her gesture said, yet I could smell the fear coming off her, rich and ripe. She was terrified: of what the pills would do; of what I would do once they had done their work; of dying. But she would not admit this fear, nor would she examine the abyss of fragility over which her life is suspended.

None of you has the courage to do that, except perhaps in the moment before you fall.

This is the reason so many of you continue with your inane solicitation of me, begging for my 'gift' as though you are Mina and I, the Count. After all I've shared in these pages, you still believe you would prefer the monstrosity of un-life rather than face the abyss and accept that this - *this* - is the gift that will set you free to live.

Perhaps I will have more luck convincing Lucy.

When the note was done and the pills had taken hold, I left Lucy sleeping. Though she didn't know it, her aunt lived only a few blocks from the hotel, in the same direction as the Cemetiére d'Auteuli. On the way over, I read the note - Oh please, as if privacy is an issue for a vampire - expecting some blatant plea for help. But, no:

> Dear Aunty M,
>
> Please forgive my sudden absence and accept my apology for any worry I've caused you over the last few days. Christian and I are having some issues, which we're trying to sort out. Hopefully this beautiful city will help us find each other again.
>
> I'm sorry to ask but, please don't tell Daddy and Mother what's going on. The last thing I need is for them to be anywhere near us; you know how they are. If they do get in touch, just tell them we've gone vagabonding for a while -

Daddy will understand that; he always was a hippie at heart, despite the suit. And please tell them that I love them and always will.

Thanks, Aunty. I hope you and Kate sorted out that stuff about the wine. Life's too short for arguing over the small things, and you two are so cute together! I love you both. See you soon, Lucy.

How sweet. How hopeful. How very, very human. Wouldn't you agree, mortal?

I read the note again as I stood outside the aunt's apartment building, and then looked up to the third floor where she lived. Could I really be bothered? What did I care if Lucy's family were beside themselves with worry for her? How was that my problem? A pang of annoyance pushed through me. The feeling wasn't surprising. I knew where it came from; Lucy had people whom she cared for, and who cared for her in return. I had no one. There it was, pure and simple; envy. One of the seven deadly sins, and how does one deal with a deadly sin?

Atonement; what else?

I made the leap to the third floor balcony and gently forced the window. The Thirst heightened my senses, bringing the colours and scents of the apartment into sharper relief. They liked to cook, these women; spices lingered on the air along with the faintly floral bouquet of a good pinot noir. Beneath these more pleasant aromas was the pungent odour of stale cigarette smoke; it leached from the furniture and drifted from the rugs in a toxic mist. I wandered through the apartment, noting the black and white photos on the walls - Lucy's aunt had a flair for the dramatic - and the paintings, mostly contemporary abstracts but, here and there, a copy (I assumed) of works from the masters: a Manet, an Ingres, and a Matisse or two.

In the hallway, books spilled from the shelves of an overflowing case, forcing me to step over Foucault and Derridra, while my eye was caught by Sartre and Camus, sparking memories of the war. I lifted my eyes higher, refusing to entertain such thoughts, and saw Simone de Beauvoir's *Tous les Hommes Sont Mortels*. I almost laughed aloud at the irony of finding the novel, here, now. How well Raimon Fosca and I would get on; two immortals who share the same outlook on this meaningless existence.

More than the philosophers, it was the inclusion of this work in the aunt's collection that decided the fate of the women I found asleep, curled together like nestled commas, in the main bedroom. I stood over them and watched them breathing, the Thirst torrid inside me, demanding as always when warm-blooded humans were within reach. But I could not kill them, these fine, intelligent women whom Lucy would need, if she survived the ordeal ahead.

I made my way to the front door - resisting the urge to steal de Beauvoir's novel as I passed the bookcase - and placed the note on the floor, angled to make it look as though someone had pushed it under the gap. When I was satisfied with its authenticity, I retraced my step through the living room where I stole a small golden brooch decorated with diamantes that was lying on the coffee table. It was not that I liked the gaudy piece, but it would prove to Lucy that I had delivered on my promise and, most importantly, that she could trust me.

I know what you're thinking; why should it matter if she trusts me? Who cares? I'm a vampire, she's a mortal - I can manipulate her mind and get her to do whatever I want, but I was (surprise, surprise) thinking long term. If I was going to watch over another human life, I didn't want to spend those years entirely on the periphery and alone. I'd done that with Didier and this time, I wanted something more.

These thoughts swirled through my mind as I crossed the city to the cemetery, where I laid out my plans to Didier. He, naturally, was silent, but as I spoke my ideas aloud, they grew more plausible and led me to the obvious question: Why couldn't I have a mortal as a friend? The truth is, I can. I'm a Shroudeater. I can have whatever I want.

Buoyed by the promise of the friendship to come, I killed swiftly, taking the blood of two vagrants and a lost Sudanese exchange student, singing them out of this world with as much kindness as I could muster. All the while, I thought of Lucy and the life that she may lead, and the conversations we would have over the length of her days.

Before I go any further, let me stop you right here, mortal, so I can make myself clear—

I don't want to be *your* friend, so don't bother filling the comments with your inane pleas and offers. You are not Lucy, and I don't need a 'back-up' friend, and even if Lucy dies, I *still* won't want to be your friend. So don't ask, ever. Got it?

Right, let's go on then—

I dropped into the alleyway behind the hotel where I'd left Lucy and froze: there was a Shroudeater nearby. Shocked to find one of my kin so close to my prize, I slipped into the shadowed enclave of a doorway and sent my senses out in an urgent search of the streets. It wasn't hard to find him; the Thirst pulsated from him like a beacon. He was hunting in a park, three blocks over and, as I pressed my senses around him, I felt something familiar, though I couldn't put my finger on what.

His thoughts were chaotic, tumbling like snow, and he made no effort to conceal them. *Was he a fledgling?* I wondered, and immediately dismissed the idea. He had none of the desperation of the newly birthed. I reached out again, probing, and realised - too late - my mistake. The Thirst receded from him along with the chaos in his mind, not because he was taking blood, but because he wanted me to see: Red Square; the tunnels beneath Mayakovskaya; the gypsy woman from the Grand-Place, drained, dead.

It was him: the Other.

I dragged my senses away and took a half a dozen steps to go after him when I thought of Lucy, alone and unconscious in the room above. *Had he already gotten to her?* A dead weight dropped through my body. Racing to the back entrance to the hotel, I ripped open the service door and, ignoring the ancient elevator, I tore up the stairs, leaping the risers five, six at a time until I reached the attic room. The door was closed, but that meant nothing; vampires rarely entered a room the conventional way. I fumbled with the key, fighting the urge to smash the lock, and eventually heard the tumblers fall.

Nothing was out of place in the room. Even Lucy was right where I'd left her, lying on her side, with a blanket covering her to the waist. The window was closed and locked. I returned to Lucy, knelt beside her and lifted her hair. Her neck was unmarked. I turned each of her wrists and checked in the crook of her elbows; no wounds. I lifted the blanket, slowly; her low-slung jeans were fastened. A rush of relief washed over me as I smoothed the bedding and stood, watching over her.

Although I desperately wanted to, I dared not send my senses in search of the Shroudeater in the park. Not even to check his whereabouts. I glanced at the window, feeling oddly nervous. Perhaps his being so close was a coincidence and, if that was so, I didn't want to lead him any closer to this room. On the other hand, I've never been a believer in coincidence, which suggested that he knew Lucy and I were sequestered in the hotel. The question was how? And why was he in Paris after all these years? And, more importantly, why had he exposed himself now? I crossed to the window and gazed at the street below, scrutinising the shadows, as the questions ran in circles through my mind.

'Who are you?' I asked the empty street.

Behind me, Lucy snuffled in her drug-induced sleep, reminding me that there were more pressing matters to which I had to attend. There was a chartered plane waiting for us at Charles de Gaulle airport, which was scheduled to depart in an hour. I picked up the phone and asked the concierge to organise a taxi. Soon Lucy and I would be eight hundred kilometres away from the Shroudeater haunting my city, and Lucy would be safe until my business with Callisto and Constantine was done. Then we would return to Paris so I could deal with this 'Other', once and for all.

Don't shake your head, mortal. It's not as though we are talking about some exotic animal here, like all the ones your kind have wiped off the face of the planet. This is not a Javan tiger, or Laughing Owl. This is a vampire who would kill you on a whim, without a thought for your future, or your dreams, or your desires. Be glad I'm going to destroy him, for I am providing you with a better chance to live and, for that, you should be grateful.

Monuments to the Dead

Cold wind buffets the taxi. Rain spits against the window. The driver curses the slow moving traffic in an indecipherable brogue. 'Welcome to Scotland,' Callisto mutters, her mood as sour as the weather.

She's irritated by a delay in our departure from Paris, which has put us twenty-four hours behind Juliana. While I understand she's worried about Constantine, her irritation annoys the crap out of me; she's not the one with a two-night deadline, after all. But, mostly what gets to me is that she won't explain why the delay occurred in the first place. When I asked her what the holdup was, she scowled and said, 'There are things beyond your comprehension, fledgling.'

Well, yeah, if you don't bother to explain, I wanted to say, but let it pass.

The driver looks in the rear view mirror and rumbles something at Callisto, his voice sounding like it's coming from the centre of a thundercloud. She nods and offers him a faint smile. 'Indeed.' His eyes slide across to me and I follow Callisto's lead, smiling and nodding. He slaps the steering wheel and tosses another incomprehensible sentence over his shoulder, followed by a barrelling laugh.

'What did he say?' I ask, taking in the buildings of Edinburgh's outer suburbs as we inch forward: phone shops, bottle shops, coffee shops, sex shops, abandoned shops, graffitied shops. I'm reminded of Paris; I'm reminded of home. *Photocopied cities,* I think, and wonder if every place humans congregate will look the same?

'Only the dead appreciate Edinburgh in the Spring,' Callisto says.

'Pardon?'

'That's what he said,' Callisto replies. She's also watching the city slip past, but it's not the view that has her attention. She's searching for Constantine.

'Can you sense him, Christian?' she asks, the irritation in her voice finally breaking.

I search the deepening twilight, but find nothing other than the hum of humanity. If Juliana has Constantine, she's keeping him well hidden. 'He's here somewhere,' I say, but Callisto doesn't respond; she is concentrating on finding her lover.

Turning to my side of the taxi, I catch sight of a sign: Haymarket. I press closer to the window. The taxi driver, misreading my interest, decides it's time for a guided tour. He points out various landmarks as we crawl along, becoming more animated when we pass a pub where he and his mates get up to their 'shenanigans'. It's the only word I understand and I nod, but my mind is on Lucy and Juliana.

What next? I wonder as we reach Princes Street.

Another rumble approximating English comes from the driver as he glances to the right, flicking his thumb towards the window. Callisto interprets. 'Edinburgh Castle,' she says, sliding across the seat. We look out together; on top of a craggy hill lit with orange lights is the old seat of Scottish power turned tourist attraction.

'A possibility?' I ask.

Callisto shakes her head. 'Juliana has a flair for the dramatic, but the castle is too obvious, and too public.'

'Are there dungeons below ground?'

'Yes, but they wouldn't suit her purposes.'

Before I can question her about where she thinks Juliana might be, I spot something in the distance. I tap the Perspex divider that separates us from the driver and point to a black structure forcing its way into the sky. 'What's that?' I ask.

The driver puffs up his chest. 'The Sir Walter Scott Monument,' he says, as though he'd built the landmark himself.

I hear 'Walter Scott' and say, 'We'll get out here,' responding to a feeling in my gut that says this is the place we should begin. The taxi weaves to the curb and I hand over enough pounds to cover the ride and the driver's commentary. Callisto doesn't move when I open the door. Her eyes are half-closed. She seems to be listening. 'Are you coming?' I ask.

She focuses on me. 'No. There's someone I need to see.' I look at the Scott monument, sensing some opportunity being lost as I grab the door handle.

Callisto holds up her hand. 'I need to go alone, Christian.'

I hesitate: Juliana wants Callisto. Lucy is with Juliana. If I let Callisto go, how will I bring these three women together? I calculate the odds - slim - and yank the door towards me. 'We should stick together.'

The taxi driver turns in his seat, garbles something at Callisto and points at the metre ticking over on the dashboard. She glances at him, a look with enough frost to cut off his complaint mid-sentence. 'I know your concerns, Christian. I won't leave you for long and, when I get back, we'll find Juliana together.'

A worm of suspicion coils through my head and I wonder if this 'someone' has something to do with our delayed departure from Paris. 'Who do you need to see?'

Callisto's expression softens. 'Relax, my child. It's just an old acquaintance who might be able to help us.' She offers a reassuring smile. 'Now, get out of the taxi before I have to sell my soul to pay for this ride.'

I laugh a little at her joke even though something still doesn't feel right about letting her go. 'Okay,' I say, stepping onto the sidewalk and closing the door behind me. Through the window, I see her give instructions to the driver. She waves as he speeds off, weaving into the traffic.

I'm on my own, again.

Despite the rain, Princes Street is alive with activity. A stream of people flow along the sidewalk: gawking tourists, briefcase toting office workers, and gangs of teens. Even with my collar up and my cap down, most of them glance at me. The more sensitive ones, acting on an instinct they can't understand, give me wide berth. I ignore them all and stare at the monument. Orange lights send beams crawling up its black turrets and over jutting gargoyles that spew water from their mouths. The highest gallery catches only a hint of light and seems to shimmer between realities.

A dark-haired girl brushes by, close enough for me to catch the faint scent of roses on her skin. The Thirst flares. I force it down and cross the street. Now is not the time for such distractions. Walking around the base of the monument, I stop to look at the statuettes tucked into niches carved into the stone before taking the steps up to the centre of the monument. Between the peaked arches sits Sir Walter Scott, dog at his feet and book in his hand, looking into the distance. I climb onto his pedestal and rest a hand on his white marble shoulder, trying to see what he sees. Instead, a memory of touching Juliana in the depths of her Parisian lair rises in my mind. I remove my hand and try not to think of my own flesh turning to stone.

I leave Sir Walter watching over Princes Street and head down the steps behind him, into the softly lit gardens. The rain has eased to a drizzle. I stand on the grass and tilt my head to gaze at the topmost turret, high above. Although it's not obvious, there is something here that reeks of Juliana; a psychic residue. She's been here, and recently. *Yes*, I think, *this is a suitably dramatic place for her to continue her game of cat and mouse.* Yet, I also get that this is not where the main game is to take place; like Edinburgh Castle, it's too public. So why leave her signature here?

As I contemplate the question, the scent of roses comes to me again and I look around; the dark-hair girl, crossing the park, alone. The Thirst rises and, this time, I make no effort to resist it. She heads towards the fence that separates the gardens from the train lines and I follow. It's been hours since I hunted and the Thirst is a blaze, made hotter by the enticing fragrance the girl gives off. She moves with confidence; this is her turf, which makes her all the more alluring.

Two young men are sitting at a stone table, sharing a bottle of something in a brown paper bag; vodka from the sharp tang on the air. Brawny, slack-faced lads, with a combined IQ of one hundred (maybe), they leer at the girl as she passes.

'Gies a gobble like ya promised, Rhona,' one of them slurs, and I begin to plan how to kill them and not lose the girl, whose blood is singing to me like a siren.

'You gotta grow a dick first, Angus,' she replies, not breaking stride. The men laugh and she shoots them the finger before slipping through a break in the fence. I move in the shadows, watching to see if they'll pursue her, but they seem content to call her a few vulgar names and swig from the bottle.

They don't see me follow the girl.

I hesitate at the top of the bank overlooking the train tracks, torn with indecision. The girl's blood calls to me with its seductive vital rush, but there is a reason Juliana wanted me at the monument and, if I leave the park, I might miss an opportunity to confront her and get Lucy back.

Choice flays me.

Trying to have it both ways, I send my senses across the city in search of Juliana while keeping my eye on the girl. At the same time, I seek out Callisto. I'm worried for her. Who is she meeting? Is it another trap? Surely, she won't underestimate Juliana's cunning again but, in case she does, I *should* stay near the monument.

The girl jumps over the train tracks, nimble as a rabbit, and the Thirst makes the decision for me.

I trek down a path of flattened grass and onto the train lines. The girl is approaching a brick building; flat roof, functional, dark. Perfect. She doesn't stop, grabs the doorknob, turns it, and slips through the door, closing it behind her. A small light flares behind the dirty windowpane. She's no longer alone. I sidle up to the wall of the shed and hear their voices murmuring inside; urgent words accompanied by quick, needful breaths.

I know exactly how they feel.

The boy groping her has the survival skills of a weasel and he almost gives me the slip, making it to the door before I grab him by the scruff of the neck and slam his head into the workbench lining one of the walls. There's a crack, like a splitting coconut, and he collapses at my feet. He'll die from the injury, but not before I've had my fill of him.

The girl knows better than to scream. Her eyes are narrowed, calculating; in any other situation, I'm sure she would make it out alive. Not tonight. I start a song and feel her resist. She backs away as I approach, but there's nowhere for her to go and when she bumps up against the back wall, her resolve crumbles. My song fills her, replacing the blood that I draw from her body, and I ease her into death with gratitude for the life she's given up to nourish me.

'Hmm, hardly an evildoer, but I do applaud your attempt at nobility.'

I raise my mouth from the girl's throat and, steadying myself for the confrontation, look over my shoulder to see Juliana leaning in the doorframe. She's beautiful. *Why does that surprise me every time I see her?* I wonder, standing. Juliana nudges the boy on the floor with her toe.

'Second course? Waste not, want not?'

That's why, I think, refusing to respond to her ugly banter. I wipe my mouth on the girl's jacket, which is lying on the bench, and repeat the question I asked her in Paris: 'Where's Lucy?'

'What took you so long to get here?'

'Ask Callisto. Where's Lucy?'

Juliana shrugs. 'Well, I had her with me at the monument, but you were late so I had to move her somewhere safe,' she says, as though it's all my fault.

I'm not falling for the guilt trip. 'You're lying. Where is she?'

'Where's Constantine?'

'He's with you.'

The look she gives me is mocking. 'Is he?'

'You know he is.'

'Okay, maybe he is here, on family business so to speak.' She smiles at her joke and then grows serious. 'But the real question is, where is Callisto? There were two parts to our bargain.'

I go on the defensive. 'She's in Edinburgh. Where's Lucy?'

Juliana laughs, though there's not much humour in it. 'How dogged you are, Christian,' she says, stepping backwards through the door and motioning for me to follow.

Outside, the rain has stopped.

Next to the building is a wooden crate that Juliana uses to jump onto the roof. She's graceful and cat-like in her agility, landing gently, barely creating a sound. Filled with the girl's blood, I jump up beside her, no less agile or soundless, but bursting with energy. I feel like I could leap to the moon. A train pulls out of Waverley station on the central line, gathering speed. It roars passed; wind buffets the building, and I grin at the sensation on my skin. It almost feels like I'm alive.

Juliana sits on the edge of the roof, staring over at the Scott monument. Something golden pinned to her jacket catches my eye; a brooch that looks familiar.

'Are you enjoying Edinburgh, Christian? It's one of my favourite cities,' Juliana says with a sigh. 'The Scots really know how to celebrate the dead.'

'Where did you get that?' I ask, sitting next to her.

She looks down at the brooch, turning it this way and that, showing it off. 'Do you like it? Lucy gave it to me.'

The fondness in her voice sets off alarm bells in my head. 'It's her aunt's brooch.'

'It was. Now it's mine.'

'Did you— Is Marguerite—' I can't bring myself to say it.

Juliana has no such qualms. 'Dead?'

My unease turns to anger and I force myself to control it. The priority here is Lucy, not her aunt - although I will make Juliana suffer somehow if Marguerite is dead. 'Yeah,' I reply, my voice tight.

Her laughter is light, closer to true amusement. 'Relax, Christian. The aunt is very much alive.' I shoot a sceptical look her way and, to my surprise, she pats my knee. 'I could've killed her, but I didn't because Lucy will need her when this is all over.'

What the hell is she playing at now? I stare at Juliana. 'Lucy will have me when this is all over,' I say.

'Will she, fledgling? So you do intend to have her birthed then?'

I shake my head. 'I told you before, that's not my intention.'

'Perhaps not,' the vampire replies, turning her gaze to the Scott monument. 'Although it really doesn't matter since Lucy is in my care. What does matter is the question of where Callisto is hiding?'

I don't like the possessive note in her tone, but I put aside my concern because she's right; the only way to get Lucy back is to give Juliana what she wants, which would be easy if I actually knew where Callisto was. I decide to put the onus back on the vampire and see where that gets me. 'You said bring Callisto and

Constantine to Edinburgh and they're here. Finding Callisto, that's your problem.'

'Is that right, fledgling? Well then, problem solved.' She grips my chin between her fingers and turns my head until I'm looking at the Scott monument. 'Do you see her?' she whispers menacingly against my ear.

Callisto is well hidden by human standards but, now that my attention is directed towards her, I spot her easily. She's tucked in beside the eastern buttress, a shadow in the shadows. The moment I see her, she moves into the open, balancing on the arm of the buttress as though it's a metre above the ground instead of over fifty. She swings down to the balcony and disappears inside the main column.

Juliana jumps from the roof.

Here we go. I race after her. She's moving fast and I pick up my pace, wondering - a little fearfully - what will happen when mother and daughter come face to face. If anyone is going down in this confrontation, I want it to be Juliana. Yet, there's a part of me that doesn't want her destroyed, mostly because she has Lucy and I need to get her back, but if I'm honest, there's also a small part of me that's intrigued by Juliana, and that part is barracking for her.

We approach the edge of the tracks. Above us is the fence keeping greenery and metal apart. I hear the subtle snap of a branch and human voices, one of which is familiar. Frowning, I look up at the spot where Callisto will come through, like some phantom from another realm, and wait for our worlds to collide. But, instead of taking the path, Juliana turns at the bank and increases her speed again. *Where the hell is she going?* I wonder, slowing as I hear shouts from the top of the embankment. Callisto's voice, cursing in French, is mingled with several deep Scottish brogues.

'Grab her, Angus,' one calls with a whoop.

'Git tae fuck, ya minky basturt,' Angus replies, his voice high-pitched with excitement.

Juliana has reached the station, presenting me with a choice: help Callisto or go after her daughter.

Lucy's face rises in my mind. *She's the vulnerable one*, I remind myself and bolt after Juliana, catching her as she shoots out of the station and onto Waverly Bridge. 'What's going on back there,' I ask, but she doesn't answer until we reach the corner of Market Street.

Here Juliana halts and looks back to where Callisto is fending off the thugs who've surrounded her. I'm surprised by the trouble she's having with them; from what I've seen, she's quick, agile, and strong. Still, she can't break the circle of men, who dart in, attacking in pairs, or swarm over her when she has one of them in her grip.

'Come on,' Juliana says, striding up Cockburn Street. I watch Callisto for a few seconds more and then follow Juliana, who has reached a long set of stairs. A sign on the building announces Advocate's Close. I look along the wide corridor of steps; there must be a hundred of them. Juliana races up and I keep pace. At the first bend, I catch her arm. She stops, amicably enough, and leans against the rough stone wall.

'Who are those men?'

Juliana's eyes sparkle red in the low street light. 'I guess you might call them minions,' she says.

'Minions?' For a second, the image of a hundred chattering yellow, goggle-wearing henchmen fills my head. I shake it way; the men surrounding Callisto are anything but adorable. As the thought departs, another occurs to me. 'They're the reason you wanted us at the monument, aren't they?'

A shrug lifts Juliana's shoulder. 'I had to get you away from Callisto. You know how she is with that mothering thing. Of course, I should have expected the Thirst would get the better of you, fledgling. I could have saved myself the bother of recruiting those losers.' She crinkles her nose as though she's smelt something disgusting. 'Now, let's go. They won't keep her occupied forever.' She pushes me towards a dark twisting section of the close, which joins a steep terraced stairwell. Near the top, I see people walking passed the exit onto the Royal Mile. Juliana tugs on my shirt, 'Slow down,' she warns, and we step out of the close like a pair of ordinary tourists.

The pretence lasts all of fifteen seconds before the herd begin to notice us. Instinctively they know we're different - dangerous - but they can't quite understand why, and they're too pacified to challenge our presence among them. Instead, they sidle away, flicking nervous glances over their shoulders. Juliana pays them no mind and strides across the road, into the shadow of St Giles Cathedral. I wait at the entrance to the close for a few more moments, hoping to see Callisto, but the stairs remain empty.

When I turn, Juliana waves me over, impatient, but my gaze is drawn passed her to the church. It's irrational, I know, especially after Sacré Coeur, but I can't shake the feeling that we shouldn't be anywhere near anything ecclesiastical. I give Juliana a nod and wander along High Street, crossing the road further down, well past the church.

Juliana advances on me; she doesn't need to be inside my head to read the expression on my face. 'You are still far too human to be a vampire,' she says, leading me to another close - Old Fishmarket - which is wider than the Advocate's Close and better lit, but the paving is uneven and slopes downward. Halfway along there is a bend in the close. I check over my shoulder; still no sign of Callisto.

'I'm curious,' I say to Juliana as we continue.

'About?'

'Your, um, minions. Are they like, part-vampire or something?'

'No, they're mortals, high on their favourite drug,' Juliana says.

I think about this, and then ask, 'You mean you gave them some of your blood?'

Juliana scowls at me. 'Seriously, Christian, where do you get these ideas? No, don't tell me. I already know. All that ridiculous fiction.' She sighs to emphasis her displeasure. 'I gave them PCP,' she says, as we come out onto the Cowgate. Juliana scans the street before turning east. 'Callisto won't touch those boys with that garbage running through their blood, but they're souped up enough to keep her busy for a little while.'

Hopefully not for too long, I think, as we head deeper into Old Town.

We are the only creatures moving along the rain-slicked sidewalk, and Juliana keeps our pace steady, unrushed. Ahead of us, spanning the Cowgate, is the South Bridge. Orange sodium light flows over the railings but barely reaches the road below and doesn't make it beneath the archway at all. An inky ribbon of shadow stretches beneath the bridge; a slash in the reality of the world; a threshold. As we stroll closer, I have a terrible Lovecraftian moment and imagine something hideous and hungry waiting for us in the dark. Then I remember what I am and a chuckle escapes me before I can stop it.

'Something funny, Christian?' Juliana asks, looking back along the Cowgate, eyes searching the rooftops.

'Lovecraft,' I say.

'The writer?'

'Master of the Monstrous.'

Juliana turns her gaze to me and I see she shares my amusement. 'Never met one of us, did he?'

'Not a chance,' I say, with a smile. It feels weird, and almost disloyal, to be sharing a 'moment' with her - she's the villain who's kidnapped the princess, after all - and I can see that she's thinking the same thing. There's an awkward pause that I end by changing the subject. 'Is she close by?' I ask.

'Depends who you mean by "she."'

Mockery laces Juliana's response and I'm relieved to be back on our usual ground. 'I meant Callisto. Who did you mean? Lucy?'

'Either or,' Juliana says, turning into Niddry Street.

I roll my eyes, wondering how the two of us could have shared anything, and follow her into the dim laneway. Two yellow lines, worn to patchiness, edge the cobbled brick road, which end in front of a row of tenements that stare down at me like a multiple-eyed monster. If Lovecraft had written *The Wizard of Oz*, this would be the road Dorothy would follow, to her detriment.

Halfway up the street, a lamp throws a circle of pale light over a metal door. I read the sign bolted into the brickwork: *The Vault*. My stomach clenches with anticipation even as I shake my head. It's so obvious now that I'm here. Lucy and I had read about the Edinburgh vaults on the Net in the weeks before we left for Paris; it was part of our fascination with all things underground. 'I should've known you would bring her here.'

Juliana lays her hand flat against the door, but exerts no pressure. 'What do you mean?'

'Lucy. You've got her in the vaults, haven't you? Ghoulish, but kind of predictable, don't you think?'

'Oh Christian,' Juliana says, her eyes lit with scorn. 'You're so far ahead of the game, it's breathtaking.' She shoves the door and stands aside to let me enter. A muted throb of music rises up a set of stairs, carried on an ostinato of racing heartbeats. I glance at Juliana as I pass her and she murmurs, 'Ready for the final round, fledgling?'

I'm not sure that I am, but it's too late not to play the hero now.

I See You, Baby

Juliana evades my grasp at the bottom of the stairs, gives a sardonic smile, and disappears into the crowd before I can stop her.

Great.

The aroma of the herd washes over me, and I grip the banister as the Thirst flares, staggering in its insistence, and I understand in an instant why Juliana has chosen this place for her final act. The Vault is a candy store and I'm a sugar addict, almost incapacitated with my need. Behind me, a wave of excited revellers flood into the club, pressing around me, driving me forward. Their scent is unbearable. Their crush is torturous, and I fight the urge to savage them as the human river carries me down the stairs, to where a long-dead pop diva is crooning about losing her self-control, the irony of which is not lost on me.

The vaults are lit with soft hues of fuchsia and emerald, fanning across the stone walls and low arched roof. Candles, fake and recessed into the rock, add a flickering golden light, their flame catching in the eyes of the humans as they lounge on leather seats, or lean over the bar to yell into the bartender's ear. Music pounds my body and circulates through air thick with human breath. The floor is uneven, but the press of bodies holds me upright. I touch their tender skin; the warmth of their blood separated from me by a tissue of flesh.

A girl, dark haired, plump with life, kisses the side of my mouth and I feel my fangs slide forward, unbidden. If she sees anything different about me, it doesn't raise an alarm. Maybe she's too out of it to care. She licks her lips, teasing, as though she knows my desire, and is drawn away by her laughing friends into one of the small vaults that open off the main corridor. A kiss floats off her fingertips towards me as the arms of some tartan-wearing alpha male, who sends me a proprietorial glare, engulf her.

I don't fight the flow of humans that pulls me away from them. There are so many others, just as delectable: wild-eyed, manic, exposing throats and wrists and thighs, and it occurs to me that this could be the vampire version of Hell. As the crowd releases me into a cavernous vault lit with pulsing red lights, I know the thought is true. The humans move as one organism: throbbing, glistening, superheated with the blood that tinges their faces a glorious, living pink.

I'm drunk on them.

Staggering into a dark corner, I press my spine into the rutted stone, dig my fingers into the mortar, anything to stop myself running at them, killing at will, bathing in their glorious, coppery, salty, sweet blood. My gaze lifts towards the ceiling. There is a balcony on an upper floor, crowded with more beating hearts. The crowd parts, like flesh for a knife. Juliana leans against the metal railing, more beautiful than any human, except—

Lucy.

The t-shirt and jeans she had on the last time I saw her are gone. She's wearing a short, black dress that hugs her like a lover. Her hair is pinned up, leaving pretty tendrils curling around her face, which is free of make-up, and expression.

Lucy: here, but not here.

Shoving away from the wall, I take a step in her direction, but Juliana holds up a hand and taps her temple. I turn *Slipknot* down and let her in. 'Look who I found wandering around,' she says.

Her playful tone grinds me, and it's all I can do to control the urge to charge at her like some feral animal, all fangs and madness. 'Let her go.' I hurl the demand across the room and see Juliana rock a little as the idea slams into her mind.

Juliana's eyes narrow. 'I think not,' she replies, wrapping her arms around Lucy's waist and nuzzling her neck, watching me all the while. Lucy lifts her head, presenting her throat. Their bodies move in time to the music and the humans dancing around them. Juliana's lips are against Lucy's ear. She looks at me and raises a hand to wave, laughing, but her eyes are empty.

It hurts to see her that way - a marionette for Juliana's amusement - and I feel a rush of guilt at my role in her being here, exposed to this danger. It wasn't what I wanted for her, and I double my resolve to get her away from Juliana and back to the safety of her Aunt Marguerite.

I wade into the swirling human pool. They grab at me, touching my face, arms, stomach, refusing to let me through. I look over their heads as I fend off their wandering hands. Juliana is amused, but I sense her alertness, the tension in her body, and understand she's ready to run the instant I break through the crowd. I stop and let the crowd push me back into the shallow vault: I can't risk losing Lucy again.

'Smart decision,' Juliana says, moving along the balcony. Lucy follows. I wonder if I'm quick enough to grab her and escape. Juliana flicks her ruby-flecked gaze my way, as though daring me to try.

Edging along the wall, I track them until Juliana stops beside a knot of humans. There are seven of them, four girls and three guys, rocking out and laughing, touching each other's faces as though they are the most beautiful people they've ever seen. I recognise the pony they're riding; how I envy their simple pleasures.

Juliana circles them. They're too into themselves to notice her. She makes another circuit, and then stops beside a blonde girl: her mark. The girl, sensing something through the mist of her drug-induced happiness, glances over her shoulder, but Juliana has faded into the dark, taking Lucy with her.

I can see her watching me. 'What?' I ask.

'Do you really have to ask, Christian?'

'Yeah, I do. What's this about?'

There's a pause. 'Love.'

I can't hide the bitterness in my reply. 'Really?'

'Of course, Christian. Everything I do is about love.'

'Cut the bullshit, Juliana. What's with the girl? And when can Lucy and I leave this dump?' Irritations press down on me: the Thirst, demanding blood; the humans, feeding my bloodlust; my fear for Lucy, gnawing at my control; the lights, disturbing, distorting. I see the ghosts of past revellers - drunks, whores, madmen - crawling out of the stonework, mixing with the living. I need to get out, with Lucy. Now.

'Okay, Christian, I'll explain,' Juliana says, as though she's speaking to an idiot child. 'Kill the girl and I'll hand over Lucy.'

I turn my gaze to the group of friends, catching them as they slam shots of some dark liquid. The girl Juliana has marked gags, shakes her head and giggles. She's a pretty thing, not beautiful, but brimming with an attractive vitality and, although the Thirst is demanding satisfaction, I have no reason to kill her. Not when there are dozens of more suitable victims on hand.

'I can't kill her,' I say.

'Then I'll kill Lucy.'

In the dark niche where she's retreated, I see Juliana tip Lucy's head. 'Wait. Wait a minute,' I say, moving onto the main dance floor, diagonally below the girl and her friends. Juliana watches me but doesn't move from Lucy's throat. 'I meant, why do I have to kill *this* girl?'

'Use those beautiful vampire eyes,' Juliana replies, releasing Lucy, who immediately picks up the beat of some mash-up song I recognise from another life, something by Rob Zombie. She gyrates and sings, joining the other voices that don't even begin to drown out the track, which is loud enough to split atoms. The girl and her friends are singing too, something about never dying.

How wrong you are, I think, taking apart her features, examining them one at a time to find the reason for her importance to Juliana, but it's not apparent until some wasted idiot body-slams into one of her girlfriends that the secret is revealed. The laughter in her face disappears as she tells the guy to fuck off, and I see the connection in the set of her mouth and the fierceness in her eyes.

Constantine.

'Don't touch her, fledgling. Moira is no concern of yours.' His voice is an unexpected intrusion, full of desperation and fury, and I realise I hadn't truly believed Juliana was clever enough to capture him again.

His daughter watches me, face impassive, her hand on the back of Lucy's neck. She's waiting for me to see her grand design.

'He's been here all along?'

She doesn't respond.

'You've been blocking him?'

She doesn't respond.

'Callisto will hear him.'

No response.

'But you don't care. You want her to hear. You want her to come.'

Silence.

'Because nothing's changed, has it? You still want them dead except, now, you also want to cause them grief - a grief to match your own.' I step closer to the stairs leading to the balcony and to the girl, who's smiling again. 'And this girl, Moira, her death is the thing that will grieve Constantine the most because she's the last link to his humanity.'

'Give the boy a gold star,' Juliana says, flatly.

As her words fill my head, I understand that whatever Juliana has planned for Callisto and Constantine, she has made room for me to share their fate. I know, also, that this has nothing to do with me; it's Callisto's suffering she wants. Callisto, mother to all of her vampire children, watching her last child starve to death. The only mercy for me in this grim future is that it won't take long. A month, maybe two.

'So Christian, it is a simple choice: his love, or yours? Which will it be?'

Simple? I almost laugh. Nothing's ever simple where Juliana's concerned, that's for damn sure. I press my lips together and try to reign in my pessimism. My fate isn't important; Lucy is the one who has to survive. She's all that matters now.

'I'll do what you ask but you have to let Lucy walk away.'

'Fledgling, *no!*'

I ignore Constantine and concentrate of Juliana.

'Walk away?' she asks.

'Into the crowd.'

Juliana's eyes travel the sea of humans below her. There are perhaps a hundred people and more in the various vaults. I know she's calculating the odds of re-capturing Lucy if she lets her go. I calculate too; they're in her favour, no doubt, but the one thing she can't factor in is Lucy.

There are two things I know about her that Juliana doesn't: she a born survivor and, once she comes out of Juliana's thrall, she'll be pissed to the max. 'If you want me to end Constantine's human bloodline, you'll release Lucy to fend for herself.' It's not much of a chance, but it's the best I can give her.

'Christian, I'm begging you. Don't do it. Moira is my family.'

'I'm sorry, Constantine. I'll do what I can to ease her passing.'

The rage I feel enter my mind is searing. I fill my head with music, closing him out, as I climb the stairs to the balcony, but I can't stop the regret that carves out a hollow space in my heart. Reaching the top step, I keep to the wall where the shadows are deepest until Juliana and Lucy are a few feet away, not to avoid the vampire but so Lucy won't see me. She's going to need all the head start she can get once Juliana releases her.

In between us is the girl I have to kill: singing, swaying, laughing. The certainty of her blood stokes the Thirst and I want to take her, even as part of me recoils at ending her life. For the moment, this part is stronger - though not by much - and I turn my gaze on Juliana. 'When Lucy's downstairs, I'll do what you want.'

'It's what you want too, Christian,' she replies, pushing Lucy towards me. She reels and stumbles and, although I want to help her, I side step, and slip in behind Moira. I don't touch the girl yet, but watch as some guy grabs Lucy's elbow, steadying her.

'Are you okay?' he yells into her ear. Lucy shakes her head, reaching for the banister. She rubs a hand across her forehead, blinks against the gaudy lights. Her rescuer scrutinises the crowd, then looks into Lucy's face, 'Are you here with someone?'

Lucy shakes her head again, points towards the glowing exit sign across the vault, and mutters something that we both miss. He leans closer, listening, and then grasps her elbow, helping her down the stairs. I follow their progress as he guides her through the crowd and out of sight.

Pressure off. Time to— *Damn it.*

Moira has slipped away while I watched Lucy. I glance at Juliana, who tips her head to the side as though she expected nothing less. *Whatever*, I think in her direction and lean over the railing, searching the crowd.

I spy the girl as she bops across the floor, dancing with strangers for a few seconds before her girlfriend drags her forward. They're laughing as they head for a metal door, which looks as though it's been lifted straight out of a bank. The door moves easily, swinging open to reveal hand basins and soap dispensers, and a long mirror reflecting all manner of girl. Moira and her friend slip inside, and I curse the female ritual of shared trips to the toilet.

I keep an eye on the door. As I see it, I have it two problems: how to separate Moira from the pack and where to take her for the kill. I want to honour my promise to Constantine and sing her out as sweetly as I can, but that'll be difficult in this place.

'I know where you can go,' Juliana says from beside me.

'What a surprise,' I reply, not looking at her.

She points to a door beside the DJ. 'Leads to the lower vaults. They're used for storage, so no one is likely to disturb you.' The bathroom door flings open, Moira struts out, feet moving to the beat, body swaying. 'I could run interference for you.' There's humour in Juliana's voice; she's enjoying her game.

I step around her. 'I'm on it,' I say, searching for Lucy's mind. She's near the entrance, close to freedom, but she's hesitating as she tries to understand how she got to the club. I urge her to go, to get away from here. I feel her frown and pull back. When I touch her mind again, she's in the alleyway.

Moira's almost across the dance floor, repeating her momentary gyrating with the guys she meets along the way. I head for the stairs, feeling Juliana's gaze on me as I catch Moira on the first step. She looks up into my eyes, and I begin to sing.

Her hand is warm and surprisingly small as it curls into mine; a child's hand. I think of Constantine and feel him press against my mind, like an army swelling against the battlements I've erected.

So powerful.

He's looking for a way in, a chink to exploit. I send Fred Durst to the wall, turn up the volume, and refocus on Moira. Bringing her hand to my lips, I taste the skin with a kiss. 'Come with me.' A dreamy smile floats on her lips and she nods, eyes locked to mine as I serenade her.

'Where the fuck do you think you're going with my friend?'

Her voice can't compete with the music, but a few people close by hear her and glance our way. I slip an arm around Moira's waist and turn to her friend. The gesture is enough to convince those nearby that what they are seeing is the usual interactions between lovers. They return to their own pleasurable pursuits.

Moira's friend is as dark as she is blonde, and with an attitude to match. It seems nothing is meant to be easy tonight. I look into her eyes, searching for her name - Caitrin - and sing again; she may be tough, but her resistance melts as my song fills her head. I wrap my arm around her waist too, and escort the women over to the door near the DJ.

The women whimper as the door closes, leaving us in darkness and I pull them in tight to my body, singing to comfort them. My sight adjust and I see in colours: the women, bright, living red; the walls covered in soft green-black moss; the floor decorated with crushed oyster shells, glittering like white gems.

I take Moira and Caitrin down the corridor, glancing through rough-cut archways into vaults of varying depth: some shallow with low roofs where the occupants would've stooped as they moved around, others deep and echoing with height. I choose a vault of medium depth; a fitting chamber for ending lives.

The snap of Caitrin's neck is cannon loud as the connection between us breaks. Moira cries out as her friend sags in my arms. I let the body roll onto the floor, regretfully, and turn to Moira. Despite my song, she's afraid, but I no longer care. The Thirst has me. On hands and knees, nuzzling, I bury fangs into her sweet pulse. Coppery perfume. Red silk, trickling down my throat. The Thirst retreats to a dull throb. Moira moans, low, almost done in, but with enough fight left to protest the end of her life, down here in the dark with a monster. A light flares, blinding as lightning in the night sky. I snarl a protest even as I recognise her scent.

Caught.

Blood on my face, near-dead girl in my arms, fangs exposed, fire of the Thirst a low flame in my no-longer human eyes.

'Oh Christian.'

It could have been a plea. Or a prayer. My song falters. Moira shivers, heaves her last breath, and cries in agony as death takes her. My heart falters. I've broken my promise to Constantine, who is hammering at my mind. I fight against his incursion out of shame and fear.

'See what your love has become?' Juliana says.

I can hide from Constantine, behind my barricades, but there's no way to avoid the eyes watching me from the entrance to the vault. On my knees, in the dirt, bodies at my side, there is nowhere to hide, nothing to say, except her name.

'Lucy.'

Convergences

'You were supposed to let her go.'

'I did.'

'Don't talk about me like I'm not right here, you freaks.'

'Feisty little thing.'

'You don't know the half of it.'

'Fuck you, Christian.'

'Charming.'

'She's afraid.'

'The fuck I am.'

Lucy is backlit by the torchlight shining in my face. To the human eye, she would be a shadow, but I can see her expression: the shock around her eyes, the worried crease furrowing her brow, the lips, pressed into a grim line. Yet, despite what she has seen, she edges closer, an inch at a time, as though she's approaching an unpredictable animal.

'What the fuck have you done, Christian?'

I look at the bodies of Moira and Caitrin, and feel an agonising shame. They were innocents whose deaths are made worthless by Lucy's appearance in the vaults. 'What the hell are you doing here?' I ask her, meeting her accusing gaze with one of my own. Lucy falters mid-step, arrested by something she finds in my face. 'I got you out safe,' I continue, as the Thirst clambers out of its pit, to hang on the black lip of my soul and survey her with greedy eyes. 'You had a chance.'

Juliana's hand descends on Lucy's shoulder. 'Actually, Christian, there wasn't really a chance—'

Before she can finish, a voice intrudes. 'Daughter.'

In an instant, Lucy is gone, whipped away like a wisp of smoke in a storm, and I am tumbling backwards, my chest stinging with the imprint of Juliana's hand. I leap to my feet and bolt after them, tracking Juliana by the ragged sound of Lucy's breathing. The vampire is moving fast, but not as fast as she could.

Fear sits in my throat: Lucy's a hindrance. A burden to be shed.

The hard earthen floor slopes downward as I run. I dodge piles of rubble where I can, scramble over others when they're unavoidable, all the time searching for Lucy in the rooms that open on the left and right of the passageway, knowing Juliana will have to abandon her if she hopes to catch Callisto.

Callisto? In the vaults?

Did I imagine the surprise on Juliana's face in the seconds before she flicked off the torch and went in hunt of our mother? No— it was there. The question is, how did Callisto know we were here, and what does she plan to do now?

The walls are wet and I hear water trickling in the dank stillness. I race past some sort of earth-moving equipment, hunkering in a corner like one of Lovecraft's monsters. Beyond its rusting carcass is another passageway. I catch a hint of Lucy's perfume at its entrance and take it, aware that the ground has pitched more sharply, taking me deeper with each step.

The air becomes noxious, carrying the flavour of old blood and disease. The ground is soggy. A cold, oily wetness seeps into my shoes and I'm glad for the darkness that, even with my vampire's sight, doesn't allow me to identify the muck I'm trudging through. Rubble is piled high in the passageway, blocking it almost completely except for a narrow tunnel that has been excavated along the left wall. No human hand has been at work here and I wonder at Juliana's preference for dark, subterranean places.

There is one small relief: the rooms to either side of the passageway are also filled with rubble, leaving nowhere for Juliana to dump Lucy. I pick up the pace, ignoring the wetness, the stale air, the scrape of rock against my arms, and focus on catching Juliana. Whatever happens next, I don't want Lucy caught in the middle of Juliana and Callisto when they come face to face.

The passageway continues downward, heading north, and as I go deeper, the air becomes more wholesome, smelling of the river and worm-turned earth, rather than of bodily filth and moral corruption. I shuffle forward as fast as I can and soon the tunnel opens into another vault. This room is larger than any other I've been in and there are a number of arched doorways carved into the rock. Standing still, I listen for a clue as to which way Juliana has gone. It's hard to be certain as the air vibrates with the slightest noise. I send my mind towards each corridor in search of her.

Of the six doorways, there are three that emit a malevolence so dark I discount them immediately. Of the other passageways, one is blocked with debris, leaving the inevitable choice of two.

Flip a coin. Roll a dice. Use my senses: *Oh yeah.*

Juliana is down the left hand corridor. I feel her excitement; she's closing in on her quarry. Lucy is with her: her mind is like a red rose in full bloom. I reach for Callisto's mind and she shies away, blocking me out, but not before I feel her confidence. I take a step towards the passageway, wondering what my vampire mother has to feel confident about when the answer steps out of the right hand corridor.

His face is a white mask looming out of the dark, the eyes flash with ice-blue streaks of rage. 'You owe me a blood debt, fledgling,' he says.

I stare at him, and then look down the passageway where Juliana has pursued Callisto, wondering if she knows of the trap that has sprung closed behind her.

The Way of the Shroudeater

The darkness is viscid; black as molasses and just as resistant to movement. I'm not afraid of this darkness. I'm not afraid of the vampire father stalking behind me; or the mother racing ahead; or the mad sister in between. I could slip away from them in this darkness, intent as they are on each other.

But—

My human father said the only thing a man need fear in life is the death of loyalty. I'm no longer a man; I am something more. I no longer have a life; I have an existence.

But—

When all is said and done and I am standing at the top of my mountain, the rock of my burden before me, teetering on the cusp of descent, when I look out at the horizon of my eternity, the thing that will sustain me - that will give me the freedom and peace of Sisyphus - is knowing I stayed loyal.

To Lucy, at least.

Luminosity seeps into the darkness; a mist that condenses into an arc of yellow light. I slow, easing into it. Ahead is a doorway, beyond which is the murmur of female voices. I slow further. Constantine shoves me forward, impatient with my caution, and I stumble into a cavernous vault. The women glance at me.

Juliana is impassive; she's been expecting me.

Callisto's gaze flicks over my shoulder and I catch the slight upturn of her mouth.

From the floor where she's been dumped, Lucy stares into nothingness.

'Christian.'

The vampires say my name simultaneously but I hear the different inflection in their voices. Juliana catches the difference too; she turns her gaze on Callisto. With the stillness of two mountains, mother and daughter face off.

'To answer your question, there is only one way for this to end,' Juliana says.

'You never were a creature of alternatives,' Callisto replies.

I inch towards Lucy, taking note of the room as I approach. The ceiling is high and hidden in shadow; the walls are rough and, like the earthen floor, are dry. Unlike the vaults above, this room has only one other opening; a narrow cavity, just wide enough for an adult, carved into the back wall. There is a scattering of bricks and rubble on either side of the small vault, and a number of old tools rest against the stone as though waiting for their owners to return.

The tools are not the only abandoned things in the chamber.

Lucy's face is filthy, her hair is mattered with mud and her dress has a ragged tear in one sleeve and along the hem. I look her over carefully, but can't see any blood or obvious wounds.

What's gone wrong in her head is a different story.

Her face has the slack look of someone who's sliding off the white horse. Her eyes are dull and unblinking: she's deep inside, which, in the current situation, is probably a good thing. I try not to think about how she'll be tomorrow, or the next day, or for the rest of her life, as I creep towards her. All that's in my mind is to get her out of here and back to the human world.

'You never gave me an alternative. You and Constantine, you're leeches, sucking away the potential of your victims,' Juliana says, over my head. 'And birthing children,' she sneers the word, 'to fed your own narcissism. But what of us?' There is a startling crack and I glance up to see her hand pressed against her chest. 'What of the monsters you make in your image?'

'No other child has struggled like you, Juliana,' Callisto says. I hear the tenderness in her voice: an offering of conciliation.

Juliana is deaf to all, but her rage. 'Don't you dare pity me,' she says. Her lips draw back from her fangs and a fierce light flares in her eyes as she curls her fingers into talons. I grab Lucy under the arms and drag her away, towards the wall, out of harm's reach.

Callisto turns her back on Juliana. As she does, I see her gaze flick over to the doorway into the vault, where Constantine fills the entry. 'Why shouldn't I pity you? You are stunted, a withered rose. Once you had beauty, and strength, and daring, but you let your love for a human crush you. Now you are an ugly shadow of the vampire you could have been.'

A hellish fury radiates from Juliana. She tenses, ready to fly at Callisto. I lift Lucy into my arms as Constantine appears beside me. 'She's right, daughter,' he says.

Juliana whirls to face him. I see the surprise on her face. It last for less than a breath before she smothers it with a cunning expression. 'How did you escape?' she asks.

Constantine shrugs. 'In order to escape, one must first be capture.'

Lucy is as light as a pillow against my body. I hold her tight, one hand over her mouth in case she rouses, and slip towards the door. 'Put the human down, fledgling.' Constantine's not looking at me, but at Juliana. 'There is still a blood debt to pay.'

I look into the black passageway, wondering if I can make it out. They'll have to deal with Juliana - *if* they can deal with her - before they come after me. It may be enough time to get Lucy to the surface.

Then what, Christian? Where would you hide her that we cannot find?

Callisto watches me with sympathetic eyes and, for a second, I feel the same anger as Juliana, although mine is born out of frustration at the Chinese Box in which they've locked me. I lay Lucy beside the wall, close to the doorway. Maybe if she comes round before this is done, she'll have enough presence of mind to try to escape, though I don't have much faith in the idea.

I stride past Constantine and stand between him and Callisto, behind Juliana. 'Now what?' I ask.

Juliana turns to me. 'Would you stand against me, Christian?' She softens her gaze, dropping a veil over her anger. 'After all, I did not bring you to this existence. If you'd followed my advice, you would be safely tucked in your bed, with Lucy at your side, with little more to fear other growing old.'

'Are you seriously fishing for allies?' I ask, shaking my head. 'We're all responsible for being here, one way or another, through the choices we've made, either as humans or vampires.'

'So you stand with them.'

'I stand on my own.'

Juliana sneers at me.

'Daughter.' Callisto's tone is gentle.

'Stop calling me that. I had parents. They were human, and they died not knowing what happened to their child,' Juliana says. Malice laces every word as she looks at Callisto.

'Will you hate us for all of eternity?' Callisto asks.

'Yes.'

Callisto's sadness hangs around her like a wreath. *So be it*, she sings.

I expect violence, and tense, ready for the battle. I have no idea how any of them expect to get out of here, but fate has rolled the dice and now I have to play this game to its end. I see Juliana draw herself inward, pooling her energies. Constantine shifts his weight, distributing it evenly. He's watching Juliana with a wolf's intensity. Only Callisto doesn't move.

'Juliana?'

At first, I think our vampire mother is revealing a new talent in her repertoire; throwing her voice to distract her daughter. Anything to gain the upper hand, but the voice is male and belongs to a figure who steps out of the aperture carved into the far wall.

Juliana draws a hissing breath. 'What is this?' she says.

'He's been with us all along.'

Juliana whirls on Callisto. 'You lie. He's dead. I was there when he drew his last breath.'

'I'm sorry, beloved,' Didier says, soothingly. 'I've wanted to come to you, to reveal myself so many times over the years.'

'Didier is dead,' Juliana says, but even as she speaks, she is drawn across the cavern as though tugged by an invisible cord. I follow her. Callisto and Constantine edge closer too.

'It was my brother, René, whom you watched over all those years.'

Bewilderment flashes across Juliana's face. 'René? That's preposterous,' she says, her eyes narrowing.

'No, my love, it is the truth,' Didier replies, lifting his hands towards Juliana; an invitation to join him. She stops, but doesn't retreat. 'I cannot express how grateful I am to you for protecting him and his family. It should have been me, but circumstances—' He raises his shoulder in a helpless shrug and even I sense the depth of his regret.

If Juliana senses the same, she appears unmoved. She flicks her gaze towards Callisto, then Constantine - she might've been surprised by Didier's sudden reappearance, but she hasn't forgotten her enemies - but when she looks at me, I see something new in her eyes, something which I think might be hope.

She returns her attention to Didier. 'If you are Didier, explain to me how this came to be.'

Didier spreads his arms in front of him. 'Can you not believe your own eyes?'

'I know what I see and I know what I know,' Juliana says, and I don't think I've ever heard her voice sound as cold. 'Now explain.'

A sigh escapes Didier. 'As you wish, my sweet. René is - was - my identical twin.'

'Twin?' Juliana asks, her tone heavy with scepticism.

'You remember, the brother my father banished because of his political alliances?' Juliana remains silent. 'He came to see my in the weeks after you vanished, wanting to mend the rift in our family, but I was too distraught over your disappearance to deal with him. All I could think of was finding you, so I sent him away.' An anguished look passes over Didier's face.

'And?' Juliana asks.

Didier rubs his hand across his mouth and over his chin, and I catch a flicker in Juliana's face. She recognises the gesture.

'René was stubborn and refused to accept my dismissal of him. He moved into an apartment in the city and continued to plead with me to be his intermediary, but I was in the grip of a black despair, useless to him and everyone else, except them.' He tips his head toward Callisto and Constantine with a fondness even I don't feel.

They respond with nods and smiles, as though we're at some grand family reunion.

Juliana is stone.

'I was on the verge of killing myself when Constantine found me and offered me a different life.'

A snort of derision comes from Juliana. 'This is no life,' she says.

'Is it not preferable to the endlessness of death?' Didier asks. His tone is soft, almost imploring, yet something about it is wrong. I watch him, trying to put my finger on what's bothering me.

'No,' Juliana replies. Whatever I'm hearing, she seems to have missed it. She steps closer to Didier. 'They birthed you and you didn't come for me?' None of us misses the anguish beneath her words.

'Ah, beloved,' Didier replies, his hand rising to touch her, 'how I've wanted too, all these years, but when I woke to this life, I was far from Paris and, by the time I returned, you were already locked into your fixation with René and his family. How could I tear you from the ones you loved after you had lost so much?'

That's it, I think, understanding what's bugging me about Didier: he sounds like Lucy when she's trying to wheedle her way around me. Not that the realisation serves any purpose for, the moment Didier's hand wraps around Juliana's arm, there is a flurry of movement beside me.

Callisto and Constantine charge forward. Hearing them coming, Juliana attempts to dash away, but Didier holds firm, dragging her backwards towards the opening in the rock as Callisto and Constantine barrel into her.

'Don't let go, René,' Constantine yells.

Juliana's cry of rage shakes flakes of dirt from the roof. 'Liar!' She slashes her nails across Rene's face. 'Filthy liar,' she spits.

I stand, riveted to the floor, torn between choices. The opportunity to save Lucy has arrived like a runaway boulder and part of my mind is yelling, *Get her out of here! Now!* But another part: the part that is Sisyphus, and Empedocles, is demanding that I help— Juliana.

Damn it.

Then the decision is made for me. Constantine's voice invades my head: *Pay your blood debt, fledgling.*

Juliana is fighting them. She's wild, gnashing her teeth, bucking her body, arching almost in half as she tries to free herself. Her eyes are red coals, filled with hate and determination.

Our parents and René are losing their grip.

Constantine roars in my mind: *I will kill the girl, fledgling.* He accompanies the promise with an image of Lucy, throat ripped open, blood spilling, flowing into her lungs, choking her, drowning her. I fly at the struggling vampires, lending my strength to push Juliana through the gap and into the blackness of the crevice.

Everything is stone.

Our bodies.

Our minds.

Our will.

We grate against each other, and I discover something: there is no singing when a vampire is to die.

We slam Juliana against the far wall, René, Constantine and I, as Callisto gathers the manacles and chains: snap, snap, snap, snap. I step away and René comes with me, watching as Juliana thrashes against the wall, the rattling of her chains deafening in the small antechamber. She hisses her rage, snarling at Callisto and Constantine as they make the final adjustments: chains around her waist, chains across her throat.

Callisto turns to me. 'Wait outside, Christian, but do not leave,' she says, and although she's as fresh faced and beautiful as ever, I can see the weariness and pain in her eyes. It has cost her much, this imprisonment of her child.

I cross the vault and sit next to Lucy, taking her head into my lap. Using the sleeve of my jacket, I wipe dirt from her face, hoping she won't wake in this place to hear the howls and curses coming from the chamber. Brushing her hair back, I wonder how much she will remember of this ordeal and if I will ever be able to talk with her again. I rest my hand against her throat, feel the heat and flow of her blood, and know the answer. With a heavy heart, I lift Lucy out of my lap and lay her on the ground again. Standing over her, I know there's one more duty, one kindness, that I need to perform for her, but after that— I let the thought go and walk away.

On the way to the crevice, I pass René as he strides through the cavern. He doesn't spare a glance for me - though I notice that Lucy draws his eye - and slips through the doorway. The instant the darkness swallows him, it's as though he never existed. *Weird,* I think, and continue on to where Callisto and Constantine are replacing the bricks that, I realise, they had removed earlier. I look into the chamber where Juliana is chained and feel a flash of shock. Touching Callisto's hand as she lays another brick, I ask, 'Why?'

She flicks her gaze over Juliana and returns to her work. 'It's our way. The way of the Shroudeater.'

The stone is the size of a tennis ball, but elongated so that it pushes at Juliana's cheeks, stretching her mouth in a grotesque parody of a clown's smile. Her teeth have snapped as the stone was forced into her mouth. Blood runs in thin rivulets down her chin. Her eyes glare at me.

You should have killed Lucy, Christian, because, when I get out of here, I'm going to feast on her, then I'm coming for you.

I'm sorry, Juliana.

To hell with you.

I watch her until the brickwork hides her from view, then I sit and listen to her shake the chains. She doesn't stop, not even when the last stone is cemented into place.

Requiem

Lucy is dead.

What a farce: the heroic rescue when death comes anyway. Her daughter posted a poem on her Facebook page:

> *My sun went out this morning, with a sigh.*
> *Leaving only darkness in my day.*
> *I pray the moon will rise tonight,*
> *to light the remainder of my way.*

She is fifteen and given to melodrama.

I didn't fall into the trap that snared Juliana. I didn't haunt Lucy. I didn't need to; that's the beauty of social networking, which allowed me to love and protect her from a distance. This was the vow I made as I carried her from the vaults, so many years ago.

Paris.

Aunt Marguerite's apartment; the next best thing to the sanctuary of home. Still, I felt guilty as I laid Lucy on the doorstep, wrapped in my filthy jacket, and reached for the buzzer. Then again, I'd never claimed to be a dashing Lancelot when I was human and the idea fit even less now that I was a Shroudeater.

Shroudeater.

The word made me shudder, bringing with it memories of my last glimpse of Juliana. I guessed she hadn't been aware of the tradition when she imprisoned her parents and kin and I wondered, as I hurried across the street, whether things would have gone differently in the catacombs had Callisto and Constantine suffered the same fate as their daughter. Would I have had the courage to remove the stones from their mouths?

As I leapt from balcony to balcony, using them as a flight of stairs to reach the roof, Marguerite opened the front door. I heard her gasp as she leaned over Lucy. She called to her lover, who appeared moments later, shrugging into a dressing gown. Together, they lifted Lucy, muttering over her like priestesses:

'She's nothing but a waif…'

'…don't understand the youth of today…'

'…drugs, do you think?'

'…when I see that little fucker again,' Aunt Marguerite said, and closed the door.

'She'll be safe now?' I asked.

Constantine rose from his haunches and stood beside Callisto. 'Safety is an illusion, especially for humans.' I gazed at him steadily. Over his shoulder, the lights of Paris continued to twinkle even as the new day erased the darkness from the sky. 'Death will find her when her time is due, fledgling, but I will not guide its hand.' He pressed his lips to the top of Callisto's head and was gone.

My vampire mother watched his passage for a few seconds before turning to me. 'There is just enough night left for you to hunt and find a place to rest,' she said, touching her cool fingertip to my arm.

'Will I see you again?'

'Perhaps, but not in Paris.' She brushed her cheek against mine and slipped away, following Constantine into the night.

I stayed in the shadows, waiting for darkness to return to Marguerite's apartment. The urge to see Lucy one last time was strong, but I fought it. I'd said goodbye to her in the narrow alley beside Marguerite's building. I'd asked her forgiveness and taken a sip of blood from her lips, all while she remained oblivious, locked in a chamber in her mind. Letting go was all there was to do. The lights went out at Marguerite's apartment, room by room.

I dropped to the street and went hunting.

Three years later, I friended her on Facebook.

I say my name is Laurent and that I meet her in Paris.

She says, 'I was out of it in Paris. LOL. Can't remember a thing. Remind me how we met?'

'It was at a bookshop. *Shakespeare's*. Ring a bell?'

'Nope, but don't let that stop you.'

I know when Lucy gets married.

And has a child— Danielle; the melodramatic one.

And contracts a ravenous disease that vampire's never worry about.

While she fights, I roam the globe, searching for a cure, for her, and for me.

Sometimes I sit in a café: in Marrakesh, or Istanbul, or Prague, or Christchurch - it doesn't matter where; they are all one city really - and I watch the living scurrying about their business, and I wonder at the futility of their lives: to what purpose all this activity when death will claim them in the end?

It's an impossible conundrum; one which Empedocles would, no doubt, understand.

I pay my bill and go out into the city to lend death a helping hand.

I don't think about Juliana, until the day they put Lucy in the ground.

Out of harm's way.

There have been extensions and collapses in the twenty-three years since I was last in the Edinburgh vaults. The water table has risen, flooding the lower passageways, before retreating again. It's a similar story for the entrepreneurs and developers: they come, they dig, they leave. No one has been to the last vault under South Bridge. I listen with my vampire senses, waiting for the rattle of a chain behind the brickwork, searching for a thought in the dark.

Silence.

How long could she last without blood? I wonder.

I know starvation can reduce a fledgling to dust in a matter of weeks, but Juliana was no fledgling when she was entombed. Still, two decades without nourishment? I follow the wall, pondering why I have come back here. Curiosity? Guilt? Fear?

Maybe.

Maybe I'm just bored.

Or nostalgic?

Or lonely?

I haven't seen Callisto or Constantine; they keep themselves hidden. Sometimes I cross the trail of another vampire, their telltale leavings easily recognisable, and I wonder if it is René or some other who Juliana missed on her crusade.

I have met no new fledglings; perhaps my parents are using prophylactics?

That leaves Juliana.

Or what's left of her.

As I approach the walled-up entrance to the smaller vault, I come across something curious: bones.

Human bones: femurs, skulls, flanges, ribs.

Not old bones: mossy, crumbling, yellowing.

White bones, pushed into a pile.

I stare at them for a while. There is only one way the bones could have come to be here; I should've guessed Callisto wouldn't completely abandon her child. A shiver works through my body as I try to figure out whether this is an act of compassion, or utmost cruelty. I walk over to the brickwork that Constantine and Callisto constructed all those years before and run my hands over the surface. As I expect, the stones, while returned with care, are loosely arranged for easy removal. I push against one and hear a pattering of mortar falling to the stone floor, followed almost immediately by the faint rattle of chains.

I feel her mind open like an Angel's Trumpet flower. She sends out tendrils of her thoughts, expecting Callisto, finding me. They wrap around my mind, testing, remembering, and then she speaks: *You woke me from my meditation, Christian.*

Abashed, I apologise and say, *I didn't know you were*— I falter when I realise where the sentence might go. How can I finish?

Still existing? She laughs; I hear no madness in her voice. Instead, there is calm resignation. Of course, she's always been good at covering her true emotions. *Have you come to rescue me?*

I sit on the ground outside her tomb. This is a good question; a Sisyphean question.

I could: leave her; free her; join her.

My moment of stasis has arrived, and all that's left to me is a choice.

Envoi of Romance

She whispers.
> 'Tell me you love me.'
> '...'
> 'Tell me.'
> And, in the dark, I do.

Blog Sixteen

The Diderot Dilemma

Hello human.

What?

Oh come on, are you *that* surprised? Did you really think I would let that young upstart have the final word? After all I've told you? After all I've shared with you? Don't you know me at all? Pah! Why do I waste my time with you?

I am being a little hard on you again, aren't I? What can I say? It's a habit; although one that is a reflection of your nature rather than mine. Nevertheless, it is true that I have been 'out of it' for a while - although that was hardly my fault - and, if the truth be told, I never thought I'd find myself back here.

In fact, for a time, I thought myself free of you, of the Shroudeaters, of the Thirst, and of this existence. Death was to be mine. It would be long, agonising, and taste like stone, but it would come and, in some small measure, for the briefest moment, I would be human again, before I passed from this world, as all things should.

But the curse of Sisyphus is not so easily escaped, or so it seems.

For she came; my selfish mother, to rescue me! From a death I *wanted*. How wicked is she? How perverse? To salve her self-inflicted wound with the suffering of her child.

I wish I could say I refused her offerings; that she had to force-feed me like one on a hunger strike, but that would be a lie, and I have never lied to you, mortal. The Thirst must be satisfied but, rest assured, I was never grateful for the quenching of that furnace, which - if she had let her justice run its course - would have consumed me.

The days after her visits were the worst, when the blood eased the Thirst and allowed me to think of other things. Did the rest of my imprisoners know what she was up to? Not the fledgling, I wagered; he would be too busy haunting his mortal, the lovely Lucy, whom I imagined quivering in my arms as I bled her dry while Christian watched. It would have saddened me to do such a thing, for I was truly fond of the girl, but *c'est la vie*, as the saying goes. Unfortunately, Lucy's death cheated me out of this small revenge. I am not concerned, however, for there will be other opportunities to punish the fledgling, especially now that he believes us to be *compagnon d'infortune*.

The vampire who interested me most during those long hours was the liar, René. Oh how I long to chain him up in the dark, to fill *his* mouth with stone - yes, I have learned the lesson well - and leave him to starve. Cur that he is! To think, I would mistake my beloved Didier for him. They may share the same features, but not the same pure heart, and I could see that in his eyes the instant he laid his hand upon me. If not for the other conspirators—

Hmm, you are right, mortal. What is the point of wallowing in the past? We are here, you and I, and the nights stretch ahead - well, at least they do for me - and the simple fact is, what has gone before changes nothing. Like the human merry-go-round you call life, my carnival goes on and the Shroudeaters will be dust, even if it takes me all of eternity.

Yes, you guessed it. Clever mortal. I *do* have a plan.

What?

No, I'm not sharing it with you.

Not now anyway, but maybe next week.

Acknowledgements

MIRA FALLING
MARIA ARENA

Mira Falling dreams of becoming a star… but achieving fame and fortune can be difficult when you're stuck in a dead-end town like Harvest Bay, and have a brilliant brother who overshadows your every move.

When Sebastian Holborn and his wealthy family move into the house across the street, Mira sees an opportunity for escape and for the fame she desires, but Sebastian's scheming twin sister, Lily, has other ideas.

Mira, however, knows there is a solution to every problem, and she will allow nothing and no one to stand in the way of her dream.

To purchase *Mira Falling,* or to read more about Maria Arena, visit: www.mariaarena.com.au

SISTERHOOD
MARIA ARENA

Abandoned by her jet-setting mother at St Mary's Boarding School for Girls, Heather Johnson thought life couldn't get much worse. She was wrong. Waiting for her behind the iron gates is an ancient evil, embodied in the insidious Sister Merce and her coven of malevolent Sisters, who thrive on the misery they inflict upon their wayward charges.

As the danger to Heather increases, a reprieve arrives with Amy, a spirited girl with a strange flair for Latin. The respite, however, is fleeting as Amy's physic abilities reveal a mystery involving two long-dead 'fallen' girls, Jennifer and Rachel. Using a diary and an amulet, and assisted by the sweet-hearted Patrick and self-destructive Caleb, the four girls are drawn into a liminal space where they must stand together and use the power within themselves to destroy the Sisterhood.

Suspenseful and enigmatic, *Sisterhood* pits the darkest aspects of human nature against its greatest virtues.

To purchase *Sisterhood*, or to read more about Maria Arena, visit: www.mariaarena.com.au